THE
ROTTEN
OASIS

THE ROTTEN OASIS

I. M. ROWETT

Published by Grey Tiger Books
GTB, 10–16 Ashwin Street, Dalston, London, E8 3DL

10 9 8 7 6 5 4 3 2 1
Text Copyright © 2018 I. M. Rowett

A catalogue record for this book is available from the British Library

Printed and bound by Clays Ltd, Elcograf S.p.A

ISBN: 978-1-912107-70-4

TERROR MORTIS

I have just only one question for you my friend: do you know what is a green mamba?

Come again?

Ha! My friend. You do not know what is a green mamba actually. Of course it is a snake. A deadly snake even. Yes and yes. But.

Let me put it like this my friend: do you know how the Devil walks among us?

Ha! Look at this, Chikomo. He jests can you believe? In this late hour during the twilight of his life our Righteous brother he jests and he jousts.

My friend. He exists. He exists as beauty and fear rolled into one long and sinuous muscle with an emerald skin, a forked tongue and the head of an assegai. That my friend is the green mamba; that my friend is our Devil in Disguise.

The green mamba rules by fear. This is true. I killed a man once long ago with just an acacia thorn and nothing more. I pricked him in the buttock and showed him my mamba, long dead but in my hand made to squirm as if in life. In the morning we found a brittle corpse twisted in agony, knotted fingers clawing its terror-stricken face. Terror mortis I like to call it.

Of course, you corner the green mamba she will bite, you will die, it's all the same. Just like the black mamba: in great pain. Body first, brain second. Your brothers will even declare you dead. You will hear them talk of burial plans and you will hear them fighting for your wives and your cows and your watch. You will try to raise your hand, just even a finger. To object, to be heard, to have your say in the matter. But your finger is dead. Your hand is dead. Then you are dead.

And yet I, I, Baba Manyoka, am the mamba's master. Do you know how it feels? A mamba's bite?

Ha! Of course you can not know. No man has felt the mamba bite and lived to tell another tale. Except me. Hear my chest? It hisses. Like an angry mamba. I have had the bite and I, I, Baba Manyoka, lived actually.

See my hands? And here on my eye. And here on my neck. And there on my arm. And here by my ankle.

And right here, next to my own mamba. Ho! Ho! Ho! Yes. They say I have the mamba blood. That I am immortal. That I am the mamba's military attaché on Earth, yes. You look away. What-for? To escape? To run away? Foolishness. That is when I strike. Never take your eyes off the green mamba.

So my friend, have you heard the green mamba scream?

Oh! Oh! Oh! This old man grows foolish. His days grow dark and his mind turns to black. My friend, you have not heard the green mamba scream. No man has heard the mamba scream and lived. Yet I and I alone have heard that scream and lived.

Let Baba Manyoka tell you. Ho! Ho! Ho! My friend, I see you are not looking sideways any more. That is good. The green mamba scream at first sounds like nothing more than a twenty-one gun salute: formidable perhaps but unremarkable; then it becomes a pair of dragons clawing at each other's eyes and their screams cleaving the sky; and then, finally, it sounds like twenty-four red-hot spikes shoved in your ear and coming out the other side, searing and tearing and ripping at your brain. It sounds like an angel being defiled. It sounds, it sounds like the Devil is paying you a

8

house call my friend. Ho! Ho! Ho! It is a scream, a shriek that splits every atom in your body. Those Nazguls? From Harry Potter you know? They would shit themselves.

Oh! Bloody fuck-sakes now I have spittled on my suit. And on you even. I see you flinch but that won't kill you. An ageing man's phlegm, that is all. No, I cannot make the venom. I am just only the humble mamba servant. The lowly mamba shepherd. Nothing more.

But that was many lifetimes ago during the reign of the great Rozwi Empire when battles were fought out in the open, warrior to warrior, army to army until death declared the victor. In this modern era of course, we do not have time to form elaborate and lasting solutions to our everyday problems. We have become crude ourselves. We want instant gratification no matter how temporary. We use guns. Like this. And this. My señoritas Smith and Wesson. Loaded with forty-fours of course. Let me introduce you to my Dirty Harriets. You know Clint Eastwood?

But a bullet don't you know. So prosaic. It explodes the head. Poof! End of story. No time to writhe, to rage, to beg, to cry, to know the absurdity of life and to welcome death as an end to the pain. How times have changed. The green mamba scream was a panacea. Refined, just like my Kilgour and my favourite John Lobbs, scuffed and bloody as they are. The mamba scream was elegant, bowing to time-honoured traditions of warcraft.

It's like this: take one big clay pot. A beer pot serves well. Fill it with our lamp oil, up to halfway. So. And then take a handful of your freshest, biggest, juiciest green mambas and drop them into the oil. So.

See the mambas they writhe and squirm. There is no need to stir this pot.

Now. Plug the top with some dry grass, garnish it with a generous lug of oil, some salt and pepper and a shot of thyme immemorial. Ready! Steady! Cook! I think I win the prize yes? Maybe we shall call this dish deep-fried death. The colonel's secret recipe indeed. Ho! Ho! Ho!

Now we place our pot of pain, our brew of brimstone into our trebuchet of terror, our catapult of calamity, our mortar of mortality, so. Then we pull the lever and secure it. So.

Take a match. We light the grass. Ho! Ho! Ho! The burning bush. Now we will hear the scream. Listen. They hiss. They struggle. They fight. They fear.

They hate.

And we launch our missile of misery. Oh! Beauty, joy and wonder, it lights up the night sky, a screaming, hissing ball of flame. Oh! Perfection, it explodes mid-air: flying mambas and burning oil. Angry mambas raining from a cloud of fire and thunder. Oh! Yes.

And lo! My brother's house burns. How his children run. Helter-skelter, hither and thither they flee. The mambas are chasing one, two, three. My mambas get them all.

And so it was.

But don't cry my friend. My brother is late and he left many children.

KAREEBER TIME

Scheme it'll rain? says Reggie. We call him Reggie, Reg, Righty, Righteous or, my favourite, Reg-gay. All sorts of things in fact. His real name's Brighton. Fuck knows how that became Reggie. He went to the Vale. Nuff said.

His face is scrunched into the setting sun, towards a huge bank of clouds towering over Bumi thirty kays across the lake. The water has that oily thickness you get when the wind dies and the air begins to cool. It's shiny and gloopy. Like mercury. Best time for catching tigers.

What does it matter? I don't care. Reggie's always doing that: making conversation.

Ya, says Bart. Over there, and he points to the clouds. I snort a laugh. We all know Reggie is shit-scared of thunder.

Arse-wipe, says Reggie and then he launches at Bart for dangling his hand in the water.

Because, Bart, it's dangerous, he's saying.

Jesus, Reg. I explain to him that a flatty isn't gay. He doesn't do cocktail parties, he doesn't do chit-chat and he sure as fuck doesn't do finger food. A croc flies at you like a harpoon, I tell him. He clamps onto you like a vice and then he drowns the fuck out of you.

I squeeze his neck and give him a good shake.

That's half a tonne of killing machine with a three thousand pound bite. So Register, my good shamwari, when you get bit you stay bit. And that's a love bite compared to those hippos over there.

I give him another shake to shut him up. He has to grab hold of the boat.

Ok man, ok. I get the picture, he says peeling my fingers back. And he shakes his head at Bart saying, Fine, shove your whole fucking arm in there.

Bart can't resist: that's what your mother said.

Oh really? You mean after she saw the size of your chipolata? Vig us some reebers, you chop.

Whatever, says Bart lobbing a beer at me.

Uh-uh my boy, Reggie says to me wagging his finger and pointing at my unfinished dop.

So it's Nyami Nyami rules all of a sardine? With these lightweights? Ooh, it's going to get messy. Fair enough, I say, and I down my reeber, crush the can and chuck it over my shoulder. Jesus does Reggie only have a hissy fit. He scoops it out the water with the net, cussing me from a dizzy height. What a laugh.

We're tied to a tree on this tiny rowing boat in the middle of the bay. A herd of impala, some zebs and a few giraffes are at the water's edge. Bart and Reggie are jizzing in their pants saying it's amazing, it's beautiful. Ooh-aah, Cantona. It's just a few stupid nyamazans you idiots. These retards know nothing about the bush.

And then, for the hundredth time today, Reggie reels in, sighs and says, Cleaned out again.

Bart then says, Tiddlers, let's move on. It's like a blerry Christmas panto with these guys.

But for once Reggie sees sense and says, Now remember what we said, Bart? If you want to go fishing with the grown-ups you have to behave.

Grown-ups Reg?

Kuff you, says Bart. Your mother said behave, and besides it's getting dark and we're miles away.

That's the best time for tiger, Ox, says Reggie. Now he's

just paraphrasing me, the dick.

Roll us a flips if you're bored, he says.

Good thinking. Give him something to do. Barty hates fishing.

Then my reel zings. That sound. Oh! That sound. Fighting talk. I yank hard: they spit the hook out if you don't wedge it into their bony mouths. He's on. Keep the line tight, tip the rod so he doesn't jump. He can still chomp the trace or just break your line with power so I let him run, then slow him down, reeling hard to keep that hook wedged and my line tight. I shout at Reggie for the net.

He's there next to me. The beer can floats away as he digs into the water to scoop up the fish. The whole boat is rocking, water splashing in as we drop him onto the floor.

Reggie is clawing at the can as it floats out of reach and sinks. I laugh and he's swearing blue hell out of me again. Bart hasn't said a word. He's on the back bench clutching the sides of the boat, legs splayed out. White as a dried turd covered in factor 50.

Jesus fucking Christ you nearly tipped us over, he says, livid. You do that every fucking time.

Maybe if you caught a fish for once, I tell him but he's not interested.

Bah! he says giving me the hand. Whatever. Reggie is standing useless above the fish so I get my pliers and extract the hook. It's wedged in there much better. We weigh him. It's a her actually, she's got eggs. Two kilos: not bad. Coons eat anything so I drop her into the keep net to make friends with the handful of bream I caught earlier. Reggie only ever goes for bream. Because at least you can eat them, he likes to say. Poofter. He's caught fuck-all so far. But his tiddlers are good bait for my tigers so at least he's got a use.

I cast out, light a fag and click over the line to start reeling in. Slowly slowly catch a monkey.

Oi! Bartpole, you great gangling galoot of an albino. One more and I'll be ready for that spliff, I say.

He needs no encouragement. His rod is away already, cleaned and slotted into a holder, and he's onto it in a flash. I have strict rules when fishing: you can dop but only beers no spirits and definitely no spliff. Turns you into a retard.

Reggie nudges me. Reeber time, Ox, he says. Sometimes he can get on a roll and there's no stopping the fucker. Then he's actually quite fun. And it looks like he's getting his stride.

What? Already? I've only had a sip, says Bart.

But rules are rules and Reggie's beer, would you believe, is finished. So we crush ours and I get three more from the box.

Ah! says Bart admiring his beer with a long contented sigh. Kaaa-reeber time. We all have a good laugh at that one – it never gets old – and then he belts out a loud soggy burp that sets the impalas on full alert: dead still apart from their roving ears and flaring nostrils.

Mmmf! And the taste, says Reggie on cue. Bart hands the lighted joint to Reggie. He takes four quick drags and hands it to me still holding his breath.

Not yet, I say returning to my line. Reggie breathes out, a plume of smoke coming from every orifice, swirling all around his face. It looks like his head's on fire.

I don't know how long we sit there, bobbing in the lazy waves. That sound of water slapping and plopping and blipping against the fibreglass hull is one of the best sounds in the world. The sun is setting a classic scene with a ghostly forest of petrified mopane trees reflected in the silky water. Nobody can deny, you don't even have to be

14

gay to know that a sunset on Kariba is the best sight in the whole fucking world. I don't care what else you tell me, that is a fact.

Reggie and Bart are chatting. I'm not following but it's a soothing sound. These okes can go at it all day and you get lulled into a daze. Probably why they're so useless.

I reel in and cast to a different spot. Tigers are predators so there's no use casting where you just caught. Light a fag, get comfy. Life jacket for a backrest. Schweet.

They giggle about something and then even Reggie shuts up. All we can hear is the water tickling the boat, and the birds: green pigeon, grey-headed gull, trumpeter hornbill, white-crowned lapwing, golden oriole, that's a bearded scrub-robin and at last a fish eagle. Aah! That sound—

Shum! Shum! Reggie shouts slapping my shoulder. Jesus I caught a skrook.

What? What the fuck's going on? I'm spinning around looking for a croc or a hippo or something.

It's time to go, he says, night falls and the sky begins to bruise. He's always doing that: dropping into posh English. I think it's from one of those stupid arthouse movies.

And the chicks are probably having a lick-fest by now, he says.

Jesus. Fine. You didn't have to make me drop my load, man.

You were zoned out, dude. We said your name three times, says Bart.

Yeah, right. I look at the state of the boat. They are all packed and ready to go. Have to admit it is getting dark and there were lots of trees just below the surface when we came here – the lake's at maximum level.

Fine. Fucking homos, I say reeling in. I clean my hook

and pack the shit away. These tenders are always knackered and I have to yank the starter cord four times before the engine farts into life blasting two-stroke fumes all over us. Actually I like that smell. I engage the prop and gun us forward. Bart topples backwards, cussing me with his usual red-faced gusto. What a laugh. Only now I realise he's had his life jacket on the whole time. What a homo.

We gurgle across the glassy water weaving between the trees, leaving a long, winding wake as we go.

***

Well, well, well. The brave hunters return. Look everyone, the savages are back with our meat, says Maria, looking down from the top deck, gin and tonic in hand, kikoyi wrapped around her waist, bikini top pure white against that dark skin. Jesus she's hot. What she sees in me. Cock, I guess. Who knows. Who cares.

We stand as Tobias, the retard deckhand, ties us to the mother ship. I grab a handful of Reggie's crotch and shout up to Maria: only one savage got meat, the other two just played with their own. Reggie swings out and connects my chest with the back of his hand. Oof! That stings a bit. He drops to his knees cussing me to hell and gone calling me fuck-arse, arse-cunt, fuck-wit, fuck-fuck-fuck until he runs out of words and just bawls into his fist. His head's on the deck, his arse is pointing up like a footstool, exposed. Teed up, wet shorts and all. Jesus, Reg, didn't they teach you anything? I wick him a bacon slice. He shrieks and falls onto his side kicking out at me like a netted duiker. Tobias is canning himself.

Maria walks away shaking her head and muttering

something to that faggot Rudi. He laughs and looks down at us and then goes back to his book. He's reading by head torch. What a homo. But for real. Rudi's a real homo.

Bart has dropped the keep net onto the bottom deck of the houseboat. He's sharing the remains of the joint and joking with Tobias that we caught him a great white for his dinner. Does he even know what a fucking great white is Bart? Tobias has never heard anything funnier. Captain Onias is parking the tender boats for the night, dragging them up onto the shore and tying them down.

Up on the top deck we drop into the plunge pool. It's lukewarm and we sink in up to our chins. Reggie's eyes are glazed with red and yellow blobs. You can always tell when these okes have been at the turbo lettuce.

And so ends another shitty day in Africa, says Reggie sweeping the water with his free hand. I think that's also from a movie. He's always quoting movies. Got anything original to say, Reg?

And so begins another dreadful night, says Bart, taking a long pull on his beer.

I let rip and a big bubble boils up and bursts the surface. Jesus that's rotten. But now I know Reggie's onto his A-game because he's gagging and laughing at the same time. Lately he would've called me an oaf or a dog or some long cuss to make him sound clever and me look stupid. Instead he just looks at me and says: Shum, you are a human turd.

Why thank you, my Righteous brother. Reckon I had a bit of follow-through there.

***

The rain did come in the night. No surprises there. We all had a good hose at Reggie pretending not to brick his pants with all the thunder and lightning. It was a cracker of a storm and we chillaxed on the top deck watching the pyro show. In the end it was lame though because instead of getting proper dopped as is right and proper on such occasions, everyone got all mellow oooohing and aaaahing over every single fucking fork of lightning. Then they went to bed. Bunch of losers. Rudi and the chicks were especially annoying. Maria said I stank and moved off to the other side of the boat where Bart and Reggie were playing cards under a mozzy net they'd strung up from the roof. Fuck them. I got wasted anyway. Puked over the edge in the middle of the night so today I feel just peachy.

It's just the two of us this morning. Tried to wake Bart. I even dropped a mouthful of gob in his ear but nothing. Dead. Would rather sleep than fish. Who the fuck doesn't like fishing? Oh. It's obvious now: homos. Rudi and Bart can bum each other to death for all I care.

The sun is up and the last bits of morning pink and orange and shit are gone. It's already hot but after last night's rain the sky is clear. Like a fucking postcard. Reggie's going for bream, Thow we can eat thomething, he says. Thinks he's goddam Jamie Oliver or that faggot farm guy, living off the land when all he ever catches is bait for my tigers. Right now he's just lying there half asleep on a pile of life vests. I bet he doesn't even have a worm on his hook.

I reach around and give his line a quick tug. He's up and lurching, waving his arms around. Oi! Hey! Oi! Got one, got one, he's shouting and he's reeling in, tugging at his rod. A chunk of weeds on a shiny silver hook breaks the surface.

I'm just feeding these fuckers, he says.

He wrestles a worm onto his hook and drops the line

back in. I'll get him again later.

Why the fuck do you even go fishing? I ask him.

I mean, the worms freak him out, hates touching the fish, can't even get the fucking hook out and twice yesterday dropped his catch over the edge.

I told you a thousand times, Shum, it's an excuse to be on a boat, he says. To do nothing and just enjoy, he says. Is that so hard to understand?

Yes, that's hard to understand. Tiny, wobbly, uncomfortable, getting gocha'd in the blazing sun. You can't even ski behind this piece of shit. Is there a point other than fishing? And as if you, of all people, need an excuse to do nothing.

Ha! You've got a point there, he says.

I go back to my line. Reggie lights up and he's sipping on a coke and munching through a pile of chips on his stomach. Leather hat covering his face. He's not even holding his rod. It's propped against the side of the boat. Only thing he's going to catch is a clap. From me.

No bites and my bait is running low. You can only cast so many times with these tiddlers and then they dissolve off the hook. Reg needs to pull finger. I wait for him to finish his chips, exposing his belly. Jesus, this oke is fit. His shirt is open and the fucker has that perfect build chicks just jizz themselves over.

I slap his stomach hard as I can.

Croc! Croc! I shout.

He's up and bent over coughing and of course cussing the shit out of me. I give him the elbow and point to a pair of nostrils poking through a film of slime in the corner of the cove.

Shum, it's a frikken log. You just wanted to slap me you—

It's a croc, man. You want to go swim there? I haul out

19

the bag of stones brought along for this very purpose.

Let's see shall we? I buzz a stone and it plops way off. The croc doesn't even move.

See? It's a log, he says. But Reggie can't resist. He lobs a weighty nut in a high arc. We watch it climb to its peak, squinting against the bright sky; it slows, it pauses, it drops like a kingfisher on full throttle and cracks the item bang on the snout with a weighty thud.

The thing thrashes out, snapping its jaws and then it drops out of sight under the slime.

Ha-haaaaaaaaaaaaaa! Got him. The fucker. We're both jumping and shouting and dancing and rocking the boat like it's on a tightrope. Total fluke, but who cares, I fucking hate all crocs. Justice has been served.

See? It was a croc, I tune him.

Tiddler croc, he says. Like your cock. Ha! I'm a poet and I don't even know it.

A poet and a fag you mean.

You wish.

Rudi wishes you mean.

We have a good chortle over that. I crack open my first reeber and get back to my line. I give Reggie a kick and say to him: Make yourself useful man, catch some bait.

Ok man, ok. Just stop assaulting me man, I'm very fragile. I have mental issues, he says. Again with the movie quotes. Sometimes I want to smash his face in. What's worse is Maria knows all those movies too and they go off finishing each other's lines. Jesus! Sometimes I want to smash her face in too.

Time to relax. We are fishing. On Kariba. Just enjoy. Count the birds. The other tender boat gurgles and whines into the picture. It's the girls, off on a cruise, all dolled up in summer dresses and clutching massive straw hats to their heads. They look bored. Jeers and taunts bounce across the water when they see us.

Hey boys, have you caught an STD yet? Did we interrupt your man-sex? Of course that's Rudi. That's all he ever thinks about. Bart has weaselled his way onto the pleasure cruise of course. Hates fishing but he sure loves the fish.

Reggie gives them the finger. And then they're gone. The nasal buzz of the motor fades to nothing and their wake gives our boat a few jolts.

Back to my line. Sometimes it doesn't matter if you don't catch anything. It's like Reggie says: to be out here is enough. I can't even be bothered moving to another spot. My last tiddler is mashed so I just drop it to the bottom and hope for the best until Reg catches some more. The silence returns. The heat presses down on us. A cicada cranks up and his chinas all join in. It sounds like tinnitus.

Dude, did you hear about Roy? says Reg.

Taylor? Ya. Got his Section 8. Fucking cunts.

Reggie sits up and he's twisted round facing me and his hat's on the back of his head. Very next day, he says, a mob is at his gate. In a fucking ZRP truck. Gave him two days to leave. And some cunt minister's cunt cousin gets the farm, lock and stock. Thieving cunts. His folks bought that farm in '96 and of course they gave the government first option, as was required.

He jabs a finger at me. Like it's my fault. Like he wants to ice me. His jaw is clenched and he hasn't blinked his bulging eyes in like half an hour. He slams the boat with his hat and the rant goes on: But no, our illustrious government officially declined the offer – opting to squander their maBritesh guilt cash on Benzes and houses for their bitches instead – so of course they went ahead and bought. Now the government coffers are dry, they just take it anyway. And all the workers? And their wives and kids? He even built a school and a clinic. Fuck, even their own soccer team. And they were good. We used to drink Skuds and watch them play home games.

He shakes his head and goes silent, just staring into the distance at nothing, brooding like those rain clouds from last night. Then he says: fucking cunts.

Heavy stuff. But seriously, this is Africa, what do you expect? Rodriguez said it best: a monkey in silk is a monkey no less. Can't say that to Reggie of course. He believes in an African democracy. What an idiot. So does Maria. What idiots.

All right, all right, keep your pants on man, don't scare away the fish, I tell him. Need to lighten the mood here. This fucker can get me down with his stories. Trouble is he knows too much. Reads too much. Keeps up with all the news. It's just depressing: serves no purpose; makes no fucking difference.

Ya. Fair enough, Shum. Lucky there's no goatbite on board, hey?

Ya. Very lucky, I tell him. Then his line goes and he's diving for his rod shouting and yelping much better. For someone who hates fishing, he sure gets into high spirits when he lands a whopper.

HURRY-UP TOWN

'How was Reebs?' Boils is asking. We're at The George, our Friday rendezvous. Spot the whitey. Concrete picnic tables in a beer garden. More beer than garden as it happens except for some ivy climbing up the Durawall and a solitary silver ash like the one we had in our garden. Harry and I used to climb it and spy on Natalie next door. My little brother: the tears well up and the chin wobbles when I think of him. Can't help it. At least he doesn't have to endure any of this shit. Anyway, we always come here: nobody bothers us and the drinks are cheap.

Hurry-up Town. Harries. Capital city of our great backyard nation and home to more single men and fewer single women than any settlement in recorded history. Or so it seems to me. Never mind we've just been on a houseboat for five days on Kariba with three other women – one was a fag, the other was a fag-hag and Shum is nyomping Maria so she doesn't count.

Everyone is shouting at the same time, 'Fuck—' 'Dude—' 'Awesome—'

'Fuck, we laughed a lot dude, it was top-dollar. You should have come man, bugger your cousin's wedding,' says Reggie.

'Weddings are junk. I hate weddings. They're the quickest path to divorce.'

'Bart, Bart, Bart.' Reggie is shaking his head. He reaches across the table and squeezes my shoulder and says, 'Weddings are the only path to divorce so of course you would hate them.'

'Ch-chck,' says Boils. And they all cock imaginary shot-guns and take aim at my head.

I slap away their arms. They are all laughing. What do they know? Pricks.

'How was it by the way?' says Reggie.

'Good. It was good,' says Boils. 'Got super-dopped.'

'There's a surprise.'

'Pulled this hot tchib from Bo'jurg. I think it was Lana's best naicha from looks days. Ended up starkers in the Cajuzzi with a tobble of schnapps.'

'Yeah right,' says Reg.

Most of the time I've got no idea what Boils is saying, talking cabwords all the time. You've got to mix the syllables more or less backwards to make a new word. Like naicha is cabwords for china and tchib of course, well, we all know what that means. I think Boils practises on his own in that little outhouse he calls home.

Shum wants details, egging him on. He says, 'That's mushie. Did you nyenga?' Boils is what we call a pathological liar. Reggie looked it up and everything. These guys love taking the piss.

'Nah, just a gons and a leef,' says Boils, looking down at his hands. And then he says to Shum, 'Shiffing any good?'

The only person in the world who loves fishing more than Shum is Boils. I think that's why Shum was so grumpy all the time: nobody to fish with. Reggie tries but I'm junk at it. It's so fiddly and slimy and I don't see the point. I get so frigging bored. Maybe if the chicks came along we'd have a bit more fun but they're never interested. The chick who likes fishing in Zims will have about a thousand okes with ready-salted hard-ons howling at her window. Mind you, every chick in Zims has that already, so why bother with fishing?

'Rubbish. These cunts were useless of course,' says Shum. Rhodies all call each other shum. Or shums. Short for shamwari, which means my friend in Shona. Rhymes with bum. And chum. As in: Howzit shum my bestest bum chum. Ha! He'd rip your head off.

Reggie objects. He caught the biggest bream, he says. At least you can eat bream, he says. Shum and Boils exchange a look. Shum snorts and shakes his head as he glugs his beer.

'I bet all they did was tug on their little peckers and mokes their stupid pips off.'

'You know it,' says Shum mid-swallow and he's coughing beer froth all over the table.

'Played cards twenty-four seven?'

'Eggs-zackery,' Shum says and then, wait for it, wait for it, here it comes, 'fucking fags.' It gets to be boring.

Here comes Maria, bomber and phone in one hand, another bomber under her arm and a rucksack over her shoulder. That's the Zims way: never arrive unarmed. Groups of men in suits clutching their own bombers – Labels of course – step aside as she cuts a river of respectful nods and earnest faces through the crowd. Everyone knows Maria: she's the people's hero. I don't get how or even why she does it. She's not even Zimbabwean. Ok, she was born here, but her parents are from Greece. Escaped the shit back there fifty years ago only to land right in it here. She can move to Europe whenever she wants to. Tomorrow even.

'Two? Two measly reebers? Is that all?'

I can't tell if he's joking or not.

'Hello to you too, Shum,' Maria says offering him a cheek over her shoulder as she sits down. 'And anyway these are both mine. Get your own.'

Reggie hoses himself at this. 'Ay! Bartles,' he says slapping my back, 'it's your round, arse-wipe.' He gets like that when Shum and Boils are around. Most of the time he's quiet as a mouse. I know he's joking but why does he have to get all macho just because these chops are here? And don't get me started on Maria. When she's around he's like a kraal dog simpering at her feet for scraps.

'Loibs.'

'Ramia.'

'Doog dehwing?'

'Ya-no, it was fine, hey. Just telling these okes, we got super-dopped.'

'No tish, what else?'

The George is filling up. The tables are all crammed and guys are standing in small circles and the noise is getting festive. A madala in overalls hobbles his way through the crowd collecting empties. He's pulling a trolley with four crates stacked up and he shuffles backwards, bent back and bandy legs in shaggy oil-stained overalls. Nobody acknowledges him. They just move aside and carry on their conversation over his head; these okes hate poor people. Makes me sad. A band is setting up inside so it's going to be a long night for him.

'Four lively ones, Chamu!'

Chamunorwa's been working here since thirty-two years if you can believe him. I have to shout and show him four fingers. He brings me four Black Label bombers. One brick each. Where else in the world do you hand over a trillion bucks for a beer? And call it a good deal at that? The minting tape is still intact. And how much is one brick worth? One U.S. dollar. One trillion Zimbabwe dollars buys you one U.S. dollar. You want change, take some sweets or a loosey – a cigarette. Carry your cash in a backpack. Take a shopping trolley to the bank.

When I get back Maria has gone to the toilet or is on the phone again and there's a lull in the conversation. Boils asks, 'So what's the plan for tonight, then?'

'Don't know, man. Scar's? The Baths were a bit dry last Friday.' Good one, Reggie. I let him get away with it though because Shum would be all over it.

'Belgravia. Beerfest,' says Shum. He burps out the word beerfest. Classy. Reggie hoots. Boils just drinks his reeber. Waiting to choose sides no doubt. Waiting for Shum's re-action no doubt.

'When will you homos realise they are the cat's tits? Cheap booze, cheap chicks and live music. What's not to like? Plus you don't get a fag rubbing his cock against your leg in the bogs neither. It's just up the road. I'm going.'

'Errr, let's see?' says Reg. 'Last time we went to one of those fuckwit-fests, Boils was tackled to the ground by a Rhodie in fellies.' He shakes his head and says, 'In actual fellies. Bart passed out in the field and a chick pissed on him. On purpose. And my "nigger lover" shirt nearly got me beaten up. Besides, Shum, I thought you liked cock?'

Uh-oh, Reg.

'Your mother likes cock,' Shum says. Phew, close call there. 'You fags can do what you like but I am going to the beerfest. I'm going to tamba to Section 8 and I'm going to get fucked. Twice.'

'Section 8?' says Reggie.

They're pretty good. Cool name. Tom was at my school. A year or two below me I think.

'That's what I said fucknut. And they are doing some songs with,' and he puts on his best Shona accent, 'Thomas Mapfumo and the Blacks Unlimited.'

'Bollocks. How do you know that?' says Reg.

'Maria told me. You know her brother owns Tamba Promotions, or her brother's friend, I don't know.'

'And they are doing a beerfest? Jeez, it's more like a music festival. Why didn't you tell us, you idiot?'

'It's a giant tent in a sports field with booze and music. It's a fucking beerfest.'

Reggie does a double-take over my shoulder and then, super-quick, his eyes flick to Shum. Shum is too busy biting his nails and scowling to notice. I turn to see what he was looking at and sure enough there's Maria. She's got her serious face on with a deep frown, eyes down, looking deep into the earth's core. So it was the phone then. Something hectic as usual. She says, 'Don't ask' whenever we ask. So now we never ask. We just hand her a drink, which Reggie does the moment she sits down. Flops down more like. Her shoulders sag and she's staring at the table. Shum gives Reggie a look that says, 'Fix this, dude.'

'So I hear Thomas is playing at a freaking beerfest tonight? What the duck?' Reggie says to Maria.

You can tell it takes a big effort but she drags herself out of the deep end and takes a big sigh and then she says, 'Far as I know it's still on. We only found out on Wednesday. Whole town is going it seems.'

'And he's playing with Section 8?'

'Yep. My brother finally twigged guys have had it with old Bud singing Run, Rhino, Run and Fraser's Rhodie anthems are as tired as he is. He wanted lively beats so I told him about Section 8. You retards don't know about this?'

'Well thanks for telling us. Now I have to cancel my hair appointment.'

Jeezo Reg. But Maria, bless her, she still manages a laugh. A fake laugh it must be said but then she runs her hand over

28

his smooth dome and says, 'You look just fine to me, Reg.'

This is awkward: Reggie swooning, Shum bristling. I have to butt in quick, so I say, 'Ok here's the plan: a few more reebers here, then we'll head over to the festival before the crowds. What time does it start?'

'Oh! So now it's a fucking festival is it?' Shum elbows my ribs – fuck that hurts, 'and suddenly, just because Maria's Limited Blacks are playing, you're all keen as mustard. Bunch of fucking benders.'

'Woo-ooooooooooo! Ay, Shum, kuss my kid, Section 8 are rad-assed mo-fos. And tchef more reebers, it's your round kufnut,' says Boils, happy he doesn't have to choose sides. This is good. By the time Shum gets back he'll be over that little incident.

'Fuck you, Boils,' says Shum but he's getting up anyway and he leaves us with a parting, 'fucking faggots,' in case we didn't get it the first fifty times.

I know the rules but I just have to ask Maria how many poor people she helped today. Genuine, I want to know, but I also need to know if she's made progress with my case. My ex-wife – ya, ya, ya, it was a shotgun, ok – she buggered off to Mud Island two years ago with my boy, Joey, far, far away from me and my green mamba. My passport to nowhere. Except maybe hell. Maria says I might qualify for asylum in the UK. He turns six in November.

Maria's face sags and she gets this faraway look. Her chin dimples and her eyes flicker. And then it's gone. She looks up taking a deep breath and says, 'Christ you won't believe the state of the judges' bogs at Court House.'

This isn't good. It means my case is a long, long way from being looked at. A father wanting to be near his son is a low priority for human rights lawyers in Snoobabland circa 2008.

The power has gone and the old man is passing out candles as he fills up his empty crates. Reggie takes one and lights it. He's bent over the table dripping wax into a pool to make a stand when Shum arrives, dumps five bombers on the table, grabs the candle and shoves it into an empty bottle and relights it. So he's still smarting. I bet that wax stung.

The stars shine bright over the dark city, chatter becomes raucous and the beer garden dances to the warm light of a hundred flickering candles.

'I hope they've got generators,' says Reggie.

Maria gives him a withering glare. 'Of course they'll have fucking generators, Reggie.'

KRINDING TO THEAD

My brain wants to erupt out my fucking temples. Jesus. Where the fuck am I? Oh. This is home. Ingocheni. The Island of Insanity in the Sea of Stupidity as Reggie likes to say. Ad fucking nauseam. He also says we're inmates not housemates. There's Bart splayed out over the other couch snoring like an old dog. He must be cooking with the sun full on his face. That frown says it all. Holy shit that beanpole can sleep. What the fuck happened last night? Why the fuck are we in the lounge?

Another fly joins the lone ranger. They collide and spin like electrons. A third fly joins in. Now a fourth and they're all on this random merry-go-round under the light bulb hanging from a shit-stained cord in the middle of the room. Why do they do that? Fucking cunts. A turtle dove is telling us to work harder and some bulbuls are heckling him. Reminds me of camping down south as a kid. Those were the days.

Boils walks in. Skinny legs and bony knees protruding from his tiny black boxers. He has a dop and he's lighting a cigarette. Dripping wet. Must've been his splashing in the pool that woke me.

Good morning, sunshine, he says to me around his fag, bouncing it up and down as he speaks, the smoke burning his eyes. He coughs, wheezes more like, sits on Bart, crosses his legs like a lady and says, Any idea what happened last night?

I'm looking up at the strange pattern on the ceiling. I rub my temples. Fuck. My head. I remember going to the beerfest and moshing to Section 8. Fragments are coming back to me. Elbowing a chick in the face. Stealing a bottle of tequila from The Europa— Maria had a cadenza.

Hey! Who were those tchibs?

What bitches?

Maria's friends, they came with us to Scar's. Pretty hot. I gave the one a leef on our way there in Maria's gee. Massive jellies, he says and he holds out his hands to emphasise.

I don't remember any chicks.

Ya, man, it's all coming back to me. One was on Reggie's lap, couldn't get enough of him, and the other sat on mine. We were seven in that car, fuck me it was grinding. I had my hand up her top and everything. She was giving it the— and he makes a grinding motion with his pelvis.

Yeah right, Boils.

Bart groans underneath him.

Uh-oh, you've stirred the beast, I tell him. He's going to want breakfast. At least you'll both get lucky for a change.

Bart is awake. He grunts something at Boils that sounds like get the fuck off me. He twists and shoves and then hoofs Boils across the room like a swatted fly. And Boils is squawking much better. Cunt gets skinnier every day. Soon he'll be nothing but cock and rib. And those fucking teeth.

Fuck me. What the hell happened last night? says Bart turning onto his side.

Well, we all got super-kuffed and then went over to your mom's house. She was her usual accommodating self of course.

Fuck off Boils.

Genuine. Shum here got his cock kussed while I saw to the business end of things. Chicken Inn. Extra mayo. Mm-mm-mm, she was on fine form last night.

Bart sighs and sits up. He sways, gripping the edge of the couch with both arms. He stares at the floor.

Fuck my head hurts, he says.

Boils offers up some of his beer. Bart waves it away as he stands up shaking his head.

Ha-ha! You did get a stonker you big bum chum, says Boils and he's humping the carpet like an inchworm. You like my bony arse, naika? You like to nyenga-nyenga with little boys, ne?

Bart is still half asleep; he rubs his face and staggers off to the bog.

Gone for a donza. Let's go wake Reggie, says Boils.

***

Boils is singing Nyama yekugocha at full volume as we open Reggie's door. I join in and we're chanting and clapping and stomping around, Woya yaweri nyama yekugocha baya wabaya, baya wabaya, and then we both jump on the lump in the bed that must be Reggie.

Rise and shine fuckface, Boils shouts punching the lump.

Get off, get off man. Get off, Reggie screams and kicks out and Boils takes flight crashing into Reggie's desk, knocking shit off it and spilling beer everywhere.

All right, all right, keep you knickers on, Jeez! Fuckin' kaiso, he says.

Boils got hurt there you can tell. Reggie's got some power in those pins of his.

Oh my fuck, says Reggie groaning and easing himself onto his back. That hurts. Everything hurts. Put some fucking clothes on you faggots.

I flick open the curtains and sunlight blasts Reggie in the face. Fuck he looks rough.

Gonna be a scorcher today, says Boils and he's singing and jumping again, Nyama yekugocha—

Stop it! Stop. Just stop. Shut the fuck up, says Reggie. Do you even know what that means?

Course I do. It means, 'We're gonna cook your flesh you lily-white bastards,' says Boils, licking his chops, then he's slapping Reggie around the head and shouting, C'mon motherfucker, get your clothes on motherfucker.

Ok, ok. Stop it. Just fucking stop it, says Reggie covering his head.

What a laugh.

What happened last night? Reggie says, still covering his head, still groaning.

Don't know, man. Nothing and everything is my guess, says Boils. He flicks Reggie's chest with a towel. What a shot. It sounds like a good-sized squib going off and Reggie doubles up, screaming. Ha-ha! He's livid, growling at us to get the fuck out of his room.

At the door Boils turns and, chuckling like Beavis the Butthead, he flicks the towel and connects with Reggie's back. Fuck me, perfect shot again: whikaah! That's boarding school for you. Reggie goes berserk screaming like a bitch as we nip away down the passage and crash into Bart coming out the bog with an empty bucket and a rotten stench wafting after him.

Jesus, Bart. Light a match.

***

We're sitting at the kitchen table with beers on the go when Reggie staggers through, red-eyed, puffy-faced and wincing as he sits down. He's bent over, moaning into his hands, one butt-cheek off the chair like he's going to bolt any moment. Poor little faggot.

We're all watching him, waiting. He lifts his head and says, Every goddam bone in my body hurts. Look at this, he says and he shows us a graze down his leg. Then he says, It feels like I was set alight and put out with a spade.

Ha! Your mother's a spade, says Boils standing up. He shows us grazes down his leg, along his sides, up his back, on his arms. He slaps a bomber in front of Reggie and opens it, spraying froth all over the place, pouring it into a plastic cup.

Jesus Boils, Reggie says.

You can't run with the dogs and piss like a puppy, says Boils wagging his finger at him.

Reggie sighs and says, Whatever. He sucks the froth and then to Bart he says, Ox, what the fuck you waiting for? Roll us a carrot.

We sit in the kitchen a while, drinking tea and beers and smoking spliffs, piecing together events from last night. That beerfest was actually not bad. Section 8 rocked. Best use of Phil Collins's goddam piss-willy whiny nasal voice I ever heard. And Thomas is a cool dude actually. He jammed with Section 8 and played some of his own songs cussing all over Bobby McGee and Co. The Rhodies were livid. Talked to the Lehman brothers for a bit. Their mullet-headed crew of tattooed bikers and beer-bellied chicks were scowling much better. Like a pack of hyenas. They try to look hard. Talked about setting fire to the tent. Wonder if they did? Ha! Just remembered the moshing and me connecting with that chick right on the snoz. Blood everywhere. And oh ya

Badza crashed the stage.

Thomas knew his poems and everything, Reggie is saying all excited, not so sore now, ay boyo? He jammed along with Section 8 while Badza mumbled shit into the mic.

Badza is this huge jungle bunny with a mop of dreads. A poet or so he likes to claim. Won some random prize twenty years ago and now he thinks he's fucking Shakespeare and the Messiah rolled into one.

That tongue, man. He cracks me up that dude.

You know he lost his teeth layping buggery?

Playing what?

Buggery. Rugby you tool.

Balls.

Struze, man. Got toobed in the chops by a Churchill guy.

Sure Boils.

I'm serious, man. Check him next time. He's huge. Played first team for Saints before he got pellexed. Savaged his way into every ruck, maul and brawl biting and scratching and kicking as he went. Even back then he was barking mad.

You think?

Ya-ya, for real. I heard he nicked his dealer's acid stash. Scoffed the lot in a day. Went benzy.

Did you see the Mono?

Ya, fuck, it's coming back to me. Getting stuck into one of the Lehmans.

Fucking slapper.

Nah-ah, she's a virgin. Waiting till she's eighteen she says.

Says to you, faggot. To everyone else she says take a number.

Jesus, we moshed the shit out of that place.

Did you see that chick I blala'd? She dropped like a sack of shit.

That was you? Reggie is giving me the shaking head face.

Not on purpose you cunt. Anyway. What is it this fuck-wit always says? Run with the dogs? It's a fucking moshpit you douchebag.

Reggie is tutting and clucking, the others are just laughing and telling more stories about last night. Fuck him. What'd she expect? I'm off for a swim. I leave these retards pulling their wires over Maria's friends who we picked up at The Europa on the way to Scar's. I fucked the one chick in the bogs. Which one? I don't know. The hot English mustard one. The one Boils claims to have felt up on the way there. She was wasted. Bet you a million bucks she doesn't even remember. Hmm, come to think of it, I only just remembered that myself. Wonder where Maria was? Swooning over Reggie's shiny dome is my guess.

The water is still cold. I swim a length underwater. That's better. Nothing like an icy dip to fix a blazing babalas. I float on my back doing starfish-stroke. Cotton ball clouds are gathering white against the deep blue sky. Fuck it needs to rain. Imagine being in the valley now? Imagine. If only some brave FTs would venture into Mad-Bob-Land I'd have some fucking work on. Meantime, I'm squatting in this shithole selling dodgy paint from the back of my car. Jesus.

They're still reliving last night when I come back into the kitchen. Reggie very much looks at the trail of water I leave behind me and shakes his head. Fuck him.

Let's get fucked, I say to Boils. Always up for it is our kwashiorkor kid.

Aay-kuffin-men to that, he says glugging his beer down. He taps the side to make it go faster. I'm digging in the drinks fridge for a cold one.

That's the last of our supplies in there, says Reggie and

him and Bart are having a fat whinge about us depleting their stocks.

Relax, says Boils burping, I've got ten crates at the garage. Plus two drums of diesel.

Boils. Nothing in small measures for this one. And for once it could be true. These sparkies have connections everywhere. I've got my own fair share of supplies it must be said, stashed at my bally's place. Just not going to share with these cunts is all.

You drink diesel?

Mmf and the taste, he says.

How's your borehole? Boils says.

Dried up in June already. Last year it went till August. Year before we had water the whole time.

Ya, man. Everyone's raping their boreholes now. The stuff falls from the sky and these frigging muppets can't even supply water in their own capital city, says Reggie.

Goatbite! I shout.

And everyone is shouting, GOATBITE!

Reggie looks like he got slapped. Oh, fuck, he says, fuck, fuck, fuck. Come on guys. Seriously okes, I'll kuffin' chunder. It's kuffin eight o'clock in the morning, man and I'm carrying a prize-winning barbie.

Tough titty, arse-wipe. Rules, my friend, is rules, says Bart sniggering like a little kid.

Boils is up and mixing the concoction already and he's dancing and clapping his hands like a Mongoloid on speed.

On special zees month, ladeez and gentlement, he says with a lame French accent— clearly he failed at school. We 'ave zee'98 Goatbite vintage, a deee-lightful concoction of, oh let's see, zee vodka yes and ah-ha yes zee skud missile.

Skud? shouts Reggie. Fuck off!

We're all chanting GOATBITE! at Reggie and thumping the table with anything we can find and stomping our feet while Boils pours a monster shot of vodka into a glass and then he tops it with a drop of skud. Looks like porridge, smells like vomit. Reggie is pleading for mercy. We're having none of it.

Drink you fucker.

And he's hyperventilating like a free-diver and still begging and bitching and whining. I lose it and shout at him: Just drink it you fucking faggot.

Twisting his face and bleating like a nanny-goat, he pinches his nose and downs it. Then he leaps up, hand to mouth and, bolting towards the toilet, he skids on the wet floor. Puke sprays everywhere. His legs shoot out and he drops, arms and legs flailing like a darted giraffe, onto his back with a solid, bony thump.

Jesus I think I shit my pants laughing. I think everyone did.

Except Reggie. He's lying in a puddle of water and puke with bits of it down his front and he's swearing us to blue hell and back and trying to get up but he keeps slipping.

Bart is canning himself, tears pouring down his face. Boils slides down the side of the counter and is on the floor rolling, howling, clutching his sides.

What a fucking laugh.

Reggie hauls himself up. Wipes some puke off his chest and flicks it at Boils but he's laughing too much to even notice or care. Then he hobbles out the kitchen and we can hear him splashing into the pool. He's gone a long time and we are just laughing. Laughing, laughing, laughing.

We are only just recovering when Reggie comes back. Someone sniggers and we crack and Bart is up, arm around Reggie's shoulders saying, shit happens, it was an accident and that he mustn't take it personally and that he just might have given us the single funniest moment of our entire lives. Reggie is just shaking his head and swearing.

Fucking cunts, he's saying which only makes us laugh more and he's complaining about how sore it was; how he landed on his hip and probably broke it.

Dude, you kuff with the toag, the toag kuffs with you.

Whatever Boils, you fuck goats for fun.

No way, man, I'm a monogamist true and true. I only nyomp your mom.

Ag, fuck you man, says Reggie and he chucks his cup of beer in Boils's face. Must've got some in his eyes because Boils is all shocked and livid, his face dripping beer, mouth open like a dead fish, wiping his face like a floppy in the deep end.

That's offsides, Reg, I say and I chuck my beer in his face only it's not beer it's tea and it's still pretty fucking hot.

If I was laughing hard before, when Reggie slipped in his puke, that was nothing. I'm fucking toppled over, falling on the floor. I try to say sorry, I didn't mean it, thought it was beer but the words can't come out I'm laughing too hard.

Reggie howls like a dragon being arse-raped by a bazooka. The whole table topples and takes Boils with it. He's trapped underneath like a dungbeetle on its back. Stop, please stop. I can't even breathe anymore. I might actually die laughing. Reggie is in a rage and he kicks me in the stomach, then he's dragging me around the kitchen by my feet, pulling me through his puke but I don't care I'm just laughing. I can't even hear what Reggie is yelling at me.

Reggie gives me one last kick and stomps out the kitchen. What a laugh.

***

We're playing that wrestling game in the pool. The kids' one where you sit on your mate's shoulders and try and get the other oke off his mate's shoulders. It's got a name but I don't know it. Of course we play a bit rougher than the kids do. Or maybe not. Those fuckers are tough. I played 'polo at school so I know the tricks. I pinch Boils under the arm every time I lunge for him and accidentally on purpose kick Reggie to try and topple them both. But Reggie is too strong despite the Bartman's height advantage. And Boils is so liquored he can't feel a thing, lashing at me like a drowning coon. He connects across my ear, on my nose – fuck that hurt – so I grab his throat and pull, twisting and shoving and Boils is gagging and Bart's yelling at me to chill but fuck him, fuck them. I haul him down and drop off Bart's shoulders pummelling Boils into the bottom of the pool. He's twisting and kicking and scrabbling at my hands. I want to shove his head into the ground. Bury him. It goes black. I feel arms pulling me and then I'm out the water, still clinging to Boils's neck and Bart and Reggie are pulling my hands off. Boils's eyes are on stalks. He's petrified. Ha-ha-ha! What a hoot. These fuckers are such fags.

Jesus, Shum, says Reggie. He's panting. We're all waist high in the shallow end and Boils is wading to the side coughing. Bart dives down to fetch his sunglasses and I

41

haul myself out of the pool.

What? I'm saying, all innocent like, just to piss him off more. Run with the dogs, man, I say.

Do you have to be so? Reggie says slapping the water. Do you have to always? Why is it? Ag! He looks up at the sky and sighs saying under his breath: fuck it, what's the use?

Boils looks at us cheeky-as-fuck and says, all groggy and choky, Let's krind to thead.

Half way there already.

I'll second that, says Bart and Boils is whooping and skipping, chuffed as a bumblebee, as we slop back to the verandah and flop on the chairs.

Dead-ants! I shout and we hit the deck, legs in the air except Bart. As per usual.

Fuck it, man. What? he says.

Beers, dickfuck.

MY BROTHER'S KEEPER

Ah! You have come to. I was worried we had overcooked our nyama there. I hope you slept soundly, yes? Alas our makeshift incarceration facility lacks certain luxuries. Please accept my humble apologies for this degrading situation. Most undignified for such a dignified dignitary as yourself. Most unsanitary actually. In fact you have about you an overpowering effluent stench, don't you know? Ammonia and human shit and fear. And wet dog. Powerful stuff. Offends the offal factories wouldn't you say?

Now where was I? Burning down my brother's house, killing his children with exploding pots of raging green mambas? Ah! Yes. That's right.

Because, my friend, it is necessary my brother's line be eliminated. Their threat vanquished. Their claims to his fortune were clamping my style so to speak. Yes of course they are my blood and kin. And I should protect them too, yes? Perhaps in your small view of the world. But not in the green mamba's ancient ways. No sah! Not in the reptilian empire where snake eat snake is the only means of survival. You know what is a mamba's biggest threat? Other mambas, yes. They eat the little ones, yum, yum, yum. Nature is cruel, yes, but nature is balanced. Survival of the fittest, yes. Compassion is humanity's achilles heel: we protect the weak, care for the sick and dote upon the elderly. Compassion, my friend, will be our species' demise.

Primitive? Primitive? Primitive you say? Spare me the objection, I can read your face like a crystal what? Like a crystal ball. Like primates you say? Like apes? Like monkeys in the trees? The very shame on you. Now you have made me strike you. That is not my habit. Look now: you put your swine blood on my hand and now I must use my last handkerchief. Tcha! Disgusting. I will have to Jik this. Next you will be saying we descended from those self-same apes, yes? No? Good. Smart boy.

Iwe! Maxwell. Bloody fuck-sakes, Chikomo. He sleeps would you believe? Maxwell you big brute, take this. Get it laundered and returned to my person. I want it bleached white. Whiter than Whiteman's what? Flour. You follow me? Good.

Filthy swine blood.

NYAMA YEKU GOCHA

Shum and Reggie have simmered down. Touch and go there. Meltdown city was very nearly upon us but they've holstered their handbags and we're now undertaking the most serious business of finishing every drop of booze in the house. Boils sniffed out a bottle of vodka and he's levelled out on a drunken plateau, high above the clouds in Zombieland. Pretty well oiled too, if I dare say so myself. Still breaking out in titters every time I think of Reggie somersaulting in a plume of his own puke. And it sets the others off as well. Reggie is not amused. In fact he's still hobbling, complaining that he broke his hip and whinging that he's going to need a hip replacement by the time he's forty and we can all go to hell and what-what. Toughies. That faceful of scalding tea probably didn't help much.

I made a bong from a Mazoe bottle and Reggie's got it bubbling away as we speak. Shum, well, he's just being Shum as usual.

'Shitsakes! What's the time?' Reggie says, coughing smoke out his mouth and nose. 'The cricket should have started by now.'

Boils springs to his feet. These garden chairs are great for that: you lean back and then catapult yourself up. Probably by design as the only way you'll get a drunken chop to stand up. Anyway, Boils's chair is still wobbling by the time he comes back.

'It's the build-up,' he says, flopping down.

Reggie is hitting the opening lines of Nyama yekugocha and we all join in on the chorus, or at least, the only line we know: baya wabaya.

'Scheme we've got a chance?' Shum says, biting his nails.

'Against England? Fuck off, we're gonn' git kuffed uuuuuuuuuuup,' says Boils.

Shum inspects his fingernail, says to Boils, 'You're gonna get fucked up, that's for sure, but I'm talking about the cricket, kuffnut. Where's it being played?'

'The Oval. There's a chance,' says Reggie all serious, 'if Henry decides to bowl on the right track.'

'Balls,' says Boils. 'Henry's not even playing, nor is Flower. They were fired for wearing black bands on their arms last week.'

'What shit you talking now, Boils?'

'Struze man, they wore black bands in a game "mourning the death of democracy" or some shit like that. Reginald, I thought you read the news?'

'News to me,' Reggie says, coughing more jets of smoke.

'Well check it.' He's nodding towards the telly in the lounge. 'Check now, you'll see. Henry and Andy are over skadovas, exiled to fuckdom come.'

'Boils, the crap you come up with,' I say to him. I mean, sometimes, he just goes too far with his stories.

'Struze Bart, you'll see,' he says.

'Henry or no Henry, Flower or no Flower, we're still going to get chopped.'

'Correct,' says Boils up-ending his vodcoke.

'At the cricket you dick,' says Shum hurling an empty can at Boils. It bounces off his head and clatters into the house.

'Your aunty's a dick,' says Boils and he's dipping his head at Shum like a Zulu warrior.

'She told me you were a chip – a fucking chipolata,' says Shum and so it goes back and forth in a never-ending test series – a cockfighting test series – that nobody ever wins.

I hated cricket at school. Everyone had to play, even numnutses like me with two left feet who couldn't catch the clap barebacking an Mbare hooker. All day in the sun with a blazing hangover praying for rain, praying the ball doesn't come to you, praying you don't have to bat, praying there's someone up there listening to your prayers. I swear if that nonce Smiffy had done his holy-Joe recruiting on Saturday mornings his happy-clapper campers club would be chockers.

Boils is cut. Blood oozes down his cheek. He grabs Shum's beer and pours it on the cut. Shum is throwing everything he can reach at Boils. Boils is laughing as things bounce off him – shirts, towels. Then Shum flicks a metal ashtray at him but Boils ducks in time and it glances off the top of his head. He's soaked with beer, bloody, and hee-hawing his toothy face off like a rabid zebra.

Reggie is lighting a fire. Boils and Shum have decided to play faces on a quest to krind to thead. One day, at least one of them will succeed, that's a fact. Could even be today.

'Ox,' Reggie says from behind the smoke, 'make yourself useful. Bring beer.'

That's my cue to join him by the fire. Better than watching these two cretins self-destruct.

'And the bong.'

Yessir.

***

The cricket is well under way. We're getting thumped as usual but not so much it's tickets. A rearguard action, I

47

think they call it. And I am officially wasted.

'Should've fielded. At least we'd get a half day in,' Reggie says. Not sure what that means but the others nod in agreement. The top order folded and it's up to some bug-eyed tailenders to bolster our meagre total. Christ that brings back memories, fending off bouncers from twelve-foot giants French-cricket style. Tip 'n' run. Get the fuck to the other end so you don't have to face.

'RUN!!!! Run, you black bastard,' Shum shouts. 'RUN! Jesus. Monkeys.'

Reggie is glued. Leg shaking double-time and he's impervious to Shum's off-colour epithets for once. Boils is rolling on his back shouting that song on repeat to nowhere and nobody in particular. Like a newborn child.

Reggie says something to me nodding at the telly.

'Ya,' I say. Whoops! Easy with the nodding. 'How much they need?'

'On this pitch? Two-forty at least. Two-sixty more like,' he says shaking his head.

And then: 'Oy!' They are shouting and jumping around. 'SIX!' The guy kind of ducked down and flipped the ball over his head, over the wicky's head, over third man's head – that was my spot, down there where the ball never comes – right over the sight screens even. Reggie is laughing. 'That's the world's best bowler,' he says, 'tonked for a six Dairy Den style by a tailender. Ha! A 'Babwean tailender at that.' Reggie chuckles like a cherub.

'Dairy Den style?' I have to ask.

'Choc ninety-nine soft scoop,' says Reggie and he mimics the shot the guy just made.

I look at the TV. The camera is zooming in on some heavy scowls and furious head shaking from the Poms on the field, then to the Zim team up in the box. They're all guffawing and high-fiving each other. The batsman is dead-pan, like it's all in a day's work. I know that look. His only concern is surviving the next ball and he's shitting bricks.

And he does it again. Reggie is on his feet, arms straight up, shouting. He jumps onto Shum's back and rides him around the room. Boils is up and screaming, 'Nyama yeku-gocha,' and making spear-stabbing motions as two chicks walk into the lounge. I get up to say hello but I topple to the floor. Reggie slides off Shum and Boils turns to them, his arm poised in mid-throw. Shum burps a sonorous 'Bu-lawayo' and from my vantage point I just see their boobs and nostrils and panicky eyeballs. They're looking pretty dubious about this tatty scene.

'Maria!' Reggie says as she comes in behind the two chicks.

'Hi Reg,' she says, 'you remember Rachel and Jill?'

They just stand there almost clinging to each other.

'From last night?' she says giving him the eye.

'Yes, yes, of course,' he says, 'from last night. Of course. How you guys doing? Helluva night, hey?'

Maria goes over to Shum. He stoops to receive a kiss on his cheek.

'Bart?' Maria says, looking down at me with a frown. 'You OK?'

'Ya-ya—' My throat gurgles shut so I have to sit up. 'Fine, fine. Howzit going?'

'Good, good. What you guys up to?'

And Boils explodes into song again, 'Baya wabaya!' making spear motions. Shum and Reggie join in locking arms over shoulders and jumping up and down. They turn to the telly to watch a replay of our man taking a wild swipe and snicking the ball for four.

49

'FOUR!' We're all up and shouting and dancing and jumping. Even me.

Reggie is shouting at the TV, 'C'mawn, my son, c'mawn my son. C'maaaaawn!'

I wonder where the chicks went.

'We're in the kitchen,' Maria shouts. How'd she know? 'Making ourselves at home, thanks.'

'Shit, Maria!' Reggie skittles through to the kitchen.

Boils is trampolining on the sofa. Blood and beer cake his face like a mudpack. Somehow he's butt-naked, chilogee flapping, drink spilling. Looks like a marionette skeleton, all teeth and bones, laughing like a full-on spazzo.

'Boils!' I have to shout over their shouting. 'Boils! Put your clothes on man.'

He stops and says, 'Eh?' He looks down. 'Oh, ya.' He's confused. Shum chortles as Boils hops down from the sofa and he's scouting around for his pants.

'Poofter.'

'Your aunty's a fucking poofter.'

'No she's not. She's fucking the good Lord almighty.'

They're at it again as a truck thunders up the driveway. Tyres screech, doors open, death metal screams, doors slam and the music is muffled and replaced by shouting.

It's Frotter and Sykes. There goes the rest of our day.

'Hello turkeys,' Sykes shouts giving Boils's bare arse a big slap. Boils screams like an impi savage and dives at Sykes who dips his shoulder and tosses him in the air. Shum runs at Sykes and knocks him to the floor, then he hauls Sykes to his feet and has him by the throat and they are snarling eyeball to eyeball like bulldogs. Frotter pulls the duelling pooches apart. Boils has found his shorts and he hoiks them up sticking his face into Sykes's.

Frotter gives me a nod. 'Huzzit,' he says. I wave a hand, too fucked to move.

'Watching the cricket?' says Boils and Frotter says, 'Of course we're watching the fucking cricket you turkey.' And then he shouts to the kitchen: 'Hey! Chop-face, your fire's out. We've got nyama.'

***

I've managed to gocha Frotter's chops to the colour of charcoal. Oops!

'Seventy-four off six overs. That's piss,' says Reggie coming out the lounge. I gave those oafs the slip long ago. I can't stand them.

'Ya. Pray for rain,' I say. Seventy-four off six sounds like a lot to me but Reggie knows his cricket.

Reggie shrugs. It's late afternoon now and we're all mighty sozzled standing around the fire poking at it with sticks. Frotter and Sykes have turned the place upside down, no doubt aided and abetted by Shum. Boils passed out long ago.

Another car trundles up the driveway. No mistaking that puke-green Datsun. It's the Porra brothers. They're pretty cool, and they've got two chicks in the back. Hooray! Gav, the younger one, or Billy Ray Cypress as we like to call him, holds a bottle of rum with outstretched arms like it's a nitro bomb or a baby fresh out the womb and he's shouting his head off something about Frotter's porno van. Nev lopes across the lawn to chat to Reggie and me by the fire. From side on he looks like an S-bend.

'Ox,' says Reg shaking Nev's hand.

'Yo dude wassappenin?' he says to me chomping on his gum and we shake hands.

'Getting chopped. Watching the cricket?'

That was dumb, does he look like the cricket-watching type? I don't think so. Reggie knows him from school, that's about all we've got in common. That and the fact we're always out same place same time getting equally smashed. He wears these imitation Vans with the white toe caps – makes you look like Goofy if you ask me – black jeans, black t-shirt, black leather jacket. Even his lanky hair is a shiny jet black and there's an oily blackness just under his skin that makes him look grey, like a cadaver.

He drops to all fours with his nose inches from the grass and he says, 'What cricket? Where's he?' He takes a big mouthy chew on his gum and says to me, 'What's he doing?'

Reggie pisses himself. Gav bounds over and climbs onto my back. We almost crash to the ground. He's squirming and shouting over my head. Gav doesn't talk, he rages. He doesn't converse, he boxes.

'Gimme some oh dat!' he shouts. Reggie has a last puff and hands him the spliff.

'Oh, Reggie, you're so fine, you're so fine, hey Reggie,' he rap-shouts bopping up and down on my back. Lucky he's a fucking midget.

'Who're the chicks?' I ask Nev.

'Dunno, man, they crashed at our place last night.'

'Nice. Did you go to Belgravia?'

'Fuck for sure, man, we saw you there, dipshit, and at Europa after and at Scar's after that,' shouts Gav. He humps my back for emphasis.

'What?'

'You guys were fucking trolleyed, Jesus. Where's Shum?'

He twists around to find him. 'Man, that guy is loco.'

A shout comes from the lounge and Reggie is off. I drop Gav and follow him inside. We watch the replays as the next guy comes in.

'What's this?' says Reggie plonking himself on the arm of a sofa. 'Suddenly they need fifty off sixteen with only two wickets left?' The others have all crowded in. Except for the Porras and their two chicks. They join Maria and her friends on the verandah. Hey, that's five chicks under one roof. On the Island no less. Cool.

'Mpofu's been slinging the nuts in, man, you should've seen it. Two maidens and now he's taken Pietersen. And these guys are fielding like their lives depend on it.'

'Thanks for calling us.'

'You want to pull your wires smoking dagga—'

Sykes is sprawled on one sofa and Frotter on the other. Boils is on the floor snoring, they must've hoofed him off. The England batsman tries to thump the next ball and misses. A hiss and a groan from the crowd, then a cheer.

'Dot ball.'

'Top nut.'

'Bowling like cheeee-ampion.'

'Fifty off fourteen. Can't do it.'

'Can. We got twenty-six off the last over.'

I haven't a clue what's going on but I can tell you it's nerves galore here at Ingocheni Island ladies and gentlemen. Don't leave your seats. Reggie is chomping his nails. Sykes and Frotter are both sitting up and everyone is transfixed by this ultra-slow-mo action. Guys are trotting around the field, having triumvirate meetings and shouting and clapping instructions all over the show. The camera flicks to the nervous faces of the Poms in their box and the crowd is all hands on heads not believing: I mean, c'mon, this is fucking Zimbabwe. Last ball of the over. He gives it a good tonk but there's a streak of red zapping across the screen and rolling up poised to throw like a hunter. Jesus you wouldn't catch me doing that in a million years. That ball is rock hard and it flies like a rocket too.

More meetings and discussions. Damn this is one slow game. How can anybody watch this shit? For five days? The umpire tells them to get a move on, so it looks, and they trot and skip back to their places. These guys do this for a living would you believe?

Reggie says to me, all earnest, 'That bit of fielding could well decide the outcome.'

'Nice,' I say. Well, I have to say something.

The commentators are incredulous. This northern git is berating the English batting; his co-commentator is trying to give credit to the Zims team but the other guy's having none of it.

Some more balls are bowled and thrashed at. There's more screaming and shouting from the lounge. The crowd at the ground has thinned out. Probably only Zimbos left. Or guys too drunk to move, which is probably also only Zimbos. Gav pokes his head in, curious about the noise levels coming near to his own standards I reckon.

Last ball now, thank fuck. I need to crap bad. Just thinking about cricket makes my stomach churn. The guy whacks it sky high. The wicky is calling for it and he runs almost to the boundary. Guys are screaming, caaaaaaatch, and the ball slots straight into his gloves. Game over. Over skadovas. The Zims team is delirious, leaping about like rutting impalas.

The lounge explodes. Sykes and Frotter are running full

tilt at each other and bouncing off their chests, tearing at the sofa cushions, spraying cotton fluff everywhere. Reggie is galloping around the lounge slapping his sides and he trips over Boils and slams face first into Shum. They both crash to the ground and everyone is shouting nonsensities at full volume.

I look at Gav. He looks at me and shakes his head. We turn and join the others on the verandah.

'So we won, I take it?' Maria says, nodding at the commotion inside. Nev is chopping up a line of coke on a CD cover with his flick-knife and the two girls on either side of him are glued, like kids watching Telly Tubbies.

SHEPHERDING THE WEAK

Now employ wisdom young man. Don't make me strike you again. I have no kerchiefs left actually and I will not abide blood – especially your rancid swine blood – on my suit, let alone my person. You follow me? I will not abide blood on my what? Suit. Let alone my what? Person. Good.

Now. Where were we? Killing the weak, yes. Concise. Succinct. To the point, indeed, yes, I like it.

I like it, hmm, yes, but it is not just the weak, you see. The strong must also kill the strong: the champion must see off all challenges. To keep the entire species strong, don't you see?

Come again? Like who? Like Maria?

How you make me sigh, boy. I have told you to be smart but you refuse. Maxwell, this impudent runt must learn some manners actually. I would like you to please see to his nose that it breaks. And if you get so much as a drop of his tainted, putrid, pigswill blood on me I will put a bullet through your foot.

HENRY IV VS.
MC THALIDOMIDE

'Hell yeah, we won,' says Reggie, dropping into a chair next to Maria – but of course – as they all come tripping out the lounge. Even Boils is up, bleary-eyed and hungover. He stumbles off the verandah, staggers across the lawn and belly flops into the pool. He just lies there face down till it seems he's never going to surface. Shum throws a beer can at him but it's too light and doesn't get anywhere near the pool.

'Nice throw Prosper.'

'Fuck off, Ox. Give me a dop.' And he digs into Frotter's cool box.

'Even me,' says Reggie holding his hands up to receive.

'Hell's teeth, Frot,' says Shum. 'Amstels? Where the fuck did you get these?'

'Hey, hey, hey,' says Frotter, 'what does this look like to you? The fuckin' Skud?'

'Shut it, MC.'

'Fuck you! What? What the fuck's MC?'

Boils is back. He collapses into a chair dripping wet. He takes the beer from Shum and downs it, one shot. He burps, crushes the can and tosses it at Frotter. 'It means MC Thalidomide kuffnut. Short arms, deep pockets you kite tunt.'

Everyone is laughing, even the girls. Frotter is fuming, shouting all kinds of fuck yous but what's done is done. At least he knows what we call him behind his back. Sykes is biting on his lip; he's known all along.

'So Herald-boy, you take the test yet?' Frotter says.

'What test?'

'Slow puncture. Henry the Fourth. The old heave ho, you homo. Look at this.' He slaps Boils on his wet chest. Damn that must've hurt. Boils is choking and spluttering, clutching at the red patch already forming there. 'All skin and bone,' says Frotter. 'Last time I saw legs like that was in a bird's nest. You need to stick your arms out like Jesus or you'll fall through your arse.'

Sykes barks a loud laugh like he's never heard that one before: he knows his place.

Boils just gives him a belter of a burp and nods to Shum, 'Vig us a reeber.' Shum digs into their coolbox. Frotter pretends not to notice and him and Sykes are heckling Boils like a pair of Jack Russells behind a fence, calling him Herald-boy because you can't trust a word he says and shit like that. Dickheads.

'So what's next?' I ask.

'Dunno man, but we're in a crisis: no more grog and these twats clearly aren't the sharing kind.'

'I'll go get more,' says Boils, his throat still croaky.

'Aguilas,' says Shum.

Not that shithole? That's Rhodie white trash central.

'That's a Rhodie shithole. We'll get the shit kicked out of us,' says Reg.

You can always count on Reg to object. Means I don't have to.

RHODIESVILLE

Reggie's whining like a bitch about Aguilas. What a dick. If Maria or Bart or even fucking Boils for that matter had said let's hit Aguilas he'd have been up and out the door like a spring hare. But no, yours truly suggests it and he's all, It's a Rhodie shithole; we'll get the shit kicked out of us. It's the same old story every time with Reg. Fuck him.

Boils? Of course he doesn't need to be coaxed.

With you all the way, Shum, he says draining his dop.

Bart? He just goes with the flow.

Why not? he says lumbering up, so I grab a handful of beers from Frotter's box.

Who's coming? Look lively fuckface, you're driving, I say to Boils tossing a can at him. He's up and swaying like a drunkard. Hang on. He is a drunkard. The drunkard is swaying like Boils. You're a good man, Charlie Brown. A good man.

Where we going? What's cooking? That's Gav, high as a kite shouting his deaf-as-shit head off.

Aguilas, you space cadet.

Ace one, ay! He's up and packing his gear: rum, coke... coke. His slappers are also buzzing. Maria's sighing and huffing and puffing. Jesus. Between the two of them.

Come on Maria, don't be gay.

She looks at me and at her mates – can't remember their names – and they're all tapping their feet and chewing their nails and humming and harring.

Fine. Stay here and suck on Frotter's balls.

That clinches it. Maria is up in a flash and the other two not far behind.

Fuck you okes, we just got here, says Sykes.

Cool, we need someone to look after the house, I tell him.

Ha fucking ha. You fucking fags, says Sykes and then he says to Frotter, Oi! Fucktard. Pack that box, let's we go.

So Frotter and Sykes are coming. Could get interesting. Maybe we will get the shit kicked out of us after all. What a laugh.

Alllllllrighty, then. One happy family going on a jolly holiday. Bart is dancing and singing and clapping his hands. Boils joins in and they do this foot-clapping dance. They stand facing each other and hop up and down like Russians clapping the soles of their feet together. Like little girls playing pat-a-cake with their feet. Only they're grown men. And they are drunk as fuck collapsing in a tangled, giggling pile of limbs. Good humour.

We pile into Boils's gee: a fucked-up Mazda B-Series. Chicks in front, okes in back. Must be twenty of us crammed in there. Five in the front and, ok, one, two, three... six in the back. So that's eleven. Sue me.

Click. Clickety-click. Click. Boils's car won't start as usual. He's got one of the chicks to turn the fucker over while he pops the bonnet with a hammer in one hand, beer in the other, fag in mouth. She's clicking away and you can hear metal clinking on metal as Boils tonks the starter motor and then it catches and chugs and farts into life and chicky at the wheel, wassername, has her foot flat and redlines the fuck out the engine. The thing is screaming its objection and the whole car, driveway and stratosphere is enveloped in black diesel fumes mixed with paraffin and oil. Sparkies: their cars are always fucked. Held together with rape tape and cable-ties and jizz.

He hops back in, whacks the jute – Ministry on full

fucking vollers – and vererses out at speed trying to skrook us but also showing off that he can use his wings only. What a dick. Who can't do that?

Sykes, I say, vig us a reeber, arse-wipe.

This time he's all generosity, very much offering to everyone. Ha! We got him good. It's only a few minutes to this place so I say, Last one to finish has to suck Boils's cock, and we all down our dops before we even hit the main road.

More dops, Bart shouts and Sykes looks dismayed so we all chant at him till he shakes his head and hands us more of his Amstels. I think he was about to cry. Gav takes his beer, nuts it, punches a hole in the side with his car key, opens the tab and crushes the item in about two seconds.

Cool, says Bart, how'd you do that?

So now we're smashing Frotter's precious Amstels into our faces and sucking at the froth until there's no more beers left. Ha-ha. Shame. Boils screeches to a stop in front of Aguilas thumping into the pavement and throwing us all in a heap. I end up on top of Reggie, kneeing him in the back. He's bleating again. Christ. We spill out the back onto the tarmac.

You see? Even the goddam suburb is called Rhodiesville, Reggie says straightening up, rubbing his back, taking in the grubby shopping centre as the others charge up the stairs.

I grab his balls and give them a good twist. He coughs and wheezes and cusses me all the way up the stairs. Good. Needs to toughen up does that one.

Place stinks of stale booze and sweat. Smoke hangs heavy in the shafts of sunlight poking through the gloom. The music is belting out. Even Gav is reduced to a mime. Proper music at last, not that ooootz-ooootz shit these faggots listen to all the time. Life is life. Much better.

Those slimy fuckers are at the jukebox already. Gav is covering Nev who's fiddling at the back. I think one of them supplies jukeboxes or vending machines or something like that. I trot over to the bar where Boils is ordering tequilas for everyone. Where he gets the cash, I don't want to know. He's always got a full rucksack. Must spend days at the bank. But who's complaining? Not I, sir. No sir, not I.

Gav bounds over and slams into us demanding tequila for the DJs and then he drags his slappers off to the toilets. Fucking junkies.

We're just soaking up the scene and next thing it's Section 8's big song, *Pamberi ne Glorious Revolution*. The Rhodies at the bar are livid. Kaffir music. You can read their lips and it's all over their faces. Ha-ha! Cool.

Phil Collins says he can feel it, he can feel it and there's this low warbling bass and a scratchy war vet bleating through a megaphone setting the scene for some kick-ass drums and ripping guitars. Not bad, not bad, but as usual with all our bands, the singing is Shiite. Cypress Hill wannabes end up sounding like Pee-Wee Herman being ripped apart by a gorilla. Got to hand it to them though: putting their necks out like that will get them waffa'd by the C-10 one-time shoeshine.

What the hell is this?

A mop of curly black hair rolls off the bar counter and looks up at me. It's the Bog Brush. I remember him from last night.

Section 8. Local band. They were playing at Belgravia, I tell him.

Section 8? He sits up and laughs a bit to himself with a little burp and says, Cool name. He's roasted. Like a beetroot that's spent all day at the cricket covered in Olivine. He's got a

Union Jack dook holding his hair back. Just cut it you moron.

Belgravia? I was there man. I don't remember this.

No shit, you were blalla'd last night pal.

What?

Saw you there man, you were off your face Shum.

Reggie pipes up, obviously listening in, Ya man they played it twice. Second time was a hectic encore. They stuck Badza in front like a mascot and brought Thomas back on. They laid into it man, you should've heard it. Awesome stuff man.

Thomas? Now he's really confused. He stifles another burp, shakes his head. He slides off his stool and staggers off to the bogs. Good luck to him if he bumps into Gav and his bitches in there. The others are cavorting about on the dance floor all by themselves. Sykes and Frotter are trying to start a mosh. They love moshing. That's all they ever want to do. Should see them when *Teen Spirit* comes on. The song is almost over so I'm not up to joining in like a girl scout, but wait, oy yoy yoy, what's this, what's this? No sooner said than done: changchang ch-ch-chang chang it's the unmistakable opening chords of the greatest song ever made. Fuck me, oh fuck me, this is heaven. We're all up and bounding onto the dance floor slamming into each other. The others come flying out the bogs and we're all giving it the full fucking Montgomery. Even the Rhodies are joining in and the whole dance floor is packed heaving up and down like a giant heart. I ram Sykes who shoves me into Frotter and we're all screaming at the chorus:

Life is stupid, and contagious, here we are now, entertain us.

There's Maria, tucked under Boils's armpit and he's swing-ing his other arm back and forth like a scythe smacking heads and faces as he swirls around helicopter-style. He looks like a grinning zombie. Reggie is bouncing around on the outside and he skips through the vortex when nobody's looking. I wait for him to cross and I dig my heel into his foot. Note to the whole stupid fucking world: don't ever go moshing barefoot.

Ha! Got him. He hobbles back to the bar, clueless who did it.

Life is stupid… Entertain us…

Fuck this shit. Fuck everything. An elbow smashes my face. I tackle the whole mosh. I'm hoisted up and then dropped in the middle. Boots, knees, I'm on my back kick-ing. I grab a leg and bite. The cloth squeaks in my head. It's Sykes I think, and he grabs my collar and hauls me up.

I know, I know, I know… Here we are now…

Reggie is at the bar with his foot up on the stool and Maria is next to him dishing out the sympathy. Fuck this. I dive into the mosh and haul myself up Bart's back and I'm rolling on heads and shoulders with fists punching me and shoving me and then I'm falling and I grab hold of some shirt and I'm dragging the whole fucking mosh to the ground and I'm kicking and punching and elbowing and now everyone's snarling and punching and pushing and shoving and we're jumping at each other like wrecking balls.

With the lights out… it's less dangerous…

I'm in the epicentre. Ringing ears drown out the noise and shadows like rocks crash into my skull and an angry red face jerks into mine and nuts collide and I'm going down, wetness, must be blood, I'm going down, down, down and the song trails off.

A denial, a denial, a denial, a denial...

People are still jumping up and down as I crawl off the dance floor and wobble to my feet. A patch of blood spreads across my shirt and I can feel it trickling into my ear. By some random stroke of genius, the next song is again conducive to a good mosh and we're all at it again. Then the next. And the next. Got to hand it to those Porras, they know how to jimmy a jukebox. But you need a good crowd to get a proper stomp going. Like last night. That was champion. Very messy. But now the jukebox hits back with some whiny bitch and only Sykes and Frotter are left moshing, running into each other like battering rams and falling to the floor.

That set the tone for the rest of the night, Reg is saying to the Mop as I come up behind Maria and grab her tits. This pisses Reggie off and he looks away. She extracts my hands. I mean it's not like I'm jealous or anything. Seriously. Any chick on Earth would tap me in a heartbeat. Maria even said that. But fuck chicks, man, I'd rather be in the bush where I belong. Once a PH – four years of hell later – always a PH. Reggie likes saying I'm a PHD. Professional hunter dog. Professional Hunter. Dog. Fuck him. He's right.

Badza rapping with Thomas last night, did you see him? says Reggie, turning back to me.

Ya-ya. Fucking k— I stop myself. Said kaffir to Maria once and, holy fuck, did she hit the roof. Reggie hates it too. He would, the fucking fag.

And Thomas even knew the dude's poems and sang one of them. What a genius that guy is, Maria says.

Ya, it was super-dooper. Let's have tequila.

No! says Maria nodding at Reg. He's a homo. Can't keep it down.

What a fag. He can go down on me if he wants, suck some real cock for a change. I shove his head into my crotch and Reggie wrestles himself free saying fuck you and fuck off and cunt.

The Mop cans himself at this.

You lads are right fahny, he says looking from Reggie to Maria to me. Yeah right, nice fake accent you twot.

Where's Boils? Maria says, looking around. This tish-hole is ready to be left, she says.

Sykes and Frotter are moshing to the soulful sounds of Rosella. Everybody's freeeeeeeeeee to feel good. What is this local night? The place has emptied out and they're sweeping the floors and putting chairs on tables. Nobody comes here these days. The barman's shirt is yellowed and fraying at the collar. Guys can't even afford clothes.

***

Where to? says Boils as we tumble down the stairs into the car park. It's full night time now and pitch black with no streetlights or anything.

I wish there was a cool club we could go to, says Reg. Here he goes again. Where we can listen to some decent tunes and actually hear ourselves talk, he says whining like that bitch on the jukebox.

66

What are you? A homo?

Maria elbows me in the ribs. Fuck her.

Fuck off, Shum, I'm just saying—

What? What are you jutht thaying, Weggie? Let's hear your gay plan. This guy is pissing me off.

Jeez, man, what's got your goat?

Fucking homo.

He just laughs this superior I-know-more-than-you-will-ever-know laugh and shakes his head. Fact is I know more than all of these retards put together. Dumb fucks think they're so fucking clever. Ever had to shoot a charging elephant bull point blank? Didn't think so.

Ok, big tough guy, Reg is saying to me, what's your bright plan for the night then? Beat up some kids at Rozza's? Pick up a fourteen-year-old. Give her one in the arse—

No. I slam him into the wall, arm to throat. One, two, three jabs to the solar plexus. Let him drop. Step back for the boot.

Boils and Bart pull me away. My kick flies into the darkness. Reggie is balled up against the dumpster choking and coughing and gasping for air.

Maria screams, no words, just screaming at me, wailing the shit off her head and pummelling me with her tiny fists hard as she can. That brings everyone to attention, even me. I grab her arms and she lets me have it.

Something about not knowing the first fucking thing about anything or anyone, only interested in myself and obsessed with my fucking stupid little gay cock and lying about absolutely everything and treating my friends like shit when they are so fucking good to me and I didn't deserve a speck of respect.

Chill tchib, says Boils and she launches at him instead,

67

how he's drinking himself to death and wasting his life and bouncing from fuck-up to fuck-up. Then it's my turn again until the rant runs dry and I'm trying to stifle the giggles.

Ah! Fuck it what's the use? We're all fucked anyway, she says hauling the mangled door of Boils's cab open. She climbs in and cranks it shut.

Good car park stuff, this. And in Rhodiesville at that.

Someone – I think it's one of the chicks blazed on charlie – titters and says, Little gay cock.

From his foetal position on the pavement, Reggie snorts too. You can see it hurts to laugh and he's trying not to. I can't help it either. I hand him up.

Fuck you, man. She said she was sixteen.

I shove him under my arm into a headlock. He's hurting I can tell. He twists away and draws himself up with a slow breath.

Ok, kuffnut, he says to me, we're going to get fucked. Proper fucked. Anywhere you like.

With whoops of delight at this new idea – and the calming of the seas – we bundle into the back of Boils's truck.

So where to? says Boils.

Well, a fucking hospital would be my first choice. Fix my broken fucking toe, says Reg. Maybe get a new spleen and pre-order a stomach pump while I'm at it.

How about the Baths?

Yeah.

Cool.

Whatever.

Thank Christ for that, says Gav pissing on Boils's tyre. For a moment there I thought we were going to fuck fourteen-year-olds in the arse at Rozza's.

Maria is fuming, demanding to be dropped off at her house. She nearly pisses herself when Boils makes for a pit stop at Chaucer's. Shame.

So she's at home nursing her wounds and we're back at Chaucer's for a few chasers because everybody knows there's no stopping a wild dog once he's got the scent. Closing time is approaching but Reggie is a man renewed after his little adrenalin rush in the car park. And without Maria to impress there's no stopping the fucker.

We take it to hell. Things go dark and then come to light, blurry and vague and then dark again. I seem to be popping up in places with different people, not knowing how the fuck I got there or what happened in between and the order of events is all fucked.

We turn Boils's car on its side. One of the Porras is screwing one of the slappers in the back so we sneak up, all six, seven, eight of us. We rope in some car guard muscle as well, and bounce the pick-up onto its side. You should hear the squawking coming from inside. Boils's car doesn't look any more fucked than before.

I'm dancing on the bar. Boils is next to me. We're butt-fucking naked.

The owner of Chaucer's, little Glaswegian fag named Geoffrey, is stroking my hand telling me we're going to have us a wee hoose paerrrty. He sends his staff home. It's a lock-in. Ah! Now I see how things have become so pancake-shaped.

The Porra brothers are doing shots of bitters.

Bart pukes in an ice bucket. He curls up around it on the bar counter.

Neville hijacks the sound system again and we turn the place upside down moshing on the tables and throwing chairs at each other using tables as shields. Sykes is hee-hawing like a peacock and Frotter's gone into full reccie mode behind a lean-to bomb shelter, buzzing beer cans at everyone.

Where's Geoffrey?

One of the chicks is doing some sort of ritual dance into the corner of the room far away from the chaos. She's fucked on coke, tripping out over that song that goes woo-hoooooooo. Good song, that.

We huck a giant inflatable weasel outside a toy shop. He's flapping on the roof as we spin through the blackness of outer space and that Sandstorm song is belting out and we're doing rave moves in the back of Boils's car and it feels like we're on a trippy merry-go-round.

Someone pisses out the back and gets a faceful of piss. Holy shit, it's me. It's me pissing out the car. I'm pissing into my own face.

What a laugh.

POP GOES WEASEL

Shish-kebab what a night. Can't remember much but I do know we nicked a giant weasel because I'm using him as a lilo. I feel like death this a.m. but it's a strange sort of hangover, the kind where you just enjoy feeling empty, like you've had a brain enema or something. The sun is up and on full power. Even through my shades with eyes closed, everything is bright red and flickering. Birds – damn me there are a lot of birds when you really listen – they're going crazy, and what's this? Oh, yes please, some decent music at long, long last. Reggie you champion.

Easy skanking, skankin' it slow
Excuse me while I light my spliff
Oh! God I need to take a—

A shadow. It's Shum. He crashes into me and we go under, tangled in Weasel's flailing arms. We struggle. I panic and kick out. Shum floats off and I wriggle free.

'Fuck man, you got me right in the balls,' he says. Can you believe this guy? He's angry with me for crying in a bucket.

'Good.'

I knew it was folly to try and relax with this oaf in attendance.

'Check the clouds, we're in for a motherfucker of a storm at last.'

I look up squinting without my shades. 'Ya, looks promising,' I say. Dark clouds are rising above the tree line and the sun will soon be blotted out. A thunderstorm is just what we need: the rains have been building for weeks now and the dry, cracking heat is unbearable. October isn't called Suicide Month for nothing. Tempers are thin, like ancient parchment, and the heat follows your every move.

Maria's little yellow Fiat farts up the driveway. She looks clean and fresh like a soap ad: Cold Power cleans better.

'Ay!' Shum shouts when she gets out. 'Come to your senses at last.'

'Fuck off, Shum. Bart? Is Reggie here?'

'Inside, making breakfast I think. You're just in time.'

'Thanks,' she says making for the house.

Shum shouts after her, 'Last time I checked you were my girlfriend, you know.'

She stops, turns and stalks back. 'Last time you checked, hey? When was that Shum? Before or after you fucked wee Geoffrey in the bogs at Chaucer's?'

Shum's head jerks back like he's been punched. He looks at me and then back at her. 'Ay? What? What the fuck you talking about? Come back here. Fucking bitch.'

I dive under for my hat and shades and wade to the stairs.

'What the fuck was she talking about, man?'

'I don't know,' I say, but judging by his reaction I think he knows full well what she's talking about. Can't wait to tell Reggie.

I dry off and flop into a chair on the verandah. Shit it's a stinker already. Where's Reggie with those eggs? I'm starving.

On cue Reg arrives with a plate piled with egg and bacon rolls. Maria follows carrying a tray with a plunger of coffee and cups.

'Welcome to the Hotel California. And finally, some decent beats.'

'Yeah those mad cunts hijacked the music all weekend. At last it's our turn. Spliff?'

'Pope shit in the woods?' I say and I'm onto it, rolling us up a nice big breakfast carrot.

'What's up with him?' says Reggie, nodding at Shum who has taken command of Weasel.

'Hey! Arse-bandit,' Reggie shouts at him. I can't help but snigger. Maria cuts me with a look. Right, right, right. Later.

'Eggy-bakey rolls,' shouts Reggie. 'Get 'em while they're 'ot.'

'So. You two kissed and made up then?' Maria says to Reggie.

'What? Oh him, ya, I don't know what his problem is. Goddam screw loose or something. Anyway, we took it to hell and back last night. You should've seen the show. It was inspiring. On second thoughts,' he says, 'maybe it's best you weren't there. Not a pretty sight and certainly no place for an angel.'

An angel? Jesus Reg, this is a new low. And Maria doesn't even seem to notice, let alone mind. Something's up, I swear it.

Shum must've fallen asleep because he blurts himself out of the water, gurgling like a blocked drain. Dripping wet he stomps onto the verandah, grabs two rolls and heads back to the pool. He didn't even look at Maria. He's lying back on Weasel, munching on a roll with his eyes closed. I guess that's the end of them two then. What a relief.

'Take, take,' says Reggie pushing the plate towards Maria.

'No thanks, just had breakfast,' she says.

'Oh ya? Where'd you go?' I ask, just to keep in the

conversation. These two will talk to each other for days if you let them.

With an effort, Maria turns to me and says all vague like, 'Oh, just IBs.'

'Cool. Who with?'

'Oh, just work. Boring crap but just as well I went home early last night. Can't deal with that shit on a hangover.'

'Fair enough. But of course, as you know, none of us have a cooking clue what that shit actually is.'

We lapse into silence. Chilling out with Bob's awesome beats on the verandah with the sun poking holes through the avo tree. Those birds are going for it all around and there isn't another sound in the world. Peace be upon us.

'Looks like rain at last.'

'Nah! Still building up. Tomorrow maybe, or the next day.'

'Hope so.'

Another silence. This is not normal with these two. Normal is me not getting a word in; not normal is me having to dredge up some pathetic excuse for a conversation. Awkward.

'So,' I say to Maria, 'looking forward to Nyanga?'

We're going camping in the mountains this weekend. Can't frigging wait.

'I don't think so,' she says, with a sharp head-tilt towards the prone Shum. He's splayed out on Weasel like one of those rats we dissected in bio class.

'Oh?' says Reggie. 'Ya, well, still not sure if I'm going either. Can't get Friday off work.'

Utter twaddle. Reggie's been going on about Nyanga for weeks. Loves camping in Nyanga and loves telling you he loves camping in Nyanga, too. Something about ley lines he says. Booked his leave yonks ago.

74

Maria is in a really funny mood. Quiet. Don't blame her really. Shum can be a real douchebag and somehow she found out about him rogering Geoffrey. That sort of news tends to take the wind out of your sails. She should just dump him, for real, and hook up with Reg because they are made for each other. But then again what do I know about relationships?

Another long silence.

'Reggie? Can we go for a walk?' Maria says and then to me on their way out, 'won't be long, Bart.'

Of course he says yes. Come rain or shine, he'll always say yes, and not just to Maria either. He's a good dude is Reg. We're best mates. Shum makes all the noise but Reg and I understand each other.

Won't be long. Yeah right, they'll be gone for ages. I fire up my spliff and wander into the lounge. Let's have some music. More of the same for sure. Let's see what discs aren't totally fucked.

Here is Shum's one and only CD: Irish Bar Songs. Typical. That guy. Ok, so Boils is the one with the drinking problem but Shum, Shum's got so many problems it makes his boozing seem normal. I mean, who the fuck goats? Shum does, that's who. I thought it was bullshit talk until I saw him do it. Just sitting there on the verandah with goddam Vic Falls pouring out his shorts onto the tiles. And he's just sitting their guffawing like a mad tramp. Why would anyone do that? Why? What's this? Oasis? Hardly. Motherfucking cesspit more like. We need some new music on this desert island. We've played all the good stuff to thead.

'Bayayayayayayayaya!' It's Reggie bounding in and dancing like a Bushman on acid. He's jumping and whooping and hollering and he climbs up on my back and dry-humps me like I'm a rodeo bull. I'm staggering under his weight and he's singing that line from The Beatles:

She loves you, yeah, yeah, yeah
She loves you, yeah, yeah, yeah

'She told me, dude,' he says as he drops to his feet and takes the spliff from my mouth. His face is lit up like a day-night game.

'Told you what, Reg?'

'She loves me,' he says. And he's off again, whooping and yee-hawing like a freaking cowboy. I can't help but be infected and we're foot clapping and singing Nyama Yekugocha and ululating like a pair of nannies bussed in for Independence Day celebrations.

A car starts up, gurgling and popping and farting, and we stop, tangled up.

'Where's she going now?'

'Off to do a few things, then she'll be back.'

Probably waiting for us to clear off, especially Shum now he's been dumped. Reggie is at the sideboard and he drops something into a drawer.

'What's that?'

'It's a thumb drive. Maria asked me to keep it safe.'

Slamming the drawer shut, he turns to me with a naughty look and says, 'Let's bomb the fuck out of that cunt.'

We creep along the wall and peer at him from the corner. Maria is inching her car backwards down the driveway and Shum wrestles Weasel round to face her. He's waving his arms and shouting, 'Maria? Maria? Where the fuck you going?' He slaps the water in a huff. Pitiful really. Maria has a grim look on her face: never been the world's best driver.

Reggie gives me the elbow and a nod and we charge out and launch ourselves at Shum for a double crunch feet first. He doesn't see us until we're almost on top of him and we shout like rabid warriors and his shriek becomes a gurgle as Weasel pops with a soft plop and Shum goes under thrashing at us, at Weasel, at everything, connecting with nothing.

Got you, you frigging cocksucker.

THE FUNERAL

Jesus, says Bart as we pull into the car park.

Place is chockers, says Boils.

Reggie hasn't said a word. Moping in the back seat.

We're late, Shum, there won't be space. See? They're already parking on the road outside.

Fuck off, Bartlejuice, watch this.

I drive right up to the entrance and hook a hard left, mounting the kerb onto the lawn right in front of the doors. A crowd milling at the steps, getting in a last fag, watches our arrival with disdain, scorn, scowls – any excuse for something to be angry about really. I'll give you something to be angry about.

Jesus fucking Christ, Shum. Why don't you just drive right into the fucking church?

This is Bart bleating for a change. Normally it's Reggie giving it the wah wah wah but it's like I said: cunt's gone mute. Makes for a welcome change. Now if only Bart would shut his dickhole.

Wouldn't fit. Car's too wide, I tell him and I give the free-flow a couple of good revs and nudge forward through the parting crowd. There we go, I say to Bart, like Moses and the Red fucking Sea: door-to-door.

I hate ties. We're all in our number ones. Or what's left of them. Boils looks like a tramp in his baggy trousers and scuffed trainers; Bart's actually wearing his school blazer. It's white. Honours for debating or bridge or some gay shit like that. Wanking maybe. Explains the colour. Reg, of course, wears a suit to work so he looks the part.

I hate churches. Way more than I hate fucking ties. They give me the creeps.

There's Steve, says Boils.

Steve is a friend of Maria's brother. He's having a fag on the front lawn. Just standing there forlorn, like a newborn goat in the pissing rain, shoulders hunched and the scowl on his face says it all. We go over to say huzzit.

Fucking bullshit, says Steve.

Fuck me, he looks like hell. His face is sagging like an elephant's balls. He grinds his butt into the grass and fishes out his smokes.

Vig us a skayver, man, says Boils with his hand out ready. Bart and I take. Reg just shakes his head.

Shitload of peeps, says Boils exhaling.

Whole fucking country should be here, says Steve with a chin-wobble and sniff and he rubs at his eyes with the ball of his hand. This oke has known Maria's family ever since forever. He looks at his feet. We all look down, up, away, at nothing. Reg is gone. Pictures, no sound since Sunday.

We watch a group of people walk in – they must've parked way down the street. They're also deadpan and the only sound is their heels click-clacking on the tarmac. One of them, a chick of course, recognises Reggie. It's Jill from the other night. Or is it Rachel?

Hi Reggie, she says, giving him a hug. His arms are limp around her shoulders and he just leans on her. She pushes him back, looks him in the face and says, I'm so, so sorry. Her face crumples at the end. Her eyes are red and puffy from bawling. Reggie's bottom lip quivers and he looks away. She snorts and wipes her nose with her arm and says to us, How you guys doing?

We shuffle our feet and mumble back, Hi-hi-fine-you?

Yeah, yeah. See you after? she says to Reggie, turning to catch up with her friends.

He doesn't even answer. I stomp my fag into the lawn and button my jacket.

Let's get this over with.

Fuck me I hate churches, says Boils as we bumble into the entrance way. This place is huge. A shuffling, whispering, hissing silence closes in. Boils pushes us all to the right, nodding towards the side aisle.

Standing room only, he says. Place is chockers.

And it sure is. People standing in the aisles, crammed into the choir box. The mezzanine is full and everyone, everywhere is staring into nowhere or whispering sombre shit to each other.

This is worse than Scarlet's on Halloween, says Bart over his shoulder as we weave through the crowd single file.

Only not so many homos, I say back. Bart and Boils snigger.

Bart looks back again and says, All right, Reg? Still with us, dude?

Reggie looks up at Bart, sighs, folds his lips inwards and makes the smallest of nods. We turn left.

Bound to be loads of room up front. Always is, says Boils.

The space fills up, pressing us forward until we hit the wall by the stage. Fucking munts. Do they have to push right up against you? No concept of personal space. And the stench. Jesus. I've got some nanny's knockers shoved against my back. I lean my body over the stage to escape.

Why a fucking church anyway? I say to Reggie.

Reggie rouses himself and looks at me. He just purses his lips again and shrugs, shaking his head.

A deep voice booms over the PA system: Ladies and gentlemen, please settle down so we may begin.

The whispers and coughs rise to a general hubbub as chairs scrape and noses are blown and coughs are expelled.

Settle down, please, the voice says again, a tall, thin black man in a shiny gospel suit. He continues, raising his voice over the noise, It is customary on these occasions for the priest of the church to preside but a very special man has requested to speak and Maria's family have kindly agreed. A brave soldier and a hero of the people all across this great country— I drift off and then he clears his throat right into the mic and says, Ladies and gentlemen, please welcome, Mr. Morgan Tsvangirai.

He finishes with a bow and the crowd erupts, stomping and whooping and cheering and clapping. The wailing women crank up the volume to full throttle.

Holy shit! Morgs? says Boils, slapping my back. He has to shout above the noise.

Morgs himself then marches across the stage to the dais, his mottled face sagging and his eyelids weighing heavy. He looks buggered.

The noise vanishes. The hall freezes. Not a whisper, not a chair scrape, not even a cough. You can hear the birds outside and the traffic on the road. Dead silence. He looks around the hall.

Friends, he says, and he heaves a sigh shaking his head to himself. He takes in the packed hall again, buttoning his jacket.

Family, he says, heaving another sigh and looking at everyone again making a slow and deliberate circuit of the entire audience.

COMRADES! he shouts, shoving his open hand high

and straight like a salute, like a punch. The hall shakes with the cry of a thousand voices: COMRADES!

COMRADES! he shouts and the crowd roars back, louder, more in time, a sharp and eerie battle cry. And again he screams, COMRADES! Spit flies, his body shudders with the effort and his feet dance to keep balance as he throws his open hand higher. The crowd responds even louder, the sound echoing off the walls and ringing in the rafters. I can't help but shout out as well. It's like war cries at the rugger, only louder. And with feeling.

He brings his hand down to command silence.

The last echo vanishes. Morgs looks at the front row of seats and says, George, Eva, Nicholas and the entire Karras family, this is a sad day for you. As sad a day as you could hope to never happen.

They were all chemaring already and this knocks them sideways, especially Maria's queen. Her bally is just sitting there like a stone, his vacant eyes fixed on Morgan's shoes. Morgs scans the upturned faces in the great hall.

And yet it has happened, he says. Zimbabwe mourns with you today because this is a sad day for democracy, for freedom, for human rights and our struggle for liberation. Maria was our bravest soldier fighting for no side but for justice.

Someone shoves me in the back, my ribs crushed against the stage and I'm about to turn and fucking bamba the shit out of him then I see it's Reggie, collapsed on top of me. The press of bodies supports him for a bit then he slides to the floor. I grab under his arms and drag him to the side wall, Boils and Bart clearing a path.

Reggie. Reggie. Wake up, says Boils patting his cheek. Bart loosens his tie and is busy trying to take his shoes and socks off. I nudge Bart and tell him to chill. Reggie's eyelids flicker and he comes back to the surface blinking at the light. He looks about him, at the feet all around and up at the faces taking furtive glances down at us. His head flops back onto his knees.

I swing round and sit against the wall next to him. Bart and Boils take his right and we just sit there looking at the legs and feet in front of us while Morgs goes on about Maria's work, about her character, her strength, her pride, her kindness, her openness, her ethics. In short, she's a fucking saint.

And she's now in heaven. Where she belongs. And who knows, maybe she took her dictaphone with her and is interviewing our fallen comrades as we speak, he says, letting the crowd appreciate his joke. A murmur of laughter and agreement and sniffing ripples across the room. Then he says, Father Makamba will now lead us in prayer as we remember Maria and how she touched our hearts and lives in so many positive ways.

Reggie's face is streaming with tears and snot. I look at the others but they won't look at me. Boils plays with his shoelace and Bart buries his head into his arms.

Here we sit, staring at arses and tits and through legs and chairs and shoes. Maria's brother Nicholas gives a eulogy that brings the entire hall to tears and wailing ululations. He caves in at the end and Maria's uncle Dimitri helps him off the stage. Uncle Dim makes a speech himself, arms flailing and feet stomping, but it's all in Greek. Now it's up to Maria's father, George, to guide uncle Dim offstage to a pair of hands emerging from the wings. You can still hear him shouting and spitting backstage. George comes back. He looks bleak. He tells us in his thick gruff accent about his early life of living hell in Greece and how they escaped the Nazis – ran away – to Zim and how proud he was of Maria for not running when this place went the same way; standing up for her rights and those of her fellow Zimbabweans; he tells us how it's up to the people of Zimbabwe to make her death mean something; to not let it be yet another futile death in the long fight for personal freedom. Jesus.

Make it count, he says in his thick accent, slamming the dais. Make my daughter's murder – for that's what it is, ladies and gentlemen – make my daughter's murder count. Take the torch, take the flame of justice that burned inside our dear, beloved Maria. His face rumples and he balls a fist to his mouth and then he wipes his eyes and says, And multiply it by a thousand thousand and put an end to this evil, this vile greed for wealth and power.

The crowd needs no prompting this time.

COMRADE! they shout foisting open hands high above their heads. We're all looking up in amazement. Boils stands up and hoists Reggie up and next thing we're all up and shouting, COMRADE! and pumping our open hands in the air with the rest of them. COMRADE!

***

It's taken an hour to get to the door. Maria's family is there greeting people as they come out. They're a wreck. Faces slumped, drained of life. Maria's mother smiles a blank smile at each and every one through a silent stream of tears.

Reggie wraps Maria's brother in a bear hug, burying his head into the guy's shoulder like a child. Boils gives Reggie's shoulder a squeeze and says, Reg. Reg. Come now. He lets go of Nick and hauls Maria's queen into a hug. She must've seen Nick getting the treatment so she knows what to do. She hugs him back and says, Bless you, my son, bless you.

You can see Nick and George are confused. You can see them thinking, Who the fuck's this guy?

Oh, fuck it. I take George's shoulder and say, I think, Mr. Karras – my chest closes in on me and I have to force the words out: Mr. Karras, this is Reggie. He would have been your son-in-law. And I burst into tears, man. Fucking tears. I can't help it. I'm blubbing, making some wailing sound that's not even real. Jesus, where's this coming from?

Someone, I think it's Bart, shepherds us away and we stumble down the stairs.

Boys, boys, says Maria's mother. We stop and turn. She's trotting down towards us and says, still blubbing, You'll come to the wake, won't you?

Yes, Mrs. Karras, we'll be there, says Boils.

PUNCH NE JUDAH

Oh! Oh! Oh! Look at this mess. Bloody fuck-sakes, Chikomo, what have you done? What do you see here? Come again? Our witness? How very perspicacious of you and on that small point I cannot disagree. My question, dear Maxwell, applies not to the object before us but to the nature of said object.

Dear, oh dear, where do they get them these days? From the zoo? Said object, my good sir, is beaten to a pulp actually. Its face is mangled. You have made sadza. Add a bowl of nyama and you have created a feast. A feast with sore eyes, yes, ho-ho-ho! Maxwell, I said render the nose broken; not the whole face. And does he need to be shackled so? Is this a tokolosh we are dealing with here?

Ah! Look at that. Pretty red bangles, those will make very nice souvenirs. Just like mine. See?

Chikomo. Back to your comic books.

Oh! And Chikomo, that bit about the nyama? It was a joke yes? A jest, a quip. The punch-line. You follow me? We don't need nyama any more than we need our prime suspect, eh, witness, turned to sadza, you follow me? Good.

Now let's we see my Righteous brother? Are we brothers yet? It seems that Maxwell, our holy water sprinkler, has developed a taste for the violence. But it is good to blood them early. Perhaps you are not ready to be our brother? Perhaps you need to discuss the matter further with brother Max?

Silence is consent, my friend, silence is consent. What is that? Lift your head off the table when you address me, my son. One must respect one's elders. This, I know for a fact, is something Baba Gabriel taught you.

Ah-ha! Now we see your face. It is good to see you respect your father and I need only mention his name and you are the perfect gentlemen ready to be our brother in arms. And I am sure Margaret would be proud, too. Proud as Punch, is that it? It does not sound right. Proud as? Help me out here, Brother Reggie, proud as what? Come again? Ho! Ho! Ho! Yes, good, good, very good. Proud as a peacock, yes. At least you can still speak. Otherwise I would have to kill that beast Chikomo.

But I prefer Punch. Proud as Punch.

So you see now, Mr. Hove, it is time to make friends with Uncle Punch. You need to tell him all your naughty little secrets. You need to tell him your what? Secrets. Good.

You are anxious to know the contents of my suitcase no? Let me introduce you to the Mamba Scream V2. Enter combination, snap, enter combination, snap. Ah! You can not beat British engineering. And here we have it: Mambokadzi Mamba. Queen of all the mambas. Here is her head, here is her forked tongue, here is her beautiful body and here is the source of her power. Without it, my friend, Ambuya Mamba would remain a slumbering serpent and we should be forced to improvise.

We clamp her tail to the terminals. So. Uncoil her forked tongue and attach her crocodile jaws to the genitalia of our subject. So. Then we just fire up the juice and, ho-ho-ho, Bob's your aunty. Chikomo?

Oh! Grief. Oh! Mercy. This one is slower than a rotting tree. Take down his trousers and attach these clips to his mamba. Hurry up Maxwell, we do not have all night.

Oh! Ho! Ho! Ho! Mr. Hove you have been keeping

Sekuru Mamba in your trousers all this time yes. Ambuya and Sekuru Mamba shall now do the dance: the waltz, the foxtrot, the cupid shuffle, the Jerusarema. You know what is the Jerusarema? Of course you know it is an ancient fertility dance.

So. I think those Koreans would appreciate Baba Manyoka's apparatus very much indeed.

Now Mr. Hove, you have certain traitorous information amassed upon a memory stick that our dear departed, but nonetheless misguided, Mizz Maria Karras entrusted to you for safekeeping. You will now tell me where it is.

DOES YOUR GOAT BITE?

'Holy shit, where'd all these people come from?' says Boils. The lawn in front of the church is full of people all dressed in their ultra-best – unlike our tatty threads – sitting in small desolate groups.

'Fucked if I know,' says Shum blipping his car open.

Madalas, frail and wrinkled, sit on low deck chairs. Women and children sit on blankets. Men stand talking in pairs and threes with sombre head-shakes and melancholy nods.

'Must be at least a thousand of them,' Shum says as we climb into his car.

'Look,' says Boils, pointing to the right, 'they've got speakers.' Massive PA-type speakers on tripods loom over the crowd. Behind the speakers, a row of half-drum fires is on the go, smoke billowing into the still air and women hovering over enormous cooking pots. These guys are pro at funerals. Plenty of practice.

'What's he doing?' says Shum. Reggie is on his haunches talking to one of the groups. They are all staring at him with earnest matter-of-fact nods and shakes.

Reggie stands and does the double-shake thing with an ancient-looking madala and he comes back to the car and climbs into the back seat next to me.

'And? Story?' says Shum.

Reggie sighs and says, 'They've come from all over. That

sekuru, Sibanda, spent his month's wages to get his family here from Mount Darwin. Took them eighteen hours and they slept at the bus shelter last night. No money left so they walked here in the morning from town, kids and all. Maria got his son, that one, out of jail. He was beaten half to death for carrying an MDC card. Can hardly walk now.'

'Jesus, Maria was a saint,' I say. Bit obvious I know but really, these guys all look gutted. Placid, calm, accepting. But gutted.

'This is where the real party's at,' says Boils. 'These okes will go through the night.' All about, men are gathering in circles opening skuds and passing them around.

'Car park's jammed. We'll never get out of here,' says Shum.

Boils opens the cubbyhole and digs among the detritus to extract a giant cone as thick as a baby's arm. 'So how about a bit of the old ganja while we wait? What do you say, chinas?' he says, all teeth and sparkly eyes.

'Boils, Boils, Boils. You are a knight in rusty armour,' says Shum snatching the spliff. He snaps his fingers at me and says, 'Iwe! Faga moto. Manje manje.'

We pass the thing round. Even Reggie joins in. The car fills with that sickly, putrid smoke in seconds.

'Jesus, I can't breathe,' says Shum turning the ignition on and opening his window.

'Wait, wait man, we'll stink the place out. They'll twig,' says Reggie.

Shum heaves round to face Reggie full-on. He shakes his head. 'You think I give a flying fuck, Reggie? You think I give a flying fuck?' he says and he turns back and takes a massive hit. Smoke billows out the car like a smouldering compost heap.

'You know what?' says Reg. 'You're right, man. Fuck it.'

'There's space now,' says Boils pointing to the exit. Shum blasts his car into life, twin free-flows ripping like a Harley – what a porn star. We thump down off the kerb and into the car park. Shum floors it to the gate, turns right, revs hard and drops the clutch. The tyres screech and slip on the tar and we leave a plume of white smoke behind as we scream down the road like a wounded dragon.

'Cool,' says Boils with that stoned chuckle of his. Reggie just shakes his head.

'Where's the do?' Shum says at the top of the road eyeing Reg in the mirror.

Reg is staring out the window. I answer for him: 'Parents' house, I presume, but no idea where that is. You ever go there?'

'Nah! I'm not exactly meet-the-parents material.'

'Dumb-fucks, it's at the Greek Club. How the fuck d'you think they'd fit all those people in their house?' says Reggie.

'All those people?'

'From inside the church fuckhead. MDC is footing the bill.'

'The whole bill? Reggie, are you sure?'

He turns from the window, drops his chin onto his chest and looks at me through the top of his head. Right, right, right. Reggie is always right; never wrong.

'Awesome,' says Boils rubbing his hands together, 'proper dhindhindhi.'

'Boils you cunt.'

'What?'

'Jesus Boils.'

'What man? I'm just saying. Fuck.'

Reggie is glaring out the window again. Shum flies along Churchill. The lights are red – must be the only lights in

91

town that work. Stop you freak. Jesus I hate it when he does this, which is like all the frigging time. Complaining just encourages him. Reggie's no use in zombie mode and Boils doesn't give a shit anyway. The lights turn green at the last millisecond.

***

Somehow we make it alive and in one piece. Shum must have a guardian angel or something. He mounts the kerb, the car rocking in all directions, heads knocking together amid loud yelps of complaint. 'Hoo-haa! I are fubar,' says Boils as we spill out the car gawking about like we've been teleported to another planet. The setting sun is blinding.

'Even me, Boils, that was one chee-ampion reefer,' says Shum making binos with his hands.

'You think we still need our jackets?'

'Yes Boils, and your fucking homework and your fucking lunchbox.'

'Fuck off you cunt.'

'Ya Reg. Chill.'

Reggie sighs. A deep sigh. He looks up to the sky, blinking the tears back. He swallows his mouth. And then, with another sigh and some big effort, he says, 'Sorry, Boils. Sorry, guys. I just... I just...'

'We know, dude. We know,' I say, shaking his shoulder.

'Just don't ruin the party. Or I'll be forced to bitch-slap you with my little gay cock.'

We all hose at that one, like it's the funniest thing we ever heard. Reggie's laughing along with us through streaks of snail trail as we bump each other up the stairs into the hall.

Maria's parents are at the door.

'Oh, Richard, I see you've started the party already.'

'Hi again Mrs. Karras,' says Shum. 'Mr. Karras,' he says shaking the old man's hand and giving Maria's mum a hug. Odd sight this: Shum being civil. 'Maria would have expected nothing less,' he says standing back and looking sincere.

'I agree,' says Maria's pops with that awesome growl. 'The bar's over there. Try not to break anything.' Looks like old man Karras was once a wild cat himself.

The noise. It sounds as if every single person – and there are a lot of people here, five hundred or even a thousand – it sounds as if every one of them is shouting at the absolute top of his voice; as if calling out to a distant boat. The noise fills every nook, cranny, corner, crevice and orifice and bounces back shooting off at different angles, crossing lines like thunder and lightning come all the way down from Judgement Day.

'Jesus!' says Boils. 'It's kuffin full tilt already.' His eyes are twinkling. Like stars. Like he's enjoying this.

The hall is filled with round tables covered in white linen each with a jar of daisies plonked in the middle next to an ashtray. Most people are standing in groups with grogs and fags chatting. Shouting more like. Others, in twos and threes, have commandeered tables and are engaged in earnest head-to-head commiserations. Some sit in silence, adrift, lost, alone. We work our way through the mob, Boils sniffing his way to the bar off the main hall.

'Will there be speeches d'you think?' I ask, looking around the bar while we wait.

'Dunno. Never been to one of these things.'

'Hey, let's scoot over there to that corner, settle in for the night.' Boils elbows his way to the far end of the bar and we wedge ourselves into the corner.

'Right. Tequilas.'

'Christ. Ok soldier.'

'Wait here,' Boils says and he bolts off his stool.

'What the hell?'

Shum shrugs and says, 'He's got some plan. Nothing comes between that oke and a krindathon.'

The bar is packed three rows deep. People shout to each other as they wait. They aren't in any rush; they're not going anywhere. Nobody is going anywhere tonight. This is Maria's night. Reggie slides onto Boils's vacant stool while Shum and I stand, hands in pockets, looking at the stream of people coming into the bar. People are ordering doubles of everything, carving their way out through the waiting rows carrying trays packed with beers and shots and mixers.

'Morgs must have some decent connections,' I say when a man with a tray of beers and what looks like gin and tonics ejects himself from the human wall. 'They've got everything. Beers, gin, vodka, tequila... probably whisky even.' I look over the sea of heads to the back of the bar. 'Yep. Johnnie red. Bull's eye!'

Boils comes back holding his rucksack in front of him, with his arm deep inside.

'Oi. Hoppit, Romeo, that's my throne.'

He extracts a bankie and chucks it at me. Jesus Boils. Then he pulls out a brick of cash.

'It's an open bar numnut,' says Shum.

Boils holds up a finger leaning over the bar. He catches the barman's eye, shows him the brick and puts it back in his bag. A minute later the barman is there.

'Four maLabels ne matequila. Choppers.' The barman nods and Boils shouts after him, 'Bombers naika.'

We're all just looking around us, too noisy to make chit-chat and anyway we're watching Boils in action. The barman is back in seconds with the beers and four shot glasses. As he pours the tequila, Boils asks him to keep his bag safe for him on the other side of the bar. The barman gives him a knowing nod and takes it into the back room.

'Well, this is where we say bye-bye, then,' says Reggie, scooping up his tequila.

'Or. Hello, mama,' says Boils as he knocks his back and, face twitching and shuddering, says, 'Morgs you are truly the people's hero.'

'I don't suppose this place runs to the odd slice of lemon or a dash of salt?' Reg says trying to see through the waiting bodies. But we've all tipped ours back already so he shudders, braces himself, and gulps it down with a grimace. His lips peel back like a baboon on heat.

'Is that tequila or petrol, man?' says Reggie wiping his mouth and glugging from his beer.

We are surrounded now. People are ordering over our heads and we just sit there drinking. Conversation is impossible. That weed has kicked in big time and we just gawk about lost in our own thoughts. God knows what these guys are thinking. The bar is a sea of unknown faces of every race, creed, colour, description and persuasion. There are foreign NGO types in their African print dresses and garish beads and copper jewellery, slick businessmen types in shiny suits, old school friends in their faded smart clothes, and arty types dishevelled and forlorn not unlike our own gang. Here are grannies, grandpas, aunties, uncles, cousins, nieces, nephews, colleagues, admirers and everywhere legions and legions of people whom Maria no doubt saved, paying the ultimate price for it herself. Fuck.

I've got line of sight over this mass of blank faces and can see Maria's friends from last Friday at a table in the main hall. The short one – the hot one – has taken a powerful shine to Reggie of course and, of course, he's oblivious as always. Even more so now. This guy doesn't need a wingman, he needs a frigging seeing-eye dog. You can tell she's scanning the hall for him but we're safe in our cocoon, this cordon of thirsty mourners eager to make full use of Morgs's open bar.

I suppose she'll nab him when he goes for a piss. Then again, the rate we're going he'll be rat-arsed before the speeches even and it won't matter.

Mbira music – Maria's favourite – is all but drowned in the din. A massive canvas print hangs above the stage: Maria, looking over her shoulder with that wide, pure smile against her dark skin and hair, beaming down on us like a pious, all-knowing, all-forgiving deity. More daisies over-flow from sconces along the walls. Technicians poke and pronk over wires, drum kits, speakers and amps, putting the last-minute fires out ready for a band. Trays of deep-fried snacks emerge destined for the tables but they are cleaned up before they get past the bar, their bearers doing immediate U-turns for the kitchen.

'Num-nums,' says Reggie, thumping my belly making me spill beer down my front. I'm cussing him but he isn't listening. 'We need num-nums,' he says.

Reggie titters like a girl as he grabs a waiter's sleeve. He says to the waiter, 'Dipe chikafu, please, shamwari,' and he's rubbing his stomach and pleading with his puppy-dog eyes.

Boils signals to the barman again. A second later he's there with Boils's bag, handing it over the bar. He says, 'Sorry, boss, we can't store your bag here. If it goes missing you make me pay.'

'No problem, shamwari,' says Boils taking the bag, 'I understand. Can we get four more beers please?'

The beers arrive in a flash. Am I hallucinating?

'Boils. I have to hand it to you—'

'Uh-uh! Not so fast,' he says, holding up a finger. He piles the shot glasses one on top of the other and drops them into his bag.

'Watch this.'

With the bag on his lap, he dips both arms in. His tongue flicks out as he fiddles about in there with a faraway look on his face. Out comes a shot of this piss-coloured liquid that can only be tequila which he hands to Reggie; the tongue flicks, the eyes glaze, and out comes another, which he passes to me.

Shum lifts the bag and says, 'What? Are you pissing in them?'

Boils hands Shum a shot and pours one for himself.

'Admire. Over there,' he nods towards the barman, 'is a very sharp man indeed.' He holds the bag open and shows us a bottle of tequila.

'Jesus. How much did you give him?'

'Twenty.'

'Twenty?'

'Fuck, dude.'

Where he gets his money, nobody knows.

We salute and drink to Boils and lurch for our beers to wash down the filth. Definitely fake but it still kicks like a mule and that's close enough.

On cue Reggie says, 'It most certainly is not real tequila but it contains alcohol. That much we know.'

He slaps my belly again, 'Dude! Dude! It's Tuku. It's Tuku. Look.'

'Jesus, man! Stop blerry slapping me,' I say.

'Tuku? Where?'

'There. He's there on the stage. Guys, guys, Tuku's playing tonight. Holy shit, Maria would love this—'

His face implodes. Like a child's balloon gone kaboom.

'Ok, new goatbite deal,' says Shum. 'Any mention of Maria or sombre talk of any fucking kind, you have to take a glug of Boils's tequila-piss. In there. You have to put your head inside his bag and take a glug. A proper glug or we'll fuck you up.'

'Deal,' says Boils, clinking his bottle against Shum's. 'We're here to celebrate Maria's life, not wallow in the tragedy of her death.'

What the?

'What?' he says, scanning our faces.

'Boils? Have you been reading Chappies wrappers?' says Shum eyeballing him sideways.

A man picks his way through the wires to centre stage. He stands there like a moron waving his hands and mumbling, 'Ladies and gentlemen,' into the microphone. Shum goes to the doorway into the main hall and whistles. It sounds like a police siren and he lets it draw out until the last shout drops from the air like a naked emperor scuttling for cover. He nods to the MC and saunters back to the bar.

'In honour of our dear, dear Maria, whom we all loved with all our hearts,' he says, patting his chest. Guys are really choked up around here. 'A very special man has flown in from England,' he continues, 'where he lives in exile—'

'See! See!' says Reg bouncing on his stool and slapping me. The hubbub in the hall returns tenfold. 'Told you, it's Tuku, man. Oh! Man. The guy fucking created the chimurenga genre and then Bob hoofs him, the cunt.'

'Goatbite!' Boils shouts above the din.

'No ways,' says Reggie, 'you said new rule was any talk of Maria and sombreness.'

'Old rules apply as well,' says Boils.

'Ya,' says Shum, 'this is an addendum.'

'A byelaw.'

Reggie looks to me for support. No way man, rules is rules as you so rightly pointed out, my friend.

'Martial law,' I say.

The announcer puts his hand up to quell the eruption and shouts over the noise, 'At great personal risk and expense he requested to play tonight to support the cause, to support the movement, to support Maria and all she stands for. Ladies and gentlemen, may I present to you the great Oliver Mtukukudzi. TUKU!'

The crowd roars to its feet as one. Everyone is shouting and jumping and laughing and cheering and making one hell of a commotion. Reggie yanks his head out of Boils's bag coughing and dry-heaving. He wipes his mouth and says, 'Jesus! Boils, what the fuck's in there, man?'

Boils takes a look and emerges braying like donkey. 'My guds,' he says with a choke.

Tuku, tall, lanky and smiling like a shy school-kid glides onto the stage with his guitar. The crowd has gone bananas, chanting his name, clapping, singing and spinning in ululations. The NGO types are high-fiving each other and giving it the polite golf clap, all smug smiles and knowing nods. What chops.

The rest of the band takes up their places – drums, bass, three buxom back-up singers, mbiras, flutes, trumpets, bongos, you name it – and then Tuku steps up to the mic and looks about the hall. There's a round of shushing and hissing and then all is silent. It's eerie. Maria smiles down at us from above Tuku's head and everyone is transfixed.

'Maria,' he says, his voice is quiet and croaky, 'we will miss you.' He reaches his hand into the air, as if holding her hand up in the heavens. His eyes are closed, like a gospel preacher, and a tear spills down his cheek. Shaking his head he brings his hand down and strums and he says, 'We will not let your life pass in vain,' and he strums again. It's the unmistakable opening chords of that song, that mournful lament of a song that even whiteys know; even Rhodie whiteys know. I've got goosebumps.

A flute joins in. Jesus! Even the kitchen is silent. Then Tuku sings one word, a long drawn out 'Neria' that sounds a bit like 'Maria' and the crowd, I swear the entire crowd, as one, just starts crying. Swaying and crying. Eyes closed. Some singing along. Others just blubbing or hugging each other. Reggie sings along word for word, tears cascading from his closed eyes, soaking his face as he sways to the music. The whole five minutes of it. I can't hold back either. I mean, one day we're having breakfast with Maria and Reggie's jumping for joy because she 'fessed up to him and the next she's gone. Gone for good. We'll never see her again. Just like that. Fuck, man, this fucking sucks. Wiping my eyes is pointless so I stop even trying to hide it and just let the tears pour down my face. Oh! Jesus, Maria. Come back. Please, you're not gone, come back. We need you. Fuck. I need you. I can't breathe. This hurts. This really fucking hurts.

A wave of gentle applause starts long before the final flute solo. Nobody has to fight back the tears now: we've all been caught on camera. No need to hide. Let it all out.

Joining in the applause at the end of the song, we're all crying, even Shum and he's not hiding it either. Reggie closes his arms around us and we form a circle. Shum picks up Boils's bag and dives inside, taking a huge swig. He staggers back gagging and Boils has to catch the bag. Shum's face is all twisted. He wipes his mouth with his arm and says, 'Boils. What the fuck is in there, man?'

Boils's legs buckle he's laughing so much and we all stagger to keep him upright. I take the bag and make a tentative sniff over the opening and, fuck me, it stinks in there.

'Jesus, Boils.'

'Now that's what I call a goatbite.'

'Holy Christ, man, you need help, son,' says Reggie. 'Bartster, vig us a spliff. We all need help.'

Meanwhile, Tuku goes straight for the jugular, singing the song that sent him high-tailing in front of a pay-rolled mob in the first place. It's called Iwe! Mkuru!

'Iwe mkuru, mkuruwe…' Hey you! Old man, step aside. It's a perky Shona song and Reggie and I hop about like dread-heads, him bellowing out the words, me just mouthing the chorus a bit because that's all I know.

'Now technically,' Boils says to us when the song ends and Tuku is speaking to the crowd some more, 'that's a goatbite offence but,' he pauses with his hand up for effect, 'but,' he says, 'luckily for you, the goatbite rules apply only to the spoken word.'

'Jesus, thank fuck for that,' says Reggie with feeling and he hucks a bar stool planting it in front of me and Boils. We've got prime position with our backs against the bar.

'I'm off for a piss,' says Shum, 'don't mokes that fucker without me.'

'Jeez, Shum's a changed man,' says Boils as we watch him weave his way through a throng of thixpence. Hoooboy, I'm pretty tanked already.

101

'I know. It's weird. But I'm sure he'll bounce back. He always does,' says Reg.

Boils sparks up the joint. Reggie reminds him about Shum's parting words but he says, 'Fuck him, there's plenty more. Besides, Shum knows everyone. He'll be gone for ages.'

***

Tuku's set is finished. Short but not without an encore of Iwe Mkuru and some other song I don't know and of course Neria. The whole place is sailing the high seas with three sheets, fuelled by Tuku's medicine and Morgan's open bar. Apparently the big man himself has prior engagements tonight but Reggie says it's for security reasons. A DJ friend of Maria's brother has taken over and is pumping out all kinds of tunes – some for the whiteys and some for the blacks, some for the oldies and some for the kids. It's just like a wedding. It all fades into the background as the noise swells and people cruise and converge, greeting each other, shout-slurring words of condolence and declaring their undying love for the already legendary Maria Karras.

The loveliest human being in the world.

A shame.

Wrong.

Evil.

Love.

Hope.

Fighter.

Funny.

Beautiful.

Kind.
Wouldn't hurt a fly.

***

'She was to be my wife,' Reggie drops an arm over Tuku's shoulder and shakes the guy's bony frame to his shoes. We are the last ones here. Tuku's army has formed a barricade at the door and Reggie, Shum and Boils are entertaining the dude like only they know how.

'Ah! She would have made a fine wife, I tell you,' says Tendai. I think he's the drummer.

'Goatbite!' Shum shouts with a madman's glee, eyes spinning and roving Reggie's panicky face like a pair of searchlights. Shum gurgles a burp, staggers, steadies himself and says it again: 'Goatbite.'

'Hey, what's a goatbite?' asks Tendai, poor fucker.

'You have to take a glug of tequila from inside my bag,' Boils says concentrating on every word. His mouth is rubbery and spit bubbles at the edges.

'It is a wake after all, sir,' says Shum offering him the bag.

Tendai frowns taking the bag. He looks around and we're all focussed on him. He shrugs and draws it over his head to take a swig and yanks it away. 'Oh, man, what's that? Some dead rat in there, man? You drinking bloody kachasu, man?' he says, gagging, and he even does a mock charge covering his mouth with his hand, eyes bulging over the top like he's about to hurl for sure. He throws the bag back to Boils.

Tuku explodes with laughter, slapping his thigh and hee-hawing with his mouth full open like a horse in a car-

103

toon hosing at its dumbass rider tossed into the air.

'Not so fast, boyo,' Shum says to Reggie who's canning himself just as much. 'I believe yours was the first infringement.'

He hands the bag to Reggie.

'Why him?' says Tuku. 'He was to be Maria's wife.'

And we hose ourselves again, Shum getting it together just enough to explain the Goatbite Rule and its Addendum. Reggie takes a deep breath and lifts the bag to his face and plunges in. The bag goes up and over his head, then it shudders and is thrown back at Boils. Reggie's eyes glaze over, like a boxer who just got smoked a headshot, and he sways and steadies himself on my shoulder, covering a sloppy burp with his hand. Then he convulses and barks a plume of vomit. All over Tuku.

'Jesus!' Tuku leaps back, his bodyguards move forward. 'What the hell?' A deep furrow folds his brow in two, his eyes ablaze, narrowed like dagger slits.

'S-sorry, sorry, sir, Tuku, I'm so sorry,' says Reggie horrified, pawing at Tuku's suit, scraping off the sludge. 'I'm so sorry Mr. Tuku, so sorry.'

Tuku bats Reggie's hand away and steps back clicking in disgust and looking from his suit to Reggie, swaying like a beacon on the high seas. Jesus, Reg, you puked on Tuku. He's glaring down at Reggie. He's tall is Tuku, and the sudden silence is startling. A chunk of chunder slides from Reggie's hand and lands on the parquet with a sludgy plop.

'Savile Row, man. Savile fucking Row,' says Tuku. He's fuming now, stabbing at the air with his spindly finger. His entourage closes in, helping him out of his suit jacket. And they are gone. Just like that and we're alone in the echoey hall. Reggie just stands there staring at the door where Tuku et al just left. Boils sniggers and soon we're all three hosing like hyenas. Reggie is stunned. He looks like a scarecrow swaying in the desert wind.

We shepherd ourselves out, bouncing off each other towards the exit. Shum slaps Reggie's chest as we pass him and says, 'Hey! You puked on Tuku. Tuku Puku.' We chant Tuku-Puku and Reggie shakes his head and staggers after us holding out his arms like a blind man in the rain.

'Wait okes,' he says. 'Hey, wait for me you guys.'

UP, UP, IT
LIFTS YOU UP

Voices coming from the kitchen. A vein in my temple wants to burst open. I can feel the blood pumping through my brain, giving my whole head a mule-kick with every heartbeat. Fucking Boils and his fucking tequila. Jesus, we took it to hell last night.

Fuck me, my entire body aches. Like I've been trampled by a horde of buffs. My neck, my back, my leg. What's this? Blood? A scab? Grazes down my leg? Ah! Now I remember. Jousting on the driveway with the pool pole and a wheelbarrow.

I hear a shout. A clang of pots. A cupboard slamming. Feet shuffling, a chair scraping. A deep, groggy growl: that's Bart. Now silence. A loud hawking: that's Boils. More murmuring and clattering and scraping. They've gone. Drinking tea on the verandah probably. Mmmm, tea, fuck I'm parched. No pills, not even water. Must've passed out. I'm on top of the bed, all my clothes on, even my shoes.

The door is shoved open, Boils bursts in and shouts, Christ, it stinks in here. Hey, fuckface, get up, we've been burgled.

Oh you have to be fucking goddam son-of-a-bitch-cunt taking the piss. Fuck sakes. Fuck this place. Fuck these cunts. I sit up, dizzy, clutching my head. Boils chuckles at me. He turns and says over his shoulder: Dead ants telling Reggie.

I slide along the passage to the bog. How come I've got a boner. Fuck. I have to stand back and piss in an arc,

106

splashing wazz everywhere.

Reggie's room stinks of booze and sweat and there's a musty, damp texture to the air mixed with his aftershave. He's also fully clothed and on his back snoring. I put my foot on his shoulder and shake him.

Wake up, cunt.

He grunts and rolls over. I shove his back with my foot.

Wake up, Reg, we've been burgled.

Jesus, that rouses him. He's up like a junkie after an adrenalin shot. Sucking in air, his eyes wild and he shouts at me, What?

I tell him Boils says we've been burgled. He looks at his desk. The drawer is a bit open. Fuck, he says, panic blasting out his eyeballs as he flies across the room and yanks open the top drawer. He stares at it for a second and claps his hands over his face. He screams and he's yelling, Fuck, fuck, fuck, fuck. He pulls at the other drawers and slams them shut. He stops, looks about his room and then he freezes like someone just pointed a gat at him.

He makes a low grunt and shoves past me shouting, No-no-no-no-no-no-no... as he runs along the passage to the lounge. Balls of fluff cover the floor, the sofas have been ripped apart, pictures are smashed on the floor, the bookshelf lies face down on the floor, torn books scattered everywhere.

Reggie is howling. He's on his knees at the side cupboard. Its doors are open and all the crap is pouring out of it – note pads, magazines, firelighters, games. The drawers are both up-ended on the floor. Reggie picks up one and turns it over. It's empty. He throws it aside and turns the other drawer over then he drops to the floor blubbing, making no sense, just screaming, crying and wailing like a

Moodley at a funeral.

The others have come into the lounge and we are all staring wide-eyed at Reggie on the floor. Jesus, says Bart, what's the matter Reg?

I drop to my haunches and shake Reggie's shoulder. He doesn't notice, still blabbering. I shake him again. Reg? Reg? Talk to me man, I'm going to have to bitch-slap you. What's going on?

He flops a feeble hand on the drawer and disappears down another spiral of wailing and sobbing nonsense. He's sucking in air, trying to speak but can't get the words out. A stick, he says wheezing, flapping a limp hand at the drawer. Maria, he says and he goes full floppy on us again.

What? Reg? Fuck sakes man, what stick? What about Maria?

Reggie is curled up into a sobbing foetus. I haul him to a sitting position by the lapels of his vomit-caked jacket and shake him. He's limp as a dead snake. I shout, What stick, Reggie? What about Maria? I give him another shake and a slap. His eyelids flicker – he's trying to figure out if I just slapped him. He looks at Bart and Boils standing there like gimps. He looks back at me and says, swallowing hard, Maria gave me a memory stick – he sobs, heaves in some air – the day she, the day she—

Yes, yes? I shake him to head off another wail. Reggie comes to but this time with a faraway look and then his face shrivels up like a chip packet in a fire.

She gave me a memory stick to keep safe, Shum. It's gone, he says and he loses it again. I shake him and say, Reggie, for fuck sakes, get a grip. But as soon as I let go he slumps to the floor, a pathetic whimpering heap of snot and tears.

A car clatters into the driveway all fumes and rattles

and a door cranks shut before the idling has even stopped.

I pick up the drawer. There's a lump under the felt. I lift the lining and pick up a black thing that looks like a big SIM card.

Knock, knock, knock! comes a loud voice from the doorway. Knuckles rap on wood. Anybody home?

I pocket the thing and step over Reggie.

Ah! Good morning officers. I take it Bart got hold of you?

Errr! Yes, yes, that's right. Bart, you say? We understand there's been a break-in?

Wow! You guys come choppers these days. Normally we have to fetch you, I say giving it my best, loudest, friendliest, most smashing voice as they walk in and see Reggie curled up on the floor like a turd.

What's wrong with him? Is he dead? says the first cop. The other hasn't said a word, just looking around, like he's bored.

Babalas, says Boils with glee and then, quieter, he says, We were at a funeral yesterday.

Yes, yes, very sad business this Miss Maria.

How did you—

Reggie rouses himself and his eyes rise from the boots at his face up the bodies and to the faces of two policemen staring down at him. He flips himself up and he's swaying with the blood-rush.

Easy, tiger, easy, says Bart grabbing his arm. I take his other arm and give him a look in the eye and squeeze, hard.

The cop looks Reggie up and down and nods. Nice suit, he says.

Officers, says Reggie with a flap of his arm, we've been burgled.

Yes, we see that, says the other one. What has been taken?

My laptop, and, and— he looks at the empty drawer.

I dig my nails into Reggie's arm and say: And we don't know what else yet, we— we've only just noticed.

The cop sniggers and says, Only just noticed?

Well, we were a bit drunk last night after the funeral and, well, our house isn't exactly neat at the best of times if you follow?

The cop laughs, patting Bart on his shoulder and says, Oh, we follow, sir. We follow very well, and he has a chuckle to himself as he says, Sergeant Chenjerai, will you search the house? Over his shoulder he says, For fingerprints of course, while I take your statements.

He says to Boils, Perhaps a cup of tea for our stunned friend? Good for shock you know.

Boils goes into the kitchen and we all sit down around the verandah table. Bart says, I'm sorry, officers, I missed the introductions. You are Sergeant Chenjerai I gather, and you are?

Oh, excuse me, sir, I am Inspector Dickens Chipenga, he says. And that is my good Sergeant Tichaona Chenjerai. Fake names and obvious ones at that. Reggie spots this as well, then he looks down fiddling with his fingers. Fuck, he's going to get us into shit, man. Chill, Reggie, just chill.

Chipenga takes a notepad from his briefcase and a clipboard with forms. Now, he says and he proceeds to complete the form in his most studious handwriting. Full name and date of birth of all the inmates of the house affectionately known as Ingocheni Island: our occupations, marital statuses, IDs, passport numbers, any previous convictions or pending cases and a minute by minute re-run of the past twenty-four hours.

And so, Bart finishes his story. The house is usually a bit of a mess – three single blazos under one roof, you know it's a problem. We don't even have a phone line, let alone internet.

Ehe, it's a problem I know for sure, says Chipenga.

That's how we didn't notice last night. Unless they came while we were sleeping but we probably only went to bed at about five so it's not likely, officer.

Oh, so now you're an investigator, a private eye. Would you like to take over the case?

Bart, still game, takes the bait and has a good laugh with the cops again. Boils arrives with a pot of tea on a tray with cups milk and sugar.

Jeez! Finally, says Bart.

Everyone having? says Boils. I'll be mum shall I? We all get our tea and there's clinking and scraping as we do our sugar and milk and then we're stirring and clunking wet teaspoons on the tray.

Chipenga sits back. He takes a loud slurp and says Ah! Good. Now the cunt's singing, Up, up it lifts you up, bright fresh Tanganda. Moron.

Good, he says. Now then. Sergeant Chenjerai, he shouts into the house, have you found anything yet? He looks at us and sees Bart's startled face. Has he twigged yet? Fingerprints, he says. Bart frowns then nods and sits back.

Yes, I think we have everything, Chenjerai says coming out onto the verandah. And I also found this.

He dumps a big bag of weed on the table. Holy fuck-shit fuck. It's like he dropped a live mamba on the table. We're all scuttling backwards on our arses trying to get away from it.

Dickens looks at us one by one. Stony faces, white as marble, frisbee-eyed and Reggie has gone back to space cadet mode. Jesus fucking Christ, Bart, I told him to find a better place for his fucking weed. Fuck. Oh! Jesus, we are fucked.

Well, well, well, says Chipenga, clicking and tut-tutting. What have we here? he says.

Sir, officer, this isn't what you think, see? We've been burgled, Bart says. And we had a funeral yesterday. We lost our friend. She was to be his wife – he jerks his thumb at Reg – and we just had a bit of fun. Maybe the thieves left it by mistake. I have a son, he crumples, and then, even more pleading, Can we talk? Let's talk. More tea, he says, lifting the pot. Boils groans. He's freaking out, climbing up his chair.

We can talk, says Chipenga, pushing his cup over to Bart for a refill. But first, let's we see what's in our pockets, shall we? He wags his finger at us to stand. Jesus fucking Christ Bart I'm going to fucking kill you. My stomach does a full backflip like I'm about to chunder. We rise like school-kids at assembly, grinding chairs back and hefting our sore and broken bodies up.

Bart and Boils, still clueless, dive into their pockets to comply. Time has stopped. I see all this in slow motion. It's like when I was charged at by that ellie in the Valley and had to drop her point blank. Everything is sharp. I can't hear shit but I see everything. Bart is speaking. His face is begging. Boils hauls Reggie up and they empty their pockets onto the table: keys, wallets, cell phones, receipts, a pebble, cigarettes, lighters, an ancient condom and a folded and tattered service pamphlet from the funeral with a picture of Maria smiling on the front and some Greek shit underneath.

Chipenga slurps his tea and his eyes flick to me over the rim of the cup. I dig my hands into my pocket. I make a cough. I throw my keys, my phone. I cough again. I feel for the memory stick thing and launch into a coughing fit tossing it into my mouth. Then I swallow it. Fuck it cuts, it burns, it's stuck half way down, Jesus fuck. I cough again, for real this time. It's getting suspicious. I can hardly breathe. I'm trying to empty my pockets at the same time and the cops are looking at me with too much interest. I raise my hand with my wallet and they look at it. I wave it in the air, waggling it so they see what I'm saying. Then I drop it on the table. Holy fuck, it burns. The cop fills my cup with tea and pushes it over to me and he says, I see you are a Mad Dog.

Eh?

He points to the box on the table and says, Madison Red. Not for the faint-hearted.

I try to laugh. It hurts to speak. I croak something and sit down, gulping down the tea. Fuck it's hot but I have no choice. Oh sweet Mary mother of God this hurts. My eyes are watering. Breathe. Stay calm, get control.

Sergeant! Chipenga says clicking his fingers, Itemise please.

The other one writes down each item in ultra-slow-motion and then puts the weed, some USB dongle thingies and two harddrives into a Ziploc bag.

Reggie sits up and says: Those are mine. Why are you taking them?

This, says Chipenga, picking up the Ziploc, is evidence. Maybe you are a dealer and have a list of contacts on here, no? Now. Are there any other little memory sticks or cards or drives or whatever you call them? Any little gifts you may have received in the not too distant past from certain recently deceased that you might be withholding from us? That might get you into a lot of trouble with the law?

What bullshit is this? says Reggie standing up. I put my hand on his shoulder and push him slowly down, looking him in the eye. I can barely speak. Wheezing like a fucking geriatric, I say to him, Reggie, I need you to sit down and be quiet. I give his arm one motherfucker of a squeeze, more to displace the pain in my throat than anything else. Reggie winces, gets the message and sits down, thank fuck. These pigs must go. Now.

Cunt, Reg says to himself as he flops down into his chair. Jesus Reg.

Chipenga gives a sly smile and says, helping himself to another cup, Oh! But I can. And I will. The law is the law, my righteous brother. Tell me, Mr., and he makes a show of referring to the police form before he goes on, Mr. Hove, have you ever been to prison?

Reg shakes his head staring at the evidence bag on the table.

I mean, real prison, here in our great nation? Not those hotels in Europe. He laughs at his joke and looks at Chenjerai who joins in.

Reg just stares at the bag.

I didn't think so. It is not a place you want to go especially. Such a fine looking man as yourself; all of you in fact – he looks around – such fine-looking gentlemen. Mm-mm, fine looking indeed. He smacks his chops like someone just plonked a bowl of sadza nyama in front of him.

And tell me, Mr. errr— he looks again at the form, he fucking knows our names, and a fuck-load more besides. Tell me, Mr. Cordoza, do you know the sentence for possession of cannabis?

I shake my head, looking down, meek as possible. You're the boss, man, whatever you say.

Ten years, he says.

114

Please, Mr. Dickens, Officer Chipenga, sir, please. Bart is in full tears here. Please! My child is in England, I will never see him again. Please. Can we work something out? We're not bad people officer. Please.

Chipenga makes a great show of packing all the forms and papers back into his folder and then into his briefcase. Chenjerai does the same and they stand ready to leave. We're all looking at each other fucking shitting ourselves. Well, all except Reg who hasn't budged. Who is still staring at the table. Where the bag used to be.

I'll tell you what we'll do, he says holding up the weed. Officer Chipenga and I will now go to the station to complete our paperwork. If we find you have withheld any memory, whatsit, sticks or what-not from us with, shall we say, state secrets upon them, you will go right straight to jail, are we together? And if you even try to leave this house, I will report this and put out a warrant for your arrest.

He shakes the bag at us.

Bart looks wide-eyed at me and Boils. Fuck he's panicking. He goes, Wha—? Wha—? For how long officer?

So now. You want to bargain? Chipenga stands, sticks his face into Bart's and says, You stay here until I say you can go.

And what about our stuff? You haven't even taken a statement about what was stolen, Boils says.

You can consider that payment, Mr. Morrel.

We are on the front steps now and Boils squeezes my shoulder and he shouts, Don't worry about our stuff, Shum, remember the n'anga? He's squeezing and looking at me with an obvious you-catch-my-drift look. It's okay, officer Chipenga, he carries on, we had Mbuya Chapo cast a spell on the house. Good will triumph over evil.

Chenjerai turns back. Now it's his turn. He says, Who? Mbuya who?

Chipenga, slaps his chest and says, Tscha! Is nonsense, Sergeant. Mbuya Chapo lives like a hyena in the mountains. She would never come to the city. But, he says turning to Boils, if it brings your stolen goods back, so much the better, isn't?

Oh it will work, says Boils. She lives on my uncle's farm in Chipinge and she comes here every year. In fact she was just here. He points to the tree overhanging the driveway. Shredded rags sway in the breeze above a pool of red goo and feathers on the paving. It's our jousting target from last night: a pillow with a crude drawing of Bob's face and a bag of tom sauce inside. Boils you mad fucking genius.

They've taken the bait. Looking super shifty now from the tree to Boils and back. Shifty fucking Shonas true to form. You should see the transformation. They're shitting themselves.

Nonsense! Tich, it is just nonsense that our mothers and grandmothers fed us kids to make us behave. Nobody believes in such nonsense any more. Come. Let's we go. We got what we came for.

Chipenga has to shove the other one towards the car. They clamber in. The car won't start. Chipenga turns it over and over and he's pumping the accelerator, the engine slipping and sliding with smoke blasting from the exhaust. He tries again, pumping harder. Oh! Jesus, he says, the car bouncing with his frantic efforts. On the third go the engine catches hold with a fart and it backfires like a shotgun. We all flinch, even the cops, and smoke envelops us as the engine screams into the red.

He grinds into reverse and fishtails down the driveway.

Bart turns to face Boils full on and screeches like a bitch at him. His voice has gone some octaves through the

116

stratosphere. What the fuck was that, Boils? Fucksakes. This house is fucking cursed? What the fuck, man? This is fucking serious, man.

A proper hissy-fit. I just laugh and slap Boils on his back and say, Boils you are a fucking genius. Mad as fuck. But a genius.

Boils is nodding and chuckling. Not quite with us but he's certainly chuffed with himself. Then his smile wraps around his face like a pair of hands – lizard hands – and his face becomes an iguana and there's a tail out the back of his head and he's grunting like a rutting bear. Jesus? What the fuck? I shake my head. I look around. Stars are flicking on and off in front of me, the house is melting, the sky has gone pink and these guys have all turned into flamingoes and they're pecking at each other's eyes. Oh fuck, what is going on? Am I dying? Is there some poison in that fucking memory stick? Oh shit! Some toxic plastic. I stagger forward and shout, Reggie! Boils! Bart! Where the fuck are you guys? What's going on?

Shum! Shum! I'm here. What the fuck's happening? I hear Reggie's voice but it's coming from a fucking flamingo, cocking its head sideways and inspecting my eyeballs. He wants to eat my eyeballs. I scream and dive at him and we spin like we're in space, tumbling and spinning and whirling for days, months, years, spinning ever faster and tentacles grab my legs and face and rip me apart like horses yanking at my limbs. We're spiralling down a zebra's arse, black and white swirling round and round and round and down and down and down and I'm screaming and lashing out and kicking and fighting and everything is black, now it's red, now pink, now green.

A panda bear is hugging me. It's a mother panda bear, squeezing me so I can't breathe. The bear is saying something. It's talking to me. What the fuck is it saying? It's saying, Shum, calm down, calm down, Shum. Listen to the panda, Shum, trust the mama bear. What the fuck's going on? What the fuck?

Shum! It's Boils, the panda is Boils. Boils is shouting at me. I hear you Boils. Am I dying? What's happening to me Boils? I try to speak but the sound is whipped away. I try to shout but nothing. And I try to scream. I scream and scream, but still no sound. I see Boils slap me. I don't feel anything and I try to scream. And then Boils is shouting in my ear.

Shrooms! Shrooms! I made shroom tea for fuck's sakes. You're tripping, Shum, that's all.

I see his face looking at me. One half is laughing, the other half is melting like wax.

Shrooms?

Yes, you fucking cunt. Jesus you've been screaming like a blatted baboon. He's laughing now. I sit up. I'm in the flower bed, covered in geranium tentacles. Reggie is cowering against the wall, staring at me in terror. Looks like rigor mortis has set in. I look at Bart. He's just standing there plucking at something in mid-air in front of him.

What? Bart screams at Boils. What did you just say?

I made mushroom tea, man.

Bart lets out this demonic howl. He turns into a fucking wolf and flies through the air and tackles Boils into the bush. They land on top of Reggie and Boils is wrestling Bart off him and the whole bush is shaking like there's some rutting rhinos in it.

Holy fuck. I had two cups. We're in for a bumpy ride.

Reggie is covered in white goo from the flowers. It looks like a bridal dress. Or like he's bleeding Malibu. We need to catch the drops, add coke, make us a delicious cocktail.

I go and give him a lick. Yep, Malibu.

Dude, I say to Reggie, we need to tap this stuff. You're bleeding Malibu.

What? Reggie says, and he wipes some off his arm and licks his finger. Fuck man, he says, spitting and wiping his mouth and scraping his tongue with his fingernails. I fucking hate Malibu. I'm howling under the bush and Reggie titters and then we're all fucking giggling and laughing and snorting and cavorting about in the geraniums and everyone's licking the Malibu off each other.

We stop. The laughter slows down to heaves and snorts. I'm hallucinating like crazy, but at least I know what it is now. At least I'm not dying. Jesus I caught a skrook there. Fucking Boils. That guy's cooked.

We're fucked, says Reggie picking a stem from his shoe and tossing it at me. We are so fucked. Looks like he's about to chema again. Why did you do that, Boils, you stupid cunt.

Yep, says Bart. He's breaking up as well. Busted for weed and then he— Bart jerks a thumb at Boils, still snorting to himself and rolling about. Fuckface over here drugs the very cops who bust us for drugs.

Fuck them. Jesus, I lose it and I shout: Boils? Boils on your fucking arse. It's your fault, you cunt. Why the fuck didn't you hide the weed before you called the cops you fucking moron?

I didn't call them, says Bart, all wounded. Boils twists and cackles into the plants. Can't remember, did he have extra tea as well? More than likely.

They said you called them, says Reggie. Shut up Boils, for fuck's sakes, man. Shut up, says Reggie slapping him.

I didn't call. We didn't call them, says Bart.

What? Then how the fuck?

119

Retards, says Reggie. They came for that memory stick. Somehow they knew about it and of course they knew about the burglary already because it was them who did it. We weren't burgled. We were ransacked you fucking morons.

What memory stick? What are you talking about? says Bart. Boils snorts again, squirming in the bushes. Shut up Boils, this is serious. What memory stick, Reggie? Holy fuck, he clutches his head, What's going on?

That memory stick Maria gave me for safekeeping, Reggie says to Bart, all eyes. You remember I came in after talking to her in the driveway and I put it in the sideboard?

Bart's face is blank.

Just tell me one thing, Reg, I say burping. Was it black? About this big, like a big SIM card?

Yes, yes exactly like that, why? he says.

Good, because I'd be fucking livid if I'd swallowed it for nothing. Almost died. And I'm laughing again and can't stop.

What? You swallowed it? When? Reggie is standing now. He hauls me up shaking me. My head almost falls off; it's hanging by a single vein and I can see the blood pumping through it. He presses his face into mine. His teeth are fangs, his eyes are forked tongues, his nose is a bazooka – hahaha! – and his tongue is a blow torch. He's green and shiny like a lizard, like a mamba.

What the fuck are you talking about, he growls into my face, scorching me with green fire. Jesus, he's going to kill me. My time's up after all. Fuck. Answer him. Quick. I let go his jacket and try to ease his hands off me but I can't. My hands are like jelly and I can't close my fingers. I just paw at him like a gay chameleon.

It was still in the drawer. The sun is blasting into my face and I have to squint. A flamingo clouds my vision. Under the lining. They missed it. Swallowed it when we emptied our pockets.

Silence. Then Reggie drops his grip on my shirt and wraps me in his arms mumbling into my shoulder, Oh Shum. Oh Shum, Shum, Shum. I love you man.

Bart cackles and he says, I'm beginning to feel unusual.

Boils lets out a shriek. I think he's actually going to split open or suffocate from laughing. He stops, he looks up, he slithers out the bush grunting and he's at our feet on his back staring up at us and he says, Dead ants fetching it, and he turns into a giant ant on its back kicking his legs and he's gone, laughing but there's no sound coming.

Oh fuck! says Reg shaking his head and blocking something from hitting him, like he's swatting at a horde of bats. Ducking and cowering he slams me into the wall and says into my face, You have to shit into a bucket. Until we get the thing. What if your stomach digests it? You need laxatives. Jesus. Everybody inside. We need to keep our shit together before this trip hits us properly.

Reggie looks around and shakes his head. We are all tripping already.

Get inside. He gives the ball-squeak like a spotty teen-ager. Now! he screams, arms straight with little clenched fists, legs flailing. He looks just like a two-year-old in full tantrum mode. That jolts us to attention. Even Boils, still braying like a donkey, climbs to his feet.

Reggie herds us to the kitchen door. Boils titters and wobbles, grabbing hold of something that isn't there, and he says, Holy fuck on a pogo stick: those mahobos had three cups each.

OF THE TIGER

Shum's gone quiet. This is disturbing. Reggie is slapping his head and saying, 'Keep it together.' He sounds like some strange bird, an emu or a dodo or something, going keep-it-together-thak-thak-thak, keep-it-together-thak-thak-thak. Boils is looking about him like he's Daniel in the lions' den only the lions are all doing their makeup ready for their Can-Can act. He giggles and looks around him some more.

'Fuck this shit,' says Boils getting up. 'I'm not going to waste my shrooms. That was for our Nyanga trip, which is obviously canned thanks to those fucking cunt pigs.'

Crashing and banging and dragging sounds come from the lounge. What's Boils doing? Putting some fucking music on he says. A giant bong fills the room. I don't really know what's going on. Music, a funky beat, oh yeah it's Cypress Hill back with the ill behaviour. Hits From The Bong. Boils sings along, shouts. He never knows the words of any song but that doesn't stop him. He bellows along regardless. A Boeing crashes through the roof, glass splintering. Boils giggles and says, 'Oh shit,' and then he's back to shouting his line but then he can't because he's laughing too much.

Reggie's gone full schizo chanting nonsense, head rocking back and forth, staring zombie-eyed at something inside the table. He has a laughing fit. Cackling like a toothless n'anga at his plopping, pink-steamed cauldron, he slides off his chair and now he's under the table, cheek pressed to the floor, sweeping his hands over the tiles.

He mumbles something to himself and for what must be an hour he's moaning and rolling about under the table.

We're using him as a footrest. Shum and I talk. I think we talk. He nods his head at me from time to time then sings a Tina Turner song right through to the end. Or is it Jennifer Rush? Not bad I tell him and we talk some more about tennis. Boils is playing the first bit of that same song. As soon as the guy says 'Hits from the bong,' he skips back to the beginning so that it's pretty much constant: hits from the bong, bubble-bubble-bubble, hits from the bong, bubble-bubble-bubble, hits from the bong, bubble-bub-ble-bubble.

Reggie's noise stops. What's he doing? His eyes ping open and he leaps up slamming his head on the table. Shum finds this funny. Reggie stands, the table tips. Whoopsie, rough weather here, batten down the 'atches, she's a-goin' over. I grab the teapot just in time. We're sitting at a table that isn't there.

Reggie is rubbing his head. 'Shit,' he says. 'Got to to to keep it together. Shit. Shit. Shit.' He slaps his head again and again. He's moonwalking up and down the kitchen and slapping his head with both hands. Shum's spaced. Reggie stops mid-moonwalk, does a half-turn – donno what he-gotoh! Mr. Roboto – and then he stoops like a giraffe at a waterhole to open the cupboard under the sink. He yelps and slams the door and flies back landing on his arse and back pedalling like a crab on rewind. This brings Shum out of his trance and he smiles upon Reggie like a holy man to a leper.

'Where's Boils?' he says.

In the lounge I think.

Shum dances out the kitchen, shadow-boxing like Rocky. Eye Of The Tiger. Now there's a song I do know. Reggie freaks out when Shum passes the sink cupboard but Shum's in the zone, ready to take on Mr. T and Drago together, and he flits straight past unscathed. Of The Tiger.

What the fuck's going on Reggie?

'Fuck!' he says groping and fumbling behind the fridge. 'Fuck,' he says again, 'did you see it? Jesus-fuck.' Jars and cans fly through the air. They spin around like flies in the middle of the room and then they crash on the floor. A mushroom cloud blasts up. He's got a mop in his hand.

'Must we tidy up the mess?'

'No you fuck. Did you see inside the cupboard?'

'No? Why? Fuck, man, what the fuck's in there? Jesus, Reggie, what the fuck's going on?'

'In there,' he says pointing with the mop. He slithers back to his position opposite the sink. He's gripping the mop as if it were a spear. He crawls forward on his haunches like a hunter. I'm standing on my chair. Reggie takes a deep breath, and another, and another.

Fuck, man.

He yanks the cupboard open and screams like a stegosaurus and he's jabbing and stabbing into the cupboard, screaming with every shot, 'Die! Die! Die!' twenty, thirty times, I lose count.

Bottles pop, liquids spray, tins fly, boxes explode and a white mist fills the air. He stops, panting, the mop still inside the cupboard. He listens. Nothing. He listens some more. Still nothing. He draws the mop out. The tip emerges and he screams again and launches it through the window, smashing the entire pane. The floor flies up and it hits me square in the face. Oof! That really hurts.

Reggie crashes backwards. He slides down to the ground, heaving for air, looking at the cupboard like it's going to eat him.

124

Why am I on the floor?

Something drops out with a clank. Reggie squeals and jumps and then stops mid-yelp, his hands by his chest, his eyes trying to open, trying to close, his face turned sideways like someone is flicking dog shit at him. We watch as a bucket rolls in an arc and rocks to a stop in the middle of the kitchen.

Holy shit.

'A bucket! Shum! A bucket! I've got a bucket, we need a bucket. Shum! I've got a bucket,' he's shouting but the music is so loud the house is vibrating. I drag myself up. Reggie crawls through the debris to the bucket, kicks the cupboard door closed and stands up. He looks around him. Ducking and shielding his face he skids out of the kitchen. I follow him, keeping a sharp eye on the cupboard. I walk as far from it as possible, crunching through broken glass and I hop through the mess to the verandah where Boils and Shum are arm wrestling. They look up and laugh together in stereo.

'What's that shit all over your face, man?'

Reggie touches his fingers to his face and looks at them. His head jerks back and he flicks his hand away from him making a low grunting noise, 'Ha! Ah! Ha!' The bucket clangs to the ground and he runs for the pool making a huge wave as he leaps in, suit and all.

Boils and Shum pause mid-wrestle to watch Reggie flailing about in the pool as the remains of Weasel float around and wrap him in a giant hug. He's screaming and fighting and kicking out, shouting for help and then he's free. He wades out the pool. Jets of water shoot from his pockets and Weasel spreads back out over the pool like an oil slick, like those lines they draw around dead people at a crime scene. Weasel got gat.

Boils and Shum return to their arm wrestle. Boils is

125

heaving and grunting. He pulls Shum's hand with both of his. His chair loses traction and he slides forward under the table, while Shum chuckles around his fag blowing smoke into Boils's face.

'Shum! Shum!' says Reggie. Shum looks up. 'You have to shit in here,' he says, holding up the bucket.

'What?' says Shum forgetting about the arm wrestle and Boils crashes his hand down on the table and both of them topple off their chairs. Reggie heaves the table on its side to clear a path and bats Shum with the bucket shouting, 'Get up you fools, get up.' This makes them laugh more.

'Get up. Or I'll piss on you,' Reggie says unzipping his trousers.

'Jesus-fuck, keep that kuffing mamba locked up, man, you'll kill us,' says Boils with a pubescent squeal.

'Vig us a hand,' says Shum holding up his limp arm and pawing at Reggie's leg. Reggie hauls him up and dumps him on the chair. Boils is laughing like a maniac. He climbs his way up the railings, picks up his chair and flops back into it.

'Holy fuck, I'm fucked,' says Boils and he's giggling again. He stands up and staggers across the lawn and wades into the pool. Holding his dop and smoke above the water, he dips his head under and then stomps back, stripping off his wet clothes.

What the hell are you talking about, Reggie?

Shum picks up the bucket and looks into it. 'It's empty,' he says.

Reggie is staring at the avo tree in the middle of the garden, its leaves rustling in the breeze.

'Reggie?' Shum waves his hand in front of his face. 'What's this for? We doing a bucket?'

'No, fuckface.' Boils slaps Shum's arm. 'The cops took

our weed, remember?'

Shum makes a single large nod of his head and points at Boils making a gun with his finger and thumb and firing it right between his eyes. 'That's a good point you make, mister,' and he jerks his head back to Reggie, like a malfunctioning robot version of Forrest Gump, and squints up at the glare.

Reggie looks at the bucket Shum is holding out for him. He takes it, frowning. He turns it over, smoothing his hand over the sides, running his fingers along the edge. He looks under it, lifting it high over his head, and he looks inside it. We all watch him.

What the fuck are you doing, Reggie?

'Awesome,' says Boils nodding his head like a stoner watching Evel Knievel fly over a line of trucks.

Shum jumps up and whips the bucket from Reggie and he's dropping his shorts. He plonks his bare arse on the bucket and lets rip.

Jesus Shum, what the fuck man? There's a fucking toilet right there.

Boils covers his face with his hands. He can't cope with breathing and laughing at the same time. Reggie is coughing like he's about to vom. You can see him thinking, is it coming? Must I run to the bogs? Can I hold it down? I think I can hold it down, I think I can, I think I can, I think I can.

Shum is oohing and aahing, and he says, 'That's the shit.' He makes plopping sounds and farting sounds and pissing sounds against the tin. His hand shoots into the air and he snaps his fingers three times in Reggie's face.

'Reggie!' he shouts and clicks fingers again. 'Bring bog roll.'

***

The air feels cool. The sun has dipped behind the trees and the effects of our trip are wearing off. Heads are drooping, like when the lights come on at Scar's and you see all the drunken soldiers slumped in corners clinging to their heads to stop the world spinning. Nobody speaks. Boils is inside, naked except for his squelching shooters. He's singing along to Toto, on repeat of course, at full volume, of course, with an air guitar strapped over his shoulder and an air mic at the ready for the only words he knows: I taste the rain down in Africa. We could do with a taste of rain right about now ourselves. He's singing with all his heart, panting from the effort, to a vast audience from his stage atop an upturned sofa rocking it back and forth.

'What do we do now?' I say to Reggie.

'We wait,' he says. 'The thing was clearly not in Shum's recent bowel movement so we wait.'

'No. About the weed? I'm not going to jail, man.'

'Fuck that,' says Shum, 'we'll just flick 'em each a twenty and that'll be the end of it. It's this tasty memory stick they're after. What the fuck's on that thing anyway? Didn't Maria tell you? Or tell you what the fuck to do with it?'

'She said it's just work stuff,' Reggie says closing his eyes and shaking his head. 'I couldn't— I didn't have the strength to— After she—' He buries his face in his hands.

'We do have a bigger problem,' says Shum.

'What?'

'When those pigs realise they haven't got it, they'll come straight back. Then what?'

'Shit,' says Reggie, standing up. 'Shit,' he says, walking towards the lounge and then stopping after two paces and

128

turning back to his seat. He flops back down and says, 'Shit.'

Boils comes onto the verandah bopping, waving his willy around like a windmill. He catches the tail-end of Reggie's rant and says, lighting a cigarette from Shum's butt, 'You said it,' blowing smoke out, laughing at his joke. 'Relax man. Fuckers won't come within a day of here. You saw their faces when I said Mbuya Chapo had done this place.'

'Yeah right, Boils. Coons aren't so gullible these days,' says Shum. 'Sorry Reg, I meant—'

'Are too,' says Boils. 'Even the taffest of taff cats visit the n'anga for demicine,' and he makes a fist and a stiff arm like a cock. 'To make them strong and to solve all sorts of problems too. Look at this,' he says and he nips into the house and comes back out with a faded copy of The Herald. Jesus did he go into that cupboard?

He's flicking the pages and then he stops and says, 'Here we go. Sekuru Juju Garwe from Chipinge. ZINATHA registered. See? They've even got a national association. Says here spells lifted, enemies vanquished, penis enlarged, debts, curses, you name it. He's a one-stop shop and there's heaps. Motora, back-pain eased. Gabarwa, HIV/AIDS cure and love spells. It's big business. I wasn't even joking about my uncle. He really did have a farm and a n'anga lived there. You should've seen the fat fucks in their Benzes and shiny suits that came to see her.'

'Well, we can't exactly rely on that mumbo jumbo now, can we?' says Reggie.

'No, we can't,' says Shum.

'Why don't you just hand it over?' I say to Reggie. Bad mistake. Holy Jesus, if looks could kill.

Shum says to me shaking his head, 'Bart, Bart, Bart.' And he sighs.

'Bart,' Reggie says to me with a grim face, 'forget the fact we're now implicated in this fucking mess. This is Maria we're talking about. And if you even think of betraying her I'll fucking kill you myself. With my bare hands. Do you believe me?'

'What? I'm just saying.' Fuck, these guys want to eat me alive. 'You don't have kids, you don't know what it's like, man.'

'Do you believe me?' he says, standing up and getting shouty.

'Yes, yes, ok, I believe you, man. I'm just saying—'

'And besides,' Reggie says, giving me this death look as if it was me who killed Maria, 'whoever did this to her is going to suffer. Hard.'

'Let's face it,' says Shum, 'whatever is on that thing is high-level shit. We hand it over, the question they will ask is: why have you fucking murungus got this stuff and where's the rest of it? And trust me, Bart, they won't accept your ignorance as an answer. Either way we are totally, one hundred cement butt-fucked.'

'Jesus fucking Christ,' says Boils. 'Why the fuck did Maria give it to you in the first place, Reg? She fucking sold us, man, like fat fucking mombes at the auction.'

'Either that or she knew Reg was the only person she could trust,' I say.

'Well then, why don't you just DHL it to someone over-seas? Like the U.N.' says Boils. At least someone's on my side.

'The Eunuch Nations? Don't be so fucking naive. And besides, why didn't Maria just do that herself?' says Reggie. 'Somehow those cops know we've got it. We need to know what's on that thing, only they took my laptop and we can't exactly waltz into an internet café with it,' says

Reggie biting his nails.

And then he slaps the table and says, 'Brucey. He'll have internet. We can upload the files and hand the memory stick over to the cops when they come back.'

'Brucey-Bruce? That homo cunt owes us two months' rent,' says Shum.

'Even better.'

'Only one snag. That fucking thing is still up my arse. And anyway we can't leave the house, remember?'

'Get Brucey to fetch it.'

'Fuck off cunt.' Shum buzzes an ashtray at Boils.

'Jesus! That would've taken my head off, man. Chill you fucking homo.'

Shum flies across the verandah clamping his hands around Boils's neck. Reggie and I have to haul him off.

'Hey! Keep it together man. This is hectic shit and we need to be solid. Okay?'

Shum glares at Boils. Boils glares at Shum.

'Okay?' Reggie shouts looking from one to the other.

Shum blinks. Boils looks away.

'Good. Now we need laxatives,' says Reggie and he looks at me. I catch his drift and go to the bathroom. Those cops emptied the cabinet onto the floor: bottles and jars and toothbrushes and razors and combs and shit everywhere. I scrape through the debris picking up likely candidates. Nothing. I go back out. Shum says we have to go and get some.

'Are you crazy?' I shout at Shum. 'We'll go to jail. I can't go to jail, man. I am not going to jail.'

'Okay, okay. Chill, dude,' Reggie says. 'Coffee. Works a charm. We'll make a stiff pot of coffee.'

'Fuck off man, I don't even drink coffee.'

But Reggie's already on his way to the kitchen, Boils shouting after him to bring beer.

'Hey puss-face,' Shum says, 'change the fucking music, man. This is shit and we've heard it a thousand times already.'

'I'll do it,' I say and I leap up to intercept Boils.

'Good.'

'What? Fuck you.'

We need something chilled here. Ground Control to Major Tom, commencing countdown engines on. Bowie's reedy voice above the rumbling bass and jangly guitars cut through the sunset like a rusty knife. Trapped in a void. That's us. Reggie returns with coffee the colour of tar.

'Jesus, I'm going to be shitting till I'm thirty,' says Shum as Reggie pours. 'I want fuck-loads of sugar in there. Fuck-loads.'

Boils gives it the anvil smile and says, 'Embassy Dark Roast: keeping Zimbabweans regular since 1999.'

'I'm hungry. Let's order pizza.'

'Good one. Dead ants!'

'Dead ants!'

'Dead ants!'

'Fuck, man, it was my idea.'

'Nobody fucks with the dead ants rule,' says Boils chucking the menu at my face.

'Yowser! You drink this shit?' says Shum. 'Bart you don't happen to have another secret stash anywhere, do you?'

'Jesus, Shum. I am fucking not going to jail, man.' I mean, there's just no way.

'It's like this Barty. Either Boils is right and they're skrooked to kingdom come or they're trawling through Reggie's laptop and memory thingies looking for something suspicious and that will take ages.'

'He's got a point,' says Reg. He would. Never heard him say no to spliff. Not that he ever buys or even rolls his own, the cunt.

'Ya, and I need a dum-cown, man. That trip was yectic,' says Boils. 'C'mon Bartster don't be a bender all your life.' Shum hoses himself at that.

'All well and good but they took my last bag.'

'Just go check, man,' says Shum, flapping his arms at me like he's shooing a bunch of flies.

Fine. Whatever.

I go to my room, lift the tile behind the door and my legs buckle. I can't believe this. I'm sitting on the floor staring at my stash, undisturbed and untouched. I know for a fact I had only one bag left because I already ordered more. This is wrong, man. Wrong. Am I going crazy? I can hear the others outside talking.

'And? What happens when they do come back?' Boils is saying.

'Dunno, man, they'll probably take us in and beat the shit out of us.'

Boils panicking says, 'What? They'll fucking torture us? Jesus man we've got to get the fuck out of here man.'

'Sit down, dick-fuck, we're not going to jail. And besides, I thought you spooked them?'

'No use taking chances now is there?'

'He's right, you know. Reg, we need a plan,' Shum is saying when I come back. I hold up my bag. I tell them the cops didn't find the weed, they planted their own. Nobody knows what to say. We just look at each other for clues. What the fuck? Then a car chugs and futs up the driveway.

Fuck.

'Shit!'

'Fuck!'

'Bart!' Reggie says. He's on his feet, shoving me into the house. 'Hide that weed. Quick. And properly. Shum! Get rid of that bucket, they'll twig. We know nothing. Got it? Nothing. Move, move.' He goes out to the front. Boils is rooted to his chair. I nip back to my room and stow my stash. Shum tosses the bucket into the hedge.

Girls' voices. I hear girls' voices. It's not the cops.

'Holy fuck! Are we glad to see you,' says Shum when Maria's friends from the other night walk through the front door. Jill and, Jill and, Jill and Rachel, that's it. Jesus, I'm shaking like a junkie. We are all heaving with the fear. I have to sit.

'That's what Reggie said. What's going on? Reggie you're still in your suit and you're soaked. What happened here? Are you renovating?'

Jill looks around anew at our faces. We're staring at her in a strange way, I can feel it. Ok, so we're still a bit baked from the shrooms and we've been at it all day but it's more than that. Flashback to being a kid gaffed roof-rattling with a torch shining in my face blinded and being assured of a sound thrashing. Fuck, I don't think we'd fool even the dumbest cop in the world. 'Reggie?' she says, turning to face him, 'what is going on?'

'Long story, really long, but we're in a bit of shit. It's to do with Maria but we're not sure how or why.'

'Basically we're fucked,' says Boils standing up, 'so I'm going to get proper fucked.'

'Boils! Put some clothes on,' says Reggie.

Shum is hosing himself. 'Get me a dop while you're up,' he says.

'And me,' I shout after him. What the fuck? May as well.

134

'We can't stay,' says Rachel. 'We just came to see if you guys are okay.'

'Reg?' Jill tilts her head at him.

'That's it,' Reggie shouts and slaps his head and then, clicking his fingers at Shum, he says, 'that's it, that's the plan.' He takes Jill's hands and he says, 'Jill, there is no way I can explain why but we really, really need your help.'

'Okay?' she says, extracting her hands and pulling her hair back. 'Sounds dodge. What do you want?'

'Jill, you promised,' says Rachel glaring at her.

'Promised what?' says Reggie.

'Nothing,' she says returning Rachel's look even harder. Huh? What's going on here?

Reggie says, 'Jill, you need to call everyone you know. They need to come here for a monster party. Everyone.' Reggie looks to the rest of us. 'All of us, we need to get everyone we know right here, right now.'

'Ha!' says Shum slapping his leg. 'That's genius.'

What for? Why? I'm confused.

'On a Thursday? Why?' says Rachel with a nervous look at Jill.

'I'm sorry, Rachel, I really can't explain. It's nothing bad or anything. We just need a cover so we can leave the house.'

'A cover?' Now they're really suspicious.

'Please?' he says and she looks up at him giving him the beady eye. Then, with a tiny nod of her head, she says, 'Okay, Reg.'

Rachel sighs and Reggie says to her, 'You'll understand, Rachel. Really you will. But right now I need you guys to muster up the biggest impromptu ever. Call it Maria's Proper Wake. With her real friends, not those flaky cling-ons she works with. Okay?'

135

'Okay, Reggie, but I swear if this cunt,' she tilts her head at Shum, that would be Shum she's talking about, 'even looks at me or Rachel I swear I'll chop both your cocks off.'

'That's my girl. That's the spirit. And besides, Shum's coming with me.'

'What?' says Shum looking to the hot chicks. 'Why?'

'Because num-nut, you're the frikken courier.'

'Oh! Ya. Ya-no fine.'

'Just say, "Ingocheni Island: Maria's Proper Wake. Right now. Come as you are. Open house." Oh, and better give the address in case.'

'In case what?' says Boils coming back out clutching a six-pack in one hand and what is no doubt a quadruple vodka and coke in the other.

'We're throwing a party,' says Reggie, 'right now. Get on your phone, everyone you know must come. They must come. Don't take no for an answer.'

'Ha-ha!' Boils does a little jump, 'Good skills!' and then he grabs Reggie's lapel. He pulls him aside and says under his breath, 'But dude, aren't you forgetting,' he nods towards the gate, 'you know? The bacon?'

Reggie pats his shoulder. 'Don't worry Boils, you'll figure it out. Meantime, call everyone you know.'

Boils thinks for a bit, then he twigs and shouts, 'Banzai!' jumping in the air. The girls shriek and Shum hee-haws his head clean off.

'And Boils. For fuck's sakes,' says Reggie, 'put some fucking clothes on.'

THREE ROUNDS WITH A LIVE TURKEY

Reggie's cooked up this cunning plan: a full-on show-down right here on the Island so we can sneak off to Brucey's house and upload the files. Whatever that means. Bart and Boils have thrown themselves into it like kids at Christmas. The first arrival is within minutes. It's that Bog Brush twot from Aguilas ripping up the driveway in his pimped out Hilux. Was he waiting outside? He's got a bottle of Smirnoff and a Skud under his arm. That same Union Jack bandana holds his mop in check. He swaggers in, chest pubes bristling through a browning undervest, giving it the awright, mate? Awright?

Fake fucker.

Maria! he shouts, throwing his head back, arms out like the preacher at a happy-clap-a-thon, and he takes a massive glug of vodka straight from the bottle. Not bad, not bad. For a Pom, or at least for a pretend Pom. He thumps the vodka on the table peeling his mouth back and then takes an even bigger glug from the Skud. Now that's impressive. Jesus that stuff tastes like shit. Like sour porridge.

Now another shiny double-cab tears up the driveway screeching tyres and a free-flow exhaust revving like a drag racer and skidding to a stop. Bodies spill out, all in black and the music almost drowns the hi-fi inside.

Who the fuck are they?

Bog Brush says he told his mates to come.

You did say open house, right, mate?

Yes but—

Boils's guffaw cuts Reggie's bleating short and he says in his most bestest mushiest muntu accent: Dhindhindhindi full time. And he follows it up with a peacock howl and breaks into his Kwasa-Kwasa moves. Classic Boils in his element. At least he's got some clothes on now.

Reggie's been peering over the wall every five minutes. Still no sign of those cops. Reckon they got their little pips deep fried by Boils's shrooms. Got their stupid noggins Boiled, no, hard Boiled. Ha! My only regret is we didn't get to witness the full humour of the trip kicking in. I'd give my right nut to see that.

***

Christ, where are all these people coming from? There's a constant stream. It's as if they were all waiting for the call. They've got coolboxes loaded with booze and ice. Most of them need two to carry. Reggie made me take my bucket everywhere. Just in case. He also said I mustn't drink. Yeah right. Guys are pouring their dops into it all the time – yes I rinsed it out, I'm not a total moron – and I'm nicking glugs from Bog Brush's vodka and Boils is helping me out whenever Reg isn't looking.

No booze, he said. We need to keep our shit together for this, he said.

Fuck him. If I need to keep my shit together, I need booze.

The Porras are here with Gav cranked up to full volume. I always thought he was permanently jacked but this is a whole new level. And Frotter and Sykes are here of course and, holy shit, there's Badza rapping some crap to Suzie, pink tongue darting in and out, head shaking his pile of dreads like a golliwog. And Suzie Bevridge. So named because he has a woman's hips and walks like he's got a Lazy Susan for a pelvis. And his surname couldn't be more apt. Already fucked, he's clapping in time to Badza's poetry. What idiots.

The noise is impressive. Like an open bar at the George and guys are super-excited getting tanked in fast-forward mode. The music was fuck-loud before everyone arrived. Now I can only hear the bass warbling in the undergrowth, probably that same song on repeat. Okes are jumping in the pool. There's a fire going. Some chicks are even dancing in the lounge. How gay is that?

Boils has revived the jousting tournament on the driveway with a new pillow hanging from the tree and a fresh portrait of His Bobness scrawled onto it with a marker: stupid Hitler tash and milk-bottle chigogs pretty much gets him down. Boils cleared the runway and all – made everyone move their cars outside.

So much the better for our cover later, Reggie had said.

A fat chick mounts Marsellus: mild-mannered wheelbarrow by day, Pegasus the Avenger by night. This should be good. The pool pole clangs to the ground, way too long for her. She sits. Gay, but still, check Boils – he's barking mad – sprinting full tilt down the driveway, his hooves flicking like a charging centaur. The chick is screaming at him to slow down. Her friends are screaming at him also and he's cackling like a rabid baboon. The pole snags on the branch and turns into one of those ancient catapults hoiking the chick, Marsellus and Boils into a heap on the driveway with a solid thump. Ha! That looked sore. Boils is rolling around. Is he hurt? Is he pissing himself? Probably both the crazy cunt. The chick is livid. She limps away to join her friends, showing them the grazes on her hands and up her legs. They're full of the righteous indignation throwing hard stares at Boils still on his back neighing to himself. But there's a fucking queue of okes wanting a go. Bob's head on a stick. Imagine. There aren't enough pillows on Earth.

I wander in the direction of the kitchen. Jill has cornered Reggie on the verandah so I loiter behind the avo tree and listen in. She's shaking him by the arms and she's all sparkly with booze. Oh! Come on Reggie, she says with a squeak. Tell me what's going on, or I'll never talk to you again. She bats him on the chest and he catches her hand and looks about, not seeing me. He sighs, all dramatic, and says, Okay fine. The cops trashed our house last night. They were looking for something.

Cops? Why? What were they looking for? Drugs?

What? No, no, nothing like that, although, and he sighs again.

Just spit it out Reg, you can trust me, she says. Jesus, suck his cock why don't you. Fucking slapper.

Woo-ooo! Jill and Reg, sitting in a tree, says the other one crashing into them and they fall against the railings.

Not now, Rachel, says Jill. Rachel. So that's her name, the one from Scar's the other night. Rachel doesn't hear, or chooses not to. Instead she stirs her drink with the straw and takes a big slurp. Then she says, Is Shum gay?

What the fuck?

What? Why? says Reggie.

Just curious, she says, sliding against the rail. She drops off the edge onto the lawn and joins in the circle standing around the fire. She still hasn't seen me.

What the fuck's that all about?

Fuck! Reggie says. Fuck-fuck! We've got to go. Jill, this might sound like some bullshit line but we have to go now and it's safer if you know nothing anyway. I need you to keep everyone here. Boils and Bart are too fucked to care.

Oh, and trash the place, he says.

What? Reggie?

We'll be back soon. I'll explain everything then, he says, shouting over the racket.

Reggie! She stomps her feet. Christ's sake. Chicks.

Reggie's by my side. He nudges me and says, Duty calls.

What's up? says Gav, or rather he shouts. We gonna do some flame-throwage jousting? Ol' Brown Eyes gonna see his ol' brown assssssss-hole. And he's giving us a full-on brown-eye for good measure.

Charlie run, says Reggie under his hand. He puts his finger to the side of his nose and says, Keep it mum, not much to go round.

Good one. Gav does a back flip and bounces straight into a forward flip, like a spring hare wired up into the ZESA. And now he's doing some crazy dance around the fire, his legs bent double, dragging his knuckles along the ground, squawking like a turkey and poking his head forward and back. You get the impression he's chuffed.

Reggie's jaw is clenched and he yanks on Gav's sleeve and says, Keep it fucking mum, I said.

Fucking whose mum? Gav shouts. Yours?

Fuck these guys are funny. No yours, fucknut, I say. Just don't tell anyone, ok?

Oh. Ya. Right. Of course. More for me, us, I mean us. Mum's the word.

Reggie goes off to get Bog Brush. I meet them round the front of the house. No sign of the cops' fucked car, thank the Bloody Mary.

Sure he'll be there? I ask Reg as we hoist our bikes onto the back of his cab.

Of course he will. It's a Thursday and those guys never leave the house anyway. They watch movies, they eat rice crackers and they pump iron. That's all they do.

Fucking homos. Bog Brush red lines it, pistons popping though the bonnet, so we jump in.

Besides I messaged him, he says and then to the Brush, Just round the corner, ok? Thanks, man, appreciate it.

Whatever dude, just make sure you score enough for everyone, he says giving Reggie a wink.

Sure, sure, we're getting plenty, says Reggie. Least I hope so, he adds looking out the window as we pull off.

The power's out in the whole neighbourhood, surprise surprise. The car lights bounce off the canopy of jacarandas and we jackhammer over the sharp humps made by the trees' roots and we thump through the potholes made by Bobby McGee & Co.

This is fine, says Reggie, just after the corner there. Remember, don't tell a fucking soul.

Gotcha mate. I gotcha.

Right, see you later, says Reggie standing at the door ready to close it.

Dude, what's with the bucket? Bog Brush says to me as I hop out onto the road.

Gag reflex, says Reggie. Carries it with him everywhere.

Hm! he says, nodding and then to Reg he says, Dude, you're wearing a suit.

He's a junkie, I say. Sold all his clothes.

Hm! he says.

Reggie closes the door and Bog Brush roars away, tyres squealing, exhaust blasting.

What the fuck was that all about?

What?

Gag reflex? You're the one with a fucking gag reflex, chundering all over the place.

And me? A junkie?

I switch on my light, Reggie rolls up up his trouser legs and then we're off, cruising along the road in silence, our lights flicking shadows all over the place.

CAN'T TOUCH THIS

Nothing. I can't believe. You delivered unto him the full voltage to the genitals? Did you test it? Don't 'what' me Chikomo, did you test the equipment? These coconut types are very crafty. Very crafty indeed. Easily he can act on the verge of expiring. Easily he can fool the dim-witted interrogator into believing he is at his own wit's end; and easily said dim-witted interrogator can believe, by process of deduction, that his subject, in fact, knows nothing actually. Take off your trousers.

You heard me. Say 'what' one more time comrade, I am fast losing my patience with you. Good. Dim you are but it seems you know my reputation. That or you have seen what a forty-four Magnum can do to your brains in fact. Good. Now. Attach the clips, I want to see your technique. Chikomo. My supply of warnings is running low. Attach the clips just as you did to our non-compliant comrade here.

Come on, come on, we don't have all night. Good. Now. Let's we engage the ZESA.

Ha-haaa! A triumph. It works. It most definitely works.

Unless you too are playing the lame duck trick? The broken-wing act. Do you know what is a lame-duck trick, Chikomo? This is the most cunning of ploys. She pretends her wing is broken that she may distract the predator from her nest, from her eggs, from her babies. The ultimate noble act: laying her life on the line to protect her loved ones. Only at the last moment does she fly away. But sometimes she is too slow, or the predator too close to her clutch, and she must take the fall that her children may live, fly, flourish and make merry. Such a noble creature. Much like our friend here, do you not think? And in turn much like our dear departed friend, too. Ah! It is a proper Romeo and Juliet tale. But I would ask them this: what is the point?

I digress. Old age, you see. Turns one towards sentimentality; to thoughts of love and loyalty. My question, Chikomo, is this: can you attest to the efficacious nature of this instrument? This instrument of what? Come again, you sound like a par-boiled frog. Torture you say? Ah! Can we not use that ugly word, an ugly word, indeed. Instrument of encouragement perhaps? Our creator of cooperation, our catalyst of compliance. I bet our clever friend here could offer us some choice monikers but he is busy putting on a good show of being dead. Maxwell. Answer my question.

Hai! Aikona. You used up my last moments of civility, Maxwell. Now you will see from whence my reputation arises. It's ZESA-time. Ha! Can't touch this bum-bum-ba-dum. ZESA-time. Ka-pow! Ka-blam! Ka-blooey! Can't touch this bum-bum-ba-dum.

Well. I can safely say you answered my question, dear, dear sleeping beauty. The device is in full working order. Unless my slumbering subaltern is destined for the stage as well? The Globe and no less for he is doing a fine rendition of a man unconscious. Oliviers and Baftas all round. Bravo! Bravo! May we have an encore? Why not. Just to be sure, of course of course. Yes. It works or I am a fool. Am I a fool, comrade? No answer came the stern reply. Very good.

Now. I wonder if that other one, that self-styled Great White Hunter, possesses such admirable loyalty and resilience? I doth doubt it verily much indeed: his oily skin smacketh of sedition, his dark eyes declare duplicity, his heavy torso trumpets treachery. And besides, he eats crayfish actually. Time to revive my blunt weapon that he may apply his charms on our hunter-gatherer friend.

How! My favourite John Lobbs they are taking such a beating. But needs must.

THURSDAY NIGHT AT BRUCEY-BRUCE'S

Plastered. Neat vodka's no walk in the park. This memory stick thing up my arse is freaking me out man. I'm scared to pedal in case I shart it out. Fucking thing's going to rip my ring apart. Swallowing it was bad enough.

Reggie's way up ahead. I can see his red taillight blinking and his front light flitting like a strobe. He's gliding most of the time, looking back at me every two seconds. I catch him up.

Jesus, Shum, you got a puncture?

Ya, slow puncture, I tune him back.

Wouldn't surprise me, he says, always the fucking prude. Always giving me uphill all the time about my what-you-ma-call-it about my extra-mural activities.

Hey! Reggie's shouting at me. I disentangle myself from him, must have veered off a bit there.

We nearly crashed, man, what's going on? You drunk? You're drunk aren't you? Jesus. And he stomps on his pedals and soon he's way ahead again. Fucking fusspot. Fuck him.

We pedal in silence through Highlands, black as an abandoned coal mine. It's dead quiet. Even the air is dead as we slice through it, tyres humming on the tarmac. We've both done this route hundreds, thousands of times. Not much at night though. Damn it's cool. Reggie has let me catch up and he darts ahead to cut through the vlei single file: duck under the low branch, hop the stones over the ditch, watch the sharp one on the right and then it's all clear because the munts have padded a silky smooth path for us over the ages. The brown grass gives off that dusty, musty October smell as it whips at our legs. Smells like we're back in the bush. Stars fill the sky as we break out from the trees.

Car! Reggie says hissing at me.

We skid to a stop killing our lights and drop below the grass. The car slows, turns and speeds off, revving the balls out the engine. Drunk kids probably.

Jesus, Reg, we don't have to duck from every fucking car we see.

Reggie whispers to me: Can't take chances. We'll hit Ridgeway and cut across the vlei to Steppes.

Why's he whispering? Fuck. That coffee, the booze, this cycling. My stomach is cramping up.

Jesus, Reg, we need to get there soon, man. My stomach.

Hold it in, dude, just hold it, says Reggie switching his light back on and clambering onto his bike.

We get to the edge of the vlei, join the road for a bit and then veer right and up past the fancy houses: ten-foot walls with electric fencing and snoring mahobos at the gates. I'm out of breath as I join Reggie at the top of the hill.

Come on, Shum, you need to push it now, he says.

Fuck pushing. If I push, I'll shit myself.

But Reggie is away already, pedalling down the long straight hill as a car turns into the road heading towards us.

Shit! I hear Reggie shout. He's looking around for a place to hide. Nothing but manicured verges. Too late anyway, they've seen us. Another car rounds the corner from the other direction.

We pedal like fuck, standing, legs pumping. The approaching car slows as it draws near and turns into a driveway; the car behind turns into the same driveway.

It's fine, Reggie, it's fine.

I'm bushed. I have to stand out of the saddle again and pedal like hell, dropping a gear and ducking my head over the handlebars. I catch up again with Reg who is waiting opposite the vlei. At least he's also panting now.

Jeez, I caught a skrook.

No shit, Lance, you tore off like a motherfucker. I tell him we should take the road instead. I'm in trouble here and I don't know this path and I need to dump. Right now. Fuck, it's hurting to hold it in.

Reggie says: Vlei's quicker and besides they could have other cops looking for us; if one spots us then checks the house—

Fuck this, no time for debates. I cross the road, dip through the ditch and into the open field then round the corner and behind the back of a house.

I hear Reggie whisper-shouting after me but fuck it we need to get there. I'm sweating like a rapist. I turn on my light and then an almighty thump knocks my brain sideways. It's so loud. I'm flying over the handlebars and someone's lashing out at me. We tumble, my bike on top of me. My face smashes into the ground and I land on a knee or something. Holy fuck-shit-cunt Jesus dogballs motherfucker it hurts. I am screaming and clawing at the ground to find a rock to smash his head in and then Reggie's by my side hauling my bike off and telling me to shut the fuck up but I don't care, I'm going to kill this cunt.

I'm gonna kill him, I'm screaming. I don't give a fuck who hears me. Get me out of this fucking bike. I'm going to fucking kill him. Where's he? The fuck. The fucking cunt. Jesus I'm going to smash his fucking face in. Ha! Oh sweet

Jesus that hurts. I can't move my arm, Reg. The pain, Reg.

Shum, be quiet, says Reggie, shaking me. Sounds like he's chewing a brick. He hoofs me in the ribs.

Motherfucker.

Quiet, he says. Oh my aching ballsack this hurts, Reg.

I make out a black heap of human. It's whimpering like a mangled KD. Reggie shoves it onto its back with his foot and it yelps out, Baas! Baas! pawing at Reggie's leg. There's a delivery-type bike leaning against the wall. Must've been about to climb on.

Serves you right, fucking tsotsi, says Reggie and he comes to me and grabs under my arms. Gaaaah! Stop. Reggie. Fuck. I think my arm is broken. Oh my fuck.

Shum, every dog within a hundred miles is barking. Neighbourhood Watch will be here any minute. We have to go.

Dogs all around us are indeed going berserk. Reggie hauls me up by my good arm and untangles me from my bike. I feel faint. I'm just standing there swaying. Then I charge over and hoof the fucking cunt in the ribs. He doesn't make a sound. I take aim at his nut but Reggie pulls me back so my next kick swings free and we both nearly topple over.

We have to go, Shum. Let's go. Can you ride? he says, hauling me up.

He kicks the bucket into the bushes, it's fucked anyway, and switches my light on. I fumble with the pedals. Change to granny gear and wobble forward, the chain clanking onto its new cog, my arm hanging limp. The black lump hasn't budged. Maybe he's dead? Good.

I hit a bump and my front tyre jags sideways and I stop dead. I'm falling. I have to put my foot out. My nuts are squished on the seat. The pain shoots up my belly. Oh! Jesus! Just kill me now for fuck's sake.

Have to walk, says Reggie.

No! I have to shit. This is faster. Go in front.

Reggie rides as slow as he can, his front light dancing side to side as he tries to keep balance at this pace. He checks my progress over his shoulder. This is a new level of pain for me. And I thought swallowing that goddam memory stick was a near-death experience.

Steppes Road at last. We free-wheel all the way down. Fuck this is tricky. One little bump and I'm fucked. I'm gripping the handlebar like I'm on the edge of a cliff. We make a slow turn right and up a steep close. I have to get off and walk the last bit, clamping my arse-cheeks together.

Reggie's bashing on the gate buzzer when I get to him. Nothing, he says. He rings again, holding his finger down and I can hear the scratchy buzz from inside the house.

Reg. I need to shit. Now.

I'm soaked. Can't breathe. It feels like there's a fist up there pushing everything upwards. Oh fuck, I'm squirming, panicking like a cornered buck. I grab hold of Reggie's jacket and yank his face to mine, eyeball to eyeball and tune him: Reggie, I fucking need to go. Right now.

Wait! he says. Hold it in, man, he says.

I'm swaying. This is agony.

The gate makes a loud clunk and then trundles open at like a millimetre an hour. I'm screaming. I don't care anymore.

Go, says Reggie. I'll bring your bike.

I can't even run. I take some breaths and step over the gate rail, then another and I'm sliding forward like Mr. fucking Bean, making all kinds of sounds I've never even

151

heard before. Reggie ducks past, chucks the bikes on the lawn and bounds up to the door thumping on it with his fist.

I shout out, Hey! Brucey you fucking faggot. Open this fucking door.

Dogs are barking all over the place and I shout again, Bruce for fuck's sake.

A light flicks on, a shadow moves across the frosted glass, latches clack, one, two, three, four. And five. Jesus. The door opens a crack and Bruce's face appears, his chin on the door-chain.

Reggie? Is that you? Shum? What's going on?

Let us in, I shout.

No ways, Reggie, you said you wouldn't bring him.

Brucey, this is an emergency, Reggie says.

No ways, Reggie.

Fuck this. I can't wait any longer. I whip down my shorts and squat on the doorstep.

What the fuck are you doing? say Bruce with a squeal. Shum, Jesus, Shum what the fuck are you doing?

I'm having a shit, Bruce.

Reggie yelps and skips away from me as, oh mothering-fuckfuck, I let rip. Oh! Mother of Mary, son of a goatfucker, my arse explodes. Bruce's yammering fades into the farthest reaches of my consciousness and Reggie is yelling at me to keep it all in one place.

Jesus, Reg, you may as well try to contain an H-bomb.

My arm is on fire. I'm feeling faint. The brickwork swims in front of me. A hand. Reggie's hand. He caught me.

I'm gonna faint, Reggie.

Steady, Shum, stay with us, he says. I grab hold of his leg. My other arm is fucked, flopping around like a donkey's dick. He's saying something to Bruce but I can't hear

152

the words. My stomach churns. My ring tears open. I can feel the fucking thing, right there by my ring. This is like giving birth. Worse even, oh my fuck. I hear this growl. Like thunder. It turns to a scream and I'm falling forwards again, the bricks racing up towards me. Reggie pushes me back. He holds me up and he shouts at me to push, get the fucking thing out, and I'm screaming and straining and clinging to Reggie's neck, his arms around me and he's shouting in my ear. Fuck. Someone is going at my arse with a razor blade, slashing it up. I strain. It burns all the way up to my eyeballs. I can't. Reggie is shouting at me to get it out. I strain. It burns. An explosion. It's out. My ring is on fire. Oh fuck me. Fuck me. I collapse, all my weight on Reggie and he's making soothing sounds that disappear into the night.

***

Help! Brucey. Help! Reggie is shouting.

Where the fuck am I? What's going on. Why am I in Reggie's arms?

Bruce, open the fucking door and help me for fuck's sake. He's fainted and his arm's broken. Come Shum, says Reggie.

He drags me to the lawn and props me up against the tap. Then he runs full tilt, leaping over my pile of shit and slams into the door with his shoulder. Two faces wince and whinny like nags and Reggie is backing up for another charge. Bruce is scrabbling at the chain to open it as Reggie flies into the door and crashes inside, sending Bruce and some other fag tumbling down the passage like a pair of skittles.

153

Oh! Good shooting, Reginald. Bravo! Nice work, son.

Shut up Shum, he says, dragging me towards the house. My buggered arm flops to the ground and sends a fucking bolt of lightning all the way up through my shoulder and into my brain. A scream tears the night apart and then I realise it's mine.

Shum. Reggie is shaking me. Shut the fuck up, he says hauling me to my feet.

And mind your crap, he says as we step over the biggest goddam coil I've seen in human history.

Jesus! A monster. Wait, Reg, let me go. We need to weigh that puppy. Could be a record.

He's having none of it and drags me into the house. We thump into the passageway. Bruce is sitting on the floor holding his head. He looks up at us, about to blub and says, Reggie? What the?

Get his shorts, Reggie says to the other fag, the one with the bulging eyeballs. The fag is frozen, just staring in horror.

Do it! Now! Reggie mock-charges, barking like a rotty and the fag jumps back like he's been slapped and then scampers out.

Brucey, help me get his shorts on. Take him from behind.

No way, man, this oke is a fucking fag. He ain't taking me from nowhere, I say.

Shut up, Shum. Brucey, do as I say and watch that arm. I think it's broken.

Bruce holds me around the torso. I can feel his goddam cock through his fucking PJs while Reggie fiddles with my feet, sticking them into my shorts.

The bug-eyed fag says, stammering, A-Aren't you going to wipe?

Wipe? Wipe? You want to wipe his arse? Didn't think

so. Reggie hoists my shorts up and twangs the waistband. Oof! Jesus, Reg.

Tiger! Tiger! Eyeballs is shouting at the dog. He's tucking into my turd.

Junior, get that dog inside and close the door, Reg says to the bushbaby. Now! He screams.

No way, man, I'm not going near that thing.

Fine. You can hold Shum.

So Junior creeps down the passage and hauls the dog off my dump and slams the door falling on his arse and the dog is trying to lick his face and he's freaking out. I'm too fucked to laugh. It's going dark and fuzzy again and I can't hold my head up.

My arm. Jesus, Reg, my arm.

Brucey, you're a physio, take a look at his arm. We had a crash on the way here, Reggie says, easing me down the wall to the floor.

Ya, fag, have a look at my armie-warmie.

It's Brucey-Bruce. Call me a fag again and I'll throw you out, he says kneeling down in front of me.

Where does it hurt?

Everyfuckingwhere. I'm panting. Can hardly talk. There. I point with my chin.

He squeezes my hand.

There?

I shake my head.

That?

No. Bruce works his way up, squeezing as he goes, me shaking my head. Then he lifts my whole arm. It's like live fucking ZESA charging through my body into my brain and then firing up a chainsaw in there and there's some cunt whizzing it around like a lasso inside my head. I scream.

155

It feels like hell is closing in on me with a flaming serpent squirming through my ear and out my chest and back into my stomach and out my arse.

I come to. Must've fainted again. I hear voices but can't see anything.

Dislocated. No break or trapped nerves, says Bruce. I can get it back in, Reg, but he'll be in serious pain. He's going to need a doctor, right away. How did you get here?

Fuck! He's not touching me, I'm yelling, trying to stand up. Reggie, tell the fag he's not fucking touching me. Reggie pulls me back down and he says, Shum, you've dislocated your shoulder. Brucey-Bruce is going to put it back.

No fucking way. You let this fucking fag touch me and I'll kill him, Reg, I'll kill him.

Reggie stands up, hands on his hips, looking down at me, livid. He says, Call him a fag again, Shum, and I'll break your other fucking arm. He is helping you so shut up and bite on this. Brucey, I assume you've got painkillers?

Sammy the bushbaby says he knows where they're kept and scampers away. There's another fag. Where'd he come from? He hasn't moved. He's just staring at me, biting his fingernails. Bare feet. Jeans. Naked on top. The floor hits my face again.

Reggie, Junior, you're going to hold him down, says Bruce. I recognise his reedy little voice.

Uh-uh. No way, man, this guy will eat me. He's a savage. I think that's the night ape speaking.

I grab Reggie. My head is about to explode. Reggie wrestles me back against the wall and says, Compared to me, Junior, he's a newborn kitten. Hold him down.

Reg? Reg? I'm stroking his arm. Please, Reg.

Shum, it's going to be fine, he says. Bruce knows what

he's doing, he says. We'll get you a bottle of something and some painkillers. It's going to be fine, he says.

Ok, Reg, I sink down. Fucked. Ok, Reg. Just get it over with.

Junior and Reggie have me in a brace. Bruce shoves his heel under my arm. That hurts. I'm writhing and Junior and Reggie are flying about clinging onto me like it's a rodeo and Reggie is shouting at Junior to hold tighter.

Ready? On four ok?

Oh Jesus.

Keep still, Shum.

On four. Right. One, two—

Wait, wait, wait, wait, wait. Junior says. I lost my grip.

Fuck sakes, Junior. Get a grip, I say. He doesn't laugh.

Ok. Ready? One-two— and he yanks. My arm is ripped off, my insides have turned to flaming liquid metal and it burns and burns and burns and, oh my blowtorched cunt, the searing goddam motherfucking pain.

I can hear myself screaming and I can feel my legs thrashing and connecting with something soft. I'm on my back. I look up and they are all staring at me. Except Junior who is curled up on the floor crying.

You said on four, you cunt.

Reggie says to Sammy: Hard tack. Fetch.

In the storeroom, says Bruce and Sammy sidles along the wall opposite me like I'm going to eat him or something. He opens the front door and a heavy-calibre bullet zucks him in the chest and he flies backwards and lands on the floor and scrabbles away from the door on all fours.

Jesus Christ! He screams at me. What the fuck, man? It stinks like rotting hell out there.

Reggie snorts and then I'm also canning myself imagining this commotion from their perspective. Sammy is having himself a nice panic attack. Bruce fetches a brown paper bag and he's hyperventilating into it.

Not exactly your standard Thursday night in, hey ladies?

***

Reggie is gagging and dry heaving. You can see his stomach trying to chuck the kitchen sink up.

Fuck off Shum, it's not funny, he says to me, his voice muffled behind the dishcloth covering his face like a cowboy. It hurts like fuck to laugh but I can't help it. He's on all fours poking at my monster pile of shit with a pair of chopsticks and a head-torch. Looks like a coal miner. Got me some mighty fine first aid: these little white pills with like a square root sign on them – Bruce refused to tell me what they were – and I'm getting stuck into the vodka despite the faggot's pansy-assed protests. Fuck him, what does he know.

Sammy has to hold the Alsation back. He wants to chow down on my dung. Dogs are awesome.

What you got there, Reg? Bit of carrot? There's always carrots Reg.

This sends him over the edge. Yanking at the dishcloth he scrabbles like a baboon to the flowerbed and is hurling and hawking his guts out. The dog wants some of this too and drags Sammy into the flowers and Reggie has to shove him away. Sammy's yanking on the collar and shouting, Tiger! Tiger! and the dog is choking and rasping and yelping and howling at all the excitement. No fair, he's saying, no fucking fair. Too much. This is too much. I can't. I can't stop. Oh, Jesus, I might just die laughing.

Ha, bloody ha, says Reggie spitting and wiping his face on his sleeve. You're cleaning up, arse-wipe.

Can't, I say and I waggle my hand in the sling. Hm! Would you look at that: it's holding a box of smokes. Don't mind if I do.

Reggie sighs and crawls back to my turd, re-tying the dishcloth over his face which just sets me off again.

And go easy on the vodka. Those pills are prescription only man, he says.

Oh don't I know it. They're kicking in now and holy balls of Jesus H. Fortesque I want some more. My whole body is numb and floating and tingling and the pain, sweet Mary mother of a cocksucker, the pain has vanished, vanished I tell you.

There, Reggie says. He holds a blob of shit up to the light and I can see edges of the memory stick.

Yep, that's the badger, I tell him. He just looks at me.

***

What the hell, man, you're going to put it in the sink? Bruce is having a hissy fit behind his hand, eyes bulging over the top. We're all in the hallway peering into the kitchen. Junior and Sammy are clinging to each other like koalas in a corner and the dog is scraping at the door and yapping his head off.

Got to wash it off, says Reg.

Just throw it away, Bruce says.

Can't. We need it.

What? It's a memory stick for Christ's sakes. I'll give you

159

one of mine. Tiger! Tiger! Sammy, shut that dog up will you.

Reggie is rinsing the thing under the tap, holding it far away from him like it's going to bite him. He can't even look straight at it, like it's cursed: he who looks directly upon thy glorious stick shall be blinded for a hundred years and grow warts on his tadza.

Get me an ice cream tub or something, he says. The fags all look at each other cowering further back into their horror and shaking their heads, no way man. Reggie shouts again so Bruce goes into the kitchen and fishes out an old ice cream tub. Reggie fills it with water and Sunlight and swirls the memory card thing in it. He lifts it out, rinses and inspects it again. Nope. Back in the tub it goes. More swirling and sloshing. Another inspection.

Bruce is back in the hallway, bristling and muttering under his breath. He stomps his foot and says, Damn it all. Now. Now listen here, Reggie. Just what the heck is going on? Huh? I mean, you message me saying you want to 'borrow some games' then you show up in the middle of the night with this, with this, oaf, yelling his head off fit to wake the dead who proceeds to take a wild, screaming poop on my doorstep and then you bash our heads open with the door and he's got a dislocated shoulder and hurling every kind of homophobic epithet he can think of. And poor Sammy got kicked in the nuts and all the while we're trying to help him, I might add. I mean, sheesh, Reggie, what the hell? Everyone knows you're a bunch of wild animals but this is ridiculous.

Huh? Reggie says, holding the stick under the tap.

Classic. I'm hosing myself again. Bruce stomps and slaps his sides. Reggie inspects the thing, shakes the water off and closes the tap.

Reggie? What is going on? Why are you wearing a suit? It's trashed. You look like a tramp, Bruce says.

Brucey, it's a long story. Let me sort this out, he nods at the thing, and then I'll explain all. Right now I need your help. I need to use your computer. Have you got a hair dryer?

Bruce looks at the floor.

Have you got a hair dryer?

Course he fuckin' 'as. All fags have hair dryers.

Jesus Christ, Shum! Bruce has lost it for proper now. He screams, just nonsense, and stomps his foot and says: Get out of my house. Right now. Just get out.

Fuck china, take a chill pill, it's just a joke.

Yeah, well it's not funny and we're tired of it, says Bruce fanning my smoke away from his face.

And steady on with that vodka, man, you're on hectic painkillers, says Reg.

I take a massive gulp, Jayziz that's harsh. I know, I say shuddering, not a fuck I'm going to let an opportunity like this slip away. I go into the lounge and there's this fuck-off sound system.

Yo bum chums, where's the music?

I'm opening cupboards looking for CDs. Celine Dion? Fuck this. I go back to the kitchen, bumping into Bruce carrying a hair dryer.

Reggie, it's one o'clock in the morning. On a Thursday, no, Friday morning, says Bruce handing him the hair dryer.

I know, I know, I'm sorry Brucey-Bruce, I'll make it up to you. Just get the bottle away from him or he'll drink the whole lot. Then we'll have a proper problem on our hands.

Oi! Oi! Don't even think of it, I say shoving my head into his face.

No Reggie, you, Bruce says with a little stabbing finger, you will have a problem. Take your memory stick and that, and that, that, monster and get the— He shakes and says, Just leave. We've had enough. Junior is crying in his room. This is all too much for him.

Reggie cranks the hair dryer on and aims it at the memory stick. It slips out of his chop sticks and onto the counter and he tries to pick it up but drops it again. He's pushing it around the counter. Fuck! he says picking it up with his fingers and holding it in the blast of hot air.

Brucey, he says, shouting over the noise, I can't explain but this is serious.

He switches the hair dryer off and says, Not just for me but for all of us, now.

What do you mean, now? What do you mean, all of us? Bruce is squealing. Jesus, he's getting on my tits. What have you involved us in Reg? I swear I'll call the cops on you.

Reggie pulls down his mask and he shoves his face into Bruce's. With his jaw clamped like a vice, he says: The police Brucey? You really think the fucking ZRP is on your side?

Jesus Reg, getting a tad worked up there sunshine. He shakes his head with a pitying look at Bruce and then he says, Take me to your computer.

LITTLE FLUFFY CLOUDS

Here we are in Brucey-Bruce Elliot's bedroom. An actual real life gay's boudoir. In the flesh. Here's his bed where he, yeugh, does his business with other gays. How many okes has he nyomped in here? It's weird: no matter how much I try, I just can't picture it. Feeling pretty goddam horny myself as a matter of fact. Does that mean I'm gay? Am I gay? Must be those pills and by God that's some simba muti right there. Makes you strong like a lion indeed. I am one hungry fucking lion. My skin is tingling and it feels like I'm floating and holy ballsack I'd fuck a goat right now.

In the corner, like a shrine, is a bank of computer crap: screens, boxes, consoles, cables, joysticks, keyboards and what-all else. It's all organised and arranged just so. Looks like an airport control tower. Probably more advanced, knowing these fairies.

The rest of the room is also spotless. Like a goddam serial killer's. Metal shelves line one wall from floor to ceiling, stacked with games, books about games, books about books about games, little gargoyle monsters and trolls still in their boxes, and fantasy novels, big fat collections of them in pristine condition and all colour-coordinated and alphabetised. A section of shelf space is reserved for a supply of jumbo-sized creatine buckets, shiny with promise. A bench press occupies the other end of the room. The wall opposite the shelves, above the bed, is covered with pictures of video game scenes and semi-naked men with torsos ripped to shreds, bodies tanned to smithereens and all of them groomed to within an inch of their lives.

So you came out the closet then? I say, gagging from another glug.

I did, Shum, and I've never looked back. You should try it.

Reggie snorts at this then he hands the memory stick to Bruce and says, I assume you've got a card reader?

Cunts. Fuck them.

Bruce recoils and says, I don't think so. He takes Reggie's shoulders in his fingers and guides him to the computer. Reggie fiddles with a little silver box. It won't go in. I can see he's shaking like a junkie. He turns the thing over and fumbles again with the little box.

Bibble-de-bip. The room reverberates. The sound comes from everywhere. Fuck. Shat myself.

Jesus. What the hell was that? Fuck me, Brucey-boy you've got speakers everywhere. They ignore me.

It wants a password, says Bruce.

May I? says Reggie, pointing to the master's chair. Or should I say, mistress's chair ho ho ho.

Yes, yes, says Bruce. I flop back, fucking dizzy, my arm slinged up and I can't feel a thing, not even Bruce's skanky bed.

Reggie sits with his head hanging over the table about an inch from the keyboard. His eyes are shut. He just sits. We all just sit. The only sound is me necking the vodka. Bruce looks from Reggie to me and back again. He's eager as a beaver to see what's on this thing, I can tell.

A head pops into the room and says something, I don't know what. It's Junior, the bug-eyed bushbaby. Bruce shoos him away and closes the door. The room goes black. He switches on a table lamp. I look around to appraise the effect. Moody, I say then I shout at Reggie, Hey fuckface, make choppers, we haven't got all night.

164

Reggie rouses himself with a big nasal suck of air. He wipes his face. I stand and drag the chair with my foot and sit down next to him. He's been blubbing and a tear rolls down his finger. He wipes it on his leg. His hand is shaking, hovering above the keyboard. He clenches and unclenches, brings it to his face again, blubbing.

Jesus, Reg!

Reggie? Are you ok? What's wrong?

He sobs. I plant the vodka on the floor between my feet and give his shoulder a squeeze. Time is few, Reggie, I tell him. Don't be a pussy.

Reggie nods through the snot and gob and tears and sits up again and with a final clench of his fist, unfurls his finger and presses a key down. It's an 'i'. He cracks up again. Christ.

C'mon Reggie, you're killing us here, man. What's the password? I'll do it for fuck's sake.

No! says Reggie. No! It's fine. I'm fine.

He puts his finger on the next key: 'l' and presses down. He is shaking and crying now, tears running free down his face as he moves to the next letter, 'o' then 'v' and he's still sobbing like a bitch, then 'e'. Jesus, he's only getting worse. Next letter, 'r' and then 'e'. Hey, man, what the fuck? Next is 'g' and another 'g' and of course an 'i' then an 'e'. I love Reggie? That's the password? That's Maria's password?

What the fuck? What the fuck is going on here?

The room blips and bleeps. The computer does some stuff and another box opens. I love Reggie? Fuck man, I knew it. I mean I knew but I didn't really believe it. That serious? And Reggie? Look at him, he's a hundred cement butt-fucked. How long? All this time? Behind my back? Not Reggie, no fucking way man. Fuck him. Fuck her. Fuck them both. Fucking cunts.

Brucey, I hear Reggie saying, his voice cracking up. He clears his throat and says, Brucey-Bruce I think it's best you don't see this.

Then I hear Bruce objecting. Reggie's telling him it's for his own safety and Bruce gets a skrook at this and he's saying to Reg what the hell has he done putting everyone's lives in danger and he's having another go at us. Reggie is silent and Bruce's rant runs dry. Then Reggie says something, I don't know what. There's a long silence and then I hear Bruce saying he'll go and make coffee.

Reggie just nods.

And you, Shum, have had quite enough vodka. Vicodin hammers your liver as it is, Bruce says. He leans over me and slides the bottle out from my feet. I look up at him and he's looking at me. His hand is on my shoulder. He looks at me funny.

The room lights up as the door opens, then it's dark again. My eyes adjust and Reggie is looking at me and he's really crying. Like fucking sobbing. Not even hiding it. He's just looking at me shaking his head and crying.

Fuck, Reg.

He says, Shum, it's not what you think. She gave me this on Sunday. Told me the password. That's the first I knew anything about how she felt. I'm sorry, man. I really am. Ok, it's no secret I loved her. But I know you did, too. That's why I never tried anything.

Shum, he says, as fresh tears spill over, you have to believe me.

How can this be? Maria? The fucking bitch. All those things you said to me, the way you smiled at me. The way you rode me, snuggled up to me. All that time you were in love with Reggie? What the fuck, man?

Reggie looks at me like I've got a gun to his head. He wipes his face and eyes and sniffs back the gob and just stares at me through sodden eyes.

Shum?

I don't know what to say. I want to smash his face in but his face is already smashed in. I rip through the books, the games, the powder-puff tubs. I pull the shelves down, stomping them on the floor. I trash the computer and fling it across the room and I rip up the bed. She's on top of me, smiling through her tousled hair with that smile, those eyes, and I smash her face in too.

Shum! Shum! Reggie is shaking me and snapping his fingers in front of my face.

Shum?

I look at Reg. At the computer. I love Reggie. He looks terrified.

Fuck it. I slap him and reach for my smokes. Let's see what's on this fucking thing, I say as I light up and wipe the fucking tears off my face.

Over a chick. What a fucking homo.

Reggie frowns at me then turns back to the screen, takes a deep wobbling breath and clicks on something.

It's all Greek to me. A list opens. He clicks on a file or folder or an archive or whatever and a picture opens.

It's a woman on a bed looking over her shoulder into the camera. Her eyes are lifeless. Strips of pink flesh shine bright against her black back. Another picture: a swollen foot, the skin stretched thin like a balloon. Next picture: Reggie flies back like he's been shot and falls off his chair going, Gah! Jesus Christ. She was raped. The room is spinning around me and I'm spinning in the opposite direction. Reggie picks his chair up, flops down and does some more clicking.

I waft out of focus, surfing on little fluffy clouds, shooting the rapids at Vic Falls, barrelling down the super tube at Waterworld.

Words squirm their way through my eyeballs and eat into my brain: abducted, tortured, assaulted, raped, electrocuted, found dead, charred remains. Jesus. Reggie scrolls to the end. Total: twelve thousandsomething. Fuck me. Reggie clicks on something else.

I'm sinking. I'm floating. The ground flies at me. The ground hurtles away from me. I have to close my eyes and put my head back.

It's some sort of legal document. Reggie scrolls down. Mugshots, eye-witness accounts, transcripts. I can't focus.

What is all this, Reg?

I don't know, Shum, but there's a shitload of this stuff. Looks like Maria was building up some sort of case against someone. Here's a whole folder on the JOC.

What's the JOC?

Jesus, Shum, he says, shaking his head at me.

And here are all the operations, he says: Gukurahundi, Murambatsvina—

Reggie, I still have no idea what you're talking about.

Gukurahundi? Fifth Brigade? The massacre of twenty thousand Matabele?

Yes, yes, we all know about that, Reg.

And Murambatsvina? The Green Bombers? Seven hundred thousand left homeless, two million lives destroyed?

Yes, yes, yes, Reg. So what?

He shakes his head at me again and turns back to the computer.

This shit's come from high up, someone deep inside the inner circle. Jesus, Shum, if this gets out. Reggie clicks again.

168

I'm underwater. It's warm. Bubbles tickle my face. I'm swimming through a shoal of rainbow-coloured fishies. Hey! There's Nemo. I found Nemo.

Look at this, says Reggie clicking the first entry of a list of names.

Col. Abel Manyoka in big black letters above a picture of a squat Shifty in a shiny suit, beady eyes sunk into a pock-marked face. Looks like a bloated iguana. The next page is a table of contents: Biography, North Korea, Guyu, National Youth Service, Training Camps, Green Bombers, Torture, Victims, Evidence, Testimonies...

Reggie's scrolling up and down all over the place. I can't follow.

Pictures hit me. Pictures of mangled faces, ballooned feet, scorched body parts, congealed blood, pus and shit everywhere. I can't breathe. It feels like an elephant is crushing my chest. The worst are the little kids with their burnt and swollen faces. And those dead eyes. They haven't had the shit beaten out of them, they've had the kid beaten out of them.

Then there's a picture of what looks like pink brains oozing from a fist-sized hole in some charred part of I don't know what. My stomach folds. I grab the dustbin and hurl, just in time, chunks of puke and goo and it looks like the picture I've just seen and that makes me hurl even more. I'm empty, gagging and retching and hawking and it feels like my insides are clawing their way out of me, blasting through my eyes. Jesus, I'm dying. Then Maria's voice fills the room.

Just talk normally, she's saying.

What the fuck? It's Maria. Fuck it's her.

Quiet, says Reggie hissing at me and he clicks back to the beginning.

I'm going to test it. Just talk normally, Maria says and

in the background are car noises, people noises, clattering noises and then a loud thump and a hiss.

No. It didn't pick you up, she says in her serious voice. I know that voice. Works fine for me; move round the table a bit; look out over the car park and lean in. Good. Your name is Mary Marimba ok? Try now.

What should I say?

Say I love cock.

There's a snigger and then: Hi! My name is Mary Marimba. You can almost see Maria reminding her what her name is. And I love cock, she says. More sniggering and another thump and a hiss.

Good, that's fine. Just act bored like you've got better things to do and do not react to anything we say.

What's up Maria?

I just got a funny feeling. Here's his car. I'll explain later but you'll be fine Busi, there's nothing to worry about. Here goes.

A long silence, just the sounds of the restaurant and cars and banging and scraping and people talking and laughing.

Hang on, what's this? Maria says cutting into the background noise. Manyoka? No-no Busi, sit, stay calm. It sounds like she's talking out the side of her mouth. Stay fucking calm, Busi.

Mizz Maria Karras? The voice is a gargling purr. Snide. Smug.

Yes? How can I help you? Maria says. It's her for sure but she sounds different. Commanding but also scared.

And you are Mizz Busi Charamba, yes?

Nothing. The background noise clatters on.

May I?

Look, Maria says. No you may not sit. Who are you and what do you want?

Me? Moi? Why surely, Mizz Karras you know outright who I am actually? And I would only talk with two beautiful maidens on this bright sunny morn. To chit the chat, chew the fat and to prattle away the day about Mizz Maria Karras and a certain high-ranking intelligence officer going these days by the name of Commander Silas Bote.

What? she says and there's a thump and what sounds like a chair scraping.

Do not move, my dear. They are watching us so do exactly as I say.

A truck clatters past.

Our great and noble comrade Bote sent me to this tryst in his stead for, alas, he is indisposed at this moment in time actually. He said to give you the code: Passed down from Lancaster? Cryptic, no? May I?

A shuffling sound.

And there it is, the crossword in today's Herald: One down. But what does it all mean, Mizz Karras?

Wha— and she stops. A waiter is at their table. She orders two cokes and there's another pause. Then she says, What have you done to him?

The CIO has pictures of you and Silas. They know about the whole operation.

The waiter is back, clanking and scraping then he's gone. Pictures of you and Silas? What the fuck, man?

What operation? What are you talking about? Who are you?

He laughs this little chuckle. Jesus, I want to smash this cunt to a pulp.

A long silence. Sounds like Maria is crying, and then he says, Good. Now. Copy everything to a memory stick or some such external device and trash the originals. Destroy

171

everything, set fire to the whole building if you have to but leave nothing behind.

I know the protocol.

And your pigeon will deliver by his, or her, own true hand to this Danazu person, yes?

Yes.

And that is?

A pause.

Ok, ok, just testing, just making sure. Of course I must not know. Not even Comrade Silas knew, err, knows. Good, good, my dear. Very good. You will leave through route three. Be at the crossing at five o'clock today. No luggage. No papers. No money. No nothing. Just you, going for your usual evening jog. Everything is arranged.

Mizz Karras? Is that clear Mizz Karras?

Yes, she says with her voice cracking like she's trying not to blub.

Go now, time is not on our side. Busi, my dear madame, you will accompany me on a stroll of the gardens. Such a beautiful day, not so?

Busi has nothing to do with this, says Maria.

I know, I know. And I give you my word she will be safe. But you must go now Mizz Karras.

A clang and a hiss and a scraping and a thump and then it's Maria saying, I'm going to test it. Just talk normally.

Reggie is slumped on the desk snivelling and his body is shaking. I haul myself up, shove Reggie aside and I'm bashing the keyboard and clicking the mouse but nothing works. I shout out for Bruce to come show me how to turn this fucking thing off.

The door opens and Bruce comes in with three cups of coffee on a tray. Jeezo, Shum, he says. Point the mouse over the window and click, yes, like that, and then click the 'X'.

Maria's voice is cut short. It hovers in the air bouncing off the walls.

I love cock—

Her last words.

What was that? Sounded very much like Maria— Bruce stops when he sees Reggie collapsed on the desk sobbing.

Reggie. Reggie, he says shaking him, you're going to ruin my keyboard. Here's some coffee. Reggie.

I pull Reggie upright. His head flops back and his face is crumpled in a silent wail, like something is being ripped from inside him and his whole body is limp as a wet towel.

What happened? Bruce says to me.

Never mind, I say, let's get some coffee in him. Bruce pulls Reggie up. I'm patting his cheek and clicking my fingers in front of him. Nothing. I shake him hard and shout, Reggie! Snap out if it.

Gone, Shum, he says curling up in the chair and climbing up it and he's rasping and wheezing from the back of his throat. His mouth is all peeled back and he's slapping at his face with floppy hands. Gone, he says like a whisper, through the tears.

Bruce and me look at each other. What the fuck to do?

Drink some coffee, Reg, I say to him. Let's get this done. It's not going to get any easier.

What is all this? says Bruce nodding at the computer screen.

Nothing, Bruce. It's nothing, I tell him.

And Reggie jumps up, roaring like a lion. The chair flies back and knocks Bruce down and Reggie's got the keyboard and he's ripped it out of its socket and he's smashing the computer with it and Bruce is yelling at him and I'm trying

173

to pull him back with one arm and he hoofs me off him and he's got the whole computer screen and he's yelling and screaming and hurls it across the room and it smashes on the bench press and he's got the box above his head and he crashes it down on the desk and he's smashing it and screaming, screaming, screaming.

Bruce has him now in a bearhug and he's writhing to throw him off and I try to help and I'm shouting at Reggie to chill and then I get my arm around his neck and I squeeze till he can't breathe and he's clawing at me and butting my face with the back of his head and all three of us flying around like we're on the Octopus and then we crash to the floor, on my fucking arm, and Reggie gives in, whimpering. He rolls onto his knees and he's curled up into a ball going, Please, please, Maria, please, come back to me, Maria and he's lost on that last please which turns into a long sob.

Me and Bruce just look at each other, panting. He jerks his head towards the door. Leave him alone for a bit he's saying. Fair do. This guy is broken. I shake him a bit and say, Reggie? Reg? You ok, china?

Nothing. He's wailing and pleading and rocking on his haunches with his head on the floor like a Moodley in prayer. He's gone. Down a deep, dark hole. Bruce's computer is trashed, his books are trashed, his games trophies, toys, creatine buckets, everything. Trashed.

The light in the passage is blinding after the gloom of Bruce's room.

He's in a bad way Shum, says Bruce closing the door on Reggie's feeble whimpering. We make for the lounge.

Tell me about it. Funny thing is: she was my fucking girl-friend. And everyone's fawning over poor fucking Reggie. Fuck it. Sorry. You don't need to hear this.

Shum, do you know what I do for a living? he says holding his gown closed as he lowers himself onto a sofa.

I collapse onto the other one. Oh sweet fucking Jesus that feels good. I am finished all of a sardine.

Never mind, he's saying and I'm drifting off and I'm at the moment when the world rushes in and flies toward you at random and Maria's saying just talk normally and I'm sucking Bruce's cock and that zaps me back to life like those shockers they use when your heart stops. Bruce looks at me and says, What?

Tell me, I say to him, why are you gay?

He sighs and looks up at the ceiling. It's the old nature-nurture debate, he says. And the next thing I know he's telling me how his dad was this big-drinking bully who called him a pansy and all sorts of shit like that. And the funny thing that's exactly my story, only it was my mother doing the dopping and the beating and telling me how useless I am. My dad was just never there. And, fuck me, now I'm telling him about the fucking school chaplain making me suck his cock.

And now? he says to me, do you get strong urges to have sex with men?

Jesus, fuck, listen to me, I'm saying, yes I do and it fucking freaks me out and I just want to smash their faces in and rip my dick off. And I tell him how just now I was sort-of dreaming sort-of awake sucking his cock. He titters and says he wishes.

But you're not gay, Shum, he says. You are suffering from guilt and shame and in fact all men have homosexual urges and it's the very fear of those urges that makes them homophobic. They fear their own latent homosexuality, which, and here is a fact, everyone has to some degree. Some more than others and that's just it.

Some more than others. And those are the guys that end up sucking cock?

Pretty much. And enjoying it too, he says, sighing. And he adds: immensely.

What about those two?

Who? Sammy and Junior? No gory stories there. They, like the rest of us, were just happily born that way. You don't have to be molested or mistreated to be gay, Shum.

Huh! Who would've thought?

You need therapy, Shum, to come to terms with your childhood trauma and move on.

Therapy? Like a shrink?

Yes, like a shrink, he says, like me.

You're a shrink?

Sort of.

I thought you were a physio.

Used to be. Now I'm a bit of both. I'll recommend someone. A woman, really good. Trust me.

Not a fuck, I say. She'll turn me into a bender.

Better a happy bender than a sad-sack straight, he says.

Fuck off, I ain't no fucking bender. You said so yourself.

Exactly. So what have you got to lose?

Well, my fucking arse virginity for one, I say.

Bruce laughs. A big, surprised laugh. He's actually just a sweet guy this oke. Fuck, maybe I will go see this chick. Talk about my fucking feelings and shit. See what happens.

The house is silent. The other fags have offed to beddy-byes, to la-la-poofter-land. I stretch out on the sofa. Bruce is dozing already. Looks like he's in a coffin. What would it be like to suck his cock? Or to have his cock in my arse? My own cock responds to this image with a little spasm. Jesus, I don't want to fuck blokes, ok. You're a pussy man you, ok? A pussy man. We like cunt. Fucking juicy cunt. Got it?

***

Reggie's face. He's shaking me. He's speaking, saying my name.

What? Fuck? What?

It's time to go.

Ok, ok, you gave me a fucking skrook, man, what's up?

He looks grim. There's this cold, faraway look about him. Not just in his face, which is set like granite and pock-marked with the carpet pattern; and not in the deadpan way he's speaking either. Something happened in there, man.

Time to go, he says.

Jesus, I am fucking broken. My arm. It throbs and each throb is more painful than the last. My arse. It burns like the worst case of piles I ever had. And now my head is joining in the party, pounding away, trying to break free of my skull.

I need more pills.

Brucey. Hey, Brucey-wucey, wake up homo.

Bruce stirs and drags his head up blinking.

What's that?

I need more pills, homo.

Suck my cock.

Fine, I tell him. Then you give me the whole box.

He smiles. Just a little smile to himself as he hauls himself up. Reggie goes off for a piss. I'm sitting on the sofa, my arm limp in my lap. Jesus, how the fuck did we come to be here? Bruce returns and tosses a bottle of pills at me. It rattles as I catch it.

I'll take a rain check, he says.

Good, I say, give me time to perfect my technique. He says I'm a big tease.

That ain't all that's big, I tell him.

He stops laughing as Reggie comes in.

What time is it?

Four, says Reggie.

Four? Jesus Reg, what the fuck were you doing in there? Have you even slept?

He just looks at me, looks through me more like, with that poker face and then to Brucey he says, Listen Bruce, I'm sorry about your computer. I'll get you a new machine and if you make a list of the damages I'll repair or replace everything. I only hope your hard drive is still intact.

Enough, says Bruce, rubbing his eyes and yawning. It was a dinosaur anyway Reg, and we can call it quits on the rent I owe you.

Reg nods and says, Fine. Then he says to me, Shum, let's move.

My eyeballs are like sandpaper. I crack open the pill bottle and tap two caps into my hand.

Uh-uh-uh-uh, says Brucey. That's very strong medication. One is plenty.

I look at Brucey and pop both pills into my mouth and then I swallow giving him a fiendish grin. He just sighs and shakes his head smiling at me. This guy's actually not bad. For a poofter.

I catch up with Reg at the front door.

So what are you going to do now, Reg? You obviously didn't upload the files, did you?

That stone-faced look.

What?

I'm going to find him, Shum, and I'm going to kill him.

Jesus Reg. Hey, are we really going to cycle back now, Reg? I mean, my arm...

Got a better plan, Shum? he says, opening the door.

***

Tiger's scoffed up all the puke and shit. Outside the air is fresh and cool with that damp-soil smell of night. I need to piss. The stars are bright pin-pricks, so many of them. A scops owl hoots and a shadow flicks across the wall.

I drop to the ground and hiss at Reggie. A tinkle. It's only Tiger scavenging for more treats.

Dog, he says.

To piss him off, I shout out, Hey! Brucey-Bruce, open the fucking gate.

Bruce is at the door. Shut up, man, he whisper-shouts at me. People are sleeping. Sammy appears behind him all kitted out in cycling gear. What a knob.

You still here? he says.

Reggie says, Leaving now, sorry about the commotion.

Yep, I say nodding to Sammy and giving him a loud burp.

Commotion? says Bruce with a shake of his head.

Well, I can give you a lift if you want, says Sammy.

Oh sweet Jesus, Sammy I could kiss you. In fact, I fuck-ing will kiss you, I say, and I march up to him with that exact intention. Sammy cowers behind Brucey and says with a squeak, No, Shum, that's fine.

Better not, Shum. Junior will eat you alive, says Brucey tugging at his robe and stretching with a loud yawn. Let's get your bikes on the rack.

We hoist the bikes onto the rack. At least, I watch while

179

Reggie hoists the bikes on and Sammy ties them down. Reggie gives them a good shake to check.

Right. Let's go, he says.

What about that memory stick?

Here, he says patting his breast pocket.

I presume you checked for hidden files? says Brucey.

Reggie looks like both his arms have been chopped off. Like he's jumped out an aeroplane and forgotten his parachute. His hands drop to his sides, his shoulders drop, his face drops, his whole body goes limp. And then he leaps around kicking at the air shouting at full volume, fuck-fuck-fuck-fuck-fuck-fuck and kicking and waving his fists about and shouting into his hands, bent double.

Hidden files, Brucey?

And he says something about invisible files and secret folders. Like I said, all fucking Greek to me.

Pity he destroyed the only computer in the house, Brucey says watching Reggie.

Reggie! I shout at him. Calm down for fuck's sake. It's done. Maybe there were secret files, maybe there were none. Whatever. It's done. I jump into the front seat of Sammy's car. Let's we go. Adios Brucey baby. It's been, what's the word? Emotional? Illuminating? Enlightening?

It's been a fucking nightmare, Shum, he says closing the door on me.

WHAT'S NEW PUSSYCAT?

Reggie hasn't moved. He's on the lawn like a drunk Buddha passed out, chin on chest.

I drop the window and shout at him: Oi! Fuckface.

Nothing.

I'm not a fag, you know. Bruce even says so.

Nada. This is getting annoying.

Iwe! Reggie! Shamwari. Maria told me.

This works. He looks up at me. Told you what?

That you were too good for her.

What?

Struze. She was trying to set you up with that other chick. Wassername? Rachel, I think it is. That dark-haired petite you left at Ingocheni. Or is it Jill?

Fuck off, Shum, I'm not falling for that.

But he's up and walking towards the car.

I'm fucking serious man. Maria's not the perfect peach you think she is. Was. Fuck. Reg. I'm saying she was also nyomping that guy in the tape. From the audio clip or whatever. That's what the guy meant when he said, They've got pictures of you and Silas.

That is fucking bullshit Shum, he says grabbing my shirt and shoving his grim face into mine.

Fuck man, you gobbed in my eye. Dude, chill, I'm just saying.

Just saying what, Shum? That Maria was a slut? Fuck you, Shum, what do you know about anything?

I pack out laughing. I can't help it. Must be these drugs. And the vodka. Truth serum or some shit because I don't give a fuck about anything any more.

Shoot the messenger, dick-fuck, I'm telling you the truth. You think I liked it? She's with me, in love with you and all the while fucking her way into the inner circle. Huh? You think this whole fucking tragedy's about you? Newsflash num-nut: you're a disposable nappy, a tampon, a little wait-for-me wanker crying all the way home because nobody wants to play with you.

Bam! What the fuck was that? Sounded like a door slamming inside my head. Jesus-fuck, he punched me. Reggie just fucking punched me. Well I'll be fucking goddamed. Reggie you stupid cunt. Stupid, stupid cunt I am going to fucking kill you now. I'm scrabbling for the door handle. I'm going to fucking rip this fucker apart. Fucking 'I love Reggie.' Cunt. I'm going to kill him. I fall out of the car and he's bouncing back. Jesus I'm going to kill this fucking cunt.

Shum. Your arm.

Whatever.

I charge at him. He's got me in a headlock, squeezing my shoulder. Oh Jesus. He'll have to kill me. I bite him in the side. I can feel the flesh through his jacket and he's wincing, screaming, squeezing me harder. He's shouting something at me. I just bite down even more and I'm reaching round for his balls. I hear another scream and here's Brucey. He's got something in his hand. He's pointing it at us.

Reggie's grip loosens and he's screaming with his face in his hands and I grab his balls and pull and then, fuck me, I'm coughing and my face is burning up and I can't breathe and the fire, oh the fire in my eyes, up my nose, down my throat. My lungs explode. We both go down.

Maced.

We've been fucking maced. Fuck me, that's classic. Could

182

you be more gay? I'm crying and laughing at the same time. Reggie's screaming at Bruce. Bruce is screaming back at him to just get the fuck out of his house.

Arms grapple me and I'm hoisted up. I can't see shit. I'm shoved into the car. The door slams after me. And here's Reggie shouting: Get your fucking hands off me, you fucking cocksucker.

Cocksucker? Good one Reg. Oh! This is too funny. I open my eyes, fuck it stings, and through a watery blur I make out Reggie swinging blind and wild with the three fags hanging onto his arms and spinning like they're on a merry-go-round.

I'm going to kill you, he screams, cracking his voice wide open.

Reggie just get in the fucking car and fuck off, Brucey shouts.

Fucking cunt.

Fuck you.

The pain. I can't keep my eyes open. I give it the biggest motherfucking whistle since my life. They stop. Works every time.

Reggie! I shout out loud as I can. Get in the fucking car. Now.

Reggie brushes off the fags, shrugs his jacket straight and stomps towards the car with his arms out, fumbling like a blind man who lost his stick. And his dog.

I call out to him, This way, Reg, right hand down. Two metres. One metre. Right hand down some more. That's my door, yes, got it. Get in the back. Good. Fuck me, my eyes are on fire now. The car bounces as Reggie clambers in. He's furious. I'm giggling. I can't help it.

Fucking maced.

Fucking mace, Reggie says yanking at my headrest like he wants to rip out the whole seat. Fucking mace.

I'm cracking up. I know. How fucking gay is that? I say.

I hear a snort, a laugh-snort and I lose it and Reggie's laughing now and we are proper fucking hosing at each other. Jesus. Fighting. Wrestling like kids. And me with a fucked arm. After all we've been through. And then maced by a fag. Oh, my sides. Over what? A fucking chick, that's what. The driver's door opens and the car bounces again as Sammy climbs in.

Reggie titters and I can't help it. I open my eyes a sec and Sammy is just staring at us both, looking first to Reg then to me and he's shaking his head as he reaches for the ignition.

Fucking animals, I hear him muttering so I howl like a wolf and Sammy flinches and Reggie puts in his maddest peacock impression and we're howling and peacocking and Reggie's got the headrest off and he's bashing me on the head with it and I lean across and start savaging Sammy's arm like I'm going to eat it off, pawing at his face and he shoves me away and starts the engine, pumping the gas to drown us out.

Tom Jones blasts out the sound system and I see Sammy leaping to kill it. Too late, too late, and before I've even had a chance to think, Reggie's onto it, saying, What the fuck was that, Sammy?

What? Nothing.

Fuck-nothing, that was Tom Jones and you know it. He whacks the back of Sammy's chair. Sammy flinches again. What the fuck we waiting for? Hit the road, he says.

Oh, Jesus, this almost tops the ecstasy incident with Suzie on Antelope Island.

The car jerks forward and stops. He's stalled. I can feel Reggie trying not to laugh. I'm trying not to as well. I mean, this guy could lose it any moment and make us cycle home. Not advisable in our current condition. I'm sniggering and Reggie's sniggering and Sammy starts up again revving the balls out the engine. I hit the play button and crank up the volume as we lurch forward, heads jerking, tyres slipping on the driveway. Reggie's sing-shouting and I join in and we're belting out what's new pussycat as we head off into the night with the faint glow of sunrise as Hurry-up Town stirs.

What's new pussycat, wo-oh-wo-oh-wo-oh

Again, again. I skip back to the beginning of the song. Sammy is scowling at us and we belt it out again. Then Sammy kills it.

Enough, he says. I can hear Reggie singing under his breath in the back, What's new pussycat, wo-oh-wo-oh-wo. And then he stops singing and claps the top of my head and he says, And fuck you, you cunt, Maria was no slag.

Guys! Sammy shouts.

Was too. Slaggy Maria. Maria the Slagster Slagheap.

Fuck off, you cunt, he says. But I can tell he doesn't mean it. He's just saying that out of habit.

I fumble at the controls and bring Tom Jones back for an encore. Sammy just sighs.

JUJU LOBBSTER

Chikomo! Chikomo! Wake up you oaf, you cretin, you imbecile. My foot can't take much more of this kicking. And neither can my shoes, my dear. Groan if you must. Curl up like a dog if you will. It will not help. The only self-assisting action you can perform at this exact juncture is to bring your entire body to a vertical position. Or perhaps you would take another kick to the ribs?

Much as I would mourn the demise of my beautiful John Lobbs, dear Maxwell, I have many, many more shoes at home, at the ancestral manse, back at the ranch, chez Baba Manyoka. One whole walk-in closet dedicated to shoes in fact. Like a shrine actually. It just so happens that these here Johnny Lobbsters are my absolute favourites. They are my lucky shoes, would you know? My lucky charm, my talisman, my Juju Lobbs actually. So I kick and I kick and I kick. And with each strike their luck wears thin and my patience even thinner.

Oh, Jesus bloody fuck-sake. Save your shoes Baba. Here's a job for Les Mademoiselles Harriets. Mizz Smith report to the frontline ASAP. Chikomo! How you smell up close. Of sweat and blood and mazondo. Must I put my mouth in your ear so you may hear? Very well. Here we are. Man-to-ear. Sotto voce I say unto you, in your ear, like a mother waking her child from a nightmare: get up sir or my ladies of the night here will blast small holes into the front of your head. And very large holes out the back of your head, to be sure.

And all over this here kitchen floor as well most like.

That will not do at all. No way to behave as a guest in another man's house. Up you get Chiko. Yes, yes, that is the sound of the hammer cocking that I may be ready to deploy a bullet at four hundred metres per second through your nose and into your sadza brain. No mambas for you my friend, no mercy. You just go right straight to death, you follow me? Ay! Ay! Wakey, wakey sunshine. Yes, yes, good boy, keep going, all the way to your feet. Steady. Good. Mind the shoes.

Good old forty-fours. They never fail. Now I don't have to shoot you and make a mess. So now let's we see how deep the loyalties of that vile murungu lie, how much agony he can endure and where his resilience ends. And what is more, let's we see how his comrade in arms enjoys the spectacle. I know I am going enjoy to it, oh-yes-oh-yes-oh-yes. Oh! Yes.

Sergeant! Don't tell me the sergeant sleeps also bloody-fuck-sake. Sergeant! What is this noise you make? Did a n'anga cast a spell and turn you into a donkey?

Enough. Sergeant, go and bring that other one in here that he may have a little chit-chat with my good friend Maxwell Chikomo. And stop that insufferable braying; it is working on my nerves so.

LUST

I can't see shit, thanks to Brucey-Bruce. This burns like fuck.

Don't say he didn't warn you. And don't say you didn't deserve it either. I mean, really.

How far are we? I shout into the blackness of my clamped eyes. No fucking way I'm opening these peepers. Not for another year. Jesus-fuck that stuff's hectic.

Glenara Avenue, says Reggie.

How'd he know? How'd you know? I shout over Tom Jones wailing about his Delilah. Sammy turns it down.

You got most of it, says Reggie and then he adds, As is right.

Fuck off you prick, you started it.

Grow up, Shum.

Ha! That's rich.

Guys.

Fuck you. Hey this is fine Sammy, right here. Stop, stop. Right here. Thanks.

But we're nowhere near your place, Reg. It's another kay at least, says Sammy.

That's fine, Reggie says. We'll cycle the rest of the way.

But your arm. Shum's arm, Reggie?

Really? says Reggie. You really give a fuck about his arm?

Ha-ha. Got him good, I'm laughing. I have to open my eyes to see this. Jesus he does actually give a shit. These fags are fucking weird. It's fine, I tell him, Reggie's gonna give me a backie. We're untying the bikes, well, Reggie is. I'm just leaning against the car smoking a fag listening to these two.

Sammy. Thanks, Reggie says.

Ya, nice one bruvva. I wave my hand about to find him, connect with the side of his head and haul him into a headlock. He ducks under and pulls away. Just like a chick.

It's fine guys. Reggie, anything for you.

Woo-oooo! Someone got the hots for Reggie.

Anyway, I hope everything works out. Whatever's going on. Stay safe.

Thanks Sammy, says Reggie.

Sammy pulls off smooth as silk this time.

Maybe he was nervous with you in the car, I say.

Can you see? says Reggie.

Sort of. If I tilt my head far back and look under my eyelids like this. I can ride.

Good, let's go.

We hop on our bikes and I'm leaning all the way back so I can see and riding with one arm and fuck-drunk and blazed on those pills. I'm weaving. I can tell.

Fuck Brucey-Bruce, the fucking fag cunt. Why'd he have to fucking blind us?

Probably saved your life.

Fuck you, saved your life you mean. I was about to close you.

Ha! Sure you were.

He's not a bad guy, actually, is Brucey.

What?

Not a bad guy. We had a good chat.

About what?

We just talked about stuff, you know.

Everything hurts. I can't see and I am fucking dog-tired. We come around the last bend, a hard left, only a hundred metres to go. My eyelids have turned to lead. I might just fall asleep on my bike right now.

Fuck me, they're still going. You can hear the bass pumping and people shouting from the house.

Chips, chips, Reggie says hissing the words. Stop. Get behind that bush. Go.

What? What?

The cops are back.

Oh! For fuck's sake. Can we just get home and sleep?

Quiet, man.

We cower down behind the bush, pulling our bikes behind us. Reggie pokes his head over the top.

What do you see?

Quiet man, they're right there. They're sleeping.

Ok, let's go then.

Wait, he says yanking me back.

Reggie lobs a stone and ducks down. Thonk! Middle stump. He looks over the bush.

And?

Nothing. Let's go.

We push our bikes out. I have to open and close my eyes to catch my bearings. We draw up beside the cop car – a fucked up yellow Datsun – and Reggie's looking in as we go past. I force a look. One is curled up on the back seat using his jacket as a blanket. The other is slumped against the window in the passenger seat.

Dead to the world. Did you see?

Reggie nods to himself. He opens the pedestrian gate and puts our bikes through and locks it after us. It's getting light.

We lean our bikes against the wall and walk into the house. Straight into the Bog Brush and he's got no shirt on, just black jeans and boots, and his bandana of course, and he's shouting at full volume like a nutter: Lust! Lust! Lust! L— Ay? What the fuck?

WAKE N' BAKE

'You wanna fuck the world.' What a song. Never mind Boils has played it about a thousand times already. Is there a better opening line? Boils is naked. Again. Screaming into his fist and prancing about like Mick Jagger, curling his lips back and gyrating, flopping his massive dong up and down like an axe. He's wired to the eyeballs. Even me. We've been at it since, I don't know, when Reggie and Shum left. They've been gone all night. Not a word from either of them. We followed orders. Boy did we: ten tonnes of dope, a racetrack of charlie and a bowser of booze. One of the sofas is burned to a congealed mass of goo on the tiles. Everyone's gone. Oh, except Jill and Rachel. They are moping in the kitchen drinking coffees. Waiting for Reggie and Shum. They didn't follow orders. They even tried to tidy up.

A commotion. Someone shouting from the hallway. Oh ya, That Idiot Martin aka TIM. He's still here of course.

'Awright lads?' Yup, that's TIM. Thinks he's Iggy Pop. We started calling him Ziggy Pop to piss him off. 'It's fucking Iggy Pop,' he says to us every time in his fake Pommie accent. Boils stops mid-song and I climb up off the floor and stagger to the front door. 'Fuck me,' Ziggy is saying. He's confused, like he forgot these guys even existed. 'What the fuck?'

'What the fuck happened to you idiots?' Boils sums it up.

They look like hell. Reggie's suit is torn and muddy and his face is kind of collapsed, the skin hanging limp on his bones, eyelids slipping off his bloody eyes; Shum's arm is

191

in a sling and he's grazed up the side of his leg and puffy face. They look like a tornado chewed them up and shat them out in the desert. Jill flies out the kitchen screaming at them where the fuck have they been, what the fuck have they been doing, and then she sees them and stops dead in her tracks and her hand flies to her mouth. 'Fuck,' she says. Then she slams into Reggie. He winces and staggers back trying to catch her little fists. She's pummelling him and screaming, 'Where the fuck have you been? What the fuck have you been doing? Have you even looked at your phone?'

She breaks into a sob and Reggie smothers her in his arms but she pulls back and shoves him away.

'Reggie, you stink,' she says, standing back and folding her arms.

'What the hell happened to you, guys?' This is Rachel, standing at the kitchen door.

'Ya, man,' says Boils. 'We've run out of charlie. And these items,' he takes aim at Jill and Rachel with his imaginary gat, held up sideways, like a gangster, 'have been going mental.' He pulls the trigger.

Everyone is shouting at him at once.

'Boils!'

'For fuck's sake.'

'Put some fucking clothes on, man.'

The girls are haggard. They exchange looks like they want to kill him. Kill all of us probably. Not our fault. We had orders.

'Did you get the charlie?' says Ziggy swaying.

'Ya, Reg, we're all out, finito, cokus endus maximus,' says Boils spinning around and winding his arms like a windmill.

'Your arm,' I say to Shum.

'Wanker's elbow,' says Ziggy. 'I get it all the time.' He stops talking, looks up, looks around and then back to the ground. He frowns.

Me and Boils have a good snigger at this. We've been menacing the guy all night. Thick as two short planks, he is.

'Neighbourhood watch,' says Shum. He's slurring and his eyes are closed. His head is tilted all the way back and he's just standing there swaying, steadying himself every now and then. 'Would you believe,' he says holding up his finger like an orator, 'that I caught a tsotsi tonight? Single-handedly. Paid for it dearly, I might add.' The hand sticking out the sling flaps about.

Reggie shakes his head and then says with a croak, 'Bart, Boils.' He nods towards the front door and says, 'A word?'

'Oh, no you don't. No! No! No! No!'

'Jill,' says Reggie with an effort. 'Two minutes.'

She closes her arms tighter and her lips press tight. 'Two fucking minutes, Reg. Two,' she says and Rachel steps aside to let her back into the waiting room.

'Woo-ooo! Looks like someone's got the hots for our stud-muffin his Excellency the Right Royal Reggae,' says Boils tucking him into a headlock as we crash through the doorway, colliding into each other. Shum holds my shoulder. He can hardly see. What the fuck happened, man?

Ziggy hasn't moved. He'll follow the chicks. Been sniffing around that Rachel's backside all night. Even followed her into the toilet.

Reggie looks back, closes the door and says to us, 'The cops are out there.'

'What? Where? Outside? Jesus.'

'Relax Bart, they're passed out. Tickets,' says Shum talking to the sky and swaying like Stevie Wonder.

'That'll be the triple dose of shrooms, maiweh,' says Boils hopping on one leg and flicking his hand bacon-slice style.

'Ya, they're out cold,' says Reggie.

'Ha! If one of our rangers is caught sleeping.'

'What?'

'What? What?' he turns in Boils's direction and shouts, 'Mahobo treatment that's what. We drop them in the middle of the bush. Ha! They fucking skrook it. Good for their tracking skills though.'

Boils's mouth peels back to reveal his sooty teeth. He cackles like a madman. 'Nice,' he says snapping his fingers. 'Very nice.'

'So what are we going to do, Reg?'

He's on his way back into the house and says over his shoulder, 'I have a plan. Put some clothes on Boils.'

So that's why the girls have been huddled in the kitchen with That Idiot Martin. Ha! Shame. We could have been having fun instead. Boils. The guy is mad.

'How do you get him into the bush without waking him?' I say to Shum.

'The rangers carry him on a stretcher. They go fucking far because it's happened to every one of them. Only once though.'

'But what about lions and stuff? I mean, he could get chomped.'

'Nah! We loiter nearby. To see the fucker's reaction more than anything. It's the funniest thing you ever saw. Every time a coconut, their first thought is the spirits put them there. They shit themselves going Heeeeeeee! Heeeeeeee! Heeeeeeee!'

Shum demonstrates, clapping his hand to his forehead

looking about like crazy. He opens his eyes wide and then cries out, shutting them tight. Jeez-o I'd love to see that. But I think I'd give the game away pissing myself. The guy would twig, straight.

'What happened to your eyes, Shum?'

'Maced,' he says as Reggie comes striding back onto the verandah. His face seems to have pulled itself together a bit now and his skin has re-attached itself to his bones. He's got this grim, focussed look about him. It's a tad unsettling.

Boils returns as well, with jeans on, thank the Pope. They are way too big for him. The waist is rumpled by his belt and the things are up around his bony ribcage. They are stained, torn, stone-washed, pleated classics. There's even a fold line down the front, boarding-school style. Gnarled feet stick out the tapered bottoms.

Reggie's got this thing that looks like a miniature apple in his hand.

'Ha-haaaaaa!' Boils is bounding up and down like he's on a pogo stick, and his face scrunches up like an evil critter from a comic book and he says, 'Nice.'

'Let's go,' says Reg. He pops his head back into the house and shouts to the chicks, 'Just fixing the gate, it's jammed.'

'What is that, Reg?'

'Jesus, Bart, where've you been?' says Shum back to Stevie Wonder mode and he laughs a sadistic snort that, in his current condition, comes across as just that teeny bit bonkers. My stomach falls through my arse. Something bad is about to happen.

'It gets better,' says Reggie. 'Come with me,' he says and he bounds over the railings onto the lawn towards the gate.

This is bad. 'Guys, no, guys. Wait. Guys, no. Come on, guys, this is a bad idea.'

Shum is hosing himself. 'Bartman!' he shouts grabbing my shoulder and giving me a good shake. 'Lead on.' He shoves me forward.

Fuck, man. What's going on?

'Reggie?' Jill's on the verandah. We've caught up with Reggie halfway across the lawn. He turns and says, 'The gate's jammed Jill. Back in a sec.'

I look back. She's watching us go. Reggie presses the remote to open the gate. He stops it and closes it then opens it making a big show of inspecting the motor. Shum shoves me forward again. 'Keep going Fido, forward march, on the double, soldier.'

We sneak up to the car.

'Have they been here all along?'

'Not sure,' says Reg trying all four doors. 'Locked. Keys are in the ignition. Get me a wire coat hanger.' He clicks his fingers back at us with his face pressed to the driver's window. Me and Shum and Boils look at each other.

I hit the deck and mouth the words: dead ants. Boils and Shum follow on cue and we're all lying on our backs pointing up at Reggie. For once it wasn't me. The trick is to be the first. That's the trick.

'Bart!' Reggie hisses at me. 'Go and get a coat hanger.'

'But the dead ants rule, Reg? Nobody fucks with the dead ants rule.'

But he just stabs a finger into my chest. His jaw is about to crack it's clenched so tight and there's a fury in his face I've never seen before.

Fuck, man. I was down first. I trot back to the house. Lucky I've got the jammed gate as a cover story. I don't fucking like this, man.

'Boils,' says Reggie, taking the coat hanger and the pliers

I took the initiative to bring. 'Open it.'

'Two seconds,' says Boils with glee.

He's made a hook at the straightened end and shoves it down the driver's door and fiddles with it. So this is how they do it? Boils yanks up. Nothing.

'Shhh! You'll wake them, man.'

'I don't think so,' says Shum and he bashes on the window shouting, 'Iwe! Mahobo. Vuka mahobo.'

I take off at full sprint. Then I hear Shum canning himself. I slink back. The cops haven't even budged.

'Jesus, Shum, do you actually want to go to jail?'

'Shut it Bart, these fucktards are comatose.'

'You try a triple dose. See how you feel after,' says Boils, his tongue working around his mouth while he fiddles with the wire.

'Ok, ok, but you don't have to actually try and wake them up now, do you?'

'Got it. Datsun Twelve Oh! Why?' he says patting the roof. 'Easiest car in the world.' Boils opens the door like a thief. The radio is on and bottles and packets cover the floor. He leans in and pulls out straightaway, waving his hand in front of his face. 'Jesus, it stinks of rotten munt in there.'

Reggie turns the ignition on, flicks the gear into neutral and drops the handbrake. He winds the window down and shoves the door closed with his butt.

'Push,' he mouths to us.

'What? Why?'

'Just do as I fucking say, Bart.'

We have to rock the car back and forth to get it off the grass verge. On the road, the car trundles along in silence, Reggie at the helm, us trotting behind trying to keep up as it glides down the gentle slope, popping over the carpet of jacaranda flowers.

'How far you going? This is plenty,' says Shum in a loud whisper to Reggie up front. You can feel the panic rising in his voice. I'm pretty jumpy myself.

'We're going to the cemetery,' Reggie says looking back over his shoulder.

Boils throws his head back and he grabs his mouth trying to stop laughing.

Fuck. The cemetery is on the other side of this block. It's miles away.

'The cemetery? Come on guys, this is far enough. Let's not be stupid here.'

'Shut up, Bart,' says Reggie. We walk-trot in silence behind the car.

We get to the T-junction and Reggie hauls the steering wheel. He looks back at us. Shum says, 'Push.'

We strain up the slope the last hundred metres to the cemetery gate. It's a back entrance we always use to mess about on the golf course. We reach the gate and Reggie turns the car. It stops dead on the grass against a bump. Boils opens the gate. Obviously it's not locked. Who locks a cemetery? In Africa?

'Jesus, Boils, get back here. I'm going to burst my poop-hole,' says Shum, veins straining, going red in the face.

'Push!'

We push.

'Back!'

We let the car roll back.

'Push!'

We push.

'Back!'

It rolls back a bit more and we get in behind and shove

as hard as we can. Up, up, up and over, the car lurches forward and the cop in front stirs.

'Down!'

We drop below the window line. Silence.

'Ok! Quick! Go.'

We heave and strain and shove and we inch the car inside the cemetery, bumping over memorial stones up to an ancient msasa.

'Jesus, this'll freak them out,' says Shum, chortling. He's in on the game now. Even me, I can't help giggling. Reggie gathers rocks and makes a line from a gravestone. We twig his plan and join in hauling stones to make a ring around the car starting from the gravestone of, let's see, one 'Emerald Baya, 1980 – 2008. May she finally rest in peace.' Well how about that?

The sun pips over the horizon.

'They'll wake soon,' says Reggie. He pulls out the little apple thing and, a-ha, it's a firecracker. He pulls the fuse up and thumps Boils on his chest for a lighter.

'Wait, wait, wait,' says Boils digging into his pocket.

He reaches into the car and grabs a half-finished bottle of coke and an empty one. He decants some coke into the empty and then drops what looks to me like a tab of acid into each one. They fizz up a bit then he screws the lids back on. He puts them both on the driver's seat. This isn't happening. This can't be happening. Shum's shoulders shake trying to stifle his laughter.

'That's good,' Reggie says to Boils and he lights the fuse. It pops and hisses. He stretches into the car and rolls it under the front seat.

Whipping his arm out he presses the door closed. We all turn and bolt. Hosing, ducking our heads like we're running under a chopper in the jungle: no colours any more, I want them to turn black. Boils throws the gate closed and we slide into the ditch behind the wall and turn to look over the culvert.

Nothing.

'Fuck,' says Shum, 'you sure that thing was lit?'

Reggie shushes him with a waving hand, his eyes glued on the car. We all watch the car. Nothing. My breathing is heavy and my heart is going like the clappers. Not a breath of wind. Not a sound in the world. The birds are even silent, watching the car, bobbing and tilting their heads for a better view.

And then it goes off. BA-BOOM! I swear the car levitated for a second. I feel a thud in my chest. I fly backwards and land on Shum. Shit that was loud. My ears are ringing and I'm dazed.

The car is bouncing with human limbs – arms, legs, heads – thrashing about and knocking into each other. Doors fly open and the cops slither out of the wafting smoke on all fours. The one cop is rolling on the ground panting and wailing, 'Heeeeeeeee! Heeeeeeeee! Heeeeeeeee!' clutching his head about his ears with his forearms. The other cop is staggering about in a drunken daze. His legs give in and he flops to the ground staring at his feet.

Shum is tearing at his face. His body is shaking. Is he having a fit? He grabs his crotch as a dark patch spreads out.

I tap Boils's shoulder. He's holding his mouth, and his eyes are straining against their sockets and veins are pumping on his temples. He looks at me blinking back the tears. I point to Shum's crotch. Boils snorts behind his hand and rolls onto his side. I have to hold my mouth closed. Reggie is on his back, curled up in a ball holding his stomach in.

'Chips, chips.' A car. It slows then speeds off. We roll onto our stomachs and watch the show.

'Iwe!' the one cop says and he's blathering in Shona. Then he stops and shouts at the top of voice, 'Iwe!'

'Eh?'

Some more blathering and shouting.

'What are they saying?'

'Shh! Shh!' Shum says. 'He's asking what the fuck just happened. They can't hear a fucking thing.'

The other cop raises his head and freezes. He goes ash grey and shouts something.

The other cop looks at him and then his eyes follow the circle of rocks. His face implodes and turns to stone. He screams and scuttles back on his arse kicking his legs out until he's pressed against the car and staring about with wild terror.

'Heeeeeeeee! Heeeeeeeee! Heeeeeeeee!' he goes, hand to face, eyes agog. Shum convulses and sets us off again.

The cops fumble for the door handles. They clamber inside, one in front, one in back and slam the doors shut, locking them. They don't say a word, crazed eyeballs tracing the circle of stones to the grave.

The sun is fully up now. It shines straight into their faces and they squint against it, looking out like they're floating on a sea of boiling lava. Must be ten minutes they've been there. Shitting themselves. An argument breaks out.

'They're saying, "you go, no you go," something like that,' says Shum through the side of his mouth.

Their voices rise. The car rocks as they slap each other and wrestle, grabbing at faces, throats, arms, ears. Then one of them stops and leaps back from the other going, 'Heeeeeeeee! Heeeeeeeee! Heeeeeeeee!' He stares about him with death launching flaming serpents at his face. He's slapping them away, slapping his head and yowling,

'Heeeeeeeee! Heeeeeeee! Heeeeeeee!'

The other cop looks about him with such fear, such pure terror. He's not just contemplating death, he's contemplating death by spirit-world; death by tokolosh; death by skinning alive and having his brain sucked out through his ears by a giant bat; death played over a million times each more grisly than the last. The other is just yowling into his arms, over and over and over.

I think I might just die. And you know what, I'll miss my boy Joey, but that's all. I can die happy. Here and now. This is the funniest thing I've ever seen. Reggie and them are also fucked. Laughing or rather dying from trying not to laugh. Oh my aching nerves, I can't. I can't.

'Chips, chips, they're coming,' says Reggie and we sink back into the long grass of the ditch. 'Oh fuck, we're fucked. We're so fucked.'

Reg elbows me in the ribs and nods towards the car. The one cop, Chenjerai I think he was called, has climbed out and is edging his way along the car like it's on a knife edge a million miles above the earth. He peers over the bonnet, bobbing and ducking his head like a nervous monkey and shading his eyes from the sun. He slides around to the front and you can see him steeling himself for the plunge like he's dropping into an icy lake, only it's not water but sulphuric acid. He takes a deep breath and lurches forward squatting in front of the gravestone. He's reading it. Then something knocks him backwards against the car, clunking his head on the grille and he scrabbles back on all fours kicking up dust and he slams his head into the open door, scuffles around, opens it and flies inside, his feet kicking out behind him like a scuba diver. Slam. Lock. He's panting much better now.

The other cop, Chipenga it must be, is pressed up against

the window, climbing up it, peeling away like a flesh-eating rhino just got in and he's yammering, clawing at the roof, at the window, at his face, at his head. The other one thumps his chest and yells something at him. He stops, hands still on his head, staring straight ahead. And then he's off again, yelling 'Aikona,' – I got that bit – and some other shit.

'What's he saying?' I'm the only one here who can't speak Shona.

'Shhhh!' They all turn and hiss at me as one.

Chipenga reaches for the ignition. The other one grabs at him, pulling him away, yelling all the more. Chipenga smacks him in the chops and presses his head into the window, shouting at him.

'Fuck, they're going to leave. We better scoot,' says Boils. We slide backwards down the ditch. I'm shitting myself now. I hear the car starting but what's this? What's this? Omygod, I never thought I'd be so happy to hear that sound: waaaaaaang, waaaang, waaang, waang, wang, wah. And then again, only this time: wang, wah. And then: tsuk, tsuk, tsuk, tsuk. Nothing.

Boils sniggers and says, 'Dead battery, oh my fuck, this just gets better and better.'

There's another shouting match. Arms waving, batting at each other like they're on Gladiators. The car jouncing on its springs.

'They're arguing whose fault it is,' says Shum. 'The one is saying run, the other is saying they'll die if they leave the circle.'

'Drink the cokes you cunts,' says Boils. 'Drink the dem- icine you stupid cunts.'

The shouting and slapping stops. They've popped like balloons. Distraught. Looking about, desperate for help, for a straw floating by in a river of blood with screaming corpses reaching out to them. Chipenga picks up a coke, spins the top open and, with the neck half way down his gob, drains it in one go. The other follows suit staring out the window as he tosses the bottle behind him.

'Yes please! Oh. Yes. Please. Now they are fa-fa-fa-fucked!' says Shum. 'Boils, you're a fucking sicko genius.'

But Boils is gone. He's on his back, laughing so hard no sound is coming out. I can't believe this is happening.

Reggie is gobsmacked, too. He's just staring at the car wide-eyed with a half-laugh on his face. 'Let's get out of here,' he says, turning to me and then to Shum. 'They must not see us.'

'Ya,' I say sliding backwards, 'let's go that way round, use the wall for cover.'

We scuttle off along the wall and everyone is laughing out loud now. I think I'll laugh forever. Shum is holding his sling in place with his other hand, swaying from side to side, laughing a deep throaty guffaw that sounds like it could go on for days. He's looking through the bottom of his eyelids, head up. Looks like he's laughing at the heavens, at God himself. Round the corner we stop, heaving for air and collapse on the ground in a pile.

'Did you, did you—' Boils says between laughs, 'did you see the legs in the air as the bomb went off?'

He cackles some more, rolling on the floor.

'And the other's head – ditsch – bolt upright,' Shum says and Boils convulses again, screaming into the grass.

'Thought his hat was attacking him.'

We dissolve again. Then Shum goes, 'Heeeeeeeee! Heeeeeeeee! Heeeeeeeee!' And that's us gone. Finished. A tangled screaming heap. And that's how they find us.

I open my eyes and there's Jill standing silhouetted against the morning glare, hands on hips, staring down at us. Her stony face is scary. I stop and sit up. One by one the others realise and they sit up, still laughing in fits.

'What?' says Boils. She's spoiling our fun and he's ready to defend our moment of glory to the death.

'You fuckers!' she screams. 'What the fuck have you been doing? Jesus fucking Christ, Reg.' She bursts into tears. 'Was that gunshot? We've been up and down every fucking road in the neighbourhood.'

'She 'as too you know. Puking too. Maybe the booze, though. Dunno,' says Ziggy.

Shum packs out laughing again and Jill cuts him down with one look. He looks away as his laugh trails off. Boils takes over and she just cries more. Reggie staggers to his feet and peels her hands from her face stooping down, looking into her face, trying to make contact.

'Jill. Jill,' and he can't help laughing, 'we've just seen the single funniest thing we have ever seen and probably the funniest thing we'll ever see in our lives.'

We all crack up again. Jill whips her hands from Reggie and stomps her foot. 'Are you fuckers fucked?'

'No! Jill, I'm telling you. The funniest thing. Two cops, legs, arms, oh my stomach. This is killing me. Come on, let's get back before they find us.'

'What cops? Before they find you? Reggie?'

'They're not going anywhere. Chill tchib we've dealt with them,' says Boils sitting up.

Jill takes a running kick and slots him in the balls.

'Don't you call me a bitch, you fucking animal,' she

screams at him. He's down, groaning and screaming up at her clutching at his knob. 'Kuffing tchib, fuck you kuffing-fuck, I'm gonna close you, you fucking tchib.'

Shum, I'm sure, pisses himself again but you can't see because of the wet patch already there.

'Reggie!' she screams, off the scales this time. 'Tell me what the fuck is going on, right now.'

'Ok, ok,' Reggie says, wiping his eyes. He nudges Shum with his foot. 'Get up fuckface. Let's get back to the house.'

I haul Boils up, still launching expletives at Jill, saying he's going to fucking fix her like he fixed those cops and then tittering to himself like a loon. Shum grabs my shoulder and we bump our way to Ziggy's truck.

We're bouncing over the road back to Ingocheni Island with the orange-brown morning sun flicking through the trees like an emergency light on a tow truck. I close my eyes and the wind blasts my face. Boils is still cussing. Shum is laughing. I think at Boils more than anything. What a night. What a morning.

AMBUYA BAYA SAYS

Right about now, those stupid cunts will be shitting in their shit-stained pants. They seriously believe in all that spirit-world ancestral shit so an acid trip in a cemetery should be just what the witchdoctor ordered. I goated. Haven't done that in years but it was that fucking funny. I think it was the guy clawing at his head going, 'Heeeeeeee! Heeeeeeee!' just like the rangers do when we mahobo them. I'm still laughing, even though Jill is trying her damnedest to ruin it for us. Fuck her. Just makes it funnier.

She barricades the front door with her arms folded and her face grim. We're all still canning as we drop off the back of the truck like a troupe of monkeys. Rachel and Bog Brush are at the door behind her. They're not finding this particularly funny, either. They're just looking at us from one to the other. I think Mr. Brush is miffed he missed out. Either that or this Rachel chick has been cock-teasing him all night and his balls are down by his knees.

Come, Jill, let's go inside, says Reggie trying to steer her. May as well try and turn a train around. She wrenches out of his arms with a double twist, flinging his hands off her like he's a blob of slime.

No Reggie, I'm not setting foot inside this house until you tell me what the fuck is going on, she says.

Fuck this, I say. I barge past, giving her a little shove as I go and she almost ends up in the flowers all flattened and broken from yesterday's escapades. Reggie has to catch her. Bart and Boils take the gap and we dart inside. Rachel and the Bog Brush step aside, like the red sea. Or is it the dead sea? Moses and shit, you know. We crash into the kitchen grabbing chairs and benches and righting the table and we flop down. Boils and Bart are still tittering, each setting the other one off. I look out the window, which isn't there for some reason, so I can hear every word of Reggie's sorry spiel.

Come inside, he says. Shame, you dig your own grave, my son. I can only see the back of her head. She doesn't say anything or even move.

I need to sit down, Jill. These past two days— He stops and sighs. I think he's even about to cry. He looks fucked. His suit's fucked. Doesn't even look like a suit. His shirt is brown and torn, the knot in his tie is the size of a pea and half way down his chest, his face is bruised and swollen, his eyes are red and puffy and his dome is sprouting a fifteen-o'clock shadow. What a sight. What a laugh.

Or is it three? he says shaking his head and wiping the tears off his cheeks and rubbing his eyes.

Jill's shoulders drop a little and she takes his arm. Oh, Reggie, she says, definite softening up of the voice there – that puppy-dog look of his will do it every time.

But you have to explain why the cops were here and all this cloak and dagger shit, she's saying as they come into the kitchen, Rachel and Bog Brush in tow.

I will, I will. But first, we need tea, says Reg and he's poking through the debris in the kitchen looking for the kettle and some cups. Boils and Bart are reliving the humour. Bog Brush is leaning against the sink with his arms folded. He looks at them and says, What? Tell us what the fuck's so funny, mate.

Passed out. Snoring. The one in the back was sucking his thumb I swear, says Bart.

So we pushed their car—

To the cemetery—

Reggie made a circle of stones—

Wait! Tell them about the tea—

Oh, shit, ya! Boils spiked their tea yesterday—

Whose tea?

The cops's tea kuffnut.

Spiked us all, you mean—

Perfect cover.

What cops? Why were the cops here?

They had three cups. Each.

We were butt-fucked from one.

Looking for Maria's memory stick, her Z-Files.

Told them the house was cursed—

Maria's what?

Z-Files. A shit-storm of intel on ZANU-PF's shifty shenanigans.

So Boils spiked their cokes before the bomb—

Bomb? What bomb? Jesus.

Cherry bomb you idiot.

And then, and then—

We can't get past the point where the bomb goes off. Someone just has to pipe up, Heeeeeeeee! Heeeeeeee! Heeeeeeee! and we're off again.

Even Jill is laughing. Sort of. She's fighting it, but every now and then she blurts out and tries not to. She's laughing at us more though, telling our story, because you can tell she hasn't got a fucking clue.

So anyway, says Reg, they were too terrified to leave the circle. The spirits had decided they'd been bad.

Ambuya Baya says you've been a bad, bad boy, says Boils wagging his finger. And he's gone. He slips to the floor, his mouth wide open, teeth dancing around his face.

Bart says, I wonder what is going through their minds right now?

He's got a point. Those shrooms were hectic. Hallucinated the cunt out of me. Then they wake up in a cemetery surrounded by a circle of stones from a random grave. And now they've unwittingly dropped acid. I can't actually laugh any more, it hurts too much and it's just too funny. Reggie is a genius.

Fuck it, says Boils, pulling himself up. I'm taking this to the next level. He's got the fridge open and he's digging out whatever food he can find.

Boils? says Reggie, What are you going to do, Boils? Don't fuck this up, Boils. They must think it's the spirits or we'll be in jail before you can say arse-rape.

Crows, says Boils. These okes are terrified of crows, according to my uncle.

Jesus Boils, don't, you'll get caught man, says Bart but Boils is already out the door and down the driveway. I'd go with but I'm fuck-knackered. All I can say is: I'd hate to be in their shoes right now.

None of this makes any sense, says Jill. Please explain. From the beginning. In English. Rachel sighs a big fucking pouty spoilt brat sigh and fucks off to the lounge. And Bog Brush? Yep. There he goes.

I catch his eye and give it the Woof! Woof! Woof! yapping at him like a lapdog. He doesn't get it. He looks at me blinking and then trots off after Rachel. Fucking prick.

Jesus, Jill, says Reggie yawning like a baboon. I am buggered. I need to sleep. Sleep. Eat. Explain. Deal?

Fuck. Me too. I am more fucked than I have ever been since my life. I might not even make it. Feels like someone swapped my blood for rubber. All my effort to just stand,

210

stagger off and crash down on my bed. Fuck my shoulder hurts. My fucking ring hurts. Everything fucking hurts.

Heeeeeee! Heeeeeee! Heeeeeee!

JUST ANOTHER DAY IN PARADISE

How! We have not much to work with here, Sergeant. Looks to old Baba M. that this one has self-destructed already. Scuttled itself. Opened its seacocks. Tscha! Look at this. Pathetic. It can't even walk by its own two feet. Shoddy goods indeed. Check the warranty on this one and return to manufacturer for a full refund.

Drop it on the floor here, Sergeant, and return to your sentinel. And stop that braying I tell you. Mizz Wesson will now get her turn. It is only fair, you see, they must both enjoy equal rights, equal opportunities. No favouritism here. No. And I do find the butt of a gun to be a useful cooperation tool when whipped across the cheekbone. Like so. Like so. Like so.

Ah-hah! It lives. The creature, it is alive. Welcome Mr. Cordoza. Watch him, Chikomo, imperialism runs deep in this one's blood. He'll have you high-stepping to his brass band before you can even say chimurenga. His grandparents settled in Mozambique, pillaged, raped, exploited their way through life but then, as is right, the scum-sucking leeches were given their marching orders by that country's brave liberators. A great pity then. A great pity indeed that their neighbours, our beloved country, were also bubonic imperialists at the time and welcomed these, these looters into its festering bosom. Thick as thieves. Now we have an infestation of these. Oh, for my snakes. Oh, the boundless joy of watching this one being rained on by an angry horde of flaming mambas.

How! All this kicking is very good exercise don't you know. Good for the heart and the brain they say. But what is this? Oh dear. Oh dear. You have really done it now, porcupine sodomiser. Chikomo, this oaf has dealt the death blow to my right shoe. Oh Baba Manyoka is very angry now. Decorum has dissolved.

Look now, he has gone and destroyed my left shoe also. A moment of silence if you please, Maxwell, mourning this sad day the demise of my John Lobbs, the loss of my Juju, and also to allow me to catch up with my breath. It is running down Rotten Row, hailing a commuter with a briefcase under its arm and a turkey round its neck.

Ah! That is better. And now. Now, you arrogant pig born of a gutter-slut, sired by a boar and raised by a colobus, now you will empty the contents of your meagre brain onto this table that we may sift through the detritus and pick up the pieces of the puzzle. Mr. Richard Cordoza, PH (Dog). I like that. The one who is called what? Shum. Short for Shamwari. Is that it? Ironic, no? Friend. Kupi ri shamwari yako izvozvi? Where are your friends now, Shum? Ho! Ho! Ho!

And who considers you a friend anyway? Your Lucky Star here, lying in a puddle of his own excrement? Ha! I think not. He considers you, and I quote, a piece-of-shit, narcissistic, racist, Rhodie, motherfucker of a cunt. No, it's true. Verbatim. I have it right here on file. You were to be voted off your beloved Ingocheni Island. Did you know that? I bet you didn't, seeing as you're a narcissistic, racist, Rhodie, cunt – sorry – motherfucker of a cunt, you were blissfully unaware of any trouble in paradise, eh? I can see this comes as news to you, young man. You are taking it

213

hard. Well. Believe it. It's true. An email, gone astray, entitled The Future of Ingocheni Island, by Brighton Hove. October fourth in the year of our Lord, two thousand eight.

Ox, he writes. I daresay you know his pet name for your pet friend, so-called friend should I say, that is called Gary William Bartholemew, aka Bart. Ox, we have to do something about that – and here it is – about that piece-of-shit, narcissistic, racist, Rhodie, motherfucker of a cunt. He won't change. He'll never change. It goes on. Quite poetic actually. Seems his chief concern is your latent homosexuality and subsequent maltreatment of his beloved Maria – may she forever rest in peace. He thinks there is some good in you, actually. May the Good Lord spare me if I can see it. To me you are less than a perverted piece of porcine pestilence. Putrid pig-fucking scum.

And most certainly nobody's Shum.

BUFFALO SOLDIER

The sun on my face wakes me or is it Boils shouting? I'm melting. Where the hell am I? I'm on my bed, fully clothed, drenched in sweat. This is my bedroom. What time is it? What frikken day is it? My head is like a giant zit ready to pop. Everything hurts. I push up to see what's going on. There's Boils on the verandah, shirt off, earphones on, bopping his head and thumping the table whenever he shouts out his lusty chorus. He's potting already. What time is it?

I roll off the bed. My legs are stiff and sore as I stagger into the savage glare. The sun is up around mid-day. We've been sleeping for ages.

I collapse onto a wonky chair at the table, taking a smoke from a sodden pack. Boils pulls off his headphones and says to me, 'Morning Bartman, mushie donza?'

Where the hell he gets his energy from I just don't know. 'The others still sleeping?' I say, my throat closing around the smoke.

'Ya. Reggie's exploring Jill's tunnel of love, Rachel and Ziggy Popsicle are curled up like dogs on the couch and Shum, like you, had to settle for pulling his wire.'

'You even been to sleep?'

'That's a negative, captain, been manning the tiller while Ingocheni Island slumbers.'

I haul myself up. Shit, my legs are like sacks of potatoes. My whole body is like a sack of potatoes. Magnetic potatoes being sucked down into the earth's core. I stagger into the kitchen.

The whole kitchen window is gone but for a few shards

hanging from the putty like icicles – blazing hot summer icicles. The floor crunches with broken glass. Cupboards dangle on their hinges. Every surface is covered with shit: bottles, cans, congealed gunk, cups with brown liquid and drowned flies, broken glasses, packets, tins, bits of food and the entire place is one giant ashtray. And the fucking flies and fucking ants fucking everywhere. Fuck this.

The tiles are stickier than a slug's arse. There's the kettle. I rinse out the least disgusting cup I can find. The tea jar, or what's left of it, is on the floor. I scratch around for a dry bag and drop it into my cup. The kettle pings and pops as it heats up. My head pounds. I have to steady myself against the counter. I'm leaning over the sink looking out the missing window. The sky is a deep blue. Not a cloud. Fuck it's hot. Where's the fucking rain?

What have we got ourselves into? I need to rewind. Re-boot. Uninstall and run far, far away from all this shit and make a clean start. From scratch. I'd rather be penniless and homeless right now. Man, this has nothing to do with me. I mean, it's sad and tragic and wrong about Maria and all that but she chose that path, she chose to put herself in front of that train; tried to stop it, to derail it with her bare hands. Me? I just want to have my place under the sun. I just want to be with my boy, Joey. An image of him laughing and twirling flashes at me. I'm cracking up. We don't want any shit. Leave us the hell alone, man. We just want to enjoy. But now. Jesus, we might fucking well go to jail. My stomach flips. I bark straight into the sink, all over the plates and pots and shit already in there. Where's Patience? Probably fucked off as soon as those cops showed up. Haven't seen her since. Anyway, the sink's so full of shit nobody'll notice a few extra bits of puke. Fuck it, I want to die. I am seriously fucked here: I can't even leave the house let alone the country because I need a fucking visa to get into South even. Takes weeks. And forget England. My fucking piece of shit Zims passport – my green mamba – is like a prison sentence. Fuck. Fuck. Fuck. Fuck Reggie. Fuck Boils. Fuck Shum. Fuck Maria. Fuck everyone, man.

The kettle rattles to its end and clicks off. I pour water onto the bag – fuck-all chance of milk. I pour sugar into the cup and go back outside. This place is fucked – like a derelict house taken over by junkies. Flies and filth everywhere. Reggie has surfaced. Still in his suit. Don't these guys ever get hot? He's sitting back from the table, leaning on his knees staring at the ground. His eyes flick up as I sit and he stirs. My God it's baking, why can't it just rain? Everything's brown and dead. Never wanted to leave a place so badly in all my life.

'Bart,' he says, croaky and sorry for himself. So someone else is having a bad morning. Good.

'Chooooooon!' shouts Boils pulling off the 'phones and handing them to me.

'No, Boils, leave it,' I say pushing his hand away.

'Just fucking listen,' he says clenching his jaw and shoving the headphones into my chest, letting go so I have to catch.

'Fine.'

'Wait, wait, wait. From the beginning,' he says, skipping back.

You wanna fuck the world.

Not this again. I yank off the headphones and hand them back to Boils.

217

'Too early for that, man.'

I flick the teabag onto the table and sip on my tea. Jill stumbles out, hair matted and stuck to her face, eyes puffy, frowning against the sun. Looks like Boils was wrong about these two. They've just been sleeping. Reggie looks up and shifts around to let her sit. She thumps down and leans back, eyes closed. She's rubbing her temples. Reggie goes back to looking at the floor.

'Is he drinking again?' says Jill, pointing at Boils.

Boils pulls the headset off, takes a long glug, smacks his chops and says, 'And how.'

'Boils,' says Reggie, 'did you? Put food scraps on the car?'

'Oh, sweet Jesus, did I. Hadn't moved. Neither of 'em. Clinging to the dashboard, like this,' he shows us, 'just staring straight ahead. Crows hit the roof soon as. Then those okes only went benzy.' He's off on a laughing fit. We wait for him to finish. 'Mad Cop was heeeeeeeeeeeeeing much better. Bad Cop just sat there shitting himself.'

'Did they see you?'

'See me? Jesus Christ I hope they did. They would have seen Dr. Death on a cloud of fire come to get them. Those pigs were taaaaaa-ripping, baby. That's hectic stuff, man.'

'I need tea, want some?'

'Fuck yes, I'll come help.'

'While-lest you're up,' says Boils waggling his beer can at Reggie and giving a naughty-Calvin grin.

'Jesus, Boils, you'll drink yourself to death.'

'My intention, boyo. Plan ay-one-ay is to do exactly that: krind to thead,' he says and he makes some kind of salute.

'That's one way to stay out of jail,' says Reggie following Jill into the house. Boils throws the empty can and it

218

bounces off Reggie's shoulder clattering into the hallway.

'The fuck we gonna do, Boils?'

'What do you mean, Bartster? Situation normal: all fucked up. Those cunts are new-trail-iced.' He makes a flatline in the air like a karate chop.

'Ya Boils, but that's not the end of it. They'll be back. Others will come. We're in deep shit here.'

'Nonsense old bean. This is the frontline. Roll with the punches. Strike while the iron's hot, get in, get out, don't fuck about. Besides, we've got grog, acid, weed. And a swimming pool. What more could a man want? Let them house-arrest us. Bring it on, I say. Balls to the wall, I say.'

This is not helping. My stomach is a fist and I need to shit. I keep picturing myself in Chiks, which makes Auschwitz look like bible camp. I saw that Carte Blanche exposé: a filthy, crowded, flea-infested, shit-caked, blood-stained cell crammed with rotting corpses and living skeletons rank with cholera and TB and HIV and syphilis and I picture this toothless tokolosh creature making me suck on his weeping leprous cock. It's too much. I bolt to the edge and yak but there's nothing left and I'm gagging bile onto the lawn. Holy fuck, it burns.

'Ha-ha! That's the spirit, soldier. Get it all out,' says Boils. 'Make room for more.'

'Jesus Bart,' says Jill.

'You ok, Bart?'

'Fine Reg. Fine.' Pious cunt.

'I'm hungry,' says Reggie. He looks into the house and says to Jill, 'I see you followed instructions to a "T". The Island is trashed.'

Glasses and bottles and shit everywhere. There's a tree in the pool and it's gone a gungy green with cans and packets

219

and bits of house floating just below the surface. Garden trampled flat with broken pot plants spilling soil and roots everywhere. Most of the verandah chairs are bent or broken and the sofa in the lounge is burnt to a sticky black blob. The house smells like it's been set on fire and put out with beer and piss.

'Rachel and I cleaned up most of it. This is your mess.'

'Ah! Fair enough,' he says.

'Reggie?' She's about to blub. Her chin is rumpling and her eyes are flickering. 'What's going on?' she says and the tears spill over.

He looks into her face. 'Jill. Things have gone from bad to worse to fucking abysmal since— since—' and now it's his turn. His forehead hits the table and he's covering his head with his hands. You can hear a hoarse wail issuing out from somewhere down there and he's sniffing and snorting and rolling his head on the table and his body is convulsing.

Jill rubs his back and says, 'Come on Reg, you can tell me.'

I look at Boils. He's got his headphones back on and is looking very much into the distance, like a queue-jumping floppy at Beit Bridge.

He sobs. And sobs. And snorts. He sits up, wipes the snot across his sleeve and paws at his eyes. 'I heard her voice, Jill. I heard it. Last night.'

Jill is furious. 'What?' she says crossing her arms and sitting back. 'While you idiots were off your faces on shrooms, you mean?' She takes me and Boils in with that and I can see Boils trying, with no great effort, to stifle a laugh. So he is listening.

Reggie's chin drops to his chest. He shakes his head and says, 'No. It was a recording.' He rubs his face and eyes and says, 'I want to tell you, but I really, really can't.'

'Oh for the love of Christ,' she says, slamming her spoon on the table. 'Fine.' She blows on her tea and takes a sip, grim faced and silent.

'Maria— Jill, it's not what you think.'

Boils sniggers.

Jill's head lurches like she got slapped. She leans towards Reggie. Her teeth are clenched and her eyes wide. 'Reggie, I don't have a fucking clue what to think. And it's Jill. My name is Jill.' She looks down at her lap and says, 'For my sins.'

'For your sins, Jill? What does that mean?'

'Hey!' Boils shouts. 'You didn't get my fucking reeber. Service here is shite.'

Fuck it. I jump up to get us some beers. May as well. Shit's getting heavy.

'Check in the freezer,' Boils shouts after me.

I hear Reggie saying, 'Ok Jill, here goes,' with a sigh, like he's going to spill all the beans.

There's a whole stash of beers in here. Ice cold. Boils must have stowed himself a crate, the fucker. I dig around the kitchen for some food. Bread bin: crumbs and a mouldy crust. Fridge: cheese dip gone green. Cupboard: a torn packet of spaghetti, spices, herbs, vinegar, tom sauce. Fuck-all, basically. Here's some cup-a-soup. Tomato flavour. I find a cup and wash it out and zap the soup in the microwave sipping on my beer while I wait, staring out the window. Fuck, man, I want an ejector seat. I want to cry. I do cry. Fuck this, man.

'Jesus, you took your time.'

Fuckwit. You don't have to shout. He takes a beer and opens it one-handed, the other hand is lighting a smoke.

'What the fuck's that?'

'You don't have to fucking shout. It's soup.'

'Soup?'

'Yes, soup.'

Reggie and Jill are staring at the ground not speaking. She looks like a ghost flew down her mouth and is busy taking a dump in her stomach. Reggie's looking grim as well.

'What's going on?'

Jill looks up at me, tears running free. She says, 'You guys are in so much shit, Bart. I mean deep shit. Do you know what Maria was even doing? Do you have any fucking clue the shit she was dealing with? This goes all the way to the top and I mean all the way.'

She's giving me the shits, man. Even Boils has taken his earphones off.

'This is serious you guys. You think it's a game but this is fucking real. You guys busy getting fucked, dropping shrooms in cops' tea, tripping out and carrying on without a care in the world. But you are all in deep, deep shit. You fuck with this lot, they fuck you up. No arguments. You've got to get help. You've got to get the fuck out of here.'

'Can't,' says Boils slurping the last of his beer. He burps and stands up. 'Another?'

Jesus, Boils.

'Shit, ya. Forgot. Fuck,' she says shaking her head. 'Fuck. What a mess. Is the memory stick safe?'

'Yes,' says Reggie, 'It's—'

She grabs his hand and says, 'I actually don't want to know, Reg, you were right.'

'Ya. Ya. Quite right. But there was a recording, Jill. A conversation she'd had the very day she was, the day she was. No idea how or why it's there. No idea why she even gave that thing to me. What am I supposed to do with it?

Might've been some hidden files with instructions but I destroyed Bruce's computer before I could check. It was her voice, Jill, talking just like normal, cracking jokes, laughing. In surround fucking sound.'

'Jesus, Reggie.'

'Two others. A man with a croaky, gargly voice who made my skin crawl. And a woman, Busi something. Also black. Good English. She was with Maria. Maria was joking and talking to her in the beginning before the other guy joined them.'

'How did she speak, this Busi chick?'

'Big, deep voice. She spoke proper. You know, like this,' he mimics the classic coconut accent, 'like she was at Chisi or Arundel or some place like that.'

'That'll be Busi Charamba.'

'Who?'

'Busi was our head girl. She worked with Maria often for exactly that kind of stuff. Translator was her official title.'

'You know her?' Reggie is on his feet.

'Of course. You do too. She's always at Scar's.'

'Call her. Now. We have to see her. Oh shit.'

'There's no way I'm going through another night like last night, Reg. No fucking way.'

'Shit! Shit! Shit!'

'What?'

'We have to see this chick, Bart, but we can't leave the house, remember.'

'Jesus, Reggie, we're in enough shit as it is.'

'If those cops really are neutralised as Boils claims, we can go and come back before their trip wears off. Bart, cover for me with him.' He jerks his head in the direction of Boils and the commotion coming from the kitchen. He's shouting 'LUST' over and over.

'What?' says Jill sitting up.

'I'm going to check on those cops.'

'I'm coming with.'

'What? Jill, no.'

'I want to see this for myself,' she says looking up at Reggie.

'You wanna fuck the woooooorld,' screams Boils coming back outside, wiping his hand on his jeans. He looks at Reggie and Jill and me and says, 'What's going on?'

'Nothing. Nothing, Boils. Jill's on her way. I'm going to see her off.'

'Fine,' he says, flopping onto his chair scowling about something. He throws the can at me.

Prick. Nearly took my head off. The can sprays beer in my face when I open it and Boils hoses himself at this.

He points his elbow at me and says, 'Buffalo! Krind.'

'Fuck, Boils.'

'Krind,' he says, standing up. His chair topples back and he's got his beer held up ready to launch at me. 'Krind or I'll take your fucking head off, cunt.' He's livid, eyes blazing at me.

'Jesus, Boils. What's got your goat?'

'Just fucking krind, you cunt.'

MIGHT FIND
SOMEONE MATEY

Pain. I can't move. Every bone hurts. Every muscle. Every nerve. Every synapse. Every fucking cell. The ceiling is fucked. There's a brown stain where the geyser leaked and the boards are sagging ready to collapse. Stupid tassels covered in fly shit on a stupid purple lampshade hanging from a stupid shit-stained wire.

Voices. Coming from outside. Murmuring and grunting: Boils shouting as usual, Bart's groggy morning voice and Reggie's sorry mumbles. A girl. And now silence. My shoulder feels like it's got a steel rod rammed through it, ready for the spit roast. Feels like I'm already roasting, flames wrapping around my whole body. I'm drenched. Basted. Holy shit, hangovers don't come any worse than this. Even my ring is on fire. How do fags do it? It must hurt like hell.

Boils is shouting some more. Now there's laughter. And murmuring and thumping. Music. Sounds like the whole Island is awake. I'm missing out but actually I don't give a shit. Those cunts are useless. And boring. And the chicks. Jesus. Turning everyone into slobbering retards when all they do is complain and sulk. Fucking chicks. Still. That Rachel chick's hot. Great fucking tits. Jesus I'd love to have another go at her with a full pass. Not in the manky bogs at Scar's but VIP access, centre court, golden circle, presidential fucking suite. Fuck me I'm horny. How's about a nice little donza then? Don't mind if I do thank you very much indeed. Rachel will be my model for today. Hi Rachel, how are you, would you like to suck my balls? Great. Oh, Jesus, fuck, arse, that hurts. And there goes the feeling, fuck it. Fuckety-fuck-fuck. I need real pussy, man. This room is killing me.

I roll onto my good side and push myself upright. Jesus, that takes some effort and the pain doubles up. I sit on the edge of my bed staring at the floor taking inventory: head, shoulder, arm, both legs grazed and stiff, fucking sphincter, Jesus will I ever be able to shit again? Speaking of which. Oh fuck me I have to go. Bad. Christ Almighty on a fuck-stick.

The toilet seat is broken. I sit on the enamel. Feels like I'm going to fall into the toilet but the cold is good. I'm breathing heavy and sweating clenching my butt cheeks. Not again. Please not again. I don't want to go through that again. I let rip.

Ha! Not so bad. Good job my stomach is rotten and I haven't eaten solids in about three days. More like pissing out my arse. This burns to fuck, make no mistake, but it's got nothing on a bad case of piles, nothing on a razor-edged fucking memory stick full of pictures of murder and torture and rape. Sweat drips into my eyes and even that goddam-well stings. Give a guy a break, man.

The bathroom is fucked. Mud-caked floor, pill bottles, razors, shaving paste, toothpaste, shampoo bottles squished and oozing pink goo, soaked towels. The basin is also cracked, shower curtain hanging by one hook. What the fuck happened in here?

Oh! Christ. No bog roll. I dig in the washing basket and find a sock. Must be one of Reggie's: no holes and it doesn't stink to the high heavens.

226

Aaaaaaaaaaaaaaaay! It's Sharty-fart-face, back from the bogs of hell.

Thanks Boils, I missed you too, but I'd prefer a cup of tea round about now.

Tea? Tea? he says pointing to the sun. Does it look like fucking daybreak to you?

He's got a point and it's fucking hot. I drag myself over to the manky pool and wade in, clothes and all, too sore to strip. Probably got my cell phone in my pocket. Too late. I turn and there's Boils flying through the air. He crashes on top of me and we go down. The pain kills me. I'm stunned. He's hauling me about. I kick out with my legs and push away from him. I wade to the edge. Boils is hooting and yelling banzai and got you motherfucker and telling me how revenge is sweet. Trying to justify himself.

Whatever, Boils.

Bart leaps over my head and does a massive bomb. The wave shoves me against the side. Feels like I've been shot. I can't even breathe. Bog Brush tries the same, ends up bellyflopping. Rachel is moping on the verandah. I haul out of the pool and stagger across the lawn and ease into a chair next to her.

She looks at me. I look at her. Jesus I'd like to fuck the shit out of you right now.

You look like shit, she says.

What shit you talking? I feel like a champion. She laughs and looks at me funny, like she's found some hidden meaning there. Fuck. Those tits. It appears my broken soldier is on the mend.

Bog Brush squelches onto the verandah and flops down,

pulling his hair back and tying it behind his bandana. Awright, mate? he says, pulling a smoke out of a box on the table. I take one.

Crazy night, man, crazy. Well slaughtered we was.

What the fuck's with this guy? He's no more a Pom than I am a fucking swan.

Rachel sniggers. Bog Brush looks at her then at me.

Make yourself useful, I say to him, fetch us some medicinal beers, there's a good chap. I know for a fact Boils has a secret stash somewhere.

What am I, mate? Your slave?

And one for me, too, says Rachel.

Comin' right up.

Nice work, Rachel, you've scored yourself a gimp.

She laughs again. She's actually not bad this chick. She shakes her head and says, Cretin.

Cretin with benefits?

She gives me the raised eyebrow, you're shitting me in the eyeball, look. Aye! Aye! Aye! Maybe there is a chance for old Shumsie to slip the lizard after all. Things are looking up.

Bog Brush returns clutching three cans, frosty cold. He flops down again, right next to Rachel this time. If he only knew. He hands me a beer.

Cheers, mate. What the hell? That just popped out. Not even taking the piss. Rachel hops up and heads over to the pool. I turn and watch. She strips off her top and jeans and dives into the water, slithers in more like, like an eel. Not a splash. She glides to the other side and comes up pushing her hair back. She looks at us. I look at Bog Brush. He's transfixed. Boils and Bart are chatting. I don't think they even noticed. Meanwhile I'm getting a bloody stonker like a goddam teenager.

So, says Bog Brush, what do you do for a crust?

For a crust? Jesus. I fuck sheep.

He's facing me but he's looking over my shoulder. Boils and Bart have stopped talking so I reckon she's getting out of the pool. I turn. Got her. Jesus-cunt, she's actually a fucking belter. She pulls her clothes back on. The white top is wet and her massive nips are showing right through on full beam. Might just pop my load right here.

She's coming back to the verandah. Bog Brush is still gawking. I pick up her beer and hand it to her so she can sit on the other side of the table, away from Mr. Brush and opposite me. Am I imagining or does she have a knowing sparkle in her eye. Oh! Oh! Oh! What have we here? One of the sailors has spotted a whale. Thar she blows. Thar she blows Shum's mighty dick.

You want to dry off?

Now why would I want to do that?

'LUST!' Boils shouts into my ear slapping my chest. Jesus I got a skrook. Then the pain arrives.

Boils. For fuck's sakes. His arm.

Oh! Jesus Shum. Sorry, man. I forgot. Shit. Sorry. You ok?

I'll live. Right now, all I want to do is take this fucking hot bitch into my room and shove my cock into her till she's sick. Till her teeth rattle.

Where's Jill, mate?

Dunno. Gone home I think. Reggie said he was seeing her off, says Bart grabbing a smoke and sitting down.

Ha! Rachel laughs and looks at me again. Jesus fucking H. Christ in a bucket of blood.

Been gone for ages, man.

Ya. Suspicious methinks. Hey! Fuck-arse. Your round.

Bart slops into the house leaving a trail of water just as Reggie comes in with Jill behind him.

Hey! It's the lovebirds. I thought you were leaving? says Boils.

Jill is smiling. She laughs and shakes her head and says, Reggie changed my mind. We paid a little visit to those coppers. She puts her hand to her face and is giggling but trying not to. You guys are insane. In-fucking-sane.

Thank you, says Boils and he tips an imaginary hat. Thank you kindly, ma'am.

Bart's handing out beers. Reggie and Jill shake their heads no and sit down.

And? Story?

Trouble is, says Reggie, there's only one cop there.

What! says Bart leaping up. Very jumpy is this one.

Yup. Looks like the main one, Chipenga I think, bolted. Door's wide open but Mad Cop hasn't budged. He's still clinging to the dashboard with eyes like golf balls going heeeeeee! heeeeeeee! whenever a bird lands on the car to peck at Boils's bait.

Fuck, man, what the fuck?

Relax, Bartlejuice, they think it's demons, says Boils. He waggles his finger and says, They've got bigger fish to fry now. He's probably hiding under a rock somewhere. He laughs and says, Or still running.

Or frecked from a heart attack. Could happen with such a bad trip, you know, says Reggie gnawing on his nails.

You think she'd come here? Jill says to Reggie.

Who?

Busi.

Who the fuck's Busi?

The other chick in that recording.

230

What recording?

Never mind.

No chance, says Reggie, that would put her in even more danger. And besides she's probably got her own police escort outside her door. He sticks his fists in his eyes and groans.

Hey, Ox, do us all a favour: have a swim.

Ya Reg, you've got a purple haze around you, man.

Fine, he says and he trundles off to the pool. He flops in, suit and all, and lies there face down, arms spread out like he's a drowned man floating on the surface.

Choons! Boils shouts and he's up and into the lounge before anyone can intercept.

Bets?

Lust, mate, lust. Fucker's had it on repeat for the past twenty-four hours.

And you would know. Hey, matey?

The Necrophiliacs – or The Bestial Graverobbers or some shit like that – blasts out the cobwebs. So the sound system survived another day. Reggie squelches his way back to the verandah. He sounds like a shower, water pouring out his pockets and shoes.

Any bright ideas, then? Jill says to Reggie.

Well no. I suppose our only option is to try and call her.

Phones will all be tapped don't you think?

What? Like this is fucking CSI?

Still, can't hurt to be safe, says Reggie. Jill, you've got her number? Call her. Invite her to your birthday party or something.

Jill fishes her phone out and is busy looking for Busi's number.

Put it on speaker. Boils! Boils!

What? He's in the lounge air guitaring his head off.

Turn it down, says Reggie waggling the phone at him.

Kuff you, says Boils giving him the double-finger but he turns the volume down anyway. The phone is on the table. We're watching it like it's a frog about to sing a nursery rhyme. It rings and rings and rings and rings then it blips off. Call ignored.

Send a text message. Tell her it's urgent.

Jill taps in the message and sends it, watching it go. I sneak a peek at Rachel's jellies still showing through her wet t-shirt. Jesus, they are massive. My balls tighten.

Now try again.

Jesus, Reggie.

He takes the phone and presses the call button. It rings once and then: Hello? The voice on the other end is timid and thin but it's her all right.

Busi? It's Jill, Maria's friend. She shouts like it's a trunk call from the old days.

I know you. I can't talk, they've tapped my phone. And they are watching my house. Fuck them. Fuck them all. Those fucking cunts can all fucking rot in hell.

The phone blips twice then silence.

Fuck me. And she's a hectic Christian.

Shit. Now what?

Do you know where she lives?

Reggie, no. If you leave the house—

Have to. Can't stay here and do nothing.

Even the Bog Brush is silent. For once.

Well, I know where she used to live when we were at school. Maybe her folks still live there.

Reggie is up and sloshing into the house and he returns with a phone book. It's ancient, from ninety-nine or whenever it was last printed, and he's flicking through the pages.

Lots of Charambas, he says, handing the book to Jill. She scans the names with her finger.

Here. Fingowrie Crescent, Chisi. That's it. We used to walk there after school for lunch and a swim. Her mum made these disgusting Scotch eggs.

Well, isn't that just the dandiest story in the world?

Shut it, Shum.

Jill is punching in the number but Reggie grabs her hand with the phone in it and says: What if they've tapped the line there too?

You think they would?

You heard Busi. Just get the story right: you want to invite her to your birthday. Your 30th, maybe? How old are you?

Old enough, she says whipping her hand away and pressing the call button and holding the phone to her ear with a scowl. Ha! Chicks and their age. I take another squizz at the tit-fest. Rachel's top is almost dry but I can still make out the shape of her nips. I have to push my cock down. She's examining the ends of her hair. Doesn't notice. Her legs are crossed and her foot is waggling.

Hi! Mrs. Charamba? says Jill in her loud phone voice. She stands up and paces the verandah. Yes— yes— no— it's nothing like that, Mrs. Charamba. My name is Gillian Draper. I was at Chisi with Busi way back when. We ate you out of house and home and swam in your pool every day.

A pause. Jill nods while Mai Charamba says something. Looks like a score.

Very well thanks, very well indeed Mrs. Charamba. In fact I'm calling because I've lost Busi's number. My phone was stolen, and I want to invite her to my thirtieth.

Another pause.

233

Pardon? When? Oh. On the nineteenth of November, she says pleading for help from Reggie. He grabs Bart's phone and thumbs the keypad and Jill's hopping up and down and then Reggie mouths to her: twenty-two.

Oh, thank you, yes, thanks. What a fool. That's the actual day of my birthday. We're having the party the weekend after. The twenty-second. It's a Saturday. She looks at Reggie in panic. He nods.

Ok, thanks, she says clicking her fingers for the pen Reggie's got ready. She calls out the number oh nine one seven something something and writes it in the phone book at the top of Busi's page.

And may I have her address as well Mrs. Charamba? I want to post an invitation.

Jesus, clutching at straws much?

Reggie hisses at me with his finger to his lips. What a laugh. Jill gives him this helpless shrug and then says, Ok, great thanks, and she writes it down calling it out as she goes.

Ok, thanks Mrs. Charamba. Yes, we're all bad daughters these days. Too much fun, I'm afraid, but I'll tell her to call you and maybe we'll come for those delicious Scotch eggs one day soon. It's so hot at the moment, isn't it? She makes a pitiful face, shaking her head.

She laughs. A pause while she listens.

Ok it's a deal Mrs. Charamba, thank you, bye, bye. Bye.

She hangs up and groans. Holy fuck, that was close. Jeez-o she was suspicious at first. Why didn't we think of a date? Idiots.

Amateurs, says Reggie looking at the address in front of him. He traces it with his finger, fiddling, tapping his leg.

Ok, says Jill.

Ok, what? says Reggie.

Ok, I'll come with you. She won't let you in on your own.

Reggie's face softens into that puppy-dog look. He says, Thank you, Jill. Like she just saved his life.

And besides I enjoyed cycling. Haven't done that in yonks, she says.

Jesus, she's laying it on thick. Wish my titty twister would be this obvious. Maybe these two will sod off now and I'll get my chance. It's odd but she's uninterested in these goings on. Before, she would have shat all over Jill for even thinking of going with Reggie.

By bike? Are you sure? Reggie says already standing up.

Yes. They'll see your cars are still here and besides it's not far. Newlands, just the other side of the golf club I think.

Jill.

Oh! Bollocks, they don't even know me.

Go, I say, it's better that way.

GENIUS BOB

Reggie and Jill have gone to find some chick called Busi. I haven't a cooking clue what's going on. Don't care either. All I can think of is my son, Joey, on the other side of the world. Him on Mud Island and me in jail. Joey's jailbird dad. And never mind what goes on inside those prison walls.

Meanwhile Boils is getting roasted – double roasted – in the blazing sun slotting the beers. Correction, he's onto the vodcokes now. That spells trouble. That's when you know he's on a mission. He's blasting the metal as usual. Shum is egging him on, not that he needs any encouragement, and Rachel is sipping a warm beer. Probably taking a mouthful and pouring it back in. Oldest trick in the book. She's bored. Hasn't said a word. Couldn't get a word in if she tried.

Joey is going round and round my head. He's all I can think of. That and a filthy, grey cement jail cell with twenty festering Gollums in it.

How come these guys don't give a shit? How can they just party on like nothing's wrong? To them this is just another fucked up day in paradise. We're besieged by psychopaths on a disintegrating Island, a rotting oasis. The pool says it all: Badza allegedly took a dump in it and judging by the colour of the water, that could be true. The bottom is littered with broken glass and cans, even a goddam verandah chair is in there and of course there's that fir tree – burnt and charred – still in its pot poking above the surface. It's fucked. the garden is fucked. The house is fucked. Everything is fucked. And yet. To look at these cretins you wouldn't notice anything amiss. It's just another day. Life goes on. So what's the point?

'Fuck this shit. Fuck all of this shit to fucking hell. I'm going to get butt-fuckingly motherless.'

'Atta boy, soldier. There's nowt left to do this day but sit back and to what? To just enjoy. Join us brother on our fabulous merry-go-down. Celebrate. Partaaaaaaay.'

'Cool, bruv, I'll sign on.'

This Ziggy character outstayed his welcome long ago.

'Oh yeah?'

'Sure. Why not? I mean. Nothing better to do, right?'

'Right.'

Fucking moocher. When I return with my stash, Ziggy's on about how pissed they were at the Tiger Tournament and how many fish he caught and how big they were.

'Biggest was a forty-four pounder man, I'm tellin' ya.'

Shum and Boils – the planet's two most avid fishermen – are taking the piss of course.

'Serious?' says Shum sitting up and blinking in fake awe. Ziggy doesn't see it at all.

'Must've put up quite the fight,' says Boils.

'Fuck, yeah,' says Ziggy revelling in the attention, 'nearly took my rod.'

Boils sniggers. Shum cuts him a look. I know what he's saying: don't give the game away yet. We haven't had nearly enough fun out of this.

'So what was your agg?'

'Eh?'

'Your aggregate, dick-fuck.'

'Aggregate? Oh yeah, course, it was about thirteen.'

'Fuck me? Thirteen?'

'Where'd you finish, then?'

'Top three, easy.'

'Top three? Shit, must've been some whoppers in at two and one. What was the winning agg?'

They go on at him. You can tell he's twigged but too far down the road to backtrack. They lured him in, baited him with juicy compliments and now they'll strike. I'm not joking when I say these guys literally live and breathe fishing.

'Hey Boils,' says Shum. Here it comes. The strike is imminent. He makes a show of getting a smoke and lighting it and then, round the side of the fag, he says, 'What's the record for a tiger?'

Boils takes a long swig, swallows, smacking his lips and then he burps and says, 'Sixteen point one kilograms, or thirty-five pounds seven ounces if that's your persuasion. Jennifer Daynes, twelfth of September 2001 at Sanyati Gorge with a Dolphin rod, Abu Garcia Ambassadeur reel, twenty pound Maxima line and a Tiger Tad lure. But, Shum, don't quote me.'

Ziggy's looking from Shum to Boils and from Boils to Shum and they are acting all casual like nothing's going on. Rachel huffs and sighs and chucks her chair back.

'I'm going for a swim. Shum? You going to join me?'

Ha! Ask him twice. He's up and almost in the pool already. This should be good. We all watch as she strips off again. Gave me and Boils an awesome show earlier: in just her white panties, white bra – and slops of course on account of all the debris. Thought I had a chance for a nanosecond. Well, if it's between me and Boils of course, but there's Shum ready to pounce. Like a hyena. Damn she's got a hot body. Ok face, but that body. Shitballs.

I toss a joint at Ziggy. He's staring like a nog at a car crash. It smacks him in the face and he skrooks, picking it up off his lap.

'For me?'

'Yup. A sympathy blunt.'

'Jayziz I love this country. Back 'ome we'd be hot-boxing a toothpick. Is this pure?'

'Course it is.'

'Fahk sakes. We have to mix with baccy to make it go. Costs a bomb 'n' all.'

'That's hash, fucknut,' says Boils, still looking straight ahead at the show. 'This is grass. Plain old buds, plucked from the earth the way mother nature and the good lord below intended. Vig us a hit.' Ziggy hands him the spliff. We're all still staring. They come up for air at the far side of the pool. We can only see the backs of their heads.

'Show's over,' says Boils. 'Back to business.'

***

Shum and Rachel are in the pool on the top step, talking. Can't hear what they're saying but you can bet your bottom dollar Shum's laying it on thick. He's got no shame. Sigh. Yet another one gets away.

Oh well. At least Mary Jane will never let me down. Let's get amongst. The sun is shining, the weather is sweet, I'm going to jail.

'Boils, I'm begging you. I'll give you a thousand dollars – of United States origin – if I can change the music.'

'Pay up, puke-breath. Money on the table.'

'Piss off.'

I go into the lounge and dig around the rubble for my Bob Marley CD. It's like sifting through a junkyard or worse, the municipal dump with smouldering tyres and melted plastic and pungent fumes. I can feel the weed kicking in already. My arms are tingling. Life is all of a sudden quite peachy, quite mellow. Fuck everything. Fuck everyone. I'll. What? I'll Abide? Endure? Persevere? There's a word but I can't remember it. I'll, I'll something, that's for sure. Here it is. Natural Mystic: The Legend of Bob Marley. My stomach does a little jump. Crank it up all the way to the max. Volume eleven. Boils even marked it on the knob. I love this opening track. It starts slow and soft, just a faint reggae beat. Speaking of whom, I wonder how he's doing? Probably just went to the vlei for a nyenga with that other insanely hot item. Now there's the total package: beautiful face, hot body and sharp as a tack. And she's up for anything. Good fun. My kind of girl, for sure. But, as always, they go for Reggie instead. Now the beat comes. Now louder. Listen to that bass, oh-oh-oh, that's good. And now Bob's rasping voice, über-fucking-cool man.

There's a natural mystic, blowing tru' de air.

Goosebumps. Again, again. I could listen to this tune forever. Next song: another classic. Could be even better. I'm swaying along to the beat in the lounge sucking hard on this joint. I need oblivion. Need to forget everyfuckingthing.

One good thing about music
When it hits you feel no pain
So hit me with music
Hit me with music

Hit me with Bob's music. Then it hits me. It really does. 'Boils! Boils!' I shout, bounding out onto the verandah.

240

'What, homo?'

'I have landed upon a mighty fine idea my friend.'

'What? You want a reach-around?'

'No you chop, we're going to have us a little compo. A little showdown. You krind to thead. I'll mokes to thead. We'll call it a thead-off. But, Boils, we do it for real.'

He puts his glass down, wipes his mouth and he looks at me serious. Then his face turns to an evil grin.

'You won't even last one round, turkey-brain. Plus I've got a head start on you.'

'What the fuck you lads on about?'

'Bartlet here has laid down the ultimate gauntlet for a head-to-head thead-a-thon but it's just big talk. Big fighting talk against the champion of the world.'

'Bantam-weight champion you mean.'

He spits into his hand, stands and proffers the gunk to me. I hawk up my most glueyest gob. It's brown. I show it to him. He puts his hand forward. It's browner than mine.

'Bring it on,' I say.

'To thead, ne? None of this foossyputting about.'

'None of this what, Boils?' says Shum reaching for a smoke, dripping water everywhere. He lights it, hands it to Rachel. She flicks her hand dry and takes it like a beginner, with scissor-fingers, and sucks a mouthful and puffs out straightaway blinking at the smoke. Trying to impress Shum. What a retard.

'No idea mate, but these two have developed incomprehensible lisps all of a sudden.'

'What Ziggy Popstar has failed to grasp,' says Boils, 'is that twot-brain over here has challenged me to a mokes-off.'

'It's Pop. Iggy Pop. Ziggy Stardust. Jesus, get it right you fucking morons. And why the fuck you calling me that anyway?'

'No dicknose,' I say to Boils, 'I smoke, you drink.'
'Swat I meant.'

***

Then my all time favourite, Stir It Up comes on. It's the ultra-cool song of the century. I bound back into the lounge and I'm slow-bopping and swaying like a feather floating along with the beat like I'm on a tube drifting down the Pungwe with the birds in the forest going crazy and the bright blue sky blotting out my vision. Boils joins in and we're giving it the gentle foot-clap. Too, too cool.

'Fuck me, Bob is my hero,' I say when that most excellent guitar solo hits us.

'Bob's your aunty you mean,' Boils shouts back at me.

I take another toke mid-bop then my head jolts back in a whiplash and I feel a sharp dig in my back and we're both crashing to the ground. Ziggy has tackled me and Boils and we're in a heap on the floor. Boils is hosing but I've had enough of this guy. Nailed me in the kidneys the prick. I hoof him hard but he's just canning himself. The moment's gone. Bob may as well be singing to himself now. Time for another joint. And that cunt's not getting any more.

Shum and Rachel have gone. The trail of water leads into the house. I've got a squintillion bucks right here says that trail leads all the way to his bedroom. Explains Ziggy's random attack.

'Boils!' I have to shout. 'Leave the music alone. Just fucking leave it.'

He considers for a moment and I'm up on my feet already. He comes out leaving Ziggy to rifle through the CDs. If that

242

dick changes the music I really will kill him.

'Jesus, that retard got me right in the back. What's his problem? Where's Shum and that tchib?'

I nod towards Shum's room.

'Ah! And then there were three.' He picks up his vodka, drains it and slops off into the kitchen.

'Bring me a coke,' I shout after him, lighting up giggle-twig number two. Oh I'm going to get so baked. Like an English scone. Like a wood-fired pizza. Like a fucking clay pot.

***

The sun is low, sending warm rays through the avo tree and speckling our table with dots of light. We're playing dice. Ziggy is motherfucked. Caught between Boils's krind-a-thon, my mokes-a-thon and his own woe-is-me-ness he's trying to out-thead us both. Boils came up with that idea. Baited him like a pro. Told him the English were a bunch of pussies. Well, that was the start of it. Now we're nailing him with the dice. He hasn't got a clue which way is up and his dice keep falling on the floor and Boils is yelling at him, 'Krind! Krind motherfucker,' and pouring him monster tots.

I roll another joint. Ok it's a tiny one but still. I chuck it at him and he's just laughing and shaking his head and saying, 'You okes, you okes.' Not such a Pom now, eh, boyo?

Shum's been nyomping Rachel for hours now. The bastard.

Boils wrestled musical control back yonks ago of course. It's Trent Reznor now. Nine Inch Nails. Slightly at odds with the warm glow of late afternoon, birds singing, pool flicking sunlight on the wall and that pure deep blue October sky that you only see in pictures. Then there's this chainsaw

243

guitar and some savage grovelling into the mic: I want to fuck you like an animal. And of course Boils is shouting along. I want to feel you from the inside, he shouts. It fucks with my brain but somehow it fits. Beauty and the beast. That's life. Love and laughter to your left, fear and loathing to your right. Always, wherever you go, wherever you live, whatever you do. So what's in the middle?

'Jesus, Bart. Shut up. What is this? Fucking philosophy classes? Shut up and play. It's your turn arse-wipe.'

I can't exactly focus. Boils seems hundreds. Ziggy is puking in the flower bed. Ha-ha! Teach you to mess with us you dick. Boils and I give each a silent victory salute and a secret high-five. Got 'im good. Happy days. Then Reggie and Jill cycle up the driveway.

***

They look serious. Very serious.

'Iwe! Kwashiorkor-kid,' I say to Boils and nod towards the door. 'Reggie's back.'

'Reggieeee!' Boils shouts and bounds up and through the house to the front clutching his vodka. 'What news from the front lines, soldier?' There's a mumbled reply, Reggie's voice. A couple of words and nothing. He looks haggard when he comes through.

'Jesus, Reg, you look fucked. What happened, man?'

He shakes his head at the joint I offer him. Shame. Looks like he needs it. And Jill. They both need a hit. They're buggered. They flop onto chairs.

'They fucked her up, Bart.' Reggie's in tears. Jill is morose, staring at the ground. 'Raped her and fucked her

244

up. Goddam nearly killed her.' He's shaking his head and wiping the tears away.

'And? Story?' Boils comes out all guns blazing. He's recharged his glass and thumps into his chair lighting a smoke. We've been chain-smoking all day. Don't mind if I do. Oh but I've got a joint on the go already. Stuff it. Double-barrel. Hit me with the music.

Reggie sighs, 'Ag! Nothing Boils,' he says staring at the ground like Jill.

'Nothing? What is this, fucking nursery school? Telling fucking secrets again?'

'Fuck off, Boils, this is serious.'

'I fucking know you cunt, that's why I'm fucking asking.'

Shum and Rachel come out, ruffled like they've been sleeping but unlike Reggie and Jill earlier this is the restful sleep of the recently rogered.

'What's the rosty? You look like shit,' Shum says, lighting up.

'Fuckface over here is too cool for school to tell us,' says Boils shaking his head and glugging back his vodka. Rachel is standing behind Shum, arms folded like she's cold, wearing his sweater, the sleeves rolled up to her wrists. Shum shrugs and turns to Rachel.

'You want some tea?'

'I'll go make some,' she says, giving his arm a sultry squeeze, the tchib.

'Fuck this. Fuck this shit. Fuck all of you. I fix those cops good and proper and what do I get? "Stay out of it, Boils, this is for grown-ups." Well, fuck you,' he says and he stands up and drains the rest of his drink.

'Who's having the tantrum now, Boils?' says Shum sniggering.

'Whatever faggot, fuck you.' Shum just laughs. That's new. 'I am going to fucking Nyanga as fucking planned and you can all go fuck yourselves.'

Ziggy lurches out of the flowerbed wiping his arm across his face. He says, 'What's going on, lads?' But nobody's interested.

Boils turns on me. 'Bart!'

'What? What have I done, man?'

'Get your shit, we're going fishing.'

'We can't leave the house, Boils,' I call after him. He's getting his car keys and his things together already. He's serious. He's off.

I look at Shum. He's looking very much at the ground. I look at Reggie. He shakes his head at me and mouths out the words, 'Just go.' I look at Shum. He shrugs. They're telling me to leave?

'Fucking cunts can suck my fucking cock,' says Boils loud enough for all to hear.

'Come on Boils, just chill. This is wrong, man. Just chill.'

'Fuck it Bart, are you coming or not?'

'Ok, ok, I'm coming man. Keep your hair on.'

'Fine. Get your shit. I'll be back in exactly one hour. Got it?'

He cranks his car for like half an hour before it farts to life. Then he backs down the driveway in a cloud of black smoke and snags our jousting target. Away he goes, car screeching and whinnying like a nag with Bob's face on a pillowcase flapping behind like a ripped mini-skirt.

'Holy shit, Boils, so long as your parachute's ok,' says Shum into the smoky silence.

MONSTER MOUSE

Boils has lost it. Threw a complete thrombie and now he's threatening to fuck off to Nyanga with Bart who seems to have gone full pussy on us. Speaking of which. Thy kingdom come, this one's a tiger. My cock is raw and my balls are throbbing. She brings tea. A big steaming pot of the stuff. And biscuits. Where the fuck she find them? Must've dug around in the dustbin. I am in love.

Reggie and Jill look butt-fucked. Their faces are sink-holes with bottomless pits where their eyes should be. They're both just staring at the floor.

Jill? Tea?

Jill gives Rachel a blank look and then she's off again with her face folding and her chin doing the frog dance and her eyes welling over. She rubs her face and looks away. Reggie is a glass-eyed statue.

Rachel pours for him too and slides the cup across the table. He looks up but he doesn't see shit. I tell her three spoons and plenty of milk. She fixes it and hands to him, picking up his arm and pressing the cup into his hand. He just stares at it. Rachel gives me a sideways look. These guys have certainly brought a downer on the mood here. Even this fucknut Ziggy Bog Brush has shut his trap. Now there's a silver lining.

We sit in silence, clinking cups, slurping tea. It's getting dark. I steal a look at Rachel. My balls tighten. Jesus fellers, give an oke a break here, let me catch my breath back. She must've felt that because she looks up at me and covers a smile with her cup, blowing on the surface. I'm squirming in my chair. Let's dust these morbid fucks. How can I get the message across to Rachel? She probably wants to look after her mate. Fuck that. We've got better things to do than play fucking nurse-maid to these two sad-sacks. Jesus, I want my cock in her arse all of a sudden. We were nearly there but she chickened out. All in good time, I suppose. Slowly, slowly, catch a monkey.

So now what? The cops are neutralised. We should be home free and celebrating but it's like a fucking funeral here. What gives? It's getting dark. The birds are doing their thing, the air is still as death. An ice cream bell rings out.

Reggie jumps up like he just had a whack of ZESA to the testicular area.

Ice cream! he shouts at me.

And me, says Ziggy, croaking like he's on his deathbed. What the devil?

And it's got to be a Monster Munch, Ziggy says tittering to himself. Jesus, he's fucked. Caught in the cross-fire I'll bet. Caught between the forces of good and evil, darkness and light, Boils and Bart. The real loser in their idiotic thead-a-thon. Or is he collateral damage? Either way, those cretins have seen him off and no mistake.

Reggie ignores this idiot's blathering and says to me: Shum, there was an ice cream bell in that recording.

Jesus, Reg, what the fuck you on about?

But he's gone. He's out the door, clambering onto his bike and half way down the driveway already, his jacket flying behind him like a witch's cloak.

I scream, you scream, we all scream for ice cream, says Ziggy. Wait! Reggie. Wait! he says, trying to shout but it's a hoarse bleat. Make it a Fatso. He turns to Rachel and says, D'you think he heard me?

248

GERONIMO, VERSE FIVE

Chikomo. Let's we begin. The electrodes if you will. Quick as you please, sir. He is losing consciousness again. You were too heavy handed with this one Chikomo. That eyeball is squished. Quite disgusting actually. Grisly in fact. And his nose? What have you done to that pretty little button nose of his? It is all over his face.

Did you know what the maBritesh did to our soldiers, Chikomo? What they did to our freedom fighters, fighting for their land – for their land – to get it back from this, this, pig-fucking scum? Oh! Oh! My decorum departs, it decreases, it diminishes. It dissolves. Ah! But we have a lifetime of retribution, revenge and restitution for the ravages of these imperialist pigs. And besides, my shoes are bloody-fucked anyway.

Let us have him up on the chair Chikomo. Naked as the day his putrid spirit entered this world. That is good. Legs clamped. Good. Arms behind. Good. How he screams. You know the drill Max. Wire him up, plug him in and fire away with our DIY ZESA.

There. And there. Good. Now. Mr. Cordoza. I shall not call you Shum. Lover of theatrics though I am, I just can not bring myself to call you my shamwari. Not even in the deepest darkest cavern of irony would I consider this jest worthy. To me you are Mr. Cordoza, interrogation subject number two-three-two-one.

Now. I take it you are MDC?

Chikomo.

Oh dear me that stinks. Chikomo, a bucket under the chair please. It looks to me, Mr. C., you are unfamiliar with our practices. Have you not seen it on the television even? On Miami Vice or CSI? I am sure you have, boy, I am sure you have. But a refresher then, to stir the mush in your skull. It goes like this: I ask you a question, you answer me, you live. I ask you a question, you do not answer me, you die. But not before we deliver several thousand angry volts to your already shrivelled testicles. So let me ask again. You are MDC?

Ah! Ah! Foolish me. Forgetting the fundamental tenet of interrogation. It must be this late hour. What time do we have Chikomo? Come again? Two o'clock? I will shoot you if you lie to me. Show me your watch. My, my, my, how time flies when you are having fun. My watch is nicer than yours, see?

Where was I, Chikomo?

Ah! Good. Yes, yes, thank you. The fundamental tenet of interrogation, Mr. Cordoza, is to extract the truth, the whole truth and nothing but the truth so help you God. You see how late it is become? You see your friend there, all but dead? You see your own fate must come soon. Must arrive before the sun comes up. Long before the sun comes up in fact for I wish to be in my small house in my warm bed next to my flaming hot mistress, and each moment you delay brings us ever closer to, not further from, your ultimate fate. Am I clear? Very good.

You are MDC?

Oh! Jesus, bloodyfuck-sake cunt. Ha! This is a new word for me that I have learned from you and your smutty little friends. Cunt. It is a good word, no? So here we go. Fire in the hole, as they say. Wikaah! That hurts, yes? And this? And this? And this? Leave off Chikomo, I know what I'm doing. I invented this apparatus. To replace my snakes, yes. And now for a bucket of reviving water.

There we go. All smiles and cooperation.

Mr. Cordoza, think long and hard over your answer to this next question: you are MDC? What? Come again? Ha! Good, good. Fast learner. Given the right encouragement of course.

Now, Mr. C. This one. This fishy friend of yours. He is MDC?

What? Come again? Of course you know, my friend.

Ha! You see that, Chikomo? It just comes naturally. Maybe this one is indeed a friend to all the creatures of the earth after all. But not in this life. Not here. Here you have no friends. Not even that one. He told me everything so you are just here for confirmation, my dear. A good science experiment must be repeatable with predictable results. I am a scientist don't you know and I am very thorough. So. That one is MDC?

Good. Now. Oh look, Chikomo, he cries. How pitiful. Do you read The Holy Bible, Cordoza? Oh, this is tiring. Chikomo! Zap him.

Thank you, good sir.

Do you read the Bible, Cordoza? No? Should I feign surprise? Your conduct is about as unholy as a serpent giving a sermon on Mount Sinai you heathen swine. Chikomo!

Thank you, Max.

I, on the other hand, am a most pious man, my dear Tricky Dicky, and thus your religious education begins. Geronimo, verse five: I, the Lord your God, am a jealous God, visiting the iniquity of the fathers on the children, and

251

on the third and the fourth generations of those who hate Me. Do you see, Mr. C.? God sanctions, nay, encourages my actions. Carrying out his retribution so that he may keep his hands Sunlight clean.

So my boy, I have it on good authority that you hate me. And that you hate all my brothers too. And so now the iniquity of your fathers is coming round to bite you on the buttocks, yes-sah!

So tell me now, Ricardo Cordoza, who is this disgusting sodomist Bruce Elliot and why are you visiting him at full volume in the dead of night?

DARKNESS

In a way, and if I'm honest, I'm quite relieved that Boils lost it and now we're effing off to Nyanga, to his uncle's farm, or whatever is left of it. Means we'll spend the whole time fly-fishing and dopping in the blazing sun but at least we'll be off The Island and out of this shit-hole of a city. I mean, really, me and Boils have got nothing to do with this mess. Maybe I should get to South and try UK from there. Joey probably doesn't even know who I am by now. And Megan's probably shacked up with some Nigerian smack dealer. Oh Jesus, my whole stomach churns like a washing machine whenever I think of him. Joey, my little boy, my pure and helpless little angel. His tiny arms around my neck when I carry him half-asleep to his bed. The warm, milky smell of him. His little grunts and puffs and sighs as he curls up under the blankets. So trusting. So carefree. Fuck this shit. When we get back, I'm on the first plane out of here. I don't care where.

Now. What to pack? A jersey and jeans for night time – it'll be nice and cool up there. Some t-shirts. Sun cream for this pale skin. Toothbrush. Deo. Hat. Rafters. Guds. Maybe we'll head to the casino, if it's still open. Better take my smart shooters and pants in case. And of course my precious bag of weed. All set. I think I'll wait here. I can hear the shouting outside. Whenever you listen to that verandah from a distance it sounds as if people are having a punching match, shouting and calling each other fuck-face and dick-fuck and cunt-arse.

Now the shouting is a chorus. Everyone's shouting at Reggie by the sounds of it. Poor fucker. I feel bad for deserting him but he's the one who told me to go. Well, fuck him then, I'm going.

What the? It's Reggie flying past my window on his bike.

I go outside and walk straight into an awkward silence. Shum and Rachel have obviously been at it all afternoon and this Ziggy twat is, finally, feeling spare. Jill is spaced out like she just dropped a roofie and Rachel is buried in her hair fiddling with the split ends. Shum is gnawing on his nails. Ziggy is playing drums on the table.

'Where the fuck did Reggie go?'

'Dunno, man. An ice cream man cycled past and he went apeshit,' says Shum.

'Jesus. Nobody try to stop him? To help? Go with? Follow him?'

'Tried, man, but he was gone in a flash. He'll be back soon. Maybe with some lollies.'

'So you're really going?' Ziggy says nodding at me.

I dump my bag on the floor and take a seat.

'Whyn't you go with?' says Shum and he spits a piece of nail over the railings.

'Bloody hell, Shum.'

'What? He'll see the country, meet some natives. Right up his donga that is.'

'It's a single cab.'

'So? He can doss in the back. Or you homos can snuggle up front, what do you say, Ziggles? Safer if you skedaddle, wouldn't you say?'

Stardust looks at Rachel, then at Shum, then at me. No way, man. We do not want this chop spoiling our trip. Boils will hit the roof.

'Awwwwright!' he says, jumping up. 'That's a rad idea.

Lemme go get my things.' He's in his car and roaring off before you can say dick-cheese.

'Nice one, Shum.'

'I'll say,' says Rachel, perking up all of a sudden. I wonder why?

Shum puts his hand on her knee and says, 'Do us all a favour, Bart. Take one for the team.'

The only one taking anything for any team is this here trollop. But I keep that to myself. I look at Jill for help but she's like a wax dummy.

Boils's battered B2000 clatters up the driveway. Even the engine is pissed off. He screeches to a stop and leans on the hooter. Shum and Rachel ignore it. Suddenly very deaf, this lot. I go outside with my bag and chuck it into the back, careful not to mess with the fishing gear – costs more than this piece of shit Mazda. I go round to Boils's door.

'Get in, fuckface,' he shouts at me over the metal blasting from inside the cab.

'We have to wait for Ziggy. He's coming with.'

'What?'

'I said, we have to wait for Ziggy. He's coming with us thanks to Shum's generous offer.'

'Ziggy fucking Stardust? Fuck off. Cunt's not invited. Get in.' He revs the engine, gushing diesel and paraffin fumes. 'Now!' He's already in reverse and looking into his mirror.

I look back into the house. Shum is leading Rachel to his room already. Boils is lighting a smoke.

'Ag! Fuck it.'

I scoot around the front of the car and crank the door open. The car stinks of smoke and booze and sweat and grease and rotting shoes. I dig a hole in the coke cans, pie tins, chip packets, cigarette boxes and greasy car parts to make space for my feet. Boils is out the driveway and half way up the road by the time I've found the seatbelt buckle and clipped in.

'Woo-hoooooo!' He's wired. 'Nyenga-Nyenga, here we come, baby. You brought the spliff?' It's dark now and, thanks to our great country's chronic fuel shortage, the roads are empty. We fly along Samora Machel. The streetlights are out. Most are bent double or flat on the ground from drunk fucks driving into them. The whole neighbourhood is dark from load shedding. Ministry on full volume. Windows all the way down, air buffeting our heads. We're like a rocket tearing across a lake in the dead of night.

'Fuck those cunts. Fuck them all to hell.'

SADZA STEW
FOR THE SOUL

Finally. That Bog Brush fucknut has buggered off. Been hanging around like a dog's bollocks for days now. Boils and Bart have buggered off as well. Jill hasn't said a word in ages so she may as well not even be here.

I waste no time. Grabbing Rachel's hand, I drag her off in the direction of my room. I hear a very big, very obvious sigh from Jill as we head inside. What? Must we babysit? Jesus-fuck I've got a stonker already and Rachel's not exactly pulling me back.

My phone rings. Fuck. It's Reggie. Fuckity-fuck-fuck. Fuck.

What?

He's panting into the phone, can hardly breathe. Oh Jesus, Shum, thank fuck. Listen to me man, you have to get out of the house, get everyone out the house. Now. Go next door. They are on their way right now.

There's a high level of panic there and I'm skrooking already. Fuck.

Reggie? What the fuck, man?

No time, he says heaving great gulps of air. Gave them the slip but they'll be there in five minutes. Less. Let me know where you—

Reggie? Reggie?

The phone blips in my ear. Rachel is staring at me in horror. Must be the look on my face.

Jill! I run out to the verandah. Jill! Wake up, we have to get out of here. Reggie just called. We have to go.

She jerks into the present tense and looks up at me. 'What?'

We have to go. Come. Help us lock up. We're going next door. I have to pull her up out of the chair and she's bleating about Reggie, that we can't leave him and Rachel's bleating about what the fuck are we doing and I'm telling them both to shut the fuck up and do as I say as we sneak out the gate.

Look left, look right. Nothing. It's totally dark anyway. We skim along the wall. I'm listening out for cars. Fuck, we can't be seen here on the road. Sitting fucking ducks. I try the neighbour's gate. Locked. Press the buzzer. No sound. Fuck. Next house. I can hear the buzzer going in the house. No answer. Fuck.

We have to jump.

There's dogs in there.

Doesn't matter, just shout at them. Go.

You go first.

I haul myself over the fence next to the gate, wobbling like that inflatable weasel with only one arm to use. Two dogs charge down the driveway, manes bristling, barking and snarling like they want to rip me apart. I go into alpha dog mode, jump down, Jesus my arm, and I run at them shouting. They go meek. Fucking labs. Useless mutts.

Ok, it's safe. Get over here.

A madala hobbles down the driveway waving his arms and rasping some shit at me.

Sekuru. Tiri kuva atandanisa. Tsotsis. In our house, they are looking for us. We are from number 48. Up the road. We have to hide.

Rachel drops down and the dogs go off again. Me and the old man silence them.

Jill. It's fine. Come over.

The fence rattles as she climbs up. Too short. Fuck. I have to climb back over, my arm on fire, and give her a boost. Rachel helps her on the other side. I hear the angry revs of a big car so I vault over the wall and hit the ground rolling onto my arm.

A scream rips out of me.

Oh sweet fucking Jesus that hurts. I'm rolling on the ground grabbing at my shoulder and biting my fist to keep quiet. The others, I can feel, are just staring at me.

Rachel kneels and puts her hands on my head.

Shum! Shum! she's saying as the car skids to a screechy stop right in front of our house up the road.

I shush her and sit up. Fuck it hurts. We listen. The car is still idling. Doors open and close, then we hear Ziggy shouting. Fuck. Forgot about that cunt. Jesus, he better get out of there.

Anybody know his number?

The girls look at me confused then they shake their heads. I can't help feeling a little triumphant at this. Poor fucker.

He'll be in deep shit if they find him there.

Who Shum? Jill is a wreck. Shum? What's happening? Where's Reggie? She's in tears now. Rachel gives her a hug and they blub into each other's hair. Ziggy's bashing on our gate calling out our names and cussing us all to hell. Then he's leaning on the hooter and revving and pressing the intercom buzzer. Must think we all fucked off to the hills without him. Played a trick. Would have been a good trick. I hear him reversing and then tyres squealing as he screams off.

He's gone. Sekuru, can we go into the back?

The old man nods and grunts and turns and we follow him up the driveway as another car slithers past, smoother than Ziggy's fuck-wagon, less of the free-flow pornstar exhaust, more of the quiet, unhurried menace. So quiet you can hear the jacaranda flowers popping under its wheels like that bubble wrap stuff. The buzzer sounds inside our house again. Fat chance we'd let you in you cunt but he's hooting anyway. On principle it sounds like. As if he wants the whole neighbourhood to let him in. As if the whole neighbourhood ought to let him in. More angry shouting and a response this time. So there are at least two of them.

What's going on? Rachel says in a terrified whisper.

Sounds like they're going to jimmy the gate.

Doors open and close. Metal clunks on metal and there's a grinding, wrenching sound, a loud clunk and then nothing.

They're inside, probably checking on the house. More shouting and then slamming of doors and the car peels off up the road in the same direction Ziggy went a moment ago.

The silence is like a lull in the ocean that makes you look up and the water's flat after being a steady roar all day. It's a weird silence. Like the next sound is going to be much, much louder. We round a hedge and into the old man's khaya. It stinks of damp soot and woodsmoke and burnt pots and toilet.

What number is this house? Forty-two, naika?

I send Reggie an SMS with the number but it bounces back: message not delivered.

Jill is seriously freaked out here. I ask the old man's wife, gaping at us like we're fucking Martians, if she will make us tea. I gesture towards the chicks, clutching at each other like those soapstone mother-and-child sculptures for sale on every street corner. She gets the picture and sets about making a fire. The old man arranges stools for us and we plonk down around the tiny flames, smoke burning our eyes as the woman blows. Jill is snivelling non-stop now, like a burst pipe, and Rachel is making cooing noises and stroking her hair and hugging her close. I must admit: what the fuck has happened to Reggie? What the fuck is going on? Never heard him speak like that. Normally it's all, if you don't mind, and, why don't you, and how about we do this, or let's do that. This was different. Get out of the house now, he said, like he knew the future. And sure enough, they came. What the fuck would have happened if we were there? Wouldn't have opened the gate but that didn't stop them. Shit. I look across the fire at the girls. They are shit-scared and our little impromptu visit sure is making an impression on this madala and his old mfazi.

A dim light from the fire flicks across the stones and up the filthy wall and into the faces of Rachel and Jill.

Wha— what did Reggie say, Shum? says Jill through her blubs, clinging to Rachel.

He just said to get out the house, to go next door because they're coming. Said he gave them the slip. That's all he said then his phone went dead.

Gave who the slip? Shum? I'm very scared.

I don't know, Rachel. I don't know what's going on. We must wait here for him. He'll come and find us.

You sure, Shum?

Yes Jill, he'll come.

They go back to staring at the fire. The woman pours powdered milk into the pot, spoons some tea leaves in, very definite with her movements counting out the ladles of sugar.

The dogs slouch around the fire, groaning as they stretch

out and murmuring with the new excitement. The commotion dies down. One last yap from the dog next door and a car on Samora with a broken exhaust farts away into the night. A stray bark. Then nothing. The smoke twirls straight up and into the darkness. The stars are thick and bright with no moon or city lights to steal their thunder. I'm very drowsy all of a sudden.

Where's the baas and madam? I say to the old man.

Holiday, baas. Souse Africa.

Where are you from, madala?

I come from Malawi, baas. I come here since twenty-two years.

Back when Bobby McGee was trying his hardest not to destroy the country.

Baas?

What made you leave there?

Ah! Baas. It is the same that makes my children go from here. Always, there are problems.

Same old story. These okes love to complain about the troubles and problems and corruption but when it comes time to vote, they run scared or, worse, they vote the same goddam shit-stealing monkeys back in. Fucking retards.

I hear a peacock call. And again. I know that sound well.

REGGIE! I shout at the top of my voice. The dogs go berserk and Jill and Rachel squawk and flap like chickens booted from their roosting spot. The old man laughs a toothless guffaw.

Reggie! Over here.

Shum? Sounds like he's on the other side of the wall and panting like a dog. Is that you? he says.

Reggie! Jill says with a shriek, leaping up. Rachel has to grab her and shush her.

No Reg, it's fucking Desmond Tutu. Hop over. Quick. Take my bike.

The bars and saddle appear over the wall and the old man helps me get it down. Reggie scrabbles up and pokes his head over, pulling himself and kicking his way to the top.

Fuck Shum, he says. He's perched on top of the wall and the dogs are growling up at him.

Jesus, Reg. I shoo the dogs away.

He slithers down and collapses in a crumpled heap right where he lands. His head is slumped against the wall and his body is flat on the ground, legs splayed out and he's breathing heavy, like he just did three rounds with Mike Tyson.

You look like shit, Reg. What the fuck happened?

He's just lying there panting like those dogs only his tongue isn't lolling out and it's not excitement that's got him going. He's freaking me out here what with the alarming call to exodus and now this, this state that he's in. In the dark I can just make out a long rip up his trouser leg.

He looks up at Jill and says, all dazed and still out of breath: You're a lot really nice girl, Jill. He pats her knee.

For fuck sakes, Reg—

Wait Shum, Rachel says, cutting me short with a look. Just let him recover.

Listen to your wise Rachel, Shum. Rachel Wise, Rachel the Vice she talks proper knowledge, Shum.

Reg. For fuck's sakes—

Shum! Rachel and Jill shout me down in a chorus, in stereo. Fine.

Reggie's body jerks and he flicks himself sideways away from us and he's curled up on the damp paving stones, his body convulsing, vomiting, coughing and hawking.

Jesus, Reg!

We all back away. He's on all fours and crawls over to the tap. It's dry of course and Reggie collapses under it spitting up and retching and sobbing. The woman leaps up and scuttles into the khaya bringing back a bowl of water. Reggie splashes it over his face and head, sobbing into the bowl like he's going to fill it up again. Jill coaxes him back to the wall.

Tea. We need more tea. Ambuya. Tii. Ambuya?

She's dumbstruck, staring at Reggie, hand covering her mouth. The old man touches her arm and mumbles something. His voice is like a gravel gargle. She flinches, coming back to life like a spring went off in her head, and she's lighting the fire and filling the pot and pouring tea leaves into the water.

The old man hauls a massive branch from round the side of the khaya. I go and get two more and we make a huge blaze next to the cooking fire. Then he fetches a blanket and we wrap it round Reggie's shoulders. In the firelight I can see scratches up his leg, blood smearing down into his scuffed shoes. He's still in shock, shuddering every few minutes. We're all silent, watching Reggie out the corner of our eyes for signs of improvement. His breathing slows and the tremors grow further apart. He's staring deep into the fire. Gone to a galaxy far, far away has our Reggie. What the fuck happened out there?

I turn to the ambuya and tell her we're all very, very hungry, that I'll come back tomorrow and pay for everything, that she must make a double, no triple, portion of sadza for us. She chuckles, shaking her head and pats my arm. She comes out of the dark khaya with tomatoes, onions, sadza and a bunch of green leaves. The old man fixes another cooking fire and in minutes the sadza pot is steaming and the onions are frying with the tomatoes and the spinach leaves. That pungent smell wafting in the woodsmoke. I could eat a horse. We're all watching these two like it's a show. Ready Steady Cook, 'Babwe-style. I chuck more wood on Reggie's fire even though it's a warm night with not a cloud in the sky.

The tea is ready. The old man takes all our cups, rinses them and pours. Reggie wraps his cup in his blanket and holds the steaming mug to his face. The tin burns your lips if you drink too quick so we're all blowing and slurping. The sweet smell of tea and sugar and milk reminds me of childhood. Even this domestic scene takes me back. I used to scoff my nanny's sadza all the time. I wonder if they minded? I was always up there with them in the khaya at meal times. Filthy with no shoes and tatty clothes. They would always make me wash my hands first. I used to bleat but there was no point. That's how I learned Shona. Spoke Shona before I could even understand a word of English. Ha! Bet my folks were pissed off with that: bringing up a little nigger-lover. Fat chance. They probably didn't even know where I was half the time.

The water in the sadza pot boils up and the woman sets about stirring it, thumping the enamel with her wooden spoon making a clunky beat. Same technique as Rosie used; same technique every munt uses the whole country over. I check on Reggie. His face has come into focus and he's blinking again. I pull the empty cup from his hands and fill it up, shoving it back into his cradle. He looks up at me and blinks again. Good sign that: blinking.

They shot the dog, Shum.

What?

But he's gone again. Tears glint in the firelight making

red-orange streaks down his face. Jill and Rachel are huddled together just staring at him, eyes like saucers. I pat him
on his shoulders and give him a squeeze. I can feel his bony
clavicle and shoulder blade sticking through the blanket.
Suddenly he feels very skinny and brittle like I could snap
him in half with my fingers. This poor oke.

Take your time, Reg. Let's get some food in you, then
we'll talk.

This rings something deep inside him and he sighs and
there's murmurs of agreement from the girls. I am so fucking hungry I'm going to eat it all. I hope this ambuya made
enough. She laughed when I said triple dose us. Everyone
must be starving by now. And the smells. Jesus. Killing me.
The sadza is sticking to her wooden spoon in big gloops.
Nearly ready, nearly ready. The old man fetches bowls and
arranges them on the floor around the pot. The woman takes
the sadza off the fire. She pours hot water from another pot
into a bowl and takes it to each of us. We wash our hands and
flick the water off. The old man dishes out piles of steamy
white sadza with great ceremony onto each plate and adds
a moat of relish, turning the sadza into a fluffy white island
in a sea of red sauce. We pass the bowls around.

'Ha! Ha! Ha!' Reggie is rolling on the floor clawing
at the inside of his mouth. The old man and woman are
chuckling at him. He's lying on his stomach, like some fucking castaway, his suit pants in tatters, skinny little ankles
sticking out of his blanket and he's shouting, 'Hot! Hot!' I
can't help it: I pack out laughing. Rachel slaps my shoulder.
My sore shoulder. That shuts me up with a wince. Reggie
rolls back and picks up his plate.

Fuck, he says. I do that every fucking time.

We all laugh. More with relief than anything. Reggie

was freaking us out there. Normally he's Mr. Cool, Calm and Collected but this. This. Anyway. All's well. We've got him back. Rescued from the brink by a steaming bowl of sadza nemuriwo and a scalding cup of tea. Not much that combo won't fix.

We eat in silence. Pull a chunk of sadza, make a ball, fingers working fast otherwise you burn. Dip sadza ball into the relish, scoop up a blob and plop the whole lot in your mouth.

Holy fucking cunt, this is good.

Shum! Watch your language, says Rachel.

Oh, right, right. Sorry. Tasty tasty, Ambuya, tatenda chaizvo.

We munch away. Break, shake, dip and chomp. A fiery-necked nightjar coos its mantra: good-lord-deliver-us. Deliver us indeed oh lord who farts in heaven, Harold be thy name. Deliver us from the pain and suffering you've lumped upon us. What? Did we take your name in cuss-form once too often? Last straw and all that? Well tough shit. Grow up you nonce.

The stars are out in full regalia. It feels like you can pull the whole lot down like a blanket and curl up inside and sleep forever. The entire neighbourhood is pitch black but for the dancing light of our fire. Rachel is leaning up against me with her arm on my leg. She moved around to my good side, thank fuck. The fire pops, sending sparks shooting and fizzing into the night. Woodsmoke and sadza and relish fill my head, and all is silent and peaceful but for that dumbass nightjar. Jesus. Can't life just be like this? I look at the old man and the woman. They are away with the fairies, glazed unblinking eyes looking deep into the fire. If they're curious they don't show it. If they're frightened they don't show it.

Reggie wipes his mouth with his sleeve. Thanks guys, he says to us and he raises his bowl to the ambuya and the sekuru and he says, Maita basa. Ndaguta manje. He rubs his stomach and puts his plate down and claps his hands together in the silent Shona thank you. They nod and murmur tatenda back to him and go back to their communion with the fire.

Jesus, Reg. We should be thanking you. Fuckers came to our house minutes after you called. What the fuck happened out there? The guy run out of Fatsos?

He chuckles. No, not exactly. Did Boils follow through? I nod.

Hey, where's Ziggy?

Sent him packing. Told him to go with Boils and Bart but he missed the boat and fucked off home presumably.

Reggie nods. Then he looks at Jill. That recording, he says, the one with Busi in it. There was an ice cream man's bell in the background. In the beginning.

What recording? says Rachel.

When I heard it again, it hit me. Why would an ice cream man be cycling through Avondale shops? Where there's a Creamy Inn, IB's is a fucking Italian deli, plus there's the Wimpy and two supermarkets. Ice cream central basically.

And besides, when last did you even see an ice cream man? They've disappeared. No ice creams to sell, no money to buy them. So I heard that bell and clicked. Something fishy. Sure enough, round the corner he stops, unhitches his ice cream box, locks it to a fencepost and buggers off, full tilt. I followed him. He went straight to this guy's house in Greendale.

What guy?

I think it's that fucker. From the recording. Busi described him to me. He's pure evil. Those beady fucking eyes. Pock-marked face. Looks like a puffed-up toad. Shum, it's the same fucker we looked at on the memory stick. Manyoka or something.

Ugly fucker? Then what happened, Reggie?

A shudder takes him. When the convulsion ends he says: I couldn't hear so I went closer. Manyoka told Ice Cream Man to bring us all in right away so I bolted. But then, stupid cunt, they saw me and jumped into his car – the typical big black SUV. A Benz.

Yup. That was the car that came here. Then what?

Well, I didn't know what the fuck to do. I reckoned they would come straight here even if I gave them the slip. Then they'd get Busi.

Who's Busi?

She was with Maria, says Jill, coming back to life. She recorded the conversation. They nearly killed her, trying to find out about that memory stick but she knew nothing.

They raped her, Shum. Reggie's got big glistening blobs rolling down his face again. Head girl at Chisi, man. You know her, she's always out. Cool chick.

Fucking animals.

They're barbaric, Shum. Medieval savages. So I called you to get out the house then my phone died so I made for Busi's to warn her.

Another round of tea is ready. We hand our cups in. The old man fills us up and we're hunched over our steaming mugs like it's the middle of winter.

How'd you give them the slip?

Easy enough. I made as if I was coming back here. Along Rhodesville, then I ducked right at the shops and doubled back to Arcturus along the back roads. Fuck I was knackered when I got there. Busi wouldn't let me in. I had to shout fit to wake the dead. She had a carving knife to my throat. Nearly sliced me in half when I told her those cops were coming. Check here.

He pulls his collar down to show us his throat.

Nah. Pussy, there's nothing there.

Shum! Rachel says giving me a nudge.

I light another smoke. Full belly. Hot tea. Hot chick. Under the stars beside a fire with my changas, my friends, my comrades. Maria would love this. Jesus, she'd be hosing at us now. Only really realising it now but that chick was motherfucking brave I'm telling you. Look at us. Scared as rats in a barrel of piss. She's been standing up to these thieving bastards since forever. Years.

Then what?

I had to wrestle her inside. Damn that's one powerful chick.

She played basketball for Zim schools. Captain I think.

Well she nearly fucking slam-dunked me, man. I had to haul her in and pull her round the back. Chucked my bike over the wall and damn near had to chuck her as well. She was kicking and shouting and screaming and scratching at me. Lucky I'd thrown her knife away.

He rubs his throat, staring into the fire. Looks like he caught a proper skrook with that knife, man.

And then? says Rachel. She's all of sudden very interested in his story. Jill hasn't said another word. She's poked.

There was this poodle going mental, I had to throw my bike at it. You know me and dogs. We scooted round to the front. The maid was having a cadenza. I had to barge in. I buzzed the gate open and then we hid in the kiddies' room. I told the maid to tell them we went through the gate. To leave it open and tell them we went that way.

Smooth.

Fuck me, a minute later, the dog's going mental again. Busi was pissing herself. Literally. Blubbing and rocking back and forth like old Badza and pissing herself.

He takes a slurp of tea. His hands are shaking and he spills on himself.

Fuck. Next thing, BAM! Louder than that fucking bomb. No more barking dog. The maid goes benzy. She locks the door and she's yammering much better and shouting, That way. They went that way, that way, that way. And she's refusing to open the door. Probably saved our lives.

He needs a break. All that soothing sadza and tea being undone.

Take it easy, Reg. Take your time, man.

He heaves a big breath. Ya, Shum. I'm ok, now. So I told Busi to stay there. To hide somewhere in the house. I told the maid to hide her and look after her. She was a wreck. They both were. Fuck I hope they're ok. Anyway, I chucked my bike over the next wall.

He sniggers.

Landed right in front of this old geyser. He was on the phone and trying to get a look over the wall, I think. Jesus he shat himself. Told me he was calling the cops. I just roared at him like a madman and chucked my bike over his wall onto the golf course. Cut across the fairway past the cemetery and round the back trying to find you okes.

Jesus, Reg.

Those cops are gone by the way. Car's still there. Doors both wide open. Nobody's going to touch that thing.

Jill's snivel cuts the silence. I realise she's been blubbing all this time and then she just can't take it any more and

271

erupts into full bawling mode. Jesus she'll wake the whole neighbourhood.

Jill, it's okay, everything will be okay, says Reggie.

It's not okay. Everything is not okay Reggie, she says whimpering into her arms now. With a big snort she sits up and screams at us: One week. One week. That's how long I've known you lot. I met you all a week ago. Not even. She takes a fancy to someone—

Me? Me? Jill, it was you who wanted to check up on the boys, says Rachel. She does that quoting thing with her fingers. Fuck I hate that.

Jill ignores this and carries on: Next thing the fucking cops are after us. We'll probably get thrown in prison, beaten, tortured—

Reggie tries again. Jill, it's not like that, he says.

Fuck that Reggie, it is. Busi was raped. Probably for fun. Just be-fucking-cause. Do you even know me? Do you know what fucking happened to me, Reggie?

She's gone shrill, off the charts.

Jill! Rachel says, cutting her with a stern face and a fair bit of menace in her voice.

What the fuck is all this about?

Jill stands up and looks down at Reggie.

I'm sorry, Reggie, it's just that I'm worried sick here. And this has nothing to do with us. With any of us. I need the toilet.

She asks the old woman if she can use the toilet. We're all stunned into silence. There's a loud parp from inside as she empties her nose. Jesus. Jill was raped. Fuck me that's heavy. She comes out apologising to us, to the old man and his wife.

No, Jill, you're right, says Rachel trying to make her feel

better. This really has nothing to do with us. It's so fucking unfair, this whole fucking thing.

Well, hey, at least you met me. I give Rachel a headlock and she digs me in the ribs.

Fuck off, creep, she says. All things considered I'd rather not have.

I have to laugh. She's got balls this one. And a point.

Reggie? Jill says, snorting back the last of her tears and gob – surely she must be empty by now. What are we going to do?

Ya, Reg, what's the plan?

We? We? he says. We are not going to do anything. I, he says, am going to figure this out. You've been through enough already.

I chuck more wood on the fire. We've almost finished this guy's stash. I tell him I'll bring more tomorrow but he just shakes his head no. Damn, it gets me every time. These fuckers are poor as stray dogs and they give us everything. Probably their whole month's supply of sadza and tea and sugar and wood. Well they'll be getting a truckload tomorrow. Make-sure.

I ask him if he like avos. He clucks, shaking his head and says with that raspy voice: Ha! Too much.

There's a lifetime's supply from our tree that he'll be getting as well.

Thank you, says Rachel to the old man.

Clap your hands. Sideways, like this. I show her.

Thank you. Tatenda, she says again in her posh English accent, clapping hands like I showed her. The old man and woman both nod and smile and clap their hands and say tatenda back.

He claps like this, Rachel says, clapping her hands

straight.

That's how men clap. Women like this, men like this. Sign of deep respect.

And she said tatenda. Doesn't that mean thank you?

Ya, but when you say it back it's like saying it's a pleasure or thank you for thanking me. There's a hundred different ways you can say thank you but no word for please. There's also no word for sorry.

So different, Rachel says. So much we don't know about each other.

I know. That's half the fucking problem.

Shum! Rachel shoves me again.

What?

The nightjar is back. Maybe it also stopped for dinner.

Where are these guys? Reggie says to me. It's the Sharpe's house, isn't it?

Jesus, I wouldn't know. Sekuru here says they're down South. Kuff sakes. Down South. Lucky tishes.

Ya.

Reg? What the kuff now?

I don't know Shum.

Are we kuffed, Reg?

His eyes dart to Jill and he says, No, Shum, we're not.

But we are. And Reggie knows it, too. You can tell.

We listen to the nightjar. The fire pops. The old man grunts as he shifts position. We're all lost in our own fucked up little worlds.

Xanadu! Reggie shouts at me. We all jump back, even the old man. It's Xanadu! he shouts again at me standing up, throwing the blanket off. We're all looking up at him, with his crazed look made all the more crazy by the firelight below, shadows chopping up his forehead and his eyes sparkling in the glow. He's got his hands to his face, fingers circling his eyes. He looks like a midnight preacher, summoning the spirits.

What gives, Reggie?

Danazu! he says, slapping his thighs. It's Danazu.

What the fuck's Danazu? What's Xanadu? Reg? Is this another Fatso run?

Maria loved talking cabwords, too, remember? She and Boils could rap for hours and you'd never know what the fuck they were saying.

Ya, so what's that got to do with Kubla Khan? says Rachel.

It's a house in Umwinsidale, I say.

Reggie is pointing and nodding at me. That's it, that's it. He knows.

We used to cycle around there when we were kids. Fuck around at the river pretending to fish. Pretending we were in Vietnam. We'd always sing that song whenever we passed the house. That fucking song.

It must be. That's where I was supposed to take Maria's memory stick. That's all I had to do. Fuck. Sorry I mean kuff. I have to go there right now.

Reg. Reg, I say pulling at his jacket. Sit down. Take it easy. It's the middle of the night. We're safe here.

No Shum. I have to go there, now. Tomorrow will be too late. They'll find us. They'll find Busi. We'll all be fucked. All of us, he says taking in Jill and Rachel with the sweep of his arm.

Fuck, Reg.

And what then? says Jill jumping up. What then, Reg? Let's say you deliver your so-called Z-Files to this so-called Xanadu person? What then? You think they'll just go away?

Leave us alone? You've seen what's on those files. They will kill you, Reg. We need to go, Reg. We need to be getting the fuck out of this country. Now. Not chasing down some mythical safe haven.

Escape, Jill? How?

I don't know. Take your car, drive across the border. Fly to England and deliver the files right into Gordon's goddam lap if you like. I don't care, we just need to get the fuck out of here. Now. Tonight.

Reggie shakes his head at her.

They'll catch us, Jill. And besides, Maria gave that thing to me for a reason. I'm not going to. I can't—

But what if it's not this Xanadu place, Reg? What if you're wrong?

I have to try. And anyway, if I'm wrong, not a fuck they'll be looking there. I'll ride. It's the best way.

He's rolling up his trouser legs already. Buttoning up his jacket.

You can't go alone, Reggie, says Jill, panic adding a shriek to her voice.

No choice, it's the safest way. This fuck's no use with one arm and they'll be watching our house so we can't go and get a car. Cycling is perfect. I can go in the dark and take back roads, cross vleis. Really, it's impossible to follow someone on a bike without being noticed.

He's right, Jill. Trust me, he's right.

And Umwinsidale is hell and gone from here, an hour at least. Fuck, I better get going. Listen, Jill, he takes her hands and just looks at her. She's looking at him and crying. He says to her, You must both get out the country if you can. They don't know you. They aren't looking for you. You'll be safe here but not for long.

Oh! Reggie! She disappears into his arms and he has her wrapped in a bear hug. Jesus, this poor oke. This poor chick. This is all fucked up.

He eases her back and she's wiping her face.

You sort this out, Reg. Then we'll all eff off together, okay? Okay?

Deal, he says and he gives her another hug.

Shum, he says over her head. You stay here and look after these two. Do not, I repeat, do not leave until it's safe.

And how will we know, Reg?

You'll know.

Reggie thanks the old woman and the old man in perfect formal Shona of course and with perfect manners. They are impressed by the power emanating from this rabid scarecrow and grateful for the honour, you can tell. He swings his bike over the fire and wheels it down the driveway. We follow in silence. At the gate Reggie turns and puts his finger to his lips to keep us all quiet. The old man unlocks the pedestrian gate. I push the door open a crack and stick my nose out. Nothing. Silence. My heart is going like the clappers. I look and listen for a full minute. At least it feels like it. Feels like a full fucking hour but there's nothing. A dog barks. Another dog barks. Then nothing.

I pull back in and give Reggie the thumbs up. He hugs Rachel. He hugs Jill, tears pouring freely down her face and trying her hardest to be quiet. And then he hugs me. Grabs my fucking shoulder, holy Jesus's balls on a hot poker. Tears well up and pour down my face. Fuck, the chicks'll think I'm blubbing for Reg. Well I'm not. Just fucking come back, Reg, ok? Just make sure you come the fuck back, ok?

I see his face in the starlight. It's set like rock. Not a tear, no emotion, deadpan. He's a man on a mission. Like a fucking marine. Like he's in Vietnam or some shit or a suicide bomber. That's what it looks like. Like he knows this is a one-way mission. I grab him and give him a hug. I try to say something in his ear but no words come out, just a silent croak and a blub. I can't help it man, he looks so helpless, so resigned. So brave and so small in his shabby suit with his skinny legs sticking out the bottom. Jesus, I just want to tell the whole world to fuck off and leave my friend the hell alone. Fuck, Reg, please come back, please don't die. Please. Rachel tugs me back. I rub my eyes dry. Reggie looks at me like he can read my mind. And I can read his: so now we are brothers.

He pushes his bike through the gate and turns to look at us. We're all huddled together blubbing and snivelling. Reggie pushes his bike forward, hops on and pedals into the night, away from us, away from Ingocheni Island. The darkness turns him into a vague shadow and then he's gone. We stand there staring in horror at the black hole that sucked him up.

The old man locks the gate. We trudge back up the driveway. Jill is crying proper now. She put up a brave face earlier for Reg, but now it's the Zambezi in full fucking flood.

Then we hear a loud voice on the other side of the gate. Something in Shona, I missed the first bit.

Eh? the voice says, louder, cutting through the night like a flaming sword.

This isn't right.

Manje, manje, I saw him. Pabhasikoro. That voice is venomous. There's a pause and then: Eh?

He's on the phone. Someone's on the phone on the other side of the gate.

Ehe. It's him. In a suit. Eh? Ok.

278

Fuck, fuck, fuck, fuck, fuck. I grab the keys from the old man and I'm scrabbling looking for the right one.

Call him. Tell him he's being followed.

But his phone died, says Jill trying anyway.

Open the fucking lock. Fuck, fuck, fuck. Reg. Jesus, Reg. I shove the gate open and run onto the road. There's a shadow flicking through the night on a bicycle, ponderous, the guy listing heavily with each pedal, like it's one of those delivery bikes. Like one of those bikes they attach to an ice cream box. Fuck. I run down the road shouting, REGGIE!

I stop and take a big breath and whistle as loud as I've ever whistled in my whole fucking life. And I'm shouting to wake the dead. My throat closes and I scream and scream and scream his name until my voice fails and I can't breathe and my head is about to explode.

I feel a touch on my arm. I jump. It's just Jill. She looks like a terrified child, eyes popping out her face.

Shum? We have to save him, Shum.

I CAN BE YOUR DEMON, BABY

My car. That ice cream guy was watching our house and now he's gone.

Rachel! Jill! Come. We're going to mow that fucking cunt into the ground.

I can't help but feel a little glee at the prospect. I break into a run.

The gate's buggered. Jacked off its rails with just enough space to squeeze through. Every dog in the neighbourhood is barking full volume and outside lights are blipping on all over the place. Not that it matters, our cover was blown long ago.

Rachel's dragging her feet. She should stay behind anyway. Jill's right behind me. I chuck the keys at her and she's looking at me confused.

Shoulder's fucked, can't drive. We need to wrench the gate.

Jill hits double-panic mode and scuttles round to the driver's side. She's tiny: barely reaches the window. She is shaking, trying with two hands to get the key in the ignition and fumbling, fumbling, fumbling. A gibbering mess.

Jill! I shout at her.

We have to save Reggie, Shum, we have to save Reggie.

Look at me Jill.

She stops and looks.

I also love him so you need to calm the fuck down.

She blinks at me. That got through.

They're on bikes, Jill. Reggie's mountain bike is way faster than a messenger bike and we have a car. They want to find out where he's going, Jill, so he's safe till they get there. We also know where he's going so we can head them off. Do you understand me, Jill? Forget about driving fast. Concentrate on driving. Ok? Ok?

Christ she's freaking out on me.

Deep breaths, Jill.

Ok, ok, ok, ok, she says hyper-venting. She gets the key in and starts the car and it clunks forward.

Clutch, clutch. It's in gear. Deep breaths, Jill. Take it easy, we've got plenty of time.

She stops, takes a deep breath, closes her eyes and tries again. The engine screams as she floors it into the red. She's looking for the light switch. I twist the stick and the lights blaze down the driveway.

Ok, now drive up to the gate. We're going to pull it with the winch so leave enough space. Go, go, go.

The car bunny-hops down the driveway to the gate and I trot after. I have to lean in and turn the winch on then pull the cable. Fuck it's slow, it's so fucking slow. I latch it on the top and give Jill the thumb. The cable whips tight as it grinds back. Jesus I'm going to get squashed. I jump into the passenger side and we watch the thing groaning and straining.

Use the car. Reverse, I say. Reverse the fucking car Jill. Pull the fucking gate down Jill for fuck sakes. Chicks. She gets the message and we're edging back and the cable is tight and the gate is buckling at the top and then it goes. A grating, grinding, crunching crash of steel and it whumps to the ground with a bounce.

Jill lets out this monster shriek.

Bleached white and squinting into the headlights, two figures walk towards us. It's Rachel and the Mad Cop. Her head is bent away from the gun pressing into her temple.

Rachel! screams Jill. I grab her arm.

Wait, Jill.

What? Shum? Oh shit, shit, shit, shit.

Shush, Jill. Let's see what he wants. We have to play this very, very cool. If one of us can get away, we must. Xanadu is on Umwinsidale Road. It's left off Enterprise just after that garage with the wavy roof, ok? Ok, Jill?

Yes. Yes, Shum. Oh Rachel, she wails.

The cop is smiling, blinking into the lights like he's on a stage. Rachel is a rag doll limp in his grip. He's shaking her like a trophy, like he just won the FA Cup. Her hair is ruffled and her dress whips her legs as she staggers to keep her footing.

I jump down from the car. Mad Cop laughs.

I found a waif. Or is it a stray? Or is it a waif and stray? Or even a stray waif? I like the sound of that: a stray wife. Hey! he says shaking Rachel, You fancy being my stray wife, hmmm?

Officer?

Officer? Officer? I am no officer. I am a street sir, a car sir, a cemetery sir, a night prowler sir. You'll find me anywhere but the office. Office sir? Were you inviting me into your office? Cup of tea perhaps?

Fuck.

Wassamatter? Run out of tea? Keep your hands up, I liked them there, he says as he waves at me with his gun. Better than at Rachel's head. Both hands, he says.

This arm's broken.

282

And what about your chauffeur, sir? Your chauffeur-sir. Ha-ha-ha! This office-sir wants to know is your chauffeur-sir planning on stepping out of the vehicle some time this evening?

I nod to Jill. Snivelling, she opens the door, the latch making an obscene sound in the silence. The cop tilts his head to watch. She turns and raises her hands.

Officer, please—

I was just explaining to your colleague here that I am no officer. No. No sir or should I say ma'am. I am neither office sir nor office ma'am. Get inside all of you.

He shoves Rachel forward and waves the gun at us.

Uh-uh. That side. You come around this way. Everyone by the strong man's side, nice and safe. His tongue flicks out and he says, Mr. Strong Man going protect you nice nice.

Ma'am?

Yes sir, please, we have to save our friend.

Nonsense, dear. He's quite capable of looking after himself, aren't you my friend?

He pokes the gun into my back.

Not him, sir, our other friend. He's in serious danger.

There's a loud noise inside my head. Now pain. Stars flick into my eyes. Pistol-whipped. The fucker just pistol-whipped me. My head is pounding and he yanks me back with a handful of shirt and hisses into my bleeding ear, And you think this one isn't?

He shoves me forward and says, In the house, quick as you can, leeeeeeefft march, left, left, left.

He swings his free arm high and marches ahead, chanting all the way to the front door where he turns to face us. The taillights cast a red sheen over everything.

Look. Officer, I say. Got to try.

Look? See? Hear? Smell? Taste? Touch? Are you telling

me to use my senses Mr. Strong Man? Am I not using all my senses?

I'm sure you are, officer, but—

The cop cocks his gun and shoves it under my chin, this time with a handful of shirt front. He puts his face right into mine, eyes bulging, his chest pressed against mine. I'm off balance and he yanks me back.

Call me officer one more time and I'll—

What? What? You'll kill me?

No, he says and he points the gun at Rachel who has shrivelled into a stick insect in the red light. I'll kill her, he says baring his manky teeth.

Then something strange happens. He ducks, looking about him like something's going to fly at him. He hides the gun behind his back and steps away from us. He stands to attention like he's on parade and shouts at the sky: Ndiri chete kuyedza ku tyisa ivo.

He's only trying to scare us? What the fuck?

Inside! he shouts at us.

What the hell was that all about? Who the fuck was he talking to?

Jill! Keys, I say and I hold out my hand. She stares blank at me, twigs, blinks and hands me the car keys. My hands are shaking as bad as Jill's. I stop, take a deep breath and slot the key in. I open the door and flick the lights on.

I see you have ZESA. You murungus are very organ-ised, yes. Stealing our ZESA for yourselves. Does it make you happy to see us living in darkness? he says ushering Jill inside after me. He pushes Rachel towards the door grabbing her arse.

Kutarira chete, he calls out at the top of his voice and follows us inside. Again in Shona. Again up at the sky.

284

What the fuck? Rachel skips away from him and presses against me.

Kitchen, kitchen, he says waving his gun. And keep those arms up ladies and gentlemen, we don't want any hanksy panksy now, do we?

We sit at the kitchen table. The cop is standing looking down at us with his hands on his hips, the gun pointing out sideways and down to the floor.

Sir. We have to save our friend, Jill says, pleading, with the tears pretty much constant now.

And why should I— He bends over double and bites his fist with a groan. Why should I— He eats his fist again and has another go: Gnnnnnnnnnnn, why should I—

Because of the ngozi, I say. Fuck knows how I remembered that word.

The cop stops, unbends himself and stands straight staring at me with a mixture of fear and wonder. Good. That worked. Jesus it was a long shot.

The curse? What do you know about a curse?

Demons. Demons everywhere. I give him a hiss and wave my arm around. In the trees, in the sky, in the grass, in your hands. In your head. I know. I know all about the demons in your head.

What? What do you know?

The cop grabs my shirt, the gun pressing into my temple. He shakes me and says, What do you know?

Easy shamwari. I push the gun away. You kill us, you will have a lifetime of hell and when you die... I laugh, shaking my head. When you die, you'll wish you were in hell. That's what I know about the demons, shamwari. You've been cursed by the most powerful n'anga on Earth and our friend, Reggie, is the only one who can lift that

285

curse. Because this is his house. You let him die, you'll be haunted for the rest of your life. And forever after.

It sinks in. He looks away. The gun drops to his side and his shoulders droop.

He looks at me. Where is he, then? He puts the gun to my head and cocks it.

Do it.

Rachel screams, No! Shum! and Jill is trying to hold her back. Good. That's good. Adds to the effect.

Do it. Pull the trigger.

Fuck, he might just do it still. I am looking deep into his eyes. They are black holes, like the hole Reggie disappeared into. He wants to pull that trigger. He's thinking about it. He's imagining my head splattered on the wall. He's imagining the tormented hallucinations he's just had. Then he goes Heeeeeeeeeeeee! Heeeeeeeeeee! Heeeeeeeeeeeee!

You kill me, the demons will take you forever, I shout over his wailing. I stand up and roar at him with all my heart: You kill me, they kill Reggie and the curse will never be lifted. Do it. Do it you motherfucker.

I can't explain but I kind of want him to do it. To send him over the edge.

Do it you fuck, I scream and my gob sprays his face. Got him in the eye and he's blinking it away. The cop looks at Rachel. Then at Jill. Then at me pressing my head into his gun. I feel the muzzle ease off my head. He un-cocks and the gun falls to his side. His shoulders slump. He slides down the cupboard and folds up on the floor. The gun clatters on the tiles in his limp hand.

Your friend is dead, he says staring straight ahead.

WHAT! Both girls shrieking in concert.

No! No he is not. I will take you, I say, shaking his

shoulder. I know where he is going. I will not tell you where but I will take you.

The cop looks up.

Shum? says Rachel. I look back at her. She holds my gaze, reading my mind I guess, figuring it out, until a tear spills over and down her cheek. She sits down again, staring at nothing and with a dying look about her.

I turn back to the cop and shake him. Leave the girls here, they have nothing to do with this. Take me. Take my truck. Now. Before it's too late.

The cop is limp and then his head snaps up and he says, How do you know he is alive?

I was with him not two minutes before you showed up. I watched him cycle into the night, followed by the Ice Cream Man.

Ice Cream Man? he shakes his head. Who is this? Never mind. Let's we go.

He waves his gun at the girls and says to me, Where are your cable ties?

What?

Cable ties. Fetch me some. Now, he says, and he presses the gun into my shoulder. I can feel my legs giving way and the needles of light flash in my face like a strobe. Oh! Fuck me, that hurts. He takes the gun away. Cable ties, he says standing up and dusting off his trousers. This house is a pig sty.

Wait! Everybody up, we go together.

Fuck, we're wasting time. I dig around in the bottom drawer. Saw some here the other day. There.

A bit small, don't you think? The cop winks at Rachel and laughs.

In there. He waggles his gun at the lounge.

Rachel and Jill stand next to the security gate.

Put your arms through, come on, come on, we haven't got all night, he says to Rachel. She's teleported herself to another planet. Put your arms through the railings like this.

He clasps a cable tie around Rachel's wrist and zips it tight. He links the next cable tie through the first and around her other wrist zipping it tight. Jill copies Rachel.

Good girl, you very good girl, he says, zipping up the cable ties around her wrists. Maybe you be my stray wife after all this, hey. He grabs a handful of tit and then screams out, whipping his hand away like he just touched a hot stove.

Feet, feet, he says pointing with his gun.

He doubles up the cable ties and zips their ankles together and attaches them to the bars.

We don't want cell phones now. Who knows what mischief you'll get up to while I'm gone. Prank calls to the police and what-what. Mustn't waste their time now must we?

He pats them both down, groping as he goes, fishing out their cell phones and Rachel's car keys.

Get me some rags. We don't want them keeping the neighbourhood awake with their screams now do we? Must be good citizens.

He follows me into the kitchen and watches as I dig around for a dishcloth.

I hope these are clean? We don't want dirty rags in their lovely mouths now do we? He makes a deal of gagging them, asking if it's too tight, too loose, just right? Rachel looks at me with petrified eyes over the gag.

It'll be fine, Rachel. Everything's going to be fine, I say.

Yeah, right. We're fucked.

Checking over his handiwork he says, Good. Now you.

Me?

Yes. I'm driving. Your hands.

He wrestles my hands together and locks a cable tie over my wrists. The pain shooting out of my shoulder is like a branding iron.

Keys?

In my pocket. I give him an evil smile. Jesus I want to bite his fucking head right off. Have a grope. I dare you.

He eyes me sideways and digs in my pocket as though I've got hooks in there. Cunt.

***

The headlights dim as the cop starts the car. The engine catches and he revs it up like Jill did, redlining it and holding it there.

Toyota. Nice, he says grinding the car into first gear and bumping over the flattened gate. Mmm-mm, those are some fine looking women you've got there, my friend. Mighty fine looking women.

That way. I nod right.

Not into the idle chit-chat? I like a bit of chitting and chatting while I drive. It makes the journey so much more pleasant. Say, what do you do for a living, err, Shum? Why do they call you Shum anyway?

Because I always say shamwari. Left.

Okey dokey. What a funny expression, okey dokey. What do you think it means?

No idea. Are you really going to drive with that gun in your hand?

Of course. You were saying?

What?

289

What you do for a living, shamwari.

I'm not your fucking shamwari. Right.

Ah! But you say everyone's your shamwari.

I'm a PH. Left.

A PH? Like a doctor?

No. Professional Hunter. Straight.

Eh! You hunt? You kill things? You have demons?

No, I don't.

So you are a game ranger?

Something like that. Keep going till the circle.

I'd like to be a game ranger.

You should. Then you can rape hyenas.

He smashes the gun into my ear. The same fucking ear. Jesus-fuck that hurts. But this is piss, I can take it.

Watch out Mr. Professional Hunter. I can be your demon if you want it. Do you want it?

Cunt's singing one of those gay boy-band songs: I can be your demon, baby.

Do you want it?

No.

Good.

He's driving like a slug. These fucks.

This better not be a wild goose chase just to save your pretty damsels.

What if it is? What are you going to do? I say. And then I shout, Uraya ini?

The cop ducks his head and his eyes dart about looking for the demons.

Let me put it to you this way, Mr. Ricardo Cordoza, sister Paula, father Miguel, mother Betty and pet dog Sharky. I won't kill you but there are plenty of professional hunters – just like me and you – who will. Now. Is this a wild goose chase?

No. I want to save my friend. Why would I take you on a goose chase?

Good answer and now back to some chit-chat. You like music?

Fuck. I'm going to smash this cunt's head through the windscreen.

I said, you like music, shamwari?

No.

Oh, come come, you sure liked Tuku at that funeral, hey?

I look at him. He sits low and small in this huge car, his hands at eye level on the steering wheel, grinning at me like a rabid skeleton as we bounce over the potholes and patches of Enterprise Road down the hill past Oriel Girls. The cop laughs to himself as he guns past a bus, belching black smoke, its back wheels trying to overtake the front. An oncoming car flashes at us and pulls off the road, the driver leaning on the hooter and pumping his fist out the window. The cop laughs and hoots back. I try to put my seatbelt on but I can't. The cop laughs at me.

It's ok shamwari, I passed my advanced defensive driving course.

Right.

How much further?

Ten minutes.

Let's we have some music.

He switches on the radio. On comes AC/DC full blast. Highway to Hell. The cop swerves in fright, scrabbling for the off button.

Yes. I see you don't like music after all, he says clenching the wheel.

EXITUS ACTA PROBAT

Of course you know him, this limp-wristed, pillow-biting, nancy-boy Bruce Elliot. You weren't exactly quiet and you damn near killed my best man on your way to his house.

What a strange name is that? Bruce Elliot. Two first names. Interchangeable front to back, back to front. Oh! Come now, do not play the koi with me. That one feigned ignorance for a while and now look at him. You know this man-girl and, I should say, you know him-her carnally actually.

I shock you? Ho! Ho! Ho! My dear boy.

Exitus acta probat. Do you know this phrase? It is Latin, actually, so of course you do not know. The end justifies the means. And I am skilled in said means. Skilled in the ancient art of knowledge extraction.

Chikomo. Tea. And biscuits. I'll wager our pudgy dandy-man has some delicious Dutch cookies stashed in his cupboard, no? Let's we just give this one a dose of ice water. Such a mess. At least it washes away the blood.

Now let me tell you a story while we wait for my tea. I was in Korea. North Korea, or should I say the Democratic People's Republic of Korea, where they do things properly. Total civilian control, much like religion actually. First comes the neural re-wiring: an absence of pain, hunger, fear is pleasure in itself and none are more eager to please than the pathetic inmates of a North Korean gulag, let Baba M. assure you of that.

Then comes the genetic re-coding: out with compassion, in with obedience. A mother will drown her own newborn on command. Is that not the most incredible story you will ever hear? And yet it is true, I witnessed it myself. A single bubble breaking the surface to indicate the job is done.

Those Koreans. But don't cry my friend, the child was mere rape-spawn and of no use to anyone.

And we traded secrets would you believe? Those noble Koreans and myself, yes indeed, they were eager to learn more of the Mamba Scream and of course my Mamba Scream Mark Two. My Snake Queen, whose charms got this one squealing like a pig, singing like a canary, bleating like a lamb and begging like a leper. He of course told me everything so you are just here for corroboration, for colour. For certainty.

Ah! Tea. Thank you my good sir. And the biscuits?

DIPLOMATIC
IMPUNITY

I am losing it here. This cunt's been driving Miss Daisy, jabbering about fuck-all the whole way. He's gone penga for sure. Boils fried his pip good and proper. What little pip he ever had. Ice Cream Man probably caught up with Reggie by now or he called that SUV-cunt, the beady fucker that Reg was talking about, and they headed him off. But hang on a sec. I said something to Jill that made sense. What was it? Think, you cunt. Think. They didn't know where he was going. They wanted, yes that's it, they wanted to know where he was going, so they could be there as well. They might have let him get to Xanadu and then waited for him to go in and followed him and... Jesus.

Hey! I say, interrupting his drivel. Can't you drive any faster? This is my car and I know it can go above forty.

He looks sideways at me, pouting and gripping the wheel tighter.

Advanced defensive driving. Speed is thine enemy. Speed kills. And anyway what's the rush all of a sudden?

I need to shit.

Pah! Disgusting. You can wait till we get there.

I know, that's why I'm asking you to hurry. Sir.

Sir? How is it respect comes from those in need to those in possession. Yes, sir.

Whatever. Just hurry the fuck up, shit-for-brains.

Woo-ooo! Mr. Shum gone crazy.

He eases his foot off the gas. We're in fifth doing thirty. He's going to stall, the stupid plug. I have to keep my cool here or I'll fuck this whole thing up.

That's better, Mr. Shum. Self-control. We will get there in good time and in one piece.

The outskirts of town drift by like we're on a boat – a fucking canoe being paddled by a lobotomised baboon. Most of the houses are in darkness as usual with the occasional light poking through the trees and hedges and massive walls. Not a single streetlight of course and we haven't seen another car since Chisi.

Left here. After the bend.

He slows down. Fuck. You can't drive any slower you cunt. He indicates. There's not a fucking car in sight. He checks his mirrors. He's braking. We are going to stall. He stalls. The engine clunks on the driveshaft and this idiot's head thonks the steering wheel.

Ah! Jesus.

He jams it into first and starts up – still in gear – and the engine pulls us up the road while it turns, tyres spinning on the loose stones and we're thrown back as it catches on the tar. This retard is giving it the full buffalo stare, looking very much ahead into the distance.

What number?

I don't know, it's a house called Xanadu.

Xanadu? Now there's a song. There's a band. The day you murungus turned your backs on ABBA was the day you turned your backs on civilisation.

How's that?

And he's singing fucking Xanadu. Can you believe it?

ABBA didn't sing Xanadu you cunt. It was Olivia Newton John, but that's ok, she's also a gay icon.

He smashes my face with the gun. Connects me on the cheekbone. Holy fuck it gets to be that you can't take any more of this shit. I clench my jaw. Shut up Shum, don't say a fucking word. I want to rip his stupid head off. I want to skull-fuck this hairless ape. Keep it together, Shum.

How dare you decry the work of Samuel Coleridge and the genius of ABBA.

The road narrows to a single lane and winds through msasa trees closing over like a tunnel and we're back at Waterworld on the tubes only at the bottom it's not a nice cool splash in a sparkly swimming pool and giggling girls in bikinis and sunshine and soapies. Instead it's, it's what? Just what the fuck is at the end of this ride? A great black mouth with giant fangs and a forked tongue and flames blasting from its nostrils.

In Xanadu did Kubla Khan
A stately pleasure-dome decree.

He's reciting now? What the fuck? And he knows the whole thing.

Where Alph, the sacred river ran
Through caverns measureless to man
Down to a sunless sea

Where the fuck did that come from? How the fuck does this idiot know poetry? Does he think it makes him civilised? Educated? Refined?

Where a monkey in silk he did see.

Come again?

Nothing. Right. Here it is on the right.

Well, well, well. If it isn't the Dutch ambassador's private residence. Well, well, well indeed.

A guard sidles out of his hut and shines a torch in Mad Cop's face. The cop flips his badge and says open up. The guard says, Aikona. Instructions to not let anyone else in.

Else? So Reggie made it. My stomach leaps into my mouth. He made it. And this is Dutch soil. He's safe. Holy fuck, Reggie, you made it.

The cop chuckles to himself. He points his gun at the guard and says, Let us in, sir, or you'll end your shift in a body bag. Then he's swatting about his head going Heeeeeeeee! Heeeeeeeee! Heeeeeeeee!

The guy bricks it and bolts back into his hut. Fucking sadza soldiers.

The gate clanks and slides open. The cop revs the balls out my car and mounts the incline and then we drop down a steep driveway that stops at eye-level with an enormous kitchen window. These Umwinsidale houses are all like that: carved out of the steep hills, their back windows are at ground level. There's Reggie sitting at the kitchen table, talking to a fat man. They look up at our car lights. Reggie freezes. You can see the dread on his face, in his entire body, from here. The fat man leaps up and his silky robe swirls about his legs as he emerges from the back door. The cop swerves left into the floodlit parking area under a flamboyant tree and this fat guy's shouting at us and shouting up the hill at the security guard.

Clarence. I said nobody else.

Clarence shouts down the hill: But he's policeman, sah, and he's got a gun, sah.

A gun? Clarence that's your job, you idiot. To stop people with guns from entering my house.

Then he says to Mad Cop all blustering and important: Who the hell are you and what the hell are you doing in my house? May I remind you this is Dutch territory and I'll have you arrested, whoever you are.

He's waving his arms about and huffing and puffing and yanking on the cord of his robe tightening it around his balloon-belly.

No need for the police, sir. I am the police. Here is my badge. I have brought with me a criminal and that one in there is also a criminal. I have come to rescue you.

Rubbish. He is no criminal. They are not criminals. What do you want?

Mad Cop jumps down from the car and walks right up to the fat man and slaps him across the face. Then he ducks down like bats are attacking him and he's going Heeeeeeeee! Heeeeeeeee! Heeeeeeeee! And he shouts up at the sky: Ku tyisa iye chete.

Reggie is at the door staring in horror at Mad Cop.

It's okay, Reg, I tell him. He's here to have his curse lifted. He won't do anything to us until the curse is lifted.

Jesus Shum, Reggie says, his voice croaky and eyes watering. He helps the fat man to his feet.

Inside. All of you, says the cop.

Just do as he says, Reg. He's harmless.

Harmless? Harmless you say? He jabs me in the kidneys with his gun. Jesus-fuck I am going to gouge this fucker's eyes out. He shoves me forward and I trip down the stairs into the kitchen: black and white tiles, bright neon light and two cups where Reggie and the fat man were sitting.

Sit. All of you. Mr. Ambassador, where are your cable ties?

What? What for? Now look here.

He steps up to the fat man, and he's heeeee-ing and ducking and swatting at his head and heeeee-ing.

I've got some.

The cop turns to me and says, Come again?

In the car, behind the seat.

He makes us all go out again.

There, behind the seat, I tell him.

I step back and he grabs a handful and marches us back into the house.

Now. Sit. Hands behind.

He clamps Reggie and the bleating Fatty to their chairs, checking their pockets and jabbering nonsense about Kubla Khan's stately dome and higher powers, and Reggie, you can tell, is spooked. Holy shit, the memory stick? What the fuck did Reggie do with it?

Oh sorry, Mr. Shum, I'm sure that hurts. But it's a fact of life, you have to crush some grapes to make wine.

Do your worst, buddy. You dug your grave a long time ago and I am going to rip you to fucking pieces. Then the spirits will get you.

Look, the fat man says, his chest heaving, just what do you want? Nobody here has broken the law. When the foreign minister hears of this, Sergeant, Sergeant whatever your name is, you will be in a maelstrom so big you won't know which way is up.

Oh, I always know which way is up. It's where the light of Jesus comes from.

BAM! A gunshot – could only be a gunshot – echoes across the valley, cracking and whipping through the silent night. And then nothing. The cop stops. Like a street-mime, his eyeballs roving the kitchen for a likely source. Then the gate clanks open and car lights blast our faces as a black

299

SUV glides down the hill and skids to a stop under the tree.

Oh, Jesus, says the cop. Oh, Jesus. It's the boss.

He trots out of the kitchen.

Good evening, sir, good evening. I have found them, sir, and incarcerated and incapacitated them for you, sir, ready and waiting. I have been chasing their tails for some days now. Very hard work. Tricky customers these. I have indeed conducted a full body search and found nothing, sir.

This fucker in a shiny suit comes round from the passenger's side. He stops in front of Mad Cop, calls him a damn-fool and says something about this being all his fault for losing Maria. His goon punches the cop in the throat, drops him with a knee to the balls and then follows his boss into the kitchen.

It's Manyoka. I recognise him from Maria's files. More like Nyoka with those snake-eyes. They skulk around his head and then lock on Fatso. Reggie nods at me, just a tiny nod. As if he needed to. Mad Cop staggers into the kitchen clawing at his throat and hawking like a cat with a fur ball.

Who are you? Where's Clarence? says Fatso twisting round trying to see up towards the gate.

So, Ambassador, the filthy rats have led me all the way to their stinking little hidey-hole and, dear me, what a stir this will create: the Dutch government colluding with terrorists to bring down the democratically-elected government of a sovereign state? Whatever next?

For the last time, who are you and what have you done to Clarence?

Tsha! Such manners, Ambassador. I am a pilgrim. I come seeking knowledge, enlightenment and fulfilment, Mr. Joseph Bergman, he says and those eyes close like he's meditating.

Or should I call you Danazu? The eyes open and fix on Fatso with a triumphant sneer.

Fatso's face whips back like he's been slapped by a priest.

Jesus, what is this? Reggie is shitting himself. Keep your head, Shum, keep your head. This is the bush: ellies, buffs, shumbas, hyena, fucking hyena. You know what to do.

Sergeant! says Snake-eyes and Mad Cop snaps to attention. You have searched their person through and through?

Yes, sir! he says with a stomp.

Good. Now take these, these pigs, these filthy excrement-eating dogs to another room and guard them while Mr. Hove and I discuss this small matter of state security. Treason and so forth.

Holy fuck. Treason? Jesus Christ Reggie? Fuck.

Mad Cop levitates into an elaborate salute and spins around. He drags Fatso, his chair screeching on the tiles, down the passageway. You can hear the guy bleating and squealing all the way. Then he's back and dragging me out the kitchen.

Snake-eyes straddles a chair and he shoves his ugly, fat face right into Reggie's and he says, I have just only one question for you my friend: do you know what is a green mamba?

MARONDEADLOSS
AND BACK

Boils is nodding off. I slap his shoulder.

'Hey! Stay awake. Imagine we peg, fleeing the scene?'

'We're not fucking fleeing, you fuck.'

Oh shit, I've set him off again.

'Those fucks shut us out.'

He's been at it for a solid hour since we left. That's how I knew he was dozing off: the sudden silence.

'We fucking fix the whole fucking thing and what do we get? Fucking stonewalled. Fuck them.'

Sigh. The countryside looms ever darker as we climb into the hills. Bushes and trees flick into Boils's wonky headlights. The road races towards us from the blackness and bugs zuck the windscreen. The wipers only smear their goo further and I have to duck down to see out. Boils is hunched over the wheel like he's straining against some invisible bungee cord.

I can't believe we're on our way to Nyanga. It's the middle of the fucking night and Boils is hammered. Of course he insists he's fine to drive. I feel bad that we deserted those guys but Boils is right: they all but told us to clear off. Reggie himself said go. So. Stuff them. We are surplus to requirements, excess baggage, dead weight.

'Vig us a dop,' he says.

'No Boils, you've got to sober up. At least till we get to Rusape, then I'll drive and you can dop.'

'Fine. Roll us a flips then.'

'Jesus, Boils.'

'Fine. Fuck you. Fuck this.'

We drive on in silence. Well, silence as in not talking. The music is so loud we can't talk anyway. Just the occasional shouting match. He's picked the heaviest of heavy metal he can find. It's just noise. Some troll eating the mic and screaming guitars and it's all torture and murder and rape. I turn it down. Boils scowls at me.

'Come on, Boils, it's giving me a fucking headache.'

'Jesus but you're a pussy, Bart.'

I look out the window. Nothing you can do when Boils gets in a mood like this.

'Oh ya, have a big sulk. Fuck you.'

He lights a smoke, veering into the middle of the road. Car lights flicker through the trees around the bend up ahead. Just my luck. He veers further. He's on the other side now. I know he's doing this on purpose. If I ignore him, he'll think he can get away with it; if I shout at him, he'll call me a pussy. I'd rather not give him the satisfaction.

'So,' I say to distract him, 'what do you think's going to happen to those guys, anyway?'

'Those guys? Who? You mean your fucking faggot friends from Ingocheni Island, the Island of Insanity in a Sea of Fuck-you-ness? They'll get thrown in jail, they'll get butt-fucked and they'll die of AIDS.'

'Or suicide.'

'Ya, maybe that.'

I can't see it. My brain refuses to see Reggie and Shum in jail. But it's also trying very hard to make me see them in jail. Trying to see them barefoot in filthy rags, in a putrid prison cell with fifty other filthy prisoners, shit and piss and blood on the floor, a frozen concrete floor they all have to sleep on, fifty to a cell. A spoonful of grey gloop for food. Lice, fleas, flies, TB, AIDS, cholera, dysentery, typhoid, starvation. Fights, stabbings, rapes. Jesus. Somehow all of a sudden my brain is letting me see them in jail.

'Boils.'

'What?'

I turn the music off.

'Boils. We have to go back.'

'What? Have you gone full pussy? Fuck them.'

We're driving through a canyon of gum trees, ears ringing in the sudden silence, past Watershed, down, up, down, round the bend, over the railway line. There's Marondera up ahead. The town is in total darkness. People walking, some drunk and staggering, women carrying huge bags on their heads, kids in tow. A few lights poke out the houses. The hotel is bursting with drinkers lit by dim naked bulbs. These are the fat cats drinking clear beer like a status symbol. The povo are dopping skuds in township shebeens.

We thump through the potholes, the mass of people parting just enough to let us through. There's filth everywhere. Plastic bags, flattened tin cans, boxes. A derelict petrol station. When last was that place in business? Shops are all barred and boarded up, paint peeling off in plates, signs faded to nothing. In the empty car park, a donkey attached to a cart waits for the second coming.

'Jesus. What a shithole.'

'Marondeadloss. I need to piss.'

'Wait till we get through town, man.'

'Fuck that. These munts will piss on their own babies.'

He pulls over, bouncing off the tar and onto the bumpier verge. I whack my head on the window as I'm thrown sideways. He's pissing into the ditch, smoking a cigarette and using his farting, gurgling car for support. The stream of people pass us by without a second glance. They are all looking down, grim, avoiding eye contact. This is not normal. Normal is these guys laughing and chatting and shouting but the town is eerie with indifference. It's making me nervous. These guys have nothing. They could drop us in two seconds and take off with Boils's car never to be found again. Why don't they? I would.

'Jesus, donkey-fucker, that feels good. Must be a Guinness world record for the longest piss ever.'

He rams the car into gear and we bounce back onto the road and push through the throng. There's a massive crowd on the edge of town all trying to hitch rides. To where? To their villages, to their homes, far away from the dead cities. Boils hoots and flashes his brights rapid-fire. 'Off the road you stupid cunts. Does it even look like I'm going to stop?'

And then we're in total darkness again. Just us and the few metres of road lit up by Boils's buggered lights.

'Besides,' he says out the blue, 'what fucking help can we be, anyway?'

'I don't know. But we've sure been pretty damn useful up to now, wouldn't you say? I mean, first we kept that party going while Reg and Shum went off on their bikes to fuck-knows-where. Then we spiked those cops. Wait, wait, wait: first you spiked them with shroom tea on the very first day, remember?'

'Ha! Fuck me, what I wouldn't give to see those stupid cunts tripping like it was the demons come to get them.'

'Well we did see them. In the cemetery.'

He's chortling and chortling to himself. Getting to the point where he can't stop.

'Ya-ya. We fucked them up, but we only saw the after-effects of that trip.'

'But then you spiked their cokes. Again.'

'That!' he says thumping the steering wheel. 'Now that was proper good humour. Those fucks tripping a second time. Oh, Jesus, they must have died. You know what? I reckon they probably did die. They probably crawled off into the bushes where they came from and curled up and died. Like dogs.'

'Motherfuckin' terrified dogs.'

He cackles some more.

'I don't know. I just feel like we're making things worse, not better. Like we need to stick together.'

'Jesus, Bart, you're a fucking stuck record. Dr. fucking Phil on repeat: "We need to help them, we need to thtick together."'

'Well? What of it? That's what friends do, man.'

'Friends? Fuck that. What friends?'

'Bullshit, Boils.' I have to shout over the engine noise and the buffeting wind. 'You don't know half of it. Did you even notice Shum sticking up for you against those fucks, Frotter and Sykes? Do you see how everyone takes care of you, puts up with you more like, when you OD on a booze-a-thon? You've got no idea, man. Those guys are your fucking friends for life whether they want to be or not. That's the thing with friends: you don't get to choose, they just happen. You spend long enough with someone, they become your friend. That's all there is to it. And I know for a fact those guys would do fucking anything for us. Anything. That's how friends are.'

'Oh! Christ, listen to fucking Hail Mary over here. Friends stab each other in the back, is what they do.'

'Fine, Boils, have it your way, but if something happens to them and we're not there.'

He looks at me. I look at him clinging to the steering wheel, and then out the side window at the trees disappearing into the blackness. My head hurts.

'We did fix those cops good and proper, didn't we?'

I can't help but laugh. 'Their faces. Schuster could not dream up anything close.'

'Schuster's pusster,' says Boils. 'That was pure slapstick genius. Next level. And Shum pissing in his pants, oh my fucking God I think I sharted.'

'You what?'

'I farted and shat at the same time. Checked some lakka skid-marks when I got home. I swear if you tell those fuckers, I'll kill you.'

'Boils, those fuckers, as you so lovingly call them, are no longer ours to call fuckers. It's over, can't you see? We've ditched them. They could get killed. Or worse: sent to jail. Do you know what a Zimbabwean jail is like?'

He looks at me, and then back at the road, chewing his nail. The dash lights make his face green and under-lit like a ghoul. The engine grinds away. The road races on. Time stands still.

'Fuck it.' Boils stomps on the brakes and the car skids across the road. He yanks hard on the wheel and we're sliding sideways towards the ditch. We're going to roll. The back spins out and he floors it, tyres screeching and ripping. Now we're charging through our smoke, burning rubber scorching my nostrils and I'm thrown back into the corner.

'Jesus Christ, Boils.'

'Bart you fuck,' he says, looking straight ahead, grim. 'If we go to jail, I'm raping you first you cunt.'

'Boils, I can't go to jail. I've got Joey, remember?'

'Jesus, Bart.'

We're going back. The bungee cord reached its limit and whipped us back. A moment ago we were flying into a black void. Now we're plummeting into the gaping jaws of a fucking crocodile; towards a cage of snarling, blood-soaked tokoloshes with throbbing hard-ons.

'Stop the car Boils, I'm going to puke.'

WAITING OUTSIDE THE HEADMASTER'S OFFICE

He screams again. A howl like I've never heard. My skin tightens, my chest clamps up. Reggie. Oh! Reggie. Jesus. Reggie. Just tell him whatever he wants to know. Fuck sakes, it's not worth it. Maria would tell you the same thing.

We're tied to our chairs in a bedroom. This wheezing fat lump of Dutchman has pissed himself, goated right there. He's just whimpering behind his bloody, tear-soaked gag.

This is a guest bedroom by the looks of it. The door is locked and Mad Cop is heeeee-ing to himself on the other side. Sounds like he's on the floor against the door and he's thumping his head against it and heeeee-ing and heeeee-ing and heeeee-ing every time Reggie screams.

What the fuck's his name? Can't remember. Clement? No that was the gate guard, the one who got shot. Fuck. Fuck. Think. Dickens, Inspector Dickens and, and, Sergeant, Sergeant Tichaona. Tichaona Chenjerai, that's it. How could I forget?

Sergeant! Chenjerai. Tichaona.

Nothing. He's heeeee-ing and thumping his head on the door so loud he can't hear me.

Another scream. Jesus. My insides are like chalk. It sounds like he's ripping Reggie's fingernails off, ripping his fingers off, ripping his fucking legs off. And I'm next. I'm waiting outside the headmaster's office all over again. It's that same feeling only worse. Much worse.

I wait for Mad Cop to stop bashing his head and heeeee-ing and I try again: Sergeant Tichaona. Do not let Reggie die. If he dies, you know what happens. Sergeant?

The door flies open and he's standing there looking down at me.

Your turn, he says.

BURNING THE MIDNIGHT OIL

'What the fuck happened to the gate?'

'Jesus. Where's Shum's car?'

'They've gone. Place is deserted.'

'Fuck sakes we came back for nothing. They've scarpered as well.'

The house is dark. Not a single light. Feels like it's been empty for years. Doesn't matter, I am shagged out. I can't walk I'm so fucking knackered. Two hours of Boils's ranting. Two hours of Boils's brain-haemorrhaging death metal. We nearly crashed about twenty times with Boils nodding off. My head hurts like there's sulphuric acid running through my brain. Every vein is full to bursting and pounding, pounding, pounding. My eyes are like sandpaper and I can't see shit. Boils's car shudders and clunks to a stop and all is silent but for the ringing in my ears. I crank the door open and roll out of the car onto the driveway. Dizziness swamps me. I have to lean on the bonnet to stay upright. My entire body aches with fatigue. It wants to just give up, lie down right here on the driveway and never get up.

Ingocheni Island. The Island. Our Island. I used to get a giddy happy feeling every time I came up the driveway. Now I feel nothing but dread. The house feels abandoned; eerie and foreboding. Like there's something inside, some monster we do not want to disturb. I've never known this place so dark and silent. A nightjar says, 'Good lord deliver us.'

Boils is also knackered. He's been hitting it hard all day. We stumble up the stairs and he's poking at the door with his key. I try the handle. It's not even locked. Typical.

I look at Boils in the half-dark and nod towards the lounge. I don't know why but I'm shitting myself. So is Boils. He shakes his head and motions for me to go and check. I'm shaking my head at him and he's shaking his head back at me and pointing and mouthing the words, 'You fucking go.' He turns to go down the passage. I grab his arm and shove him towards the lounge. We go together.

He's pushing back against me as we round the door and this shriek hits me like a whale-sized owl is fucking my head and ripping my entrails out and I'm flying through the air. Everything is cloudy and there's a loud thump and I'm staring at the ceiling behind a charred sofa. I'm on the ground. Where am I? Boils's face is next to mine and he's smiling at me and slapping my face, not hard, not sore but it's loud inside my head.

'You fainted, fuck-face.'

Rachel and Jill's faces loom into the picture above Boils, looking down at me like I'm on an operating table. They are haggard, like they've been pulled through a thorn bush into a cave of vampires.

'What's going on?'

'These two were tied up to the security gate. Thought we were baddies coming to get them. Screamed to give us a skrook.' He laughs and looks up at them. 'Think it worked.'

It must've: Boils is white like a maggot and he's all of a sudden wide awake again.

'Come on gaylord, up you get.'

I have to steady myself on his arm. The whole room is spinning like I've had ten turns on the Octopus.

312

'Bart we have to go right now,' says Jill.

'What? Now? But we just got here.'

'We'll explain on the way,' says Boils.

'On the way? On the way where? Jesus Christ, man, we just got here. Can't we just—'

'You can stay if you want, but we have to go save Shum and Reggie.'

'Save them? Why? What happened? What's going on?'

'Are you coming or not?'

Joey flashes in front of me. That cage of tokoloshes dances around my head. All three of them are looking at me waiting for a verdict.

'Fine. Fuck.'

I clamber into the back of Boils's car, onto a sticky piece of foam. It smells of diesel and oil and damp. Rachel hops in after me and Boils is already flying backwards down the driveway while I pull the canopy shut.

Rachel hasn't said a word.

'What's going on, Rachel? Are you ok?'

'I'm fine, Bart. He took Shum, Bart. This crazy cop, talking in a strange way. We came back to the house to get Shum's car to go and rescue Reggie. Then this cop shows up looking for Reggie to lift some curse so Shum said he'd take him to Reggie and the cop tied us up and, and, and…' She bursts into tears. 'They've been gone for ages, Bart,' she says gasping for air.

Boils is flying down Glenara. Tyres squeal as we hook a right onto Enterprise. Not a car in sight. Not a light in sight. The car creaks and thunks over potholes. Boils is yammering something to Jill up front. Can't hear. Doesn't look like Jill can either. Not over the sound of his fucking music.

'So what happened to you guys? Why'd you come back?'

'I dunno.'

I look at Rachel. She nods to herself. I look out the window again. What the fuck are we doing? Where are we going? What the fuck's going to happen to us? This is crazy.

'So where are we going, exactly?'

'I don't know,' she says, sniffing and wiping her eyes. 'Some place called Xanadu. Reggie reckons that's the safe house. It's somewhere in Umwinsidale. He left hours ago on his bike but we saw someone following him, also on a bike. Shum knows where it is so he took that crazy cop there. To "get the curse lifted", whatever that means.'

'So why the fuck are we all going?'

'Jesus Christ, Bart. Are they your friends or not?'

'Well, yes, but. I've got a son, Rachel. I'd do anything for these guys but—'

It's too much. I'm blubbing into my hands. We are flying under full canvas straight into the storm. I'm in a cage hanging onto the bars and we're spinning round the edge of a whirlpool. I can see to the bottom where giant snakes writhe in a sea of blood and they're leaping up trying to pull me down, snapping their teeth and cutting each other up with razor blade scales and hissing fire.

'Bart! Bart!'

Rachel is rubbing my back and shaking me. I've been wailing like a child, I can feel it. My face is drenched. My body is drenched.

'I'm sorry, Bart. I had no idea you had a son. Jesus. I'm sorry, you shouldn't be here.'

'Neither should you. Neither should any of us.'

She sighs and sits back.

'I just keep imagining if it was me instead of Reggie. Or Shum.'

We fly through the night, Boils's exhaust futting and farting fumes, the engine whining at full throttle. I hope he doesn't kill us before we even get there. We're out of town and it's even darker without any houses. The air is dry and dusty. Diesel and dust. How can we sleep while our beds are burning? Those were the days.

I slide the cab window open. It honks of cigarettes and booze and diesel and rank fear-sweat.

'Boils! Boils! For fuck sakes, turn the fucking music off. What the fuck are we going to do when we get to this Xanadu place?'

'We are going to kuff them to hell and gone, Bart. To hell and gone.'

I can't see any faces but I can feel the fear like a boa constrictor coiling around the entire car and it's crushing the car, squeezing the breath out of us. I didn't know snakes could laugh.

BANGERS
AND MASH

Mad Cop is a bleating waste of space, braying like a fucked donkey as he drags me back along the passage towards the white glow of the kitchen. My arm is on fire, my face is on fire, my ear is on fire. Everything is on fire and I'm tied up with red-hot chains and headed straight for the fucking furnace.

The sight of Reggie, slumped on the floor in a heap, hits me like a baseball bat to the face. There's a puddle of blood under his head and he's pissed himself. And shat himself: the kitchen stinks of it. Those skinny legs poking out from his ripped trousers, his jacket flap open, an arm stretched out across the floor. He's face down, his cheek squashed out, his nose mashed and his lips bloody and swollen.

'How! We have not much here to work with, Sergeant,' says Snake-eyes. He's all jovial, and he's jabbering about something, very pleased with the sound of his own voice. Mad Cop throws me to the floor. The pain makes me scream. I need a sign of life. Is he breathing? I swear. If Reggie. If they've— Oof! That hurts. More pistol-whipping. It's fine. You go wild. Do your best. Because I am going to tear you apart. I am going to eat your fucking eyeballs out you little… I am going to rip your arms off and shove them down your fat fucking gob, you pathetic little fuck-face. Jesus-fuck, he's kicking me now. Oh, fuck me. Must self-preserve. Must live.

316

I can feel fresh blood oozing down my face. I'm hauled up and dumped onto a chair. Try to focus on what he's saying. What is he saying? Some shit about Reggie voting me off the Island. What the fuck's he talking about? My eyes are closing up, things are going watery and blurred. They're ripping my clothes off and this fucker's still ranting about colonialists, rapists, and looters. Whatever, cunt. As if you're any better.

What? No, no, no, what the fuck, man? No, no, no. Electrodes? This isn't happening. No, no, no, this is not happening. I lash out but I'm tied up. Hands clamp me down. No. They can not do this. They are not going to do this. It's a threat. It's a show. They aren't doing this. Oh dear God fuck me, please help me, oh my fuck they are not doing this. They are not doing this. They are shouting in my face, foul breath, rotting teeth, rough hands. Cold sharp clamps on my balls.

They did it. They fucking ZESA'd me. But I'm alive. I survived. Just. Jesus that hurts. What's this cunt saying to me? Am I fucking MDC? Of course not you cunt, you think I'd vote for any of you fucking monkeys?

Haaaaaaaaa! Jesus, I must've screamed the house down. I can see Reggie's eyelids flickering. My screams. He's trying to see if I'm ok. He can't even move.

What? Yes ok I'm fucking MDC you cunt. Full on, hundred percent card-carrying, Morgan-humping MDC. I love MDC. They don't electrocute people.

And him?

Sure. Whatever. Look, fuckface, this has nothing do with us. We're just—

Fuck. Did I pass out? Cunt fucking zapped me again. Jesus. Now he's quoting the bible. Go for it you retard.

You and my fucking pederast priest can fuck each other to death in your very own creation of hell. Maybe it's heaven for you two.

He's straddled a chair with his blotchy face pressed up into mine. I look into his dead eyes. I am going to eat you alive. I am going to slice you up with razor blades and pour boiling oil into the cuts and then I'm going to take you to The Valley and drop you into a pack of hyenas.

Some shit about the iniquity of my fathers. He laughs at me, picking at his yellow teeth bringing his cunt-face even closer. Come on, one inch more and I can nut you.

So tell me now, Ricardo Cordoza, he says hawking up a gob and swallowing it, who is this disgusting sodomist Bruce Elliot and why are you visiting him at full volume in the dead of night?

What? Oh! Fuck.

THEY CALL IT XANADU

We're at the garage with the wavy roof. Just around the bend we'll turn left into Umwinsidale. My heart is pumping out a million beats per second and I can't breathe. Rachel is silent too. The road goes narrow and snakes its way up into the hills. We hit a steep rise. Boils slows then accelerates past an elaborate gate with bright lights and a pink neon sign that says Xanadu.

'Fuck! That's it. That's it. You've gone past it you fuck.'

Boils looks at me in the mirror and tells me to shut up. He pulls off the road and Jill jumps out to open the canopy, the car idling and farting on the edge of stalling.

'We know, we know. We saw it too,' says Boils. 'We can't just waltz in there and say, Hi! Can we have our friends back, please?'

'So what do we do now?'

'I don't know.'

'We have to get in there. Right now.'

'Ya, no shit Sherlock.'

'Can't we just drive down? The gate's wide open.'

Boils shakes his head and says to Rachel, 'Didn't you fill him in?'

'I did. Sort of. He was crying.'

'Jesus.'

'Fine. I'm going to have a look. You lot wait there.'

He slinks along the wall, crouched down in Vietnam mode. He's at the entrance, his shadow flicking across the road. He's lit up like a prisoner caught escaping. He's peering round the gate, like a cheeky monkey. His head jerks back. He looks again. He jerks back and now he's sprinting along the road back towards us.

'Fuck. There's a dead mahobo in the guard's hut,' he says.

'What?'

'A night watchman.'

'Dead?'

'Fucking head blown off. Jesus. Fuck.'

Boils is skrooked.

'I saw Shum. In the kitchen. Tied to a chair. The window's at ground level. And there's two cunts in suits.'

'So what now? What the fuck now?'

'Dunno Bart, you got any bright ideas?'

'Can't we sneak in?'

'No ways. Place is lit up like a fucking prison.'

'Fuck.'

'Ok,' says Boils, 'here's the plan: we all get in and drop down the driveway and ram into that big black Benz. Bart, you and Rachel must drop out the back before they know what's going on. Use the cars as cover to sneak round the other side of the house. Jill and me will act all drunk and stupid like we've come to the wrong house looking for an after-party or some shit like that. We'll distract them as long as possible. You guys have to find a way in and get Reggie and Shum, ok?'

'Boils. That's crazy. What then? We sneak round and then what? We all get tied up and killed?'

'Got any better ideas, Bart?'

'Well no, but—'

'It won't work,' says Jill. 'They know you.'

'Fuck. Ok you and Rachel in the front; me and Bart in the back.'

'Boils?'

320

'Get in, quick,' says Boils and he's climbing into the back already. Jill's gone into a full tailspin groping at the driver's door, eyes like balloons.

'Boils! This is madness,' Rachel hisses at him. 'We'll all get killed,' she says but she climbs in anyway.

Jill's trying to pull the seat forward, yanking on the lever and wiggling her bum but it won't budge.

'Pull your side as well Rachel,' she says and they're both bouncing up and down on the bench seat and the car's wobbling on its creaky springs but still nothing.

'Fuck sakes, Jill, just drive,' says Boils through the cab window.

'Come on Boils, there has to be a better plan.'

'Shut it, Bart. Get in.'

Jill scooches forward and she's trying to find reverse; she's revving like a drag-racer and the car stalls. She fumbles for the keys. Click. Click. Click. The fucking car won't start.

'Fuck. Pop the bonnet Jill,' Boils says climbing out the car. 'Rachel, hammer. There. On the floor. By your fucking foot, Rachel. Jesus Christ! Jill. Pop the fucking bonnet for fuck's sake.'

'Jesus Boils, you want them to come running up the hill?'

'Just pop the fucking bonnet. It's there by your left knee. Pull it.'

'Fucking pull it, Jill'

'I fucking am pulling it, Boils.'

'Pull it fucking harder.'

'I'm pulling as hard as I fucking can, Boils.'

I shove my head through the window. Can just reach the lever and I give it a hard pull. Nothing.

'It's stuck Boils. Jesus, man.'

'Out. Out. Out,' says Boils opening Jill's door. He slides

in and he's yanking the lever back and forth and cussing and shouting and we're all telling him to be quiet and this only makes him shout louder and yank it harder. Then it catches and clunks with a loud twang. Boils scoots round and Jill climbs back in.

'Turn the engine,' he says, lifting the bonnet.

Jill cranks the motor and it's skidding and slipping and whinnying. Nothing.

'Put some fucking gas, Jill.'

She cranks again and floors it. The engine takes with a screaming roar and a cloud of diesel smoke and we're hissing at Jill to keep quiet.

Boils launches himself into the back. 'Go. Go. Go,' he says.

'Come on Boils. There has to be a better way.'

'No time. Get in, Bart. Let's go. Let's go.'

Fuck this. Fuck this shit. I clamber in and I'm pulling the canopy shut. Boils says leave it open and Jill's reversing, revving the balls out the engine.

She's doing a fucking three-pointer. And strapping herself in. Rachel, too. Jesus. Boils reaches into the cab and fires up his death metal on full volume. Rachel flinches and she's scrabbling for the off switch.

'Jesus Boils! What the fuck man?'

'Shut it, Bart,' he says batting Rachel's hand away. 'They're a distraction remember?'

We roll forward, picking up speed down the hill. We reach the gate and Jill heaves left. There's the black Benz in the floodlights. Jesus, are we actually doing this? We're not. We can't be going in? The car slows on the level and stalls with a thunk.

'Fuck!'

There's the security guard. Slumped on his chest, head half gone, blood and bits everywhere. There's the kitchen window and I see a black man in a suit drinking tea peering up at us.

'Fuck!'

'Jill? What are you doing?'

She's cranking the engine in gear and we're humping forward.

'Jill! Don't.'

The back tyres bump over the gate track and Jill is shouting at the car to start and we're all shouting at her to stop and we're moving faster and Jill is shouting at the car and now we're free-falling down the driveway. The steering locks and Jill is hauling on the wheel with all her weight.

We're going to miss. We're going to miss. Jill screams. Rachel screams.

Time stops.

Jill's knuckles poke through her skin, and her forearms are long streaks of bursting sinew, and her jaw is clamped shut. She looks like a wax dummy. Rachel is shrieking and screaming at Jill to stop and there's Shum. Naked. Tied to a chair, doubled over, covered in blood.

It's happening.

We smack into the side of the Benz with a head-splitting explosion of metal. So loud. It's so fucking loud it's like a crane fell out the sky. We bounce off it and we're rocketing straight for the house; straight for the fucking kitchen window.

It's happening.

We shoot over the cliff's edge, over the daisies and we're soaring like human cannonballs over a vast canyon and now we're plummeting, spinning, swirling, tumbling, down,

down, down into an abyss of boiling blood and snakes and flaming erections.

It's happening.

We're going to die.

Fuck it.

MARSELLUS CRASHES THE PARTY

Fuck, fuck, fuck. What a fucking moron. He fucking got me. Jesus, he knows about Brucey. Knows about everything. Fuck.

He's at it again. Boasting about his torturing prowess, all the shit he's learned in North Korea and the shit he's done to people.

He knows about Brucey. Maybe he doesn't. Maybe he's bluffing. Would Reggie have cracked? He hasn't moved. The blood has stopped and it's making a dark brown patch on the white tiles around his head. Like a rusty halo. Would he have cracked? Would Reggie crack? Reggie, what did you tell this fuck?

Reggie is alive. So long as he's alive he knows something. If he tells, if I tell, we're both dead.

You fucking idiot. This is Reggie. Reggie and Maria. Maria did not crack and neither did Reggie. This little fuck knows nothing. It's a bluff. His rambling trails off.

Ok, says a voice. Where the fuck did that come from? Reggie? Ok, he says, bubbles of blood frothing around his mouth.

No, Reggie, shut the fuck up man.

It's gone, he says panting and straining and then he shouts, it's gone. To The Hague. Your damn-fool cretin got here too late.

No, Reggie, don't tell him anything, he'll kill you. He'll kill both of us. Shut up, Reggie.

And you. You fucking cunt. You are going to rot in hell.

Reggie—

A hand slaps my face.

Continue, says Snake-eyes.

I uploaded the files. The ambassador has sent them to The Hague already. You are fucked, Reggie says sitting up.

Then he shouts with all his might: SO NOW YOU CAN KILL ME, YOU FUCK.

He slides back to the floor, panting and he points to Snakey and says, I'm finished and so are you, Colonel Abel Manyoka, aka The Green Mamba.

Snake-eyes blinks. He slurps on his tea and looks at Reggie on the floor, covered in blood, eyes closed, chest heaving.

He chuckles to himself and says, Let us see, shall we? Chikomo?

He clicks his fingers at his goon, the Ice Cream Man.

Sah!

Shoot that one, he says, taking another slurp.

Sah?

The slurping stops. The eyes flick over the cup at the goon.

Ah! Yessah, he says unclipping his gun and walking over to Reggie.

I'm screaming at Reggie to get up to say something, save himself, to fucking do something. We fucking know nothing you cunt, leave him alone, we don't know where the fucking thing is, leave Reggie alone you fucking cunt.

Chikomo.

The goon points his gun at Reggie's chest.

Reggie!

BAM! Jesus Christ. Reggie! I'm screaming and bawling and the cable ties are ripping through my skin and then the goon falls forward. He lands on top of Reggie and fresh blood spreads across the tiles. What the?

Heeeeeeeee! Heeeeeeeee! Heeeeeeeee!

There's Mad Cap, standing at the door with a gun pointed at Snake-eyes and his other hand clapped to his forehead and he's yammering, Heeeeeeeee! Heeeeeeeee! Heeeeeeeee!

Sergeant? I'm surprised at you. You are supposed to be standing guard over the ambassador back there. Not shooting my personal assistant. What's gotten into you my good man? Have you gone and lost your marbles?

BAM! Another shot blasts my head in. This one sounds like a fucking cannon. Snakey's massive gun is smoking at the barrel. Hey! Just like the movies. My ears are ringing and Mad Cop is down. A finger of blood reaches out to Ice Cream Man's pool. They're nearly touching. What the fuck is going on? What the fuck is going on? What the fuck, man? It's the curse. Reggie dies, Mad Cop is cursed for life, or so the stupid fuck thinks. Thought.

So now it's just this fat fuck left. Let's see how tough you are now, cunty.

He laughs and says, You think you can take me on now? You think I'm nothing without my strongmen? My strongmen who have spontaneously combusted in a most perplexing case and one I shall lose no sleep in dissecting. My protégés are a dime a dozen you know. First it's the pitiful pay cheque I wave under their snotty noses. But then, once they've had the taste, they would do this for nothing, free, gratis and no overtime. The only trouble is, keen students though they are, they are not so bright you see. They copy my every word but they can never learn what experience teaches: to maintain the calm demeanour in high-stress situations. That is what North Korea did for me. Gave me strength to remain passive under the greatest duress. He shakes his head and laughs again. Sonny boy, you'd wither and quack in your own puddle of excrement if you knew how far our little slant-eyed comrades go to maintain the peace.

Try being a PH, you faggot.

Maybe you think a professional hunter is hard Mr. Tough-nut To Crack PH, he says as he puts his teacup on the table. Still got his gun. I'm going to get that gun. He's standing behind me. He grabs my buggered shoulder and squeezes. Jesus, lightning and fire and red-hot fucking javelins. Stars. Blurry. I go down, screaming, with my head on the table begging, stop, please, please.

I smell his breath by my face.

But as you can see, Mr. pig-fucking Scum, I, I, I have what it takes actually.

I whip my head back like I'm doing a backwards somersault; I flick back with everything I've got. A thud knocks my skull. I hear the crunch and squeak of bone and cartilage giving way to a broken nose. He staggers, hand on face, blood pouring down onto his white shirt.

He's woozy, maybe going down. Is he going down? Is he? Is he? Nope. Fuck it I am dead now.

BAM! It's louder and sorer than anything I've ever known. And again, BAM! He's got the gun by the barrel and he's pounding my head. Don't go down. Stay up. Stay alive. Take the beating. Take it. For Maria. For Reggie. For everyone. He's shouting nonsense and spraying gob and blood at me. He stops, panting, and I'm hanging by a thread here. My face is in my lap, blood pouring like someone's running a tap over my head. Fuck, that was stupid.

Very clever, Mr. Scum. You think you got one on me,

eh? Sounds like he's got a cold. Well, let me tell you. I am going to kill you. It will be slow and painful. I don't care for mercy but I do care for the information you have inside that vile head of yours. So it's a showdown. A battle of wills. A duel to the death. Your death, of course. He picks up his tea and turns to the window, inspecting his nose in the reflection.

He winces, flicks his blood at me and slurps on his tea, scowling much better. I try watching him from the corner of my eye but everything is red. Now it's grey and spinning and flying at me.

I'm losing consciousness here.

I hear a shrieking, a screaming horror and it's getting louder. Mad Cop stirs – what? he's alive – he hears it too and he's squirming and heeeee-ing on the floor blowing bubbles in the blood. Snakey hears it too, and he's frowning and peering out through the window but all he can see is himself.

The screaming drills into my ears, into my brain and there's this enormous grinding crashing sound pummelling my head. Then the window explodes. Shards of brilliant white light burst into the kitchen and the air is blasted into a million dazzling, glittering, shimmering stars. A crystal stallion rears up with a terrible roar. Its flailing black hooves block out the light and crush my body into the ground. I'm floating. I'm spinning. Floating and spinning through a black silence towards a tiny white dot.

Marsellus? That you?

PASSED DOWN FROM LANCASTER?

Ancestral? What bloody-fuck nonsense is this? The clue? One down? Passed down from Lancaster? The clue to what?

Where are you going? Don't go. Come back. Please come back. Baba Manyoka has lots of money. Great wealth. He can offer you millions. Houses, diamonds, cars, oh dear Lord above, save me. Sweet Jesus, I am pinned beneath this bleeding motor vehicle. Help me. Immunity. Baba Manyoka can grant you full immunity. Help me, kind sirs, sweet madams. Please, don't leave me here to die.

Ambassador? Can you hear me? Are you still there? Please. Save me, I beg you, save me from this vengeful monster, this spiteful half-pig. Sergeant? You are still alive? I can hear your braying. Get up.

My legs. They are crushed. I cannot move. I am bleeding. My mamba blood. Oh! The pain. I am dropping out of this world. I am leaving this world. I have to see my baby girl one more time. I have to hold her in my arms. I have to see my son and tell him be a man, be proud. I have to hug my children; I have to tell my children that I love them. My children.

You swine. Oh! Jesus, bloody fuck-sakes please, I beg you, help me. Use the car jack. Help me. Please Reggie, I will set you free. Set you all free. You will be a millionaire. Your friends will be millionaires.

Where are they going, Reggie? Don't leave me here to

330

die. This is inhumane. You can not leave me here to die. I will kill you.

What are you doing? Get out of my jacket. Those are my keys for my car. Oh coward, kick a man when he's down. Where's the ambassador? I can hear him calling you from the bedroom. Go to him: your lover. That is my wallet. Those are my cards, my money. You can't take that you thieving half-caste. All the same. All of you. The same. Ambassador, stop this bastard. Ambassador? Ambassador, help. Ambassador?

Oh, Jesus. My mamba blood. My mamba blood is spilt. It spreads about me. Oh, Jesus. This savage is leaving me to die, Ambassador.

Help me, Ambassador. No! No! No! Ambassador, he is setting alight this vehicle, Ambassador. It burns. Oh! how it burns. They are leaving. They are leaving me here to die. Oh! The pain. This is not happening. It is but a nightmare; a torment from another life.

The flames they are growing. You loathsome creatures. You will die a thousand deaths and spend the rest of eternity in hell you vile, blood-sucking, pig-fucking maggot parasites. Oh! Jesus bloody fuck-sakes my mamba blood.

But what is this? It cannot be? A green flame-serpent rising out of the ground? You are not real. You were not real, just a story ambuya told us. You are a fragment of my imagination. Stand down. I am the mamba master. I command you to stand down, soldier. That is a direct order. Stand down, this instant I tell you. I am your master.

Heeeeeeeee! Heeeeeeeee! Heeeee—